THE

AND

THE PURE

HOME OF THE DAMNED LTD

THE EVIL

AND

THE PURE

DARREN DASH

The Evil And The Pure

by Darren Dash

Copyright © 2014 by Home Of The Damned Ltd

Cover painting © Stephen Toomey

First published in an electronic edition by Home Of The Damned Ltd February 1st 2014

First physical edition published by Home Of The Damned Ltd February 1st 2015

The right of Darren Dash to be identified as the Author of the Work has been asserted by him in accordance with the Copyright, Designs and Patents Act 1988.

All rights reserved. No part of this publication may be reproduced, stored in a retrieval system, or transmitted, in any form or by any means without the prior written permission of the publisher, nor be otherwise circulated in any form of binding or cover other than that in which it is published and without a similar condition being imposed on the subsequent purchaser.

All characters in this publication are fictitious and any resemblance to real persons, living or dead is purely coincidental.

www.darrendashbooks.com

www.homeofthedamned.com

in the beginning

Tulip sat in the room with the corpse and stared at the ceiling, dry-eyed.

She'd wept when she woke and wandered in from her bedroom to find her father lying close to the window, doubled over, eyes open, impossibly still. Throwing herself down beside him, she'd called his name, hugged him, tried to shake life back into his cooling form.

She wasn't sure how long she had held him, tears streaming down her face, oblivious to everything else. All she could recall now was moaning "Daddy," over and over, head buried in his chest so that she didn't have to look up into that dreadful stiff mask of his face.

Eventually the tears ceased. She didn't release him for a long time. There was no rush. Once she stood and made the phone call, control would pass to her brother and she would become a bystander, a thirteen year old girl ("Almost fourteen," she automatically murmured internally, as she had been doing for some months now) who would be expected to wail and mourn but play no more of an active role than that.

When she felt ready, she pushed herself back and smiled sadly at her father. She touched his lips with trembling fingers. "Daddy," she said softly. "I love you."

She almost broke down again, imagining him blinking and replying, not really dead (as she knew he must be), merely comatose, emerging out of his daze to call her name and wrap his arms around her and tell her that he loved her too.

But she staved off the tears. She had always been a practical girl, maybe a result of losing her mother at such a young age. She didn't think this loss would hit her as hard – nothing could be as hard for a little girl as having to face the death of your mother – but it had come as more of a shock. There had been lots of warning with her mum, maybe too much warning, all those months that she had fought the cancer, when they'd lived in a fog of desperate hope.

Her father, on the other hand, had seemed fine the night before when she'd gone to bed without kissing him, having stopped doing that a year or more ago. He had been a normal, healthy man as far as she was aware. There had been no talk of problems or illness. She was sure that he had been taken by surprise, that he hadn't anticipated this sudden collapse. He would have talked about it with her if he'd had even a notion. Death was something they had learnt to deal with together. He wouldn't have been afraid to discuss it with her.

She poured herself a drink, a tall glass of milk, and drank a third of it before calling Kevin and breaking the news to him. Her voice wavered as she told him that

Dad was dead, that she'd come into the living room this morning to find him sprawled lifelessly on the floor. But she didn't cry, even when Kevin asked if she was sure, in a tone that suggested he didn't believe she was old enough to make such a terminal call.

Kevin was at work but he told her he'd come immediately and be with her as quickly as he could. He asked if she needed anything, if she wanted him to ring one of their neighbours or the police. She told him she was OK, she didn't mind waiting for him by herself. He suggested she go to a local park or café, but again she said that she was fine.

She did a bit of tidying up, cleaning her room, giving the surfaces in the kitchen a wipe, keeping busy so that she didn't have to think too much about her dead father and how her life was going to change. But her heart wasn't in it and in the end she returned to the living room and sat in her daddy's chair. She stared at the corpse for a while, then fixed her gaze on the ceiling and tried to let her brain shut down. She wished humans had a standby mode, like computers, so that she could simply blank out.

It felt like hours before she heard Kevin inserting his key into the lock and pushing open the front door, but she knew it was far less than that. Her mind was playing tricks on her, that was all.

"Hey," he panted as he stepped inside, as if he'd run to get here.

"Hey," Tulip replied softly.

Kevin crossed the room and stopped in front of their motionless father. She heard him gulp and thought he was going to cry. That brought fresh tears to her eyes, but they hovered in the corners, not flowing yet.

"Dad," Kevin moaned, bending to check, to make sure. He searched for a pulse, rolled one of the eyelids all the way up, opened the dead man's lips and peered inside. Tulip watched with morbid fascination. She had never seen anything like this before. She wanted to know what Kevin was looking for, how to decipher the signs that would confirm for certain that they were orphans now. But she didn't ask. She couldn't. She had choked up and knew that she would burst into tears as soon as she tried to speak.

Kevin let out a long, shuddering breath, then turned. He wasn't crying but he wasn't far from it. He smiled shakily, hopelessly, and held out his arms to her.

It was what Tulip had been hoping for, and with a heartbreaking cry she hurled herself forward into his embrace, wanting him to wrap her up into a small, shivering bundle and take all of her pain and fears away.

The tears came now, full force, but she didn't care and she didn't try to hold them back. This was a time for crying, and though it seemed hard to credit, she knew that it would pass, as it had when they'd lost their mother. Kevin was here now. He would handle all of the difficult decisions and calm and soothe her. With his guiding hand she would pull through. He'd be her guardian, her pillar, her friend and mentor. She could trust him completely and he would steer her through the awful days, weeks and months ahead. There was no escaping the pain that must be endured, but with Kevin's help she would find a way to deal with it and move on. He would look out for her and be her rock every slow, stuttering step of the way.

After all, that was a loving big brother's job.

september 2000

ONE

Big Sandy lay buried beneath a mound of newspapers, XXXL cap pulled down over his eyebrows, a third-full bottle of cheap scotch in his lap, sprawled across the floor of an alley, watching soft yellow light through a chink in the curtains of a child's room in a house across the way. His jumper was filthy and it stank. His trousers were stained with liquor and piss. Old, scuffed boots. His fingers twitched by his sides. His feet jolted sporadically. Every now and then he mumbled to himself, grunted, cursed.

Foot traffic was sparse, the occasional local from a nearby council estate. They passed him with no more than a glance, noses wrinkling. Most steered clear in case he made a lurch for them. Braver souls stepped over him indifferently. One woman paused, bent and dropped a pound coin in his lap. Big Sandy muttered a weak thank you and saluted drunkenly, smiling loosely. When the woman was gone he sniffed, pocketed the coin and fixed his sights on the chink in the curtains again, waiting for the light to dim.

Finally the light in the room turned a darker yellow, hit black, came up again slightly and stopped. Just enough light for its five-year-old resident to negotiate by if he woke in the night. A shadow flickered as an adult exited, leaving the boy alone.

Big Sandy made sure no one was present then checked his watch — twenty past seven. He didn't look drunk any more. The tremors were gone from his feet and hands. He pushed the cap back. His eyes were dark grey, hard, focused.

He stretched beneath the newspapers and scratched an itch. He didn't rise. Not yet. The boy was confined to his room but his mother had the run of the house. Big Sandy didn't want to make his move while she was there. Sarah Utah was taking a night course in computer programming. Her class started at eight. She shouldn't be in the way much longer.

On cue, the back door opened and Sarah emerged, late twenties, a brassy, good-looking black woman, dressed in jeans and a loose shirt. She shouted something at her husband – Big Sandy heard a muffled reply – then grabbed a bag from a table to the left of the door and set off, a bounce in her step, eager to make her class.

Big Sandy gave it ten minutes then rose like a mountain. He shed newspapers, took off his cap, ran a hand through his lank, sandy hair, scowled at the stench of his borrowed clothes, then went to kill Tommy Utah.

He slipped on a pair of light gloves and tested the

door — locked. But the window to the right wasn't latched. Careless. Tommy Utah all over.

Big Sandy slid the window open. It was a tight squeeze – Big Sandy six-foot-six, built like a wrestler – but he sucked in his gut and forced himself through into Tommy Utah's office. Lots of highbrow books on the shelves — Shakespeare, Dickens, a gulag load of Russians. Tommy Utah an educated man. That was his problem. He'd decided he was smarter than Dave Bushinsky, that he could rip off the Bush without anyone realising. Big Sandy was here to show Tommy Utah what happened when educated people tried to outsmart his boss.

Three giant strides took Big Sandy to the door. He pressed an ear against it. No sounds outside. With a massive paw he opened the door and stepped into the corridor. Concealed on his person was a hunting knife, an untraceable handgun, knuckle-dusters, a short iron club. He didn't think he'd need any weapons – he planned to kill Tommy Utah with his gloved hands – but it was best to come prepared.

The corridor was deserted. Music played softly somewhere. Two lights broke the gloom of the upstairs landing, the dim yellow light from the boy's room and a stronger light from the other end of the house. Big

Sandy moved forward to climb the stairs, then stopped. The steps were uncarpeted. He snarled with disgust. Tommy Utah would have to be deaf not to hear a man of Big Sandy's size coming up.

Big Sandy checked his watch again — seven fifty-two. Sarah Utah's class lasted an hour. A twenty minute walk. But it might finish early. Somebody might give her a lift home. To be safe, he had to be out of here by nine. If she walked in on him, he'd be forced to kill her too. That wasn't part of the plan. Business was business. Tommy Utah had this coming. But Big Sandy didn't kill innocent women. Not if he could help it.

He'd give it forty-five minutes. Wait for his mark to come down. If he didn't, Big Sandy would storm up the stairs and strike quickly. Noisy, dangerous, clumsy, but Tommy Utah had to die tonight. The Bush wouldn't tolerate a delay. Withdrawing into the shadows at the side of the stairs, Big Sandy waited.

A quarter of an hour later, a door creaked. A shadow passed on the landing and another door creaked — Tommy Utah checking on his son. Big Sandy waited neutrally, asking nothing of the fates. When he was younger, he thought he could influence the actions of men by concentrating his will and forcing his desires upon the world. Time had taught him that he couldn't make himself the centre of the universe just by wishing it so.

Footsteps at the top of the stairs. Tommy Utah coming down. Big Sandy lowered his head and sucked in his gut, trying to appear smaller, eager not to give his position away, not to have to chase his prey up the stairs, making noise which might wake the child.

Tommy Utah was whistling softly. He stopped near the bottom of the stairs. Big Sandy tensed — had he been seen? Then Tommy yawned and took the last few steps with a soft hop, landing smartly. He half-turned toward the kitchen, smiling, his white teeth startling in a face otherwise almost entirely black.

Big Sandy lunged, grabbed Tommy Utah's throat and thrust him against the wall, knocking over a small table loaded with magazines. Tommy got off a squeal. He kicked out wildly and struck Big Sandy's shin. Big Sandy ignored the pain and pressed Tommy hard into the wall, searching for the vulnerable flesh of Tommy's throat. Tommy got off a shout – "Fucker!" – then choked as Big Sandy's fingers tightened.

A sleepy moan overhead made both men pause. "Daddy?" Fear flooded Tommy Utah's eyes — but also hope. Big Sandy saw it, saw that Tommy meant to scream and wake his son, hoping it would drive off his attacker.

Big Sandy said softly, "If he sees me, he dies."

"You... wouldn't," Tommy Utah croaked. "Not... a child."

Big Sandy didn't answer. He let his expression say it for him. Tommy Utah stared into his assailant's cold grey eyes. He gulped and felt the huge, scarred fingers gripping his throat. He started to cry — but quietly.

"Daddy," came again from upstairs, mumbled this time. Then silence.

Big Sandy's fingers crushed Tommy Utah's throat like a cardboard toilet roll. His eyes bulged. He slapped feebly at Big Sandy's arms and his legs thrashed — Big Sandy leant in, pinning them to the wall with his knees. Moments later Tommy Utah's eyes clouded over and he went limp. Big Sandy flexed his fingers, then squeezed again, making sure, before gently laying the corpse on the ground, resting Tommy Utah's limp hands on his stomach, pausing to close the dead man's eyes, mindful of the wife who'd be coming home in forty minutes give or take.

Big Sandy stepped back and glanced up the stairs to check that the boy hadn't woken up and come to find his father.

The boy was on the landing, rubbing his eyes and

yawning.

Big Sandy felt a sickening tremor ripple through him. He hadn't expected this. He was sure the boy would sleep through the violence. The Bush hadn't told him to kill the child if he got in the way. He hadn't needed to. Big Sandy knew better than to leave behind any witnesses.

Big Sandy quickly moved up the stairs, blocking the child's view of the corpse. He tried a shaky smile as the boy lowered his arm and stared at him. The boy was clutching a Noddy doll in his other hand.

"Where's my daddy?" the boy asked.

"Sleeping," Big Sandy answered without thinking.

"Who are you?" the boy asked.

"I'm his friend," Big Sandy said with a straight face, taking another three steps, moving in on the blinking child.

The boy stared at Big Sandy. He looked confused but not afraid. Then he said, "Will you read me a story?"

Big Sandy paused. He was within reach of the boy. He knew what he should do. Grab the child, snap his neck, leave him with his father. It would send out an even stronger message than just killing Tommy Utah — if you fuck with the Bush, we won't just kill you, we'll kill your loved ones too. Maybe wait for Sarah Utah to come home and break her neck as well, kinder than leaving her alive to mourn the loss of her son.

But the boy was looking at him hopefully, trustingly. He wanted a story. The worst thing he could imagine was the stranger refusing to read to him. He had no idea that this was a monster far worse than any he might have dreamt of hiding under his bed or in his wardrobe.

Big Sandy gulped and said, "Sure, I'll read you a story. Go to your room. Pick a book. I'll be right in."

The boy didn't smile. He simply went back to his bedroom. Big Sandy wanted to flee but then the boy would come out again, see his dead father and scream. Big Sandy checked his watch. He still had time. Time enough for a short story anyway.

Big Sandy stepped into the boy's room and found him in bed, holding out a picture book, *Where The Wild Things Are*. Big Sandy wasn't familiar with it. He'd once had a girl of his own, but she had been taken from him before he'd had a chance to read many books to her. Besides, this didn't look like a book that a sweet little girl would enjoy.

The boy pointed to a large grey monster with horns and claws on the cover. "That looks like you," he giggled.

"Yeah," Big Sandy grunted. Then he sat on the edge

of the bed, took the book from the boy and started to read.

The boy stared at Big Sandy as he read slowly and carefully in a deep, low voice. His eyelids dropped almost immediately, but kept flickering open until the story was about two-thirds finished. Then they closed and stay closed.

Big Sandy read another couple of pages, just to be safe. When he was sure that the boy was asleep, he lay the book on the bed, stood and gazed down at the slumbering child. He thought about taking one of the pillows and smothering the boy, but his hands shook at the mere thought. Big Sandy had done a lot of bad things in his life, and he'd probably do a lot more before he died. But he didn't want to truly become a horned, clawed monster. Even a man of darkness had to draw the line somewhere. Besides, how much could a five year old describe to the police? A big man came and read him a story. He wouldn't be able to tell them much more than that.

The Bush wouldn't like it but he'd understand. If the boy turned out to be some kind of genius who could sketch Big Sandy's face, there would be consequences and Big Sandy would bear them. But if the boy was just an ordinary kid, the killer should be in the clear.

Big Sandy eased his way down the stairs to the back door. He stopped with his hand on the lock, took a hat from a hook – Tommy Utah had a *penchant* for hats – tried it on, checked in a mirror, smiled at the ridiculous sight of the hat looking like a thimble on his immense head. He replaced the hat, opened the door, stepped out, pulled it shut, rolled off his gloves and pocketed them, walked away. He thought of the boy and shivered, then went to report to the Bush.

The party was being held in a gentleman's club recently opened to members of the fairer sex, a five minute walk from Covent Garden station. Big Sandy wasn't dressed for the occasion, but two of the Bush's men were on the doors. They waved him in despite the disapproving glares of the staff. One of the watchmen was Eyes Burton — steeliest eyes Big Sandy had ever seen. Eyes wasn't a large man, but he could wear most people down with his stare alone.

"Any problems?" Eyes asked, handing Big Sandy a tie and helping him into an oversized jacket that the Bush had had the foresight to supply.

"Clean," Big Sandy said. He would tell the Bush about the boy, leave it to him to tell the others if he saw fit.

"Wife? Kid?"

"Clean," Big Sandy said again, pushing past, tugging at the arms of the jacket, slipping on the tie. The tie and jacket didn't match the jumper and piss-stained trousers. Big Sandy didn't care.

The party was confined to two rooms. The other rooms were filled with middle-aged men, grey hair, hand-tailored suits, the scent of expensive aftershave. Those who caught sight of Big Sandy – and he was a hard man to miss – frowned reprovingly but said nothing. They knew who Dave Bushinsky was, the standard of man he employed.

The atmosphere in the party rooms was distinctly different. Young men and women, flashily dressed. Loud laughter, the chinking of glasses, coke-glassed eyes, talk of horse racing, Formula One, the stock market, money money money. They also stared at Big Sandy as he circled first one room, then the other, in search of the Bush. He didn't mind. He was used to the attention.

Big Sandy paused a couple times to acknowledge the greetings of those who knew him, but didn't stop, eager to deliver his report and evacuate the building. Parties weren't Big Sandy's scene.

He spotted Lawrence Drake larging it, impressing a group of giggling girls with tales from his pop star days and current work on a TV soap. Drake was a small fish in a very big pool, but he knew how to play to a crowd. He was a regular at the Bush's parties. Not because he was indebted to or friendly with the Bush — he just knew that he could score high quality coke and women, with no journalists sniffing around.

"The Big S," Drake boomed, waving Big Sandy over, shoving one of the girls aside to make room for the giant. Big Sandy reluctantly slotted into the space and smiled tersely at the self-proclaimed star.

"Lawrence. Good to see you."

"Hey, I told you, it's Larry. How you been?" Before Big Sandy could answer, Drake had turned to his entourage. "The stories I could tell you about this guy. But hush!" He put a finger to his lips and rolled his eyes. "Walls have ears."

"Have you seen Mr Bushinsky?" Big Sandy asked politely, wishing Drake would do something to piss the Bush off, so that he could squeeze him a bit.

"The Bush man? No, not recently. But have *you* seen his niece?" Drake wolf-whistled. "Sorry ladies, but Shula Schimmel is definitely the belle of this ball."

"Shula Schimmel?" Big Sandy repeated.

"Mrs Bush's niece," Drake explained. "Flew in from Switzerland yesterday. This party's in her honour."

"I was in Switzerland last year, skiing," one of the

girls remarked.

"Me too," Drake smirked. "Spent most of the time flat on my back."

"On the slopes?"

"In my bed!"

Big Sandy excused himself and pulled clear of the group. The tie felt tight around his throat. Remembering Tommy Utah, his eyes when Big Sandy threatened to kill his child, the sound of his last wheezing breath, the crackle of the cartilage in his throat as Big Sandy crushed.

Claustrophobia seized Big Sandy but he shook it off and bee-lined for the bar. A double vodka, straight, no ice, tossed back quick. A second, this one to sip, and his hands stopped trembling. The panic attacks had alarmed him the first few times — he'd shook like a leaf, wept in public — but he'd learnt to control them. He was always fine when he killed, detached, professional, cold. The shakes hit after an hour or two. Not every time, but often enough. When they struck, he knew he was in for a long hard night, but by morning he'd be in control of himself again.

A hand on his left shoulder. "How's the vodka?"

Turning, smiling, relieved. "The best. As usual."

"Why settle for anything less?" Dave Bushinsky

grinned broadly at his ogre-like henchman and ordered a red wine. The Bush had turned fifty a couple of years earlier but he looked forty. Lean, tanned, jet black hair, alert dark eyes, a casual suit, soft leather shoes, discreet diamond rings and a gold St Christopher dangling from his neck — no matter that he was proud of his Jewish roots, he'd been given the St Christopher by a friend when he was a young man and had worn it ever since.

"Have you met my niece?" the Bush asked, testing the wine, frowning and handing it back. The barman scurried away to locate a superior vintage.

"No. Heard the party's for her."

"Yeah. Alice's niece. On holiday from Switzerland. First time in London since she was a kid. We're showing her the sights, introducing her to the right people."

"Hear she's a looker."

"Judge for yourself." The Bush pointed with a jerk of his head and Big Sandy turned, spotted a young woman in a yellow dress, smiling as she chatted with the Bush's wife. Alice was a looker herself, but Drake had spoken truthfully — this girl stood out from all the others.

"Stunning," Big Sandy said.

"Yes." The Bush raised a finger. "But she's barely eighteen, so back off."

"I'll hold my charms in check," Big Sandy

deadpanned.

"Want to meet her?" the Bush asked.

"Not dressed like this," Big Sandy said, and the Bush's smile faded as he recalled where his right hand man had been earlier in the night.

A man in a dark green silk shirt, with swimming eyes, clapped the Bush on the back and congratulated him on the party. The Bush endured his good wishes and smiled thinly until the stoned guest wandered away to bug someone else. The barman arrived with a fresh bottle. This one proved acceptable.

"Take care of business?" the Bush asked softly, studying the red wine, not looking directly at Big Sandy.

"Yes."

"Clean?"

"Yes. But there was a problem. The child saw me."

The Bush stopped swirling the wine. "Saw you with his father?"

"No. It was after. Before I could leave."

"What did you do?"

"Put him back to bed. Read him a story."

The Bush gawped at Big Sandy. "And then?"

"He fell asleep. I left."

The Bush looked troubled. "If he can ID you..."

"He's five," Big Sandy said. "He was half asleep. I

don't think he'll be able to tell them anything they can pin on me."

"But if he can..." the Bush pressed.

"It's a risk," Big Sandy said. "I'll accept it, take what's coming if it blows up on me."

The Bush smiled. "I wish I had a hundred men like you."

Big Sandy grunted, uneasy with the compliment.

"Do you want to leave town for a while?" the Bush asked.

"No," Big Sandy said. "I don't think I need to. I'll keep low for the next day or two. If the boy can tell them anything, we'll hear about it and you can deal with me before they track me down."

"You're a cool customer," the Bush laughed.

"We make choices," Big Sandy shrugged. "We've got to live with them."

The Bush shook his head with admiration, then slipped Big Sandy a plain brown envelope, padded with bills. Big Sandy pocketed it without looking inside. There was never a fee when he killed – he received a regular salary, paid direct into his bank account – but the Bush often slid him a bonus.

"Have a good night on me," the Bush said, knowing Big Sandy was sometimes edgy after a hit, that he might need to get drunk to unwind. "Drop by the house when you sober up tomorrow. I've some more work for you."

"Enjoy your party, boss."

"I intend to." He squeezed Big Sandy's shoulder then went to show off his niece and steer her away from the horny male wolves who were circling.

Big Sandy thought about ordering another drink, decided against it. He could get a chaser at his next port of call. He departed, tearing off his tie and shrugging loose his jacket as he stomped down the stairs, thrusting them at Eyes Burton on his way out.

"You didn't stay long," Eyes noted.

"Long enough," Big Sandy replied, turning left as he exited, to hail a taxi, heading for Sapphire's.

Sapphire was an Asian American, long dark hair, surprisingly thick eyebrows, late thirties (the same as Big Sandy), a Londoner for twelve years, doubted she'd ever return to the States. Twenty pounds overweight but she didn't care. She'd worked hard in her prime, set a lot of money aside, established her own house in Earl's Court, ran a discreet service, only taking on clients who had been recommended by existing customers. Sapphire rarely entertained her guests personally any more – that was a job for the younger women – but she still graced a few favourites with her pleasures.

Big Sandy usually went with one of Sapphire's girls when he visited, but she took one look at his face when he entered, stooping so as not to bash his head on the doorframe, and knew this would be one of his hard nights. Sapphire preferred to service him on nights such as this — she knew what to expect and how to handle him. Big Sandy was a lamb most of the time but he could get violent when morose, and a violent Big Sandy was a handful.

"Come on through," she drawled in her light Texan accent, taking his hand and leading him to her *boudoir*. When he was sitting on the bed, she kissed his cheeks, forehead, finally his lips. "Take off those revolting clothes and burn them while I fetch the vodka."

"I needed the clothes for a job," Big Sandy protested.

Sapphire sighed. "I'm sure you'll tell me all about it."

Big Sandy went to work on his laces. When Sapphire returned with a pitcher of vodka and two shot glasses he was naked, torso rippling with muscles, body ripped with scars, scabbed cuts, lumps from old bruises. But not his face. Almost none of Big Sandy's opponents over the years had been tall, fast or lucky enough to strike him in the face.

Sapphire bagged the soiled clothes and hung up a

dressing gown, then poured the drinks and silently toasted the giant on the bed. Without a word they tossed back the vodka. Sapphire poured a second glass for Big Sandy, he took it gingerly, lay on the bed, set the glass on the side table, rolled over. Sapphire massaged him, working hard on the bunched muscles. No oils — Big Sandy wasn't into oils. No conversation either. In this mood he didn't like to talk, not right away.

It took about twenty minutes for Big Sandy to relax. When Sapphire felt the stiffness sap from his massive frame, she slapped his buttocks playfully. "Turn over." He obeyed, the bed shaking as he fell flat on his back. His penis was coming to life. Sapphire smiled. When Big Sandy was really bad, he couldn't get an erection. This was a good sign. She wouldn't have to nurse him as forcefully through the night as she had feared. "Close your eyes."

Big Sandy shook his head, muscles tightening. "Dark."

"It's OK," Sapphire said. "I'm here. I'll protect you." Crazy, a five-foot-two elf (albeit a pudgy elf) offering to protect a man-mountain, but it was what Big Sandy wanted to hear. He allowed his eyes to close and Sapphire went to work on him with her lips and tongue, first his chest, stomach, the insides of his thighs, slowly and teasingly working back up his body, before heading south again. Big Sandy groaned and gently clasped her head while she pleasured him. His hands could crush her delicate skull but she wasn't frightened, she knew how to control him.

She eased off when he was approaching climax, then climbed on top, slipped a condom on and mounted him. His hands automatically went to her flanks, fingers gripping her tightly, and he thrust, eyes still shut. His grip tightened as he bucked and Sapphire gasped painfully. Her legs would be bruised in the morning but she didn't mind. Big Sandy paid well and his boss sent a lot of business her way. She could live with a few bruises.

Big Sandy came with a juddering shout, fingers digging into her flesh, causing her to shriek. He released his grip immediately, though he went on thrusting, and Sapphire thrust with him, letting him decide when to end the moment, not rushing him. When he eventually subsided and opened his eyes, she smiled, kissed him, slid off, removed the condom, binned it, returned to cuddle him.

"Did I hurt you?" Big Sandy asked, concerned.

"A few love bruises won't break me." Sapphire studied his eyes and read his mood, considering her approach. Sometimes Big Sandy didn't invite questions. Other times he wanted to be interrogated. She decided this was such an occasion and broke the silence with, "Want to tell me about it?"

Big Sandy's lips turned down and he shook his head, but she could tell this was a delaying tactic, that he did want to talk, so she pressed him. "Come on, tell Sapphire all about it. I won't let you touch me again until you do."

Big Sandy grinned and reached for her breasts. She slapped his fingers away and he grimaced with delight. "Spoilsport," he grumbled.

"I want to know what happened." A pause, then a gamble, based on what he'd said to a girl the last time he was here. "Was it Tommy Utah?" Big Sandy stiffened and she sensed she'd said the wrong thing, but she didn't panic, kept smiling.

"How do you know about Tommy Utah?" Big Sandy snapped.

"I know everything that happens," she smiled. "You aren't my only customer. Everyone talks when they come to see Sapphire." Protecting the girl who'd told her about Tommy Utah, letting Big Sandy believe he wasn't the source of the leak.

"He crossed Dave," Big Sandy sighed, picking up his

glass of vodka, twirling it so it caught the rosy light of the bedside lamp. "He used to fence for us, good at his job, but he started skimming thirty, forty percent."

"How did he think he'd get away with that much?" Sapphire asked, nibbling at Big Sandy's nipples.

"Money fucks up people's thinking," Big Sandy said. "I've seen it happen to dozens like Tommy Utah. Smart, ahead of the game, all the benefits and none of the cons. They start to feel that they deserve more and they set out to fleece the men they work for. They never think they'll be caught. They always are."

"How did you kill him?" Sapphire asked, sliding another condom over Big Sandy's hardening penis and mounting him. He often came three or four times in quick succession when he'd killed a man.

"Hands," Big Sandy gasped, closing his eyes again. "Strangled him. Quick. Clean. Crushed his throat."

Sapphire trembled – death disturbed her when it was described so plainly – but Big Sandy thought she was reacting to him and he thrust harder, pulling her close, kissing her, clasping her tight, rolling over so that he was on top, powering away, Sapphire crying out with pleasure and pain, urging him on, losing herself to the passion, but not totally, always in command, a child controlling a bear.

*

Later. Most of Sapphire's girls had retired for the night. Big Sandy was stretched out like a beached wreck, drunk, head swaying, limbs shaking. Sapphire held him and stroked him, hearing his confession. He was telling her about Tommy Utah's boy, how he'd woken after Big Sandy had killed his father, reading to him. "I should have killed him," Big Sandy moaned. "He's a witness. He can describe me to the police. I should..."

"But you couldn't," Sapphire cooed, brushing his hair back with her fingers, kissing his forehead and eyelids, trying to soothe him. "And you were right not to. You can't go round killing children. You're not a monster."

"Horns," Big Sandy croaked. (Sapphire had no idea what that meant but she didn't ask.) Tears trickled from Big Sandy's eyes, the sign that the night was drawing to a close. In this mood he always cried at the end. Sapphire was glad — it had been a long day and she craved sleep. Big Sandy began telling her about the story he'd read. Then he told her again about Tommy Utah. He told her about others too, men and women, their crimes, their punishments. She let him babble, kissing him, caressing him, telling him he wasn't evil, just doing his job, someone else would have killed them if he hadn't. Eventually he mumbled his way to sleep and lay snoring, head in Sapphire's lap, her fingers entwined in his hair.

Sapphire stayed like that, sitting up, cradling the giant, not wishing to disturb his sleep. As she tried to doze, she thought about Tommy Utah and the other people Big Sandy had killed. She knew too much. Big Sandy wasn't the only one of her clients who talked in bed, but he told more than most when he was in one of his death-fixated dips. If Dave Bushinsky knew what Sapphire knew about his pet killer – even a fraction of it – he'd kill her to protect himself. Sapphire knew that and accepted it. It was part of the risk she ran to live the life she desired. Hers was a wonderful but terrible world. As long as she sold herself to men like Big Sandy – men of crime and violence – it always would be.

TWO

Clint Smith mingled with the rich, glamorous and infamous, wishing with all his being that he was one of them. While he thrived on parties like this, he hated them too. As he drifted around the opulent rooms of the League of Victoria, ignored by his peers, he was reminded at every step of his true insignificance. In dingy pubs and clubs in East London he could strut and impress. But here the reality of his position was clear — he was a nobody.

Clint plucked a canapé from a passing tray, watched how those around him were eating – nibble or munch? – then copied them. He paused beside a group of stylish twentysomethings and eavesdropped as they discussed Aspen, Epsom, the Groucho, how gauche Harrods had become, how difficult it was to find a decent bottle of bubbly. Clint was the same age and he yearned to join in the conversation but he'd never been to Aspen, Epsom or the Groucho, he thought Harrods was the coolest store in London, and he knew nothing about champagne. After a while he drifted on, aware that the young men and women were eyeing him suspiciously, whispering behind his back, "one of Bushinsky's boys," "think he's a gangster," "doesn't look dangerous," "gives me the creeps."

Clint wasn't a gangster, though he dreamt of becoming one. He had an insatiable appetite for movies and TV shows about the Mafia. He would commit chunks of dialogue to memory, mimic expressions and gestures. One day he'd cross the Atlantic and take America by storm, make it his own, establish a dynasty. But not until he'd made his mark here. He wasn't interested in going to New Jersey or Chicago as a nobody. He wanted to hit the States like a meteorite, perhaps as a liaison between cousin Dave and his American counterparts.

Cousin Dave was Dave Bushinsky, Clint's entry to the underworld. Related through Clint's mother. Clint hadn't seen much of the Bush when he was growing up but he'd heard all about him, whispered tales, gossip. When Clint left home aged seventeen, sick of his humdrum life and a job in Tesco's, he targeted cousin Dave, looking for work. Dave laughed when Clint said he wanted to be a gangster, told him he didn't have the balls for it. "But don't worry," he'd grinned as Clint's dreams threatened to crash around him, "we'll find something for you."

Clint spotted Lawrence Drake, surrounded by sensual women, acting out a scene from the TV soap in which he was currently appearing. Arms wide, exaggerated expressions flitting across his face as he told of a run-in with a producer, the whimsical demands of his co-stars, his behind-the-scenes adventures. His audience hung on his every word, enthralled. Clint did too. Clint knew Drake was a small-timer enjoying fifteen minutes of semi-fame before slipping into obscurity, but right now Drake was moving in dreamy circles, with access to actors, singers, producers. Like everybody else, those people partied and got stoned, but they were prepared to pay more than most. If Clint could use Drake to gain access to them, it would be like plugging directly into the national grid and draining off as much current as he cared to.

Drugs were what Dave Bushinsky had *found* for his gangly, nervous, pale-faced cousin. He was sure that Clint Smith would never amount to anything, and he didn't trust the boy – eager to get ahead but totally unsuited for the life he craved, the sort who fucks it up for everybody if you let him get too close to the action – but blood was blood, even if Clint's mother despised the Bush and phoned Dave constantly, begging him to "release her son before his soul was corrupted".

Having observed Clint for several weeks, Dave decided he would be a liability in a position of authority, so he set him up as an independent dealer — lots of opportunities to make money, even the chance to come into the organisation for real if he matured and proved himself worthy. But it also kept him at arm's length, away from the heart of the Bushinsky empire, where he could do no harm. If Clint ran into trouble, there would be no comebacks. He'd burn alone.

Clint was wading closer to Lawrence Drake, waiting for a line he could seize upon and use to slide into the conversation, when all of a sudden Drake burst out with "The Big S!" and waved Sandy Murphy over. Clint stepped aside swiftly. He didn't like Big Sandy. Clint had moved into Kennington when he first went to work for his cousin, close to Cleaver Square where Big Sandy lived. Big Sandy collared him one night outside a pub. "Don't deal here," he'd said softly but firmly. "If I catch you dealing on my patch, I'll break your legs, I don't care whose fucking cousin you are." Clint had transferred to a flat in the Borough. He'd had nothing to do with the giant since then and that suited him fine.

Clint had little contact with men of Big Sandy's ilk. His business was narcotics, and while it was by no means a clean profession, he liked to believe it was civilized. He struck harmless deals, not with junkies, but with clubbers, executives looking to unwind, people in search of a good time. He joked with his customers and had social drinks with them. He didn't carry a knife and had never fired a gun. He abhorred tools of violence, despite the fact that it was his dream to one day rule men of destruction and profit from misery and conflict. And that was all Big Sandy was — not a man, but a tool. He disgusted and terrified Clint.

Clint circled the room, waiting for Big Sandy to split — he had a feeling the brute wouldn't linger long with Drake and his admirers. A few minutes later Big Sandy slipped away and Clint closed in. A beautiful young woman in a lemon low-cut dress intervened. "You're Clint Smith, aren't you?"

"Yuh-yes," Clint said, eyeing the blonde beauty nervously, unaccustomed to being approached by such visions out of the blue.

"I think we're cousins, kind of," she said.

"Eh-excuse muh-me?" Clint only stuttered when he was anxious or unsure of himself, which was more often than he wished.

"My name's Shula Schimmel. I'm Dave's niece. I understand you're related to him too?"

Clint smiled, relaxing, delighted to have been singled out. "Yes, through my muh-mother. But you're not Dave's ah-actual niece, are you?"

"No. Alice is my aunt. But I always think of him as an uncle. So a cousin of his is a cousin of mine, in my view." She smiled – beautiful, captivating, innocent –

and offered a tiny white hand. Clint wasn't sure whether she wanted him to shake or kiss it. He went for the shake.

"Have you been here long?" he asked, releasing her slim fingers and making eye contact. She had deep blue eyes. She was even paler than Clint, but hers was the paleness of rich marble, and her face was flawless. She didn't need the layers of make-up that so many of the women in the room relied on. Her flesh was clean and glowing, merely highlighted in a few places with some lipstick and eyeliner.

"I flew in yesterday," Shula replied brightly as Clint's gaze shifted so that he could study the rest of her. She had the body and poise of a model, even though she was not fully formed, still maturing, an alluring but incomplete eighteen year old. He remembered what he had been like at that age and winced at the memory.

"Having a good time?" Clint asked.

She laughed. "I never expected anything like this." She waved around at the party. "It's so beyond!"

"Dave loves to throw parties," Clint grinned. "Any excuse."

"Can I ask... you've probably been asked a thousand times already... but your name..."

Clint chuckled. "My dad loved westerns. I was always

going to be Wayne or Clint."

"Did you get teased about it in school?"

"Not much. It was cool to be named after Clint Eastwood."

They chatted about films for a while. Shula hadn't seen many westerns, so Clint did most of the talking, telling her about some of his favourites. He began to get confident. He hadn't much experience of women, certainly none like Shula, but that didn't mean he couldn't dream. He imagined her warming to him as he told her about *The Wild Bunch* and *The Good, The Bad And The Ugly*. Maybe she would fall for him. Sure, she was beautiful, but that didn't mean she was cold. She was young, from a country where maybe the women weren't as quick to judge as they were here. It didn't take much to set Clint dreaming. A kind word was all he required, though it was seldom that he got even that much from a woman like this.

"Are westerns what you mostly watch?" Shula asked.

"Actually I'm more of a gangster fan," Clint admitted.

Shula's eyes sparkled. "Me too," she exclaimed. Then she leant forward and squinted, lowering her voice, trying to sound like Marlon Brando. "*I'll make him an offer he can't refuse.*"

Clint laughed with genuine delight. "Isn't that a

brilliant film? I could watch it forever."

"Me too," Shula smiled. "My parents think I'm too young for such films, so I have to watch them in secret. The bloodshed repels me – I always look away when Sonny is killed – but the characters fascinate me."

Clint thought she might ask about Cousin Dave at that point, if he was anything like the cast of *The Godfather*, but she had probably been warned against such queries, and instead they just talked about the trilogy and other such films, Clint feeling warmed with every passing minute, hardly able to believe that he was holding her interest like this, his dreams solidifying, standing a bit straighter, no hint of a stutter now, confidence lending him a certain handsomeness that he never saw when he caught his reflection in a mirror.

There was a lull in the conversation when they ran out of steam on the movie front. Clint tried to think of something else to say, loving the way the lights caught Shula's blonde hair, imagining running his fingers through it, sniffing her scent when it was just the two of them, what she'd feel like in his arms as he leant forward to kiss her.

Then Shula said, "I saw you heading for Lawrence Drake. Do you know him? Could you introduce me?"

Clint shrunk in an instant as he realised she had

collared him to meet Larry Drake.

"Do you get his show in Switzerland?" Clint asked miserably.

"Yes, on satellite. He's such a rogue." Her blue eyes bright, shining at the thought of meeting Larry Drake. Clint didn't blame her for using him to get to Drake. He was just disappointed.

Hiding his feelings, Clint smiled and took hold of Shula's sleeve, waving her towards Drake and his entourage. "After you, muh-madam."

"You don't think he'll mind?"

"Larry Drake lives to be adored," Clint muttered bitterly, then guided her into the ranks of Drake's entourage, apologising for interrupting, asking if he could introduce the guest of honour. They already knew who she was – Drake's eyes lit up with lust – and welcomed her with gushing kisses and "I love your dress!" and "What do you think of London?" and...

Clint listened for a while, smiling blankly while he was roundly ignored. Then he slipped away, leaving the beautiful, wealthy, influential Shula Schimmel to the other beautiful, wealthy, influential people. He struck for the bar, seeking solace with fellow anonymous outcasts.

*

Clint was nursing a Bacardi Breezer, brooding on the injustices of the world, when Dave Bushinsky stepped up beside him and called to the barman, "The same as before." He turned to Clint with a swiftly refilled glass of red wine. "That's a woman's drink," Dave noted, clinking Clint's bottle with his glass.

"Leave me alone," Clint groaned.

"Life treating you badly?" Dave smirked.

"I met your niece," Clint said.

"Nice girl, yes?"

"Lovely. But all she cared about was meeting Larry fucking Drake. I could have been on fuh-fire for all it would have mattered to her."

Dave shrugged. "Girls like actors and singers. What are poor schmucks like us to do?"

"I know," Clint sighed, "but if I had more cash, better clothes, the power to get things done…"

"Angling for a promotion, cousin?"

"I've worked hard," Clint grumbled. "I bring in decent money, play it clean, don't hold back on you. I make good contacts and –"

"No," Dave interrupted softly. "You don't." Clint stared at him, hurt. Dave took pity on him and elaborated. "Good contacts are people who spend thousands every month feeding their addiction. They bring in others with similar tastes and funds. They're people of authority and influence, who can do favours for our friends. Bankers, lawyers, MPs, entrepreneurs. You sell to passing trade. Fifty pounds here, a hundred there, nothing constant, no big scores."

Clint stared at his shoes, ashamed, hating his cousin, hating himself, hating the whole damn world.

"I'm not criticising you," Dave continued. "I respect the work you do. But don't make yourself out to be more than you are. If you want to get ahead, get serious. This city's full of dealers no better or worse than Clint Smith. Show me you're worth more than them, *then* talk to me about promotion."

Clint trembled but said nothing. He had never been able to take tough advice. This wasn't the first time Dave had told him to push himself, gamble and expand, but Clint never listened, just went on dreaming about emulating his screen idols, wanting success so badly it hurt, but unwilling to actively pursue it.

Dave sipped his wine and observed his cousin in silence, hoping he'd show some backbone. When Clint only slumped glumly over his Breezer, Dave sighed and lowered his voice. "Phials is horny." Clint blinked and looked up. "He asked for Tulip. You can take care of it?"

Clint nodded slowly. "I'll have to ch-check that she's

available, but if she —"

"No buts or ifs, cousin. What Phials wants, Phials gets. If you can't secure the hooker for him, I'll find someone who can."

"It's duh-duh-difficult," Clint said, reddening. "She's not really a huh-hooker. That's why he likes her. But..." He gulped and nodded fiercely. "I'll get her. Free or not, I'll muh-make her come."

"That's what I like to hear," Dave smiled. "Take him some weed too, but only let him smoke what he can while you're there. Don't leave any behind."

"I know the rules," Clint sniffed. "You don't have to remind me."

"I hope not," Dave grunted. "Phials is your one true *good contact.* If you do well with him, there's hope for you yet. Screw it up..." He didn't need to finish. "Phials won't be free before eleven, but if you want to leave early to set things up, I'll understand."

"Consider it done," Clint grinned, rising, glad of the excuse to leave with a purpose.

"Clint," Dave called him back. "Larry Drake — you think Shula's got a thing for him?"

"No," Clint said. "She just wanted to rub shoulders with a celebrity. She gets his show on satellite in Switzerland."

"She's eighteen," Dave said. "Hasn't seen much of the world. Drake's a pussy-hound and he likes it young. I would not approve of a relationship between him and my niece. Should I be worried?"

Clint sensed an opportunity and made his play. "I don't think so, but I can keep an eye on her if you like, be her escort, stick close to her."

Dave considered it, then waved his worries away. "Thanks for the offer. I'll monitor the situation myself. But if I think she needs a guardian, I'll bear you in mind." Dave touched his cousin's left hand. "Fast Eddie will pay for the weed, the hooker and any other expenses. Make sure he recompenses you for your time too."

"My time's your time," Clint replied with a shit-eating grin.

"You're learning," Dave winked and returned to the party. Clint left his drink unfinished and hit the street, heading for Charing Cross, fishing out his mobile, dialling Kevin Tyne, making plans.

Clint didn't like to waste money on taxis. He'd rather catch the Tube, claim the taxi fare back at the end of the night, make a small profit. A man like Dave would sneer at such penny-pinching, but it all added up. So he caught the Bakerloo line to the Elephant & Castle, then the Northern line to Borough. A short walk to his third-floor flat. Untidy inside, clothes strewn across the floor, dirty washing in the sink, an overflowing laundry basket, flies buzzing around boxes from a Chinese takeaway two nights ago which Clint hadn't disposed of yet. He ignored the mess and cut straight for a loose panel in the floorboards under the rug in the bedroom. Clint had several stash points around London, in public lockers, but he always kept a small supply of grass and pills at home, in case he needed to get his hands on some gear in a hurry.

Clint flicked on his TV and surfed the channels, but paid little attention to the shows, thinking about Shula. He replayed their conversation, reading more into her responses, playing out scenarios where she didn't ask about Larry Drake, where they kept on talking, where the interest she'd shown in him deepened, where he told her of his dreams. Some of the scenes ended with her coming back here and getting down and dirty with him, but in most they innocently strolled the streets together, hands linked, just talking.

Clint was a lonely young man. He was making a good living as many judged such things, but he had nobody to share his success with, nobody to impress with his plans for the future. If he had someone like Shula to come home to, maybe he'd work harder, not just settle for easy scores, set out to truly impress cousin Dave.

By the time Clint turned off the TV he had developed a serious crush on Shula Schimmel. It had been a long time since anyone (with the exception of his clients) had spared him a gentle word or graced him with a few minutes of their time. Shula's small gesture of friendship had touched him. Always quick to latch on to a vague dream, he began to see her as the answer to his prayers. With her by his side he could rule the world. She would give his life meaning, encourage him when he flagged, adore him when he did well. He could do anything with a woman like her. For a woman like her.

Dreaming idly and wildly, he changed into casual clothes, pulled on a pair of trainers and let himself out. He could have got the Tube to the Elephant & Castle again but it wasn't a long walk and he had time to kill. It was a dry September night, just right for walking, and he could fantasize about Shula en route.

Clint made good time to the Elephant, strolled up Walworth Road, passed the Heygate Estate, kept walking, eventually took a left on to a side-street, then another left to the lab, putting thoughts of Shula aside as he drew near.

The lab covered almost one whole side of a cul-de-sac. The houses on the opposite side were owned by Dave Bushinsky, deserted or occupied by approved tenants. The lab buildings were once a garage, a warehouse and four two-storey houses. From the outside they still had this appearance, six separate structures, the garage and warehouse long shut for business, windows boarded over with planks and aluminium sheets, ghost houses, ground floor windows boarded over, the glass in the upper windows shattered. What the public didn't see — all six buildings were linked on the inside, garage and warehouse converted into a state-of-the-art laboratory, the houses home to those who lived and worked in the complex. There was a computer room (no internet access), a gym, sauna, games room with pool tables and table tennis, underground basements for the Bush's beloved hounds.

Clint paused at the sliding garage door, spun the tumblers of a rusty old combination lock, freed the chain, slid the door open, stepped inside and pulled the door shut. A second door nestled within, a couple of metres further on from the outer door. No handle on this side, just a button in the wall. Clint pressed the button and stepped back, whistling jaggedly, always nervous when he came here, thinking of the creatures beneath, imagining them on the loose, having devoured Phials, Fast Eddie and the others, waiting for fresh flesh — for Clint.

A series of heavy clicks, then the door slid open. Fast Eddie Price emerged, a large man, almost as tall as Big Sandy but not as broad. Fading grey hair, crooked nose, a squint in his left eye from an old boxing injury, missing several teeth. Wearing a purple tracksuit, sleeves rolled up, a fluffy headband, but looking dangerous regardless. "Dave told me you were coming." Strong Irish accent, even though he'd moved to London more than twenty-five years ago.

"Kevin and Tulip aren't here yet?" Clint asked.

"No. You know the procedure."

Clint spread his arms and legs, subjecting himself to a fast but thorough body search. Rules of the lab — everyone was searched, no exceptions.

Fast Eddie finished checking him, motioned Clint through and closed the inner door.

"Why aren't you at the party?" Clint asked as they set off through the outer corridors of the lab, skirting the sealed rooms where Tony Phials and his assistants weaved their narcotical charms.

"Someone's got to babysit the professor," Fast Eddie grinned, his gap-toothed grimace a ghastly facsimile of a normal smile.

"Is he still working?"

"Nah. He's in his bedroom. You brought the hash?"

"I never leave home without it." It was crazy, bringing a baggie to a lab where they could manufacture any kind of chemical intoxicant. But the products they cooked up here were for export only. Ultra strict on that point. Phials was their resident genius, the source of Dave Bushinsky's recent dramatic rise, the Bush gone from a middleweight to heavyweight in the space of four short years. But he was also a junkie, a man who couldn't be trusted, who had to be kept under lock and key, plied with marijuana when the shakes hit bad, otherwise kept clean.

Past the concealed doors to the basement, home of the Bush's monstrous pets. Clint shivered, imagining their howls. He hated any dog that was bigger and more aggressive than a poodle. The hounds were his perfect nightmare come to fanged life.

Up the stairs. Guards on the door outside Phials' bedroom. Armed. Alert. They parted for Fast Eddie and he knocked hard with his knuckles. A high-pitched cry from within. "Enter!"

"I'll bring up the Tynes when they come," Fast Eddie said, opening the door, gesturing Clint into a dimly lit room.

"Thanks," Clint said as the door closed.

Dr Tony Phials was sitting on the end of his bed, black skin almost invisible in the gloom, fuzzy dark hair sticking out in uneven clots, thin slivers of eye white shining in the dull light of the cloth-covered bedside lamp.

"That you, doc?" Clint asked, half-afraid.

"Sure as shit hope so," Phials replied, his accent unmistakable, New York, the Bronx, Scorsese, DeNiro. It always gave Clint a thrill. Phials whipped the cloth away from the light and stood. He was wearing a satin dressing gown, hanging open. Naked beneath. Penis long, black, erect, curving to the left. "Resting my eyes," Phials said, striding forward to shake Clint's hand. Clint tried not to stare at Phials' exposed cock but the doc caught him glancing and grinned. "Viagra. Couldn't wait. Needed a hard-on. I can cover up if it bothers you."

Clint laughed edgily. "Nothing I haven't seen before." Phials was often naked or half-dressed when Clint visited. It always unnerved him.

Phials led Clint to the bed, bade him sit and asked what he wanted to drink. Phials had a fully stocked bar in the bedroom. He could be trusted with alcohol — he had a weak stomach, couldn't drink much. Clint said a beer would be fine. Phials fetched a glass and poured, the perfect (half-naked) host.

"You know I despise bluntness," Phials said, passing Clint his drink, "but I'm feeling utterly wretched tonight, so I'll cut straight to the chase. Have you brought something to make me happy?"

Clint produced his baggie and shook it.

Phials nodded approvingly. "High quality, I trust?"

"Only the best for you, prof."

"Could you do the honours? My hands are trembling."

While Clint rolled a joint, Phials asked half-heartedly if Clint had anything else on him. "Afraid not," Clint smiled. "You know the rules."

"Who'd know?" Phials grumbled. "A few E's to give me an extra bit of a buzz."

"I'd do it if I could," Clint apologised, "but I'm searched every time I enter."

"You could sneak a few pills past Fast Eddie and his crew," Phials insisted slyly. "You're smarter than them. I bet you could slip a hog past that lot if you set your mind to it."

"Maybe," Clint chuckled, "but if they found out I'd crossed them, it would be bad news for both of us."

Clint finished rolling the joint, lit it, handed it over. Phials took it reverently, eyes narrowing, the tip of his penis seeming to rise towards the spliff like a divining rod. Settling it gently between his lips, he inhaled softly, breathed out, then took a deep drag, toes curling inwards, his whole body focused on the joint, greedily devouring the smoke, holding it in as long as he could. When he finally let it out and coughed, he was smiling sagely, at one with the world and the prison of the lab. "Good shit," he said, paying the traditional homage.

Clint watched Phials smoke. As the chemist reduced the joint to ash, his left hand crept to his penis and lightly stroked it, drawing his fingers back over the tip in time with each inhalation, reversing course as he let the smoke escape. Clint looked away, red-faced.

Phials' eyes went vacant when he was done and for a couple of minutes he said nothing. Clint sat in silence, waiting for the doc to speak. Finally Phials gazed at his young dealer and smiled lazily. "You'll have to forgive me if I'm not my normal verbal self. It's been a long day. A long week. The pressure I'm under, Clint, the strain… You don't know what it's like."

"You have it hard," Clint said automatically, fake sympathy, secretly thinking, *I'd love a place like this, servants bringing me women, drugs, whatever I wanted. The bastard doesn't know when he's well off.*

Phials appeared to read Clint's thoughts. "You envy

me," he said. "You think I have it sweet. Lots of money, people to kiss my ass, power." He leant forward and reached out to grip Clint's knee but stopped short. "A prison's a prison, Clint. No matter if the bars are made of solid gold, they're still bars."

"You could leave," Clint said uncertainly, not sure if Phials could, not knowing what sort of a bind Dave Bushinsky had over the American.

Phials blinked dumbly. "And go where? Who'd take me? Who'd protect me from my enemies or from myself?"

Clint didn't answer. Couldn't. As he sat uncomfortably, trying to think of a reply, there was a knock at the door. Phials almost exploded with excitement. "Tulip! Is it Tulip? It must be. Let her in, Clint, let her in."

Clint went to open the door. Phials covered his erection, drawing his dressing gown tight around his waist, plucking at his uneven hair like a nervous schoolboy. Clint eased the door open. Kevin and Tulip Tyne were outside, Kevin an inch or so less than Clint's five-eleven, gaunt, stiff dark hair cut short, dressed in dull black trousers and a shirt, looking like a man at a wake. Tulip was five foot nothing, plump, curly auburn hair, smiling sadly, clutching an expensive leather handbag (a gift from the doc), wearing the green school uniform which Phials favoured (the real deal, Tulip having only recently left school), complete with scruffy plimsolls.

"Kevin, Tulip," Clint greeted them, stepping aside, waving them forward.

"An angel," Phials gasped, striding from the bed, meeting Tulip halfway there, taking her hands and kissing her cheeks. "Kevin, you've brought me an angel. She looks more beautiful each time I see her."

"I'm a growing girl," Tulip said softly, no cynicism in her tone, even though she had reason to be cynical. Clint had never seen her bitter.

"I'll leave you to it," Clint called to Phials. "I'll roll a couple more joints on my way, leave them with Fast Eddie, you can –"

"Stay," Phials interrupted, circling Tulip, studying her intently, besotted. "We always have room for one more, don't we, my angel?"

Tulip didn't answer but looked uncertainly at her brother. Kevin Tyne coughed into a fist. "That's not part of our deal."

"So we'll strike a new deal," Phials smiled. "The more the merrier. Money's not an issue. I've named my vice — name your price."

"I don't –" Kevin began.

Clint cut in quickly, heatedly. "I don't want to stay. Not my scene." Sweating at the thought of unrobing in front of Phials and Kevin Tyne, not much sexual experience, not wanting to be exposed as a relative innocent.

"If you're sure..." Phials mumbled, right hand settling on Tulip's left breast, squeezing it through the fabric of her jumper and its school crest. Clint turned gratefully for the door. Phials called to him, "Drop by sometime, Clint. Don't be a stranger. You don't have to wait for my summons."

"I'll do that, doc," Clint said.

"I mean it," Phials insisted. He glanced up briefly. "I consider you a friend. Call whenever you wish."

"I will," Clint said, honestly this time, tickled by the offer. Phials nodded, then fixed completely on Tulip Tyne, forgetting Clint, the lab, Fast Eddie, everything. Clint paused just long enough to catch Phials kissing Tulip, his thick lips covering her small pale mouth completely, then he spun, exited, closed the door.

Fast Eddie was waiting for him. "You should have stayed."

"I don't pay for my women," Clint said gruffly.

"What women?" Fast Eddie chuckled.

Clint didn't rise to the bait. Instead he sat in one of

the spare chairs to the left of the door, a few metres from the guards with the rifles, and rolled twin joints, concentrating on his fingers, willing them not to shake. He laid the joints on the chair when finished, pocketed the almost empty baggie, walked back through the complex accompanied by Fast Eddie. He paused at the exit. "The doc said I could come vist if I wanted. That on the level?"

Fast Eddie shrugged. "The professor can invite anyone he wants. Long as you come clean, you can visit whenever you like."

Clint nodded, thinking about Shula, wanting to do something that would provide him with the means to impress her, figuring he might be able to get some mileage out of the professor if he came more often, not just when summoned. This could be one of those opportunities that Cousin Dave was always urging him to seize. Inspired by dreams of winning the heart of Shula Schimmel, he decided on a whim to get proactive and seize it. "I'll see you soon then."

"Looking forward to it," Fast Eddie deadpanned. He pressed a button and the door slid open. Clint stepped through and hit the streets, obsessing about Shula and the life they might share.

THREE

Kevin Tyne hated London Bridge station. Grotty, claustrophobic, a non-stop flow of commuters and tourists, everyone in a rush, everyone snappish. He used to work in Southfields, much more relaxed. But London Bridge was a ten minute walk from his apartment on Long Lane. It meant he was close to home, close to Tulip. He'd requested the transfer, and though the last sixteen months had been torture, he wouldn't have it any other way. Having ready access to Tulip made up for the rest of the crap that he had to endure.

Kevin had recently *celebrated* ten years working for London Underground. He'd joined them after dropping out of college three months into his first year, unable to connect with his history tutors and fellow students. Originally a stopgap while he cleared his head, re-evaluated his ambitions and chose an alternate course. A decade later he was still issuing tickets from behind a glass window and answering the most mundane travel questions, no imagination required, a robot's job. One slight perk — he didn't have to smile. Nobody expected Tube staff to be courteous.

Today he was manning the Northern Line northbound platform. He had to spend his time endlessly directing people, clearly and politely telling them how to find their way out of the station to the London Dungeon, the Globe, London Bridge, HMS Belfast. Also which lines and stations they needed for Buck Palace, Covent Garden, Oxford Street, Harrods. Surrounded by the crowd, a constant press, the same questions over and over, exhausting.

At least the days never dragged. In Southfields he would often get bored, his eyes glued to the teasing hands of his watch, wishing the day would pass quicker, glumly looking forward to another quietly desperate night — bland dinner, a walk, TV, perhaps a pub. He'd wonder for the millionth time how he'd lost touch with all his friends from school, why he had such trouble making new associates, what he should be doing with his life, whether it was always going to be this humdrum. Worrying about Tulip towards the end of his spell there, fearing exposure, sickly certain that he'd come home to find her gone. He'd dash out to phone her, even if she was in school, heart beating, fighting to hide his anxiety when he spoke with her, telling her he loved her. Then he'd hang up reluctantly and return to watching the seconds drag, waiting for night, wanting to be with her all the time.

After a dog of a morning he relished his first break. One of his colleagues flashed him a sympathetic grin as he headed for the escalators to daylight. Kevin wandered up through the station to Tooley Street, then a short stroll to clear his thoughts. Pausing in the doorway of a building he slid out his mobile and rang Tulip. She answered on the third tone. "Hello?"

"Me. Everything OK?"

"Sure."

"We need milk."

"I got it."

"You've been out?"

"Yes."

"To the shops?"

"Yes. I got a Mirror and Sun too."

"You should have told me you were going. I'd have left more money."

"I had enough. How's work?"

"Awful." He laughed, not caring now that he was talking with her.

"What do you want for dinner?"

"Didn't you get anything?"

"Thought I'd check with you first. I fancy a takeaway. Fish and chips?"

"Maybe. We'll discuss it over lunch."

"Want me to make some sandwiches?"

"No. I'll buy rolls. Chicken tikka?"

"Yes please. And a Pepsi Max."

"That's bad for you. I'll bring orange juice."

"There's no sugar in Pepsi Max."

"The bubbles are bad for your teeth."

"Don't be silly. Pepsi Max."

He laughed. "You win. See you soon."

"Thanks." She waited for him to disconnect — he didn't like her putting the phone down first.

Back to work. Cheerful after his chat with Tulip. Daydreaming about her in his few quiet moments. Perfection in his mind's eye, even though she was overweight, her front teeth crooked, her hair poorly styled. He wanted to drift with his thoughts, devote his day to her, worship at the altar of his imagination, plan an impossible future where they were together forever, happy, content, one. But customers kept intruding, spilling out of trains, asking for directions, complaining, getting lost. Kevin wanted to scream at them, tell his boss to go fuck himself, storm out, find Tulip, seek the comfort of her arms.

But he had bills to pay. They had to eat and drink. Tulip needed new clothes, shoes, books, CDs, videos. *Drugs.* They made a lot of money out of their late-night appointments, but Kevin only loaned out his sister reluctantly, to a chosen few, those who could play the game, whom he could trust. She wasn't a whore and he wouldn't treat her like one. Couldn't. They needed a regular income. It was his job to provide.

So he kept a neutral expression. He answered questions courteously, never lost his cool, even when customers were losing theirs. Gave directions, apologised when people complained, handed out free information maps, manned his platform efficiently and quietly. Until lunch... freedom... home... Tulip.

She was on the tiny balcony of their top floor apartment, waiting for him, basking in the weak September sun. Kevin kissed her forehead, told her not to get up, handed her a chilled can of Pepsi Max, took the rolls to the kitchen to unwrap and place on plates. The kitchen was small, like the two bedrooms, the living room, the bathroom, the spare room which used to be Kevin's when he was growing up. The apartment was once a council flat, the family home since Kevin was seven years old. He moved out when he was eighteen. Returned two and a half years ago when Dad died unexpectedly, to look after Tulip. The flat was theirs by that stage, bought from the council in the early nineties. The plan had been to move in, take care of Tulip until she finished school, sell the flat, split the proceeds evenly, use his half of the money to get out of the Underground trap, go into business, go back to college, just *go*.

Kevin joined Tulip on the balcony and gave her the chicken tikka roll. She thanked him and started munching, cheeks bulging, making quick work of it. She used to be a light eater, Mum always worried about her before the cancer gave her more substantial problems to worry about. Practically starved herself after Dad's death, crying, lonely, picking at her food like a sparrow, Kevin urging her to eat more. Now she was ballooning, had gained a stone in less than six months, no sign of slowing down. Kevin thought that she was trying to make herself fat and ugly, so nobody would want her. But he couldn't tackle her about it. He lacked the spine to make open mention of the issue. Afraid she'd confirm his suspicions. Terrified of what that would mean, what it would do to them, to *him*.

They discussed the evening ahead. Kevin suggested a movie but there was nothing at the cinemas that Tulip wished to see and they'd watched videos the last two nights. She didn't want to sit through a third. "Theatre?" Kevin asked, but Tulip didn't enjoy plays. She liked to munch popcorn and slurp soft drinks while watching a show. "We could go to a pub." Tulip was sixteen and looked it, but most bartenders served her when she was with Kevin, or turned a blind eye while he ordered and she hovered in the background.

"How about a long walk after dinner?" Tulip asked. "We could go by the river, walk to the London Eye and back." Tulip loved walking along the bank of the Thames to the Eye, where she'd buy a hotdog, sit for hours and stare at the tourists, wondering where they'd come from, where they were going, what their lives were like. The Eye itself didn't appeal to her – they'd been up on it once and she'd expressed no interest in a second trip – just the people it attracted.

"Again?" Kevin groaned. "We were there at the weekend. How about Hyde Park? Nice evening, fresh grass, open air..."

"Maybe," Tulip said, and by her sullen tone he knew she had her heart set on the Eye, which meant they'd be going. Kevin couldn't bear to disappoint his sweet little sister.

They agreed on a fish and chips supper. Kevin would collect the food on his way back from work. Then the Eye.

"Got to go now," he said, wishing he could stay.

"Already?" Tulip checked her watch and pouted.

"The afternoon will pass quickly," Kevin laughed. "You have your shows on the telly. And..." He cleared his throat.

Tulip sighed. "Do I have to?" she muttered.

"Of course not," he said quickly. "You know I'd never force you. But you'll get the shakes if you don't. You know what you're like. If you leave it until later, the night will be spoilt and you won't be able to come out."

"Go on then," Tulip sniffed. "Fetch it for me."

"I'm not your slave," Kevin protested.

"Of course you are," she giggled and they smiled at one another.

"Come inside," Kevin said. "I don't want anyone to see."

"Nobody's watching."

"Still. It will be safer inside."

Tulip rolled her eyes but rose and followed him through to the bedroom. She sat on the bed while Kevin retrieved the box from a cubbyhole at the back of the wardrobe, dully watching him as he removed the tin foil, the lighter, the heroin. His hands were much steadier than hers. She sometimes chased the dragon all by herself, but Kevin prepared her fixes more often than not.

Kevin carefully melted down the powder, then beckoned Tulip forward. She picked up the foil tube, shuddered as she thought about what she was doing, then leant forward and inhaled. She despised the drug and would have refused if she could. But its lure was powerful. She had smoked often (at Kevin's sly bidding) and become addicted. She'd suffer withdrawal pangs if she went without. Besides, it helped numb her to what she had done with Kevin and their clients, what she would no doubt be asked to do soon again.

Kevin left her in front of the TV, only vaguely focused. He kissed her goodbye and hurried back to work, feeling the cold, dark station walls close around him, cutting him off from the world and his sister, hating the place more than ever, surviving by imagining it was three years from now, the apartment sold, working in a rural rail station or embarked on an exciting new career, living in the countryside with Tulip, a cottage of their own, no one to interfere, alone except for when they entertained a few wealthy, understanding guests, Tulip having come to accept, enjoy and depend upon the *appointments* as much as he had. Bliss.

Busy all afternoon. A couple of customers picked arguments with him. One had lost her purse and wanted her money refunded – seventy-four pounds, eighty-six pence exactly – while the other was an American in his sixties, moaning about the train schedules. Kevin could deal with most complaints himself, but these two kept yapping, wearing him down until he had to call his superior. Dan Bowen hated facing the public even more than Kevin, and always took it personally when one of his staff called him to the front lines — he thought they were doing it to spite him. Kevin knew Dan would spend the rest of the week thinking up ways to pay Kevin back. Once, after a similar incident, Dan had sent him down five nights in a row to clean the platforms. The fact that he'd have to sit and take Dan's shit depressed him even more. He shouldn't have to scrape to his boss' petulant whims, but Dan's father was a major player in the union and his brother was highly placed too, so there was no recourse there.

Eventually the day ended and Kevin was free. Before clocking off, he tracked down Dan and apologised — probably wouldn't do any good, but worth a try. Dan sniffed and said it was just part of the job, he didn't care. Kevin knew that was bullshit, but maybe his grovelling would satisfy Dan and he'd get off lightly this time, just have to work at the weekend or do some unpaid overtime.

Home to Tulip, stopping for fish and chips in Long Lane, fresh, piping hot, excellent. Marco chatted with him while he was wrapping the food. He wanted to know how Kevin was and what his beautiful sister was doing.

Kevin stiffened automatically, then relaxed. "Looking for a job," he lied.

"She not going back to school?"

"No."

"Not good," Marco tutted. "Education so important today, young people should go as far as they can. You want her to end up working for me?"

"At least I'd get free meals," Kevin grinned.

"Don't even believe it," Marco snorted. "Tell her to go back. She listen to you, eh?"

"I'll try." Kevin smiled guiltily. Tulip had wanted to go to college. She wasn't a great student but she was bright and able. A-levels appealed to her, maybe uni too. Kevin had quashed her hopes over the space of a year, arguing with her softly, at great length, offering all sorts of reasons why she should quit — college was a waste of time, there was lots of quick money to be made, she could take her A's as a mature student and enjoy them more. But never the real reason — his fear that he'd lose her if she stayed in school. His only hope of possessing her indefinitely was to keep her home, make her dependant on him, make himself the centre of her world and push everybody else out to the edges.

Tulip was alert and hungry when he came home. They tucked into the fish and chips, Tulip smothering hers in vinegar and ketchup even though they were bad for her skin, wolfing the fish as steam rose from its delicate white heart. Kevin ate slowly, with his fingers, breaking bits of batter off the fish and nibbling at them like sweets. Tulip licked her fingers clean when she was finished. Burped, then laughed. "So can we go see the Eye?"

Kevin sighed. "You're sure you wouldn't rather a park?"

"Eye," Tulip giggled, rubbing the end of his nose with a greasy finger.

"OK," Kevin collapsed. "But a rest first – I'm exhausted – and a shower."

"Me first," Tulip squealed, pushing herself away from the table.

"Be quick," Kevin said.

She pulled a face. "Amn't I always?"

Tulip ducked into her bedroom to disrobe. Came out a minute later totally naked, heavy breasts dangling over her protuberant stomach. A thick pubic mound where two years earlier there'd only been a light furze. Kevin watched her bouncing buttocks as she made her way to the bathroom to run the shower, no lust in his eyes, seeing pure beauty in every line, every curve, every mole.

Tulip looked back at him before she entered the bathroom. She squeezed her breasts together and winked lewdly. "Fancy a shag?" she said, fake husky.

"Do you have to be so crude?" Kevin scowled.

"I am what you made me, brother."

He glanced at her sharply but she wasn't trying to hurt him. Just the truth. Two years ago she'd been innocent, a virgin, untouched by the world. He'd taken that away from her — not her virginity, which she'd lost herself, but her innocence, her joy. Now she was a junkie and something worse than a whore. And it was all his work.

Kevin disrobed while she was showering. He waited close to the bathroom door, as naked as she had been. This was an established routine of theirs, a test devised by Tulip, her single hope of one day being offered an escape from the nightmare of his creation. As she came out, hair wrapped in a towel, she glanced down at his penis — soft, lifeless, harmless.

Tulip sighed. She accepted Kevin's excitement during their appointments, but if he'd shown any here, in what she termed normal time, he was sure she would have walked away. But limp as he was, she had nothing to complain about. They were, on the surface, just a brother and sister, at ease around one another, even in the nude. Nothing more sinister to it than that. On the surface.

They finished drying at the same time and pulled on fresh clothes. Tulip wore a short skirt and revealing top, carrying a sweatshirt in case the evening grew cool. He wore jeans and a light jumper. They set off arm in arm for the London Eye, clean, fresh, rosy, to all appearances a happy man and his happy young sister, their secrets, sorrows and strange practices hidden in a safe, shady place where they could for a while be ignored.

To the top of Long Lane, left on to Bermondsey Street, a short walk, crossing Tooley Street and through the Hays Galleria, circling the giant mechanical fish in the open centre of the complex. Left when they hit the Thames, strolling along the Southbank, detouring away from it only when the path demanded it of them. They passed pubs, tourists sitting overlooking the river, soft laughter, couples making out, boats drifting by. A perfect night.

Past the Globe. Kevin kept meaning to take Tulip there – history, the magic of Shakespeare, transportation to the past – but they hadn't made it yet. Perhaps next year, when summer rolled round again. He could take a day off work, they'd walk here together, maybe stand in the pit with the unwashed masses.

Past the London Weekend Television studios, the National Film Theatre, Royal Festival Hall, Jubilee Gardens, and at last the London Eye. Crowds queueing up, despite the month, despite the hour, despite the clouds creeping across the sky and casting the city into gloom. Always queues for the Eye, but they were processed quickly and unless you were dumb enough to come during the peak hours in the middle of summer on sky-blue days, you usually didn't have to wait too long.

Kevin and Tulip walked past the Eye, cut through a line of customers scurrying to get on, past the impressive buildings of County Hall, up to Westminster Bridge, where they viewed the Eye in silence, shining, majestic, beautiful, dwarfing and eclipsing the traditional tourist draws of Big Ben and the Houses of Parliament. Back through the crowds, stopping to buy hot, chocolate-coated peanuts and a bottle of lime juice. Kevin looked for a bench but Tulip preferred the grass of Jubilee Gardens, so they found a clean spot and sat, Kevin making Tulip lay her sweatshirt underneath, mindful of the damp. Kevin reclined, a hand over his eyes, breathing in the scent of the grass, the buzz of the crowd a soothing background noise. Tulip sat to attention, scrutinising the tourists, trying to guess where they were from, how far they'd travelled, what exciting and taxing adventures they'd endured along the way, creating stories inside her head.

A child lost its helium balloon and turned on the tears until an exasperated parent went looking for a replacement. An elderly couple hobbled off the Eye, awed, speechless, vanishing swiftly in the crush of the crowd. A woman argued with her boyfriend, threw her bag at him, stormed off, boyfriend following meekly, clutching the bag, trying to apologise. A clash of punks sauntered by, hair spiked and coloured, jeans and leathers carefully ripped, studs, chains, pierced all over, looking adorable and cuddly despite their apparent viciousness. Two PCs, male and female, smiling, confident, helpful, handsome — like the punks, there to play up to the tourists.

Kevin lost track of time. The sky darkened, the air chilled, the crowds thinned, but he and Tulip remained. Kevin felt totally calm, like he could lie here forever, or at least until morning, silent, thoughtful, at one with the world. The peace disrupted by the screech of his mobile, the theme from *Raiders of the Lost Ark*. Tulip went stiff the instant she heard it, knowing it wasn't personal, anticipating the end of the pleasant evening. Kevin fumbled the phone from his pocket, checked the incoming number, thought about not answering, then thought about the money. "Hello?" A short conversation.

He hit disconnect and looked at Tulip sheepishly. She stared back expressionlessly.

"We have an appointment. We have to leave now."

Tulip nodded. Stood and brushed her skirt with a hand. "Who is it?"

"Phials. I can tell him we're busy if –"

"We have to go back to the flat," she said in monotone, knowing he didn't mean it about putting Phials off. If she said she didn't want to go, he'd nag at her until she caved in and agreed to the visit. She'd learnt to avoid the dramatics — they didn't wash with her brother. "I'll need my uniform. Lubricant and condoms. Some coke to get me in the mood."

Kevin flinched and stood. Reached for her hand. She brushed him away and set off. He looked at the Eye, shining like a skewed UFO, the elongated shadows of its passengers indistinguishable from Greys. Turned and hurried after Tulip, ashamed but excited, penis hardening, mouth dry, fantasizing about the night to come.

No rush. Tulip sat in her bedroom, the room she'd slept in before Kevin installed her in his own bed, preparing herself for the appointment, applying light layers of make-up, not interested in looking beautiful, just presentable. Kevin hovered, drifting around the flat like a ghost, nervous, stomach tight, breathing thinly. The wait was always a joy and a strain, the best and worst part of the experience. Anticipation was sweet but guilt soured it, and fear that things could go wrong — these were dangerous people, dealers, thieves, killers. Phials was harmless but Fast Eddie Price and the others were cold-blooded thugs. They could kill Kevin, keep Tulip as their slave. A gamble the pair took each time they ventured forth on an appointment. Part of the thrill. Kevin wouldn't have it any other way.

He checked his watch, checked with Tulip – a cool "I'm ready when you are" – then rang for a cab, one of four local firms he split their custom between. They always took a cab when working, but never the same firm twice in a row. Tulip emerged wearing her green school uniform, tight in places but still a comfortable fit. Phials had a thing for the uniform. Kevin never admitted it, but he did too. He would have liked Tulip to wear it to more of their appointments, but he never openly influenced her choice — one of the rules they operated by.

Tulip rooted her old plimsolls out of the cupboard where their shoes were kept. Sat on the chair by the phone to pull them on. Kevin saw between her legs as she raised her left foot to tie the laces — no underwear.

That excited him. He turned his gaze away quickly in case she noticed. Deep breaths, thinking about work, Dan Bowen, his schedule for the rest of the week, willing himself soft.

"How do I look?" Tulip asked, standing and twirling.

"Fine," he grunted, feigning disinterest. "You have everything?"

Tulip shook a leather handbag at him. It was a present from Phials. "All here, except for the coke. Will you get that from Clint?"

"I have some from last time."

The phone rang — the cab was downstairs. Kevin hurried to the door. Tulip didn't follow. She stood staring at him, faint hope in her light brown eyes. "We don't have to do this," she whispered. "You could cancel. We could go away. You could get help."

Not a standard spiel, but not new either. She'd tried it before. She would try it again. Her plea tore at his heart but he ignored it. His urges were stronger than his shame. "We'll go shopping on Saturday," he said. "Oxford Street. Buy you something nice."

"That's no compensation for letting Tony Phials fuck me," Tulip said, the swear word almost as hard for her to say as it was for Kevin to hear. "Thinking of a new dress or shoes won't make me feel any better when I'm on my knees sucking his cock."

Kevin stared at his sister, appalled, trembling, on the verge of tears. He almost capitulated. Almost ran to her, clutched her, begged her forgiveness, promised her freedom. But he'd *almost* spared her many times in the past. *Almost* was as far as he ever got. The lust was absolute — the *almost* always fleeting.

In a shaky, shamed voice he croaked, "Let's go."

Tulip's eyes went bleak, detached, dead. "I have to pray first." She turned her back to him, knelt, pressed her hands together, muttered words of remorse and hope to the God she still childishly believed in. Kevin stood by the door, wretched, helpless. He wished he had a god *he* could pray to for strength, understanding and forgiveness, but there was no god in Kevin Tyne's life, except perhaps the god of warped, twisted lust.

The cab dropped them on the Walworth Road and they walked the last hundred metres or so to the lab. The outer sliding door was unlocked. Once they were sheltered from any prying eyes, Kevin gave her the coke. She preferred this to the heroin. It was how he'd started her off. A few friendly snorts to begin with, a big brother letting his sister have some fun, no harm intended, everybody did it.

Tulip sprinkled the coke over the back of her left hand. Snorted deeeeeeep. The other nostril. The lazy smile that Kevin had come to know so well. She wiped her nose clean and nodded at him.

Kevin pressed the button and the inner door opened shortly, Fast Eddie Price standing inside, impassive. Kevin and Tulip entered. Fast Eddie searched them then led them through the lab to Phials' room. Kevin wasn't sure what they manufactured here. He rarely asked questions. Didn't want to get involved.

Fast Eddie knocked on the door of Phials' room. An excited squeal from within. Clint Smith opened the door, thin, nervous, dark hair, shifty eyes. Clint was their go between, their connection to Phials and a few others. He'd been Kevin's dealer to begin with. Now he was much more.

Clint greeted them and they responded neutrally. Kevin's heart beat fast as Phials met Tulip in the middle of the room — "Angel!" was all he heard the chemist exclaim — and he struggled to control it, to hear, to function.

Clint was leaving but Phials asked him to stay. Kevin froze — that was unacceptable. "That's not part of our deal," he said through chattering teeth.

"So we'll strike a new deal," Phials smiled, gaze fixed

on Tulip. "The more the merrier. Money's not an issue. I've named my vice — name your price."

"I don't —" Kevin began.

Clint interrupted. "I don't want to stay. Not my scene." Phials tried persuading Clint to change his mind, but he was resolute. Kevin relaxed. Phials told Clint to drop by sometime, then Clint was gone, the door closed, the three of them alone, Phials already kissing Tulip, thick lips hungrily seeking hers, no speaking, soft moans, two desperate men and a frail young woman.

Kevin rounded Phials and Tulip, watching light-headedly as Phials' robe slid open to reveal a long, firm penis. Phials was a viagra freak. Kevin had tried viagra but didn't enjoy the falseness of it. Nothing compared with the natural erection he got watching his sister with another man.

Phials broke contact, stepped away from Tulip and removed his robe. Tulip stood with her hands crossed demurely, the way Phials liked. He launched himself at her, lips fastening on hers, fingers exploring, moving his lips to her chin then down her body.

Kevin focused on Phials, watching intently as the excited chemist worked a hand up under Tulip's dress. He unzipped, freed himself, masturbated softly, not wanting to come too soon, a long night ahead, Phials capable of going for hours.

Kevin studied everything as Phials took Tulip in all the ways that her brother wanted to but never could, knowing this was as close as he'd ever get. Gasping, circling, telling them what to do, Phials grinning, letting Kevin direct him, Kevin undressing, gliding around the lovers as they writhed on the bed, imagining he was Phials, head exploding with the lights of desire, groaning as he climaxed, Phials taking control as Kevin slumped against a wall, disgusted, loathing himself, but already looking forward to the next rising of his flesh.

Several minutes later he staggered back towards them, taking control again, not meeting his sister's tormented gaze, consumed by evil lust, sacrificing himself to it, burning on an incestuous altar of his making with a savage, sex-fired smile.

FOUR

Gawl McCaskey took a pew near the back of the Church of Sacred Martyrs and waited for Fr Sebastian to summon him. Staring with disinterest at stained glass windows, statues of Christ and the Virgin Mother, the stations of the Cross, remembering the stories from his childhood, reared a good Scottish Catholic, whipped if he couldn't name all the apostles. He started growling to himself at the bitter memories. *Fucking apostles. Who gi'es a fuck. Dead fucking saints — fuck 'em all.*

His blasphemy didn't worry him, even coming in a house of the Lord. Gawl believed in God but didn't care. Suspected there was a devil but wasn't fussed. Religion was for the weak and gullible. He was determined to wring all of the pleasures from this life that he could. Fuck whatever came next. Deal with it when he had to.

Gawl studied his knuckles — cracked, creased, stained, scarred. A labourer's hands. Fighting hands. He had beaten men senseless with these fingers, built roads and houses with them, destroyed with them. A life on building sites and in pubs, laying blocks and breaking skulls. All his history there. Christ needed two rows of documentative paintings but Gawl could see every day of his past in the red lines and ugly lumps of his fingers.

Gawl chuckled. A woman two rows forward glanced

back at him with a frown. He stared her down, grey eyes cold, smiling leanly. This wasn't his patch. He didn't want to draw attention to himself and sour the sweet deal he had going with Fr Sebastian, but if the bitch gave him grief, he'd grab her by her scrawny fucking throat and choke her within an inch of her life.

She looked down at her rosary beads. Gawl sneered. *Yellow fucking hoor, piss the fuck off and take yer Saviour with ye.* Resting his arms on the back of the pew, cherishing his minor victory, beaming around the church, master of the house.

Not many in attendance. Some old ladies at the front, the bitch near Gawl, a few men on their last breaths sitting alone, a couple of bored kids praying by a row of candles. Gawl felt overwhelming contempt for all of them. Anyone who needed a crutch like God was a hopeless case. Gawl stood alone, asked no favours, faced the world on his own terms. God and his angels, Satan and his demons, saints and sinners — they could all go fuck.

A middle-aged woman in tweed stepped out of the confessional. A long pause, then Fr Sebastian stuck his head out, checking to see if anyone else required his services. He spotted Gawl in the recesses of the church and his lips tightened, his face reddening above the white collar. Gawl started to wave but stopped — he'd be a fool to alert the parishioners to his relationship with the priest. Scratched his head instead. Parry disappeared back inside the confessional.

Gawl grinned to himself in the gloom, remembering Leeds, his introduction to Fr Sebastian Parry in a brothel. It was a gangbang. Parry stoned, naked from the waist down, sanctifying bread by dipping it between a laughing whore's legs, passing it around a group of horny punters and giggling prostitutes, all partaking of the *holy host*, Parry deadly serious, praying for their souls, weeping for his own. Gawl refused the bread — he didn't put anything in his mouth that had been in a whore's snatch. He took Parry home afterwards. Thought about rolling him for the contents of his wallet, then thought again — the priest could be a profitable ally, ripe for exploitation. So Gawl fostered a friendship with the straying servant of God. Sober, Parry tried to avoid the brutal Scot, banned Gawl from his church, threatened him with hellfire if he didn't steer clear. Gawl just laughed and kept sniffing round, waiting for Parry to fall prey to his weakness again, ready to lead him to another brothel, fix him up with heroin, protect him, escort him home.

They had it sweet in Leeds. Not long before Parry was dancing to Gawl's tune, doing his bidding, slipping him names and addresses. Always repentant, floods of regretful tears, begging God for strength. But weak, unable to resist temptation, pleading with Gawl to lead him further into his ugly but scintillating world. Super fucking sweet until Parry was caught molesting a choirgirl. The priest was spirited away by his superiors, the scandal hushed up. Gawl thought his goldmine had run dry, that Fr Sebastian would be locked away in an isolated friary. He should have known better — the church always loathe to castigate one of their own, eager to forgive and offer stray sheep a fresh start.

Six years after Leeds, two months after his return to London (Gawl had lived here when he was younger, when he first left Glasgow), he heard a rumour about a crooked priest who was willing to act as a fence, a priest who accepted goods as payment, *goods* being female, young and willing to oblige.

Gawl thought it was too good to be true — it couldn't be Fr Sebastian. Then he remembered one of the Christian tenets he'd had drilled into him as a bairn — *God moves in mysterious ways*. But Gawl didn't. He moved directly, no fucking around. He tracked Parry down to Sacred Martyrs, worked his way back into the priest's life, dangled drugs, women and adventure in front of him. Parry was reluctant (he already had a dealer and some seedy contacts) but he couldn't resist. Gawl had been prepared to blackmail the priest but it never came to that. Parry was soon lapping like the junkie whorehound dog he was. Gawl triumphant. *Yes, you fucker!*

Rising, shuffling his way to the end of the pew, slipping up the side of the church to the confessional. Six-two, lean, tightly muscled, ginger hair turning grey, freckles, face scarred and marked by more blows than he could count, top half of his left ear missing, gnarly at the edges, chewed off in a fight many years ago. He was in his mid-fifties but had the build, stride and passions of a younger man. Chequered work shirt, dirty black jeans, heavy boots. It looked like he'd come from a building site, though he hadn't worked on the sites since pairing up with Parry — richer pickings to be made in church.

Tucking into the confessional, closing the door, air musty, Parry's face distorted by the thick gauze separating the priest from his sinners. "Forgi'e me, Father, for I have sinned," Gawl chuckled. "It's been fuck-knows how long since my last confession."

"Don't blaspheme," Parry hissed. "This is sacred ground. Respect it or get out."

"Don't play high and mighty wi' me, Father," Gawl growled. "I don't gi'e a fuck where we are. I'll speak as I please, right?"

"Have you no fear of God?" Parry sighed.

"Away wi' yer fucking god," Gawl snorted. "Have ye a name for me? I'm low on cash."

"I gave you money last week."

"How the fuck long d' ye think I could survive on what ye squirrel away?" Gawl laughed crudely. "Ye'd be a great man if ye was rich, Father, but as it stands ye're only good for a few nights on the piss. I need a name."

"But it's only been three weeks since the last job," the priest objected. "We agreed you wouldn't hit too often, in case —"

"I know what we agreed," Gawl interrupted sharply. "I also know I'm down t' my last fiver and've been living within my means for the last fortnight, which is fuck all fun. My new motto — bollocks t' budgeting. Gi'e me a name and quit yer fucking whining."

Parry fell silent. Gawl let him mull it over, then said softly, "There's a new girl at Kate's." He heard the priest stiffen. "From Yugoslavia, Bulgaria, some fucking place like that. Fourteen, slim, pretty, speaks no English. Kate's keeping her for special clients, breaking her in slowly. She's no virgin, but ye won't have much trouble imagining she is."

Parry shook, indignant but thrilled. "I take no

pleasure from the corruption of the innocent," he hissed. "My yearnings lead me down dark, lonely roads, but I've no wish to hurt, no desire to –"

"Save it for the big guy when ye die," Gawl cut in. "It's three hundred an hour. Interested or not?"

"Three hundred?" Parry gasped. "I can't afford that."

"Ye can once ye've fenced the goods I'm gonna get from the name ye're gonna gi'e me," Gawl whispered. "I'll cut ye in for thirty percent, same as always. But we have t' move quick, tonight, t' get the money before Kate sells the girl on."

"Sells her on?"

"Whores are like second-hand cars, Father. Traders like Kate buy and sell as the market dictates. The girl will be fifteen soon. She's depreciating every day."

"That's barbaric," Parry moaned. "It's slavery."

"*You* could buy her freedom," Gawl said slyly. "Take her out of her misery, show her the light, install her as yer housekeeper."

"Don't mock me, sinner," Parry snarled, a fierceness in his tone which was rare. Gawl paused uncertainly. He could control Parry most of the time, but when the priest snapped back it worried him. He wasn't sure how to play it.

"Come on, Father," Gawl said, soft this time. "D' ye

want the lass or not? I've told Kate ye're interested, and she's promised t' hold on t' her till the end of the week, but I need an answer t'night."

A long, troubled silence. Then, meekly, "Fourteen?"

Gawl relaxed, confident again. "That's what the girl says. Could be a year or two older — or younger. Good looking girl, Father. Not my type – I like 'em ould and hairy, like my granny – but for a man of yer refined tastes..."

A slow blurring motion on the other side of the gauze — Parry crossing himself. "We'll burn in hell for our sins, McCaskey," he whimpered.

"Aye," Gawl laughed, "so we'd better make the most of the good times while we can, right? A name, Father. I can do it t'night, ye can fence the goods, take yer cut straight from the profits, be enjoying the lass this time t'morrow."

Another long pause. Then, quietly, desperately, "Janet Adams. A widow of just three months. Lives in a small terraced house in Islington. Not much cash but lots of silver and gold trinkets. Her husband didn't trust the banks."

"Alarm systems?"

"I don't think so but I'm not certain."

"I'll tread careful then."

"If you wait a couple of days, you can do it while she's out," Parry said. "She goes to bingo every –"

"No waiting," Gawl snapped. "I hit t'night."

"But it would be safer –"

"Leave the safety lessons t' me, Father. Her name and address — write them down."

"Can't I just tell you?"

"That's not the way we do it. If ye tell me and I'm caught, I can't shop ye t' the police t' get a reduced sentence — it'd be my word against yours, and we both know which way that'd go. But if ye write it out nice and clear…"

"You're an evil man, McCaskey," Fr Sebastian said bitterly.

"Aye, but I don't pretend t' be anything else. And as bad as I am, I don't fuck children." The priest flinched. "Now gi'e me the fucking address."

Fr Sebastian sighed, asked God for forgiveness, then produced a pen and paper and started to write.

Gawl didn't study the scrap of paper until he was on the Tube, surrounded by strangers, invisible in the crush. Unfolded it casually and checked the address. North London wasn't his usual territory. Not sure whether he should case the house or hit it straight. He tucked the paper away, undecided, figuring he'd make the call when he got there.

Gawl could have taken the Northern line direct from the Elephant & Castle to Angel, but he had a social call to make first, fishing for connections, so he took the Bakerloo line to Picadilly Circus then walked to the League of Victoria, where he stood outside the lobby, gazing in at the receptionist and pair of guards, before crossing the road to shelter in the doorway of the building opposite. He watched guests arriving and leaving, killed time by trying to guess which were there for the Bush's party and which were regular members. Enviously eyeing the women in their fine dresses, taking the measure of the men with them — strong, determined, resourceful. Men Gawl respected and feared. Men he wanted to work for. Knowing he was too old, too common, too blunt to ever be part of the elite inner circle, content if he could hover at the edges and be thrown a few scraps to keep him sweet in his old age.

He saw Big Sandy enter and depart. Didn't know much about the giant, except he was Dave Bushinsky's strong right arm, did the Bush's dirty work for him, the sort of work Gawl could do if he had the backing of a boss like Bushinsky. All his life he'd been in search of a true master. He'd worked for many violent, powerful men in many cities – Glasgow, London, Berlin, Melbourne and Sydney during his Australian years – but always short-term, never taken into their confidence, always on the outskirts, expendable, unprotected.

For a long time that had been enough – he liked to boast that he was slave to no man – but secretly he'd always envied the likes of Big Sandy, Fast Eddie Price, Eyes Burton. They were part of a crew, they didn't have to watch their backs every minute, always a lawyer on hand to bail them out of trouble and smooth things over with the police.

And now Gawl was getting old, slowing down, vulnerable. Still a tough son of a bitch, tear apart any fucker in London if he had a mind to — but for how much longer? What when his fifties became his sixties and his hands shook and his legs didn't always support him and young wolves sensed his weakness and closed in on him? He needed a boss who would shelter him. The only alternative was a big score to see him through his twilight years, but *big scores* were the province of crime thrillers. Men like Gawl McCaskey didn't rob a bank and see out their days in style. If they were lucky they earned enough to scrape by and found a safe haven where they could grow old quietly and die of natural causes. Most were denied even that, preyed upon by jackals and vultures, picked clean, left to rot in gutters and doss-houses.

Gawl would rather die than end up like that, begging for change, sleeping rough, shat upon by the world and all those in it. But he hoped to avoid death — his plan was to get in with the Bush or some other well-placed crook, work hard, earn the respect of his boss, stash away enough cash over the next decade to pay for a room in a retirement home. He'd been sniffing around since returning to London, but no luck yet. Had a good feeling about the Bush. He knew Eyes Burton, one of the Bush's bodyguards, and thought that maybe Eyes could get him in.

Waiting patiently. Eyes was a chain-smoker, sixty a day. It was only a matter of time before he slipped out for a puff. On cue — the door of the club opened and Eyes slipped out, lighting up as soon as his feet hit the pavement. Gawl let him smoke the first fag and light up a second before pursuing him, calling as he crossed the road, "Hey, Eyes, those fuckers'll kill ye."

Eyes stared hard at Gawl, impossible to read since he always looked the same — pissed-off. "Gawl," he muttered neutrally, dragging on his fag.

Gawl pulled up beside Eyes Burton and smiled his warmest. "Good party?"

Eyes shrugged. "What I've seen of it."

"I expected an invitation. I'm disappointed."

Eyes smiled thinly. "Must have got lost in the post."

Gawl was nervous, trying not to look it. "How's the Bush?"

"Mr Bushinsky to you," Eyes said.

Gawl's smile slipped but he ploughed ahead. "Have ye told him about me?"

"I've mentioned you." Eyes sniffed. "He made enquiries. Heard bad things from Glasgow."

"Ye cannae trust the fucking Scots," Gawl joked, heart sinking, wondering how much those bastards had told the Bush, if he'd have to move on again.

"You're not popular up there. You didn't tell me."

"Nobody talks about their bad shit unless they have t'," Gawl said quietly. "If ye'd asked, I'd've told. I never lied."

Eyes nodded. "But you made me look bad by not mentioning it."

Gawl scowled at his feet. "So no chance of a fucking job?"

Eyes puffed deep and drew the moment out. "It's a bad time. Dave's talking of going legit. Even if the reports hadn't been negative, I doubt he'd have found a place for you. He's not looking for trouble right now."

Gawl nodded sourly. "So it's thanks, Mr McCaskey, but fuck off."

"Basically." Eyes stubbed out the cigarette and turned back towards the club. "My advice — hang in there. Make yourself busy. Prove you're not the crazy fuck that the Glaswegians claim. If things change, I might be able to push some work your way."

"Thanks." Gawl offered his hand and Eyes shook it. "Stay in touch?"

"Sure," Eyes said and headed back into the club, leaving Gawl to glare at the wall, hands clenched into fists.

Fucker! Jewish prick! Fuck Dave Bushinsky and his scum-fucked stooges! Gawl didn't need them, bigger sharks in the sea, the Bush a fucking nancy. Trying to go legit? Fuck that. Gawl was better off clear of the fool. This wasn't the first time he'd seen this happen. It never worked. Bushinsky would get the brush-off from the legit world, same as all the others who'd tried to clean up their act. Let him come crawling to Gawl when the suits gave him the big fuck-off. Gawl would tell him to go fuck himself, spit on him as he said it.

Gawl stormed away, cursing Bushinsky, Eyes Burton and their kind. Marched to the Tube station, barging past a group of teenagers at the entrance, knocking them aside, ignoring their cries and shouts, down beneath the ground where monstrous steel slugs burrowed through the earth. North to Angel, fuming all the way. Back on the streets, face dark with hatred, fishing in his pocket for the address, not sure of his direction, getting lost, backtracking, rage increasing as he got frustrated, Gawl deliberately working up a head of vengeful steam, feeding on his fury.

Eventually he found it, a small house as the priest had said, a light in one of the rear ground rooms, houses on either side both dark downstairs. Gawl checked his watch — nearly twenty past eleven. The old bitch could be in bed, the light just to scare off burglars. He stood on the doorstep uncertainly. Then he saw a moving shadow inside — she was awake. Steeling himself, he knocked brazenly. A pause. Then footsteps, hesitant, the old bitch rightfully wary. She switched on the light in the hall and called to him shakily without opening the door, "Yes?"

Gawl masked his strong Scottish accent. "Mrs Janet Adams?"

"Yes."

"Police, ma'am. One of your neighbours said they saw someone loitering behind your house. They asked us to check that you were all right."

"Loitering?" She sounded confused.

"Is your back door secure, ma'am? Your windows?"

"Yes, I think so."

"It's probably nothing, but we'd like t' check, if that's OK with you."

"Of course, officer. Do you need to come in?" Guarded, suspicious.

"No, ma'am, I'll go around the side. I don't want t' disturb you any more than necessary. I just wanted to warn you, in case you heard me back there and got scared."

"Don't be silly," she chuckled, guard dropping, opening the door. "Come on through, it's much quicker and –"

Gawl didn't wait for the door to open all the way. Barged in, knocked her over, grabbed the door and shut it swiftly, careful not to let it bang. Janet Adams on the floor, frizzy grey hair, red dressing gown, furry white slippers, gasping, shaking, too shocked to scream. Gawl crouched over her and snarled, "Keep yer fucking trap shut and ye won't be hurt." Her eyes round, glassy. He grabbed her shoulders and shook hard. "I don't want t' hurt ye. I'm just here for the money. But I'll kill ye if ye fuck wi' me."

"I... I... I..."

Gawl kissed her roughly. She stared at him, amazed, when he broke the kiss — but no longer shaking, momentarily too astonished to be afraid. "That was t' calm ye down," he chuckled, wiping his lips on the back of his hand. "Ye needn't think this is yer lucky night — I'm not into saggy auld cunts."

Her features stiffened indignantly. Gawl's words calculated to reduce the threat — an angry victim was easier to control than a frightened one. Now that she was thinking straight, she'd realise that the sooner she gave him what he wanted, the sooner she could be rid of him.

"What do you want?" she hissed.

"Money if ye have any, jewellery or anything else that I can sell."

"I don't have anything. I'm a widow. You should –"

Gawl slapped her, just hard enough to sting. She cried out softly and covered her cheek with her hands. Gawl pointed a finger at her. "If ye fuck wi' me, missus, ye'll regret it."

"You shouldn't have done that," she sobbed. "You should never hit a woman."

"I'll do more than hit ye if ye piss me off. Now, what's downstairs that I can sell?" She didn't answer. He prodded her face with his finger, forcing another thin cry. "Last chance t' cooperate."

She stared at his eyes. Saw his intent. Nodded weakly. "The drawing room... photographs... silver frames. Some small trophies. Nothing valuable."

"We'll have a look all the same," Gawl grunted, picking her up and shoving her forward. "Which door?"

"This one," the old woman said, grasping the handle to steady herself, shaking, sobbing, but not cracking. Opened the door and reached towards the light switch.

"Not so fast, Annie Oakley." Gawl pulled her back, checking to make sure the curtains were drawn, then turned on the light himself. He pulled her into the room, pushed her at a chair, made a quick appraisal of the goods on display. As the old bitch had led him to believe, photo frames and trophies, nothing worth taking. Didn't want to leave empty handed though — had to drive home the point that this was a burglary, keep her cowed. He found a nice lighter on the mantelpiece over the fireplace. Worth a few quid. He pocketed it and turned on Janet Adams, who was still rubbing her slapped cheek, staring at him like he was a monster. Walked past her, not letting her fix on his face too closely, and muttered, "Upstairs."

Janet followed the intruder out into the corridor. Her eyes fixed longingly on the telephone as they passed.

She wondered if she could reach it, dial for the police and warn them about the man in her house before he could stop her. Played the scene through several times, each time the same unfavourable result. She was too old, too slow, too close to him. Safest bet — do as he said, let him take what he wished, phone the police as soon as he left.

The landing at the top of the stairs. Three bedrooms, a bathroom and a closet. Gawl kept hold of the old woman and pushed each door open, checking all the rooms, making sure they were alone, taking no chances. Satisfied, he began with the spare rooms, full of photographs of the bitch's dead husband and two grown-up sons. Nothing of any great value, but he found a lavish pen-knife in one room, some gold medals in the other. Then Janet's room — payload. Jewellery boxes stacked on the dressing table. Gawl raided them, having first made Janet face the wall so she couldn't study him at length. Lots of necklaces, rings, bracelets. Good shit, easy to fence. Gawl hummed *We're in the Money* while he filled his pockets.

Once the boxes had been emptied, valuables stashed, cheap junk ignored, Gawl turned his attention to the drawers. The first — a bible, rosary beads, mass cards. Gawl stared at the bible, then at Janet Adams. He grinned bleakly, still stinging from the Bush's rebuke, needing to make someone feel worse than he felt. He reached for the bible, stopped, half-closed the drawer. Save it for later. Work came first. He searched the other drawers, found loose cash in a purse – less than forty pounds – more rings, a verrrrry nice necklace hidden under a pile of tights in the lowest drawer on the left, the highlight of the lot, should fetch a few hundred.

Gawl ran his gaze over the table one last time, making sure he hadn't missed anything, then faced Janet Adams and smiled like a snake. Decided to tease her a little. "Where's the safe?" he growled.

"I don't have one," Janet said, not turning around.

"Don't lie t' me," Gawl shouted, then thought about the neighbours and lowered his voice. "Tell me where the safe is or I'll cut yer tits off."

Janet made a weird sound, half-sob, half-laugh. "Good luck," she sneered with unexpected strength. "Breast cancer. Both had to be removed."

Gawl's face dropped and he snarled, "Think ye're fucking clever?"

"No," Janet said quickly, resilience fading as swiftly as it flared.

"Come here."

Janet half-turned, stalled, faced the wall again.

"Please," she sobbed. "You have what you came for. Leave me alone."

"Don't tell me my fucking business," Gawl hissed. "Get over here." When Janet didn't obey, he crossed the room, grabbed her by her neck and dragged her to the dressing table. She cried out with pain and fear. He squeezed tightly to silence her, then shoved her to the floor. As she wept and shook, he opened the drawer where the bible was nestled and yanked out the holy book.

"Are ye religious, Janet?" he asked slyly. She moaned in response. "What was that?" He kicked the floor by her stomach. She winced and sucked her body away from him as if he'd connected. "Speak up, girl. D' ye believe in God?"

"Of... course," she gasped, sobbing, covering her eyes with her hands, wishing the horrible intruder gone, fearful of what he intended.

"D' ye think he's looking down on us now?" Gawl asked conversationally. "D' ye think he's watching, thinking I'm an awful wee man, feeling pity for ye?" Janet shook her head and didn't answer. "What was that? I didn't catch it."

"I don't... know," Janet wheezed. "Please... don't hurt me."

"Hurt ye?" Gawl blinked innocently. "D' ye think I'm gonna rape ye?" Janet moaned. "Silly auld cow. I already told ye that wasn't my thing."

"Please," Janet sobbed. "You have everything. Go. Don't hurt me."

"I'm not gonna hurt ye," Gawl laughed. "I just want t' pray wi' ye before I go."

The old woman's sob caught in her throat. She stared at the tall, evil man. "You want... to *pray*... with me?"

"Aye." Gawl shook the bible. "Let's say a wee prayer and ask God t' forgive me. Is that OK, Janet, or would ye rather not pray wi' a miserable sinner like me?"

"I... I'll pray with you if you're serious," Janet said, wiping tears from her cheeks, half-hopeful. Perhaps the brute could be redeemed, maybe he'd see the error of his ways, return the objects he'd stolen, reform, put the wickedness of his past behind him and...

"That's fucking brilliant," Gawl beamed, then dropped the bible, undid his jeans and exposed himself. Janet moaned and shut her eyes, bitter at herself for her foolish surge of hope. "Open up," Gawl cooed.

"Go away," she snapped.

"That's not very Christian of ye," Gawl tutted. "I'm giving ye the chance t' save my wretched soul. Don't ye want t' save me?"

Janet opened her eyes and gazed hatefully at the man who'd brought mockery into her life. "All sins are paid," she whispered. "You'll suffer for your arrogance and crimes, not only in the next world, but in this. God punishes. You're a fool if you think he doesn't."

Gawl's eyes narrowed. She had no right talking to him like that. It wasn't her place to lecture him. He could kill her. He'd killed before and had been waiting a long time to strike again. He took a step towards the woman, fingers spreading, nostrils flaring, the taste of murder thick on his tongue, penis hardening as he pictured her throat between his hands, choking, tongue sticking out, eyes bulging. He'd release her, let her think he'd stopped, then fall upon her again and...

"No," he groaned aloud, stopping short of the terrified Janet. Fr Sebastian knew he was here. If he killed her, the priest would have an unbreakable hold over him. Gawl had been careful all his life, almost never succumbing to his murderous impulses, killing only when it was safe, when he couldn't be held to ransom.

"Did ye think I was gonna get bloody on ye, Janet?" Gawl chuckled sickly, making a joke of it. "Ye have t' learn t' relax — separate the real fears from the bullshit, right? Now, let's pray." Gawl looked down, located the bible, stepped over it so that it lay a few inches on the floor in front of him. "Kneel, Janet," he ordered. "Hands together on yer knees." When she didn't react, he barked at her, "Kneel!" This time she obeyed, face haggard, weeping fresh tears. "That's good. Now, repeat after me. 'I believe in one dog...'"

"'I believe in...'" Janet started, then stopped.

"Go on," he urged her.

"No," she croaked. "I won't take the Lord's name in vain."

"Say it," Gawl said softly, "or I'll slit yer fucking throat, right?" Bluffing, but she didn't dare test his resolve.

"'I... believe in... one dog,'" she moaned, silently begging God to forgive her, praying he'd take mercy on a poor old woman too frightened and weak to be a martyr for her beliefs.

"'The alsation almighty,'" Gawl chuckled.

"'The alsation... almighty,'" Janet sighed.

"'Creator of howls and piss,'" Gawl said and urinated on the bible, a steady yellow stream, howling softly so as not to disturb the neighbours.

Janet closed her eyes, blessed herself, then muttered sickly, "'Creator of howls and piss.'"

Gawl laughed and went on pissing, power in the defilement, showing Janet Adams how strong he was, how free he was. Showing God, Dave Bushinsky and Eyes Burton. Showing the world and everybody who'd crossed him over the years. Showing himself. Showing them all.

october 2000

FIVE

September bled into October, shortening days, weather turning, London gearing itself up for the coming winter. Big Sandy busy, something new every day, the Bush deploying him wherever he could be of use, making the most of his violent talents.

Two of the Bush's men accepted a shipment of heroin which had come a long, twisting route through Europe. The Russian sellers were new contacts, the Bush not sure he could trust them, so Big Sandy was sent along armed to the teeth. He stood silently on the sidelines while the deal was going down, ready to wade in if the Russkies tried to pull a fast one.

A woman from the Bush's old neighbourhood complained to him about her husband. Eric Flowers was a drunk who beat her and their children. She was sick of it but couldn't go to the police — the pair were pickpockets, they worked pubs and clubs together, he could rat her out if she had him sent down. Big Sandy waited for Eric at their home one night, wife and kids gone on a short vacation. A painful lesson, cracked ribs, shattered nose, the two smallest fingers on each hand snapped. It ended with Eric's head in the gas oven, left with the threat that if he hit his wife again, he'd be suffocated next time. Big Sandy walked away pleased with his night's work. He despised wife-beaters. Wished he could kick the shit out of scum like Eric every night.

A rabbi associate of the Bush's in east London was having a hard time. Local thugs had been making sporadic attacks on his synagogue, trying to drive him out. Not the Bush's turf but he agreed to help, keen to foster closer links with civic leaders now that he was going legit. Big Sandy was dispatched to the synagogue, long nights waiting within, dark and lonely, Big Sandy resting in the shadows, brooding, patient. He was Catholic but many of the Bush's men were Jewish and Big Sandy was accustomed to synagogues, so he wasn't fazed by the job.

Sixth night — stones came flying through the windows. Laughter outside. Big Sandy jogged to the door, burst out swinging a thick length of chain. Took three of them down before they knew what was happening. Two more put up a brief, ill-advised fight. The last guy fled. One of the downed anti-Semites was unconscious, skull ripped open by the chain. Two of the others were badly injured, screaming. He focused on the final pair, grabbed them by their collars, dragged them inside, stood over them, chain held taut between his giant hands. "Give me your wallets." They didn't react. Big Sandy's chain snapped and found flesh. Screams, then wallets were hastily dug out of pockets. Big Sandy studied names and addresses. "If this place is targeted again, I'll come find you."

"Fucking kike," one of the men wept. Big Sandy grabbed him and stuck four fingers in the man's mouth. The bigot gagged. Big Sandy jerked hard, left then right. The man's cheeks ripped like cloth. Big Sandy released him and left him to moan and bleed. The other man was ashen.

"This synagogue's protected," Big Sandy said evenly. "Stay away." He ushered them out, kicking their legs and arses, licking their backs with his chain, set them loose to gather their colleagues and stumble to freedom. Mopped up the blood. Phoned a glazier, left a message for him to come in the morning to repair the windows. Phoned the rabbi, said he'd sorted things out, to contact them again if there were any comebacks. The rabbi thanked him and said he'd pray for him. Big Sandy didn't reply. Got a cab home, staring out the window at the sleeping city, wondering if helping a rabbi in some way compromised his standing as a Catholic.

The day after. Big Sandy woken by the phone, the Bush calling to thank him. Big Sandy yawned and made little of it. The Bush asked if he had a suit. "Yeah..." he said cautiously. "My niece, Shula Schimmel, is still here.

Supposed to return to Switzerland last week but we can't get rid of her. I've been keeping tabs but it ain't easy, an eighteen year old girl in London with a taste for parties and clubs..."

Big Sandy remembered the beautiful young woman. That had been the night when he'd read to the boy after killing Tommy Utah. As he'd figured, the boy hadn't been able to tell the police anything about the man who'd killed his father, so life rolled on as normal for Big Sandy. But it wasn't a night he'd forget.

"You want me to look after your niece?" Big Sandy grunted.

"I've had younger men on the job but they keep going gooey-eyed and losing her. You probably won't have any more luck, but if you can trail her around for a few nights, try and make sure she doesn't get into trouble..."

"Sure. She's staying at your place?"

"No more she's not," the Bush sighed. "She's in a hotel near Gloucester Road — the Harrington Hall. Alice said the girl needs her independence and who am I to argue?"

"Does she expect me?"

"She expects some handsome, stylish guardian angel like the others I've sent to watch over her. Doesn't know

I'm sending a yeti this time."

Big Sandy grinned. "Give me her room number and a list of the places you want me to steer her clear of. I'll do what I can."

Shula was decidedly unimpressed when Big Sandy turned up. She stared at his craggy face, the dusty suit, his untidy hair. "If uncle Dave thinks I'm stepping out with you, he's crazy," she snorted, dashing upstairs to make an emergency call. She returned ten minutes later, sullen. "He said I go with you or stay indoors."

"Be a lot easier on both of us if you stayed in," Big Sandy noted.

She tried withering him with a look, saw that it was wasted, and smiled. "Come on then, we might as well make the most of it. Try not to look too conspicuous."

In the car she asked for his name. "Big Sandy."

"I mean your real name," she laughed, tugging at the tight material of her dress, breathing heavily to direct her small but effective breasts at him, eyes twinkling.

"Just call me Big Sandy." Staring neutrally at her, not looking away, not ogling her either.

"What's your surname?" she pressed.

"Murphy."

"I'll call you Mr Murphy then."

Big Sandy shrugged and the cab rocked gently. "If

you want."

First port of call was Notting Hill, trendy pubs, Shula connecting with lots of new friends, kissing cheeks, introducing a few of them to Big Sandy, who hovered in the background, quiet, polite, teetotal, alert. Some of her friends (a few egged on by Shula) asked Big Sandy what he did for a living, where he got his hair cut, was he a gangster, who was his tailor. Big Sandy ignored them. Spoilt rich kids or students, their ignorance understandable and acceptable. The only time he reacted was when a girl asked if he could hook her up with a dealer. Big Sandy frowned and his grimace sent her scurrying from the pub, so flustered that she forgot her purse and had to return, giggling shrilly, to fetch it.

Shula was mildly upset that Big Sandy didn't feel belittled. "They're laughing at you," she told him as they cabbed between pubs.

"I don't mind."

"You could stop them. You're big, tough. You could make them respect you."

Big Sandy shook his head. "No, they'd only fear me and laugh about me behind my back instead of to my face."

"Doesn't it bother you?" she asked.

Big Sandy smiled. "They're kids. Let them laugh."

They hit a party up the West End. Shula lost Big Sandy in the crush and he had to circle, searching for her. Spotted her on a couch with Lawrence Drake, the pair talking softly, Drake's fingers drumming Shula's knee. Big Sandy paused — break them up and make a scene, or stand back and keep watch? He chose to stand back. Nothing serious went down — Drake leant forward a few times, trying to kiss the teenager, only for Shula to laugh and peel away — but Big Sandy didn't like it.

"He's too old for you," he told her as Shula relaxed in a cab on their way to a club.

"Hmm?" Eyes opening drowsily.

"Drake's bad news, a borderline paedophile. Your uncle won't approve."

"Larry's fun," Shula yawned. "I know he's a lech — that's what makes him so amusing. I know how to play him. I won't let him *deflower* me." She squinted. "Will you tell uncle Dave about him?" Big Sandy nodded. "Nobody likes a snitch," Shula sniffed.

"I'm paid to observe and report," Big Sandy retorted coolly.

"You don't have to report everything."

"No, only what's relevant. Larry Drake's relevant." A pause. "But I'll tell him I didn't see anything untoward, you know how to handle yourself, and he probably doesn't need to worry."

Shula smiled. "You're a sweetheart." She leant across and pecked Big Sandy's nose, then half pulled away, eyes hooded, inviting a response.

Big Sandy laughed. "You're a sweet thing, aren't you?"

Shula pouted. "That was meant to be provocative, not daughterly."

Big Sandy bent and kissed her nose. "That's what made it so sweet."

Shula smiled, thinking, *He could have bitten off my nose!* Feeling like a girl in league with a wild bear. She snuggled up to him, but not teasing him now, hugging him like an uncle. Big Sandy saw this and reciprocated her hug, but gently, careful not to crush the tender girl.

SIX

Clint had started shadowing Shula Schimmel. Nothing stalker-level, just trailing her around at night sometimes, watching her mingle, hovering at the edges of her world, dreaming about one day being part of it.

Dropping by cousin Dave's house one day not long after the party – unusual but not the first time he'd visited – he managed to get chatting to her for a few minutes and casually asked if she was enjoying London, how often she went out, the places she frequented.

It was easy to keep tabs on her after that, and he had a legitimate reason to pop up in the pubs and clubs, dealing as he went. Occasionally she noticed him and said hello – that always put a big smile on his face – but more often than not he hid in the shadows, watching in silence from across a busy room. It was easier to believe in the dream if he viewed her from afar.

There were all sorts of things that he wanted to say to her, and he would spend his down time rehearsing, running lines through his head, sometimes practising out loud. But whenever their paths crossed and she smiled at him and instigated a short conversation, he would feeze, mutter something inane, fail to make the most of the moment.

As besotted as he was, he didn't let that distract him

from business. This was a good time of year, students returning to college, loaded at the start of a new term, desperate to get high, lots of them not sure how much they should be paying, easy to con. Although Clint cut some nice deals while trailing Shula, he didn't want to do too much business in the places she frequented, in case the Bush heard — he might not want his wife's niece to be involved, even in passing, with anything major.

So Clint peeled himself away and did the campus rounds, hitting student pubs, smartly dressed and worldwise compared to the fresh-faced teenagers, feeling much older, like a real gangster. Making good deals wherever he went, E's selling themselves, coke and grass trickling through his fingers. Not much of a demand for heroin, but he was able to offload that to his regular hardcore junkies. He was making a lot of money and investing most of it in cousin Dave's various operations — good business bets, high returns, and the Bush approved of his men sticking their cash back into the organisation.

Clint also started to spend more time with Tony Phials. The chemist was crazy, but smart, funny and friendly. Eager to worm his way into the heart of his cousin's empire, to make more money and get closer to Shula, Clint had taken the doc up on his offer to hang out and swung by one slow evening in the middle of September, expecting to be turned away. To his surprise, Phials was delighted to see him, took Clint to the games room, treated him to all the drinks he cared for. They shot pool, smoked some grass (Clint normally didn't indulge but the prof refused to smoke alone), bullshitted. Clint returned a few days later and had been coming two or three times a week since.

They watched movies together on Phials' 55 inch widescreen TV. The doc had seen more films than Clint ever would. "I'm an insomniac," he explained. "If I get three hours sleep it's cause to celebrate. I grew up in a small town, nothing to do in the dead of night but sit up and watch movies on cable."

Like Clint, Phials loved gangster movies, though his favourites were the black-and-white flicks of the thirties and forties. Clint didn't know much about films before *The Godfather*. Phials introduced him to the originals, a new slate of actors — Bogart, Cagney, George Raft, Paul Muni, Edward G Robinson. Clint not as keen on the oldies as the doc was, but he enjoyed them.

He started mentioning the movies when he met with Shula, telling her about them. She was interested and he bought a few DVDs for her, which she watched and liked. She was starting to spend more time on him now when their paths crossed. Most of the talk was confined to the old films they were watching, but that didn't bother Clint. He was delighted just to have an in. He didn't care what they discussed just as long as he got to share those personal moments with her.

He discussed Shula with Phials sometimes, late at night, dizzy from too many Buds or Millers, talking big, making plans. He'd impress the Bush, make lots of money, earn Shula's love and respect, then whisk her off to America. He was in love with the idea of America. He'd always dreamt of moving there, becoming part of the American dream. He felt he'd fit in more easily across the ocean, especially with a beautiful wife by his side. For a long time he had only dreamt idly of the move. Now he was seriously considering it, looking for ways to make it happen, Shula the spur for his reawakened desire to do more with his life.

Phials listened with a wry smile when Clint rattled on about Shula and the States, saying little until Clint would ask him to describe America, its cities, its people, its gangsters. Then he'd talk for hours, recalling the good times, boasting of the power he'd wielded, the success he'd enjoyed — money, women, sports cars, part-ownership of a night club. All lost to the demons of addiction, wealth squandered, trusts betrayed, deserted by his friends, forced to flee the country, hounded for debts he owed and lives he'd ruined.

"I did terrible things," he said one night, eyes glazed, staring at the blank TV screen after a Bogie double-bill. "Designer drugs have always been my thing. I was cautious, tested my product thoroughly before releasing it to market. But as I got hooked, I lost control. Towards the end I pumped experimental drugs out on to the streets. People died. I hear their cries sometimes when I dream."

"Is that what you're making now?" Clint asked.

Phials squinted. "Hasn't your cousin told you what I do?" Clint shook his head. "You haven't asked about me?"

Clint shrugged. "I didn't want to pry."

Phials smiled. "You won't get rich that way. You've gotta take an interest in people if you want to use them."

Clint laughed edgily. "I don't want to use you." Then, curious, "How could I?"

"I'm a money machine," Phials said softly, staring deep into the blank screen. "I invent. I'm a magician. If you wanted to live dangerously and take a gamble, you might try and find out what I was working on, double-cross your cousin, try and cut a deal with me, maybe take the shit off my hands and sell it yourself."

Clint grinned weakly. "I cuh-couldn't. Dave's been guh-good to me, he trusts me. Besides, if I did, and he fuh-fuh-found out…"

Phials silent, no response. Then, "Know what I want?"

"What?"

"Tulip. Is she free?"

"I don't know." Clint produced his mobile and chuckled, confident now that he was back on familiar territory. "But I can soon find out."

Kevin and Tulip Tyne — an unexpected goldmine. Jack Mack had introduced them. Jack supplied dealers like Clint with coke. One of his guys used to sell to Kevin but he'd got busted. Jack Mack gave Clint the unfortunate dealer's list of contacts. Kevin was one of the names. The pair met a few times, business as usual, Kevin just another client as far as Clint was concerned.

Then Clint arrived one afternoon to find Jack Mack sitting in his garden with a business associate, both men high, talking sex. Jack wanted to hear about Clint's sex life. Clint invented wild tales to appear the equal of the others, babbled about threesomes, nymphos, the mile high club. Jack Mack told him he could top all that.

"You sell to Kevin Tyne. Nice guy, huh? But I bet you

don't know about his sister." Nudged the other guy in the ribs. "This shit you *won't* believe."

Jack Mack told them that the brother and sister provided sexual services to a small group of hand-picked customers, very exclusive, very hush-hush. The girl was young, fifteen or sixteen, and would do whatever you wanted, but only as long as the brother could watch.

"He drifts about, watching you fuck her, takes off his clothes and jerks off."

"That's all he does?" Jack Mack's guest – he never gave his name – frowned. "He doesn't get it on with you or the sister?"

"Never touched either one of us," Jack Mack giggled. "I only did it once, to see what it was like — a hell of an experience, but not my scene. Most of their clients are sick fucks who need to be watched, who get off on it."

"Can't be much demand for something like that," Jack's guest mused.

"You'd be surprised," Jack Mack laughed.

Clint thought about Kevin and his sister a lot over the next few weeks. He met Kevin a couple of times to sell to him. Clint wanted to verify the story but was afraid that Kevin would take his business elsewhere if Clint offended him. He couldn't afford to lose a regular client like Kevin Tyne, so he kept his mouth shut.

A couple of months later, at one of Dave's parties, he heard his cousin talking about some chemical genius who worked for him. "Getting itchy," Dave sighed. "Locked up too long. I supply him with all the hookers he asks for, but he likes it kinky. I haven't found any who can hold his interest. I've thrown him every type going. Phials takes them all then asks for more. I don't know what to send next."

"Actually," Clint coughed, seizing the moment, atypically daring, "I know a bruh-brother and sister, weird fuh-fuh-fucking sh-shit. I could suh-set him up with them if you wuh-wuh-wuh-wanted..."

At his next meeting with Kevin, he nervously admitted to having heard about Kevin's sister and their act, careful not to mention Jack Mack. Kevin was angry, denied it, thought Clint was trying to entrap him. Clint calmed him down, said he'd known for some time, didn't care, wouldn't have brought it up except he had an offer for Kevin, a client who was discreet and could pay handsomely. Kevin eventually agreed to visit Phials for a trial session.

Clint met Phials for the first time the next night, at the lab, when he made the introductions. Kevin and Tulip were edgy, Phials bemused, not sure what he was letting himself in for. Clint lingered outside while they were having sex, waiting to take the Tynes home, nervous, wondering how cousin Dave would react if the chemist complained. Phials emerged naked, buzzing, beaming. Clasped Clint's shoulders and barked, "I want them again. I don't care what they cost. Give me your number."

The Bush surprised and impressed, Clint elated. That was when the world had started to open up a little for him. Then Shula had entered his life and Phials had invited him to hang out. It was all coming together. Clint was gathering momentum and there was no telling where it might end. Today a mad doctor and a couple of incestuous sex fetishists, tomorrow Shula Schimmel (*Mrs Clint Smith*) and the U.S. of Clint.

SEVEN

It was late when Clint phoned. Tulip was sleeping. Kevin thought about refusing the appointment, but Phials was a valuable customer and Clint had set them up with a few of Dave Bushinsky's other associates recently. He couldn't risk queering the deal, so he shook Tulip awake. She grumbled, tried to dissuade him, but he persisted. An hour later Tony Phials was sweating, thrusting in and out of Tulip, her eyes fixed on the ceiling, detached, silent, Kevin circling voraciously.

Afterwards, while Tulip was dressing and Phials was flaked out across his bed, Kevin collared Clint, who as usual was waiting outside. "Do you know a guy called Martin Laskey?"

"Heard of him."

"We have an appointment with him tomorrow. East London. His place."

"So?" Clint asked.

"He knows how we work but I'm not convinced he'll abide by the rules. I think he only wants Tulip, that he might try to force me out of the equation."

"Why don't you sack him off?"

Kevin scowled. "The money's *good*. He kept upping the offer when I said no. It's hard to resist."

Clint shrugged. "What do you want me to do about it?"

"Alone, I can't stop him if he throws me out. But if we had a bodyguard..."

Clint frowned. "You want one of Dave's men to go with you?"

Kevin nodded reluctantly. "This isn't the first time I've had reservations about an appointment. In the past I've cancelled or taken the risk. If we had someone to protect us, it would make life simpler."

"Protection isn't cheap," Clint drawled, not sure if it was or wasn't.

"I'll meet any reasonable price," Kevin said.

Clint cracked his knuckles, trying to exude confidence. "I'll talk with Dave and sort something out."

The Bush was interested when Clint called in to see him the next morning in his Whitechapel office, one of several dotted around the city. "Forget payment," he said. "We'll provide protection for free."

"So that he'll owe us a favour?" Clint asked.

"Partly. But mostly to find out who their clients are. Vice is power. A man's weaknesses can be used against him, especially if he's a public figure."

"But Kevin's willing to pay," Clint said, eager to make a quick profit, wanting to get a new suit so that he might catch Shula's eye the next time she saw him.

The Bush smiled patiently. "If we make them pay,

they'll ask for assistance only when it's imperative. If we throw in a bodyguard for free, they'll make use of him all the time. We'll learn a lot more that way."

That night Kevin opened the door to Clint Smith and one of the largest men he'd ever seen. Clint introduced him as Big Sandy Murphy then left them together, anxious to be out of there, still nervous around Big Sandy, wishing his cousin had sent another of his goons.

Big Sandy smiled reassuringly at Kevin as the door closed. "It's OK," he said. "I'm house-trained."

Kevin smiled weakly. Tulip stepped out of the bedroom, paused when she saw the giant. He nodded politely and Kevin told her who he was. "Nice to meet you, Mr Murphy," she said, shaking his hand, hers almost invisible in his.

"Call me Big Sandy," he said, studying the small girl, her sad eyes, the gold cross around her neck, wondering why she did this, if her brother forced her or if she volunteered. Not too concerned either way. None of his business.

"Can I get you something to drink?" Kevin asked, not liking the way Big Sandy was staring at his sister.

"Just water," Big Sandy said. Tulip returned to the bedroom to prepare. Big Sandy followed Kevin into the tiny kitchen. "Tell me about tonight."

"You don't know?" Kevin asked, surprised.

"I know what you do. But tell me about Martin Laskey, why you're nervous. The more I know, the more I can guard against."

Kevin shrugged. "I just want to make sure he honours our bargain."

"You want to make sure he lets you watch him fuck your sister."

Kevin blushed angrily. "Yes."

"OK," Big Sandy nodded. "I can take care of that."

A long cab ride east, Big Sandy up front beside the driver, Kevin and Tulip in the back, everybody silent. Kevin spread a line of coke across his knee when they stopped. Tulip leant over and snorted. Big Sandy said nothing, though his lips puckered with disapproval. It was a shame to see a young life wasted. Tulip couldn't be much older than the daughter he had long ago lost contact with. Girls that age shouldn't be snorting coke and fucking for cash. Seeing Tulip sell herself cheaply like this made Big Sandy worry about his own girl.

Laskey opened the door of his apartment, smiling lazily. His smile disappeared when he saw Big Sandy. "Who's this?" he snapped.

"I'm with the Tynes," Big Sandy answered before Kevin could.

"I know you," Laskey growled. "You work for Dave Bushinsky."

"Tonight I work for the Tynes," Big Sandy responded calmly.

"Why's he here?" Laskey asked Kevin. "You want him to watch too?"

"I –" Kevin began.

"The Tynes are associates of Mr Bushinsky," Big Sandy interrupted. "He asks me to accompany them on certain occasions."

Martin Laskey grinned broadly. "You're a bodyguard. That's OK. I thought the kid wanted to make it a foursome. In that case, come in, you're welcome, my casa's your casa. Drink?"

"Just show me where I can wait."

They left Big Sandy in Martin Laskey's study. Laskey escorted the brother and sister to his bedroom, a four-poster bed, a table beside it like a doctor's operating table, laden with sex toys, dildos, rubber masks, a nurse's costume.

"What's this shit?" Kevin yapped.

"We're here to have fun, right?" Laskey smiled lewdly.

"No accessories," Kevin said stiffly, feeling Tulip tense beside him.

"Don't be prudish," Laskey laughed. "I'm paying enough to be entitled to a few extras." He reached for Tulip. Kevin stepped between them.

"We do it straight or we call it off."

"Don't fuck with me, Tyne." Laskey's face hard, eyes narrow. Alone, Kevin would have been terrified. But they weren't alone.

"Don't make me call Big Sandy," he said softly.

Laskey hesitated. "Kevin, don't take it the wrong way, I want to have fun, I don't mean to threaten you or –"

"Straight sex. Me watching. That's all." Strong, knowing he had Big Sandy to back him up, standing firm, not afraid.

Laskey pulled a face. "At least have her put on the nurse's uniform."

Kevin checked with Tulip. She shrugged. "OK." Laskey beamed.

Kevin waved Tulip forward and shut the door, feeling bigger than he'd ever felt before, knowing he didn't have to fear Laskey or anyone else any more, already thinking about how he could manipulate his newfound power, calculating where it could take him, what it could free him to do.

EIGHT

"*Rangers fucking scum!*" Gawl screamed, lobbing a half-full pint glass at the stranger in the Rangers t-shirt. The man had entered the pub twenty minutes earlier with three friends. Gawl had been eyeballing them ever since. It was ten forty-five, he'd been drinking since seven, itching for a fight, the t-shirt a red rag to a Celtic bull.

The Rangers fan was taken by surprise. There had been no build-up, no banter, no warning. One second, drinking with his friends, laughing at a joke, enjoying the night. The next, a glass shattering against the back of his head, toppling sideways, a large, scarred, bellowing maniac lunging at him through a quickly parting crowd, rough fingers squeezing his throat. His friends stared, shocked, then dropped their drinks and waded in, tugging Gawl off, kicking and punching him.

Gawl turned on the man's allies, snarling, spitting, elated. Threw wild punches, rammed one in the groin with his head, bit into another's thigh. The other customers in the bar watched with interest or weariness. The barmen screamed at Gawl to stop. The younger of the two tried to leap over the bar, grabbing a crowbar from beneath the counter. His older colleague stopped him, shaking his head — let them wear themselves out, easier to break apart and herd away.

The Rangers fan was back on his feet, blood pouring from where the glass had shattered, face contorted with hate. He reached into a pocket and produced a knife. "Hold him still," he shouted. "I'll cut the fucker open from bollocks to brain." Gawl heard the threat, saw the knife, laughed and pulled a knife of his own, twice the size.

Gawl howled, "If that's the way ye want it, ye wee shite!" He slashed. One of the men's arms opened, blood spraying.

The four men retreated warily, the one with the slit arm crying with pain, the Rangers fan jabbing at Gawl with his knife, warding him off, looking for the exit. Gawl hurled curses at them, challenged them to stand and fight, tried slipping within range of the dancing knife. When the men broke and raced for the door, he stumbled after them, saw he wasn't going to catch them – too drunk – and hurled his knife at the man bringing up the rear. It stuck deep in his lower back and he fell out of the pub, shrieking, dragged away by his friends, trailing blood.

"Fuck!" Gawl shouted, angry at having wasted a good knife. He should have thrown a glass or a bottle of beer.

Gawl turned back towards the bar, thirsty, buzzing, grinning. Saw the barmen, one holding a crowbar, the other on the phone to the police. "Get the fuck out," the older barman snapped, covering the mouthpiece with a hand.

"Make me," Gawl retorted. The younger barman slapped the crowbar into the palm of his hand. Gawl laughed, delighted — the stupid wee fuck thought he had the beating of the Scot. Gawl wouldn't be long putting him right.

He was stepping forward to take on the barman when his self-protective drive kicked in. The older barman was too calm, he must know that help was on its way, maybe he paid for priority service. Gawl was certain he could take the younger man – and any others who fucked with him – but he'd done enough jail time and was in no hurry to go back. Spitting at the barmen, he lurched from the pub, wiping sweat, blood and beer from his face, trying to look casual, making for the safety of the underground.

Swinging into Hampstead station. Stomach lurching as the lift dropped — the deepest shaft in London. He vomited in the lift. The other passengers were disgusted. A woman berated him. Gawl ignored her, vomited again, wiped his lips clean. The lift hit bottom. He went searching for a train headed south. Chuckled as he staggered along. A good laugh of a night.

*

Noon. Gawl woke, bladder bursting. He rolled off his creaking, stinking mattress and shuffled to the bathroom. He pissed, yawning and scratching his stomach. His penis shuddered and piss flew across the toilet rim, splashing the wall and floor. Gawl took no notice, shook himself dry, returned to bed, dozed until three.

Depressed when he woke again. Hungover. Parched. He searched the floor and found an almost full bottle of cider — Gawl liked to plan ahead. Gulping greedily from the bottle, he spluttered some of the cider over his chest and the mattress. He coughed, cleared his throat, finished the bottle. Sighed happily and belched. Stared at the light shining through the curtains. Tried to check his watch, remembered he'd lost it on a bet a few nights earlier (something to do with football, he couldn't remember exactly), looked to the alarm clock on his right. Groaned when he saw the time — he'd hoped it was later. Gawl didn't like drinking before nine (last night had been an exception, the thirst had hit early). Nobody of any merit came out before nine. What was he supposed to do for six fucking hours?

Mulling it over, Gawl stared moodily at the ceiling, reflecting on the past few weeks. A lousy time, one setback after another. Rejected whenever he enquired about a job. Word had spread that he was too violent, unpredictable, had stirred up trouble in Glasgow, was an enemy of men who might take exception to him being offered employment. No nearer to finding a boss than when he'd first hit London.

Getting drunk every night, fighting, mostly winning but occasionally losing, beaten bad when he did, sometimes unable to walk for days at a time, pissing blood, spitting blood, blood trickling from the corners of his eyes while he slept, lids caked together when he woke, having to bathe them with warm beer before he could prise them apart. A shite apartment, no hot water, no gas, furniture falling to pieces. It had electricity, cold water, a mattress and some battered old chairs, and that was all. He hated the dive, but he'd been kicked out of his previous apartment and this was where he'd wound up. The flat had been recommended by a guy in the King's Head. Minimal rent, no hassle, the third floor from the top of one of the Heygate's ugly blocks. Gawl could have found some place better if he'd looked – London was full of hovels – but he hadn't bothered. Maybe later this month, or November when the cold hit — he didn't plan to sit here all winter and freeze.

Gawl lay in bed for an hour, studying the torn wallpaper and cracked ceiling, scratching his testicles, thinking about what to do with the afternoon. He crawled to the bathroom at four, nose crinkling when the stench hit him. He opened the tiny window to let out the worst of the fumes, then squatted over the toilet.

He washed out his mouth with rusty water, splashed a couple of handfuls over his head, trying to recall the night before, vague memories of a fight, being sick in a lift, getting gloriously drunk in a local pub with a late lock-in, stumbling home, singing and swearing, a kebab and chips to round off the night.

Slightly refreshed, Gawl wandered back to bed, sour, unsettled, wishing it was night, trying to think what he could do to fill the next five hours.

Eight o'clock. Bored out of his brain. Enough! He pulled on his jeans and a damp t-shirt – lacking a washing machine, he washed them in cold water in the bath and hung them over the broken radiators to slowly dry – grabbed his denim jacket and stormed out, pacing down the landing to the lift, pausing when he got there, recalling the drop in Hampstead the night before, stomach growling at the memory. He thought about taking the stairs but his legs were wobbly. Hit the button for the lift, slumped against the rear panels when he entered, deep breaths, out quickly once he reached the ground, brightening as he left the tower block behind, lungs filling with the street air, licking his teeth and gums, hungry, heading for a café on the Walworth Road, toast, beans, chips and a burger, fine greasy food, gorging himself, three cups of black coffee, the waiter ignoring his unhealthy scent, accustomed to Gawl's binges — the Scot stumbled in unshaven and stinking of cider and urine, four, maybe five nights a week.

From the café Gawl continued up the Walworth Road, past rows of shoddy small stores and grim off-licences. Left on to East Street, birthplace of Charlie Chaplin, home to a bustling street market most days of the week. Gawl sometimes bought crabsticks at a stall near the top of the street. A pub stood near to where that operated from, a favoured haunt for some of the local gangsters. Gawl had been coming here a lot, sniffing for an opening, buying rounds, ingratiating himself with the regulars.

The pub was a third full. A woman in her late forties stood by the bar, dressed like a teenager, smoking a long thin cigarette, hands trembling. Gawl made a quick assessment — an alkie, not a hooker, but needed money bad, would fuck for spare change or a bottle of scotch/vodka/whatever. He'd seen her here before, usually near the end of the week when she'd drunk all her dole money and was desperate. Must have got through it quicker than usual this week. Her name was something like Alice or Annie. Probably riddled with disease. Gawl circled the alkie (here for business, not women) and chose a spot at the bar with a good view of the pub. Drank alone for an hour until a familiar face walked in, Little Zippy, small and wiry but a tough fucker. Knife-man for Johnny Baggs. Baggs a far cry from Dave Bushinsky, but any fucking port in a storm.

"Zippy," Gawl said, smiling grotesquely. "What're ye drinking?"

Little Zippy studied Gawl distastefully, repulsed by the ugly low-life Scottish scum. But – looking quickly round the bar – there was nobody else who'd stand him a drink. He forced a thin smile, took off his jacket and draped it across a chair. "Gawl," he nodded.

"Heineken?" Gawl asked, careful to always note what people drank.

"Cheers." Sharing a drink with the Scot, chatting dully, Gawl asking what he was up to, what the buzz on the streets was, if Johnny Baggs was going well. Little Zippy grunted noncommittally, mind wandering while Gawl blabbered.

Ten to eleven, bar half full, as full as it was going to get tonight. Johnny Baggs strolled in, a dishevelled bodyguard with him. Two young bits of skirt by the bar pushed away the men who'd been pestering them, making eyes at Johnny, hot shit around here, good for a new coat or dress, maybe a necklace or a small diamond if he really liked you. Johnny sidled up to them. He was pushing sixty, fat, bald, hands covered in warts. The girls cooed over him, kissed his cheeks, whispered in his ears, Johnny loving it. Gawl watched enviously. *If only.*

Little Zippy grunted a farewell at Gawl and went to talk with Johnny. One of the girls rubbed his head with her tits. Little Zippy shoved her away, no sense of humour, sensitive about his height. If a man mocked him that openly, Little Zippy would gut him. Different rules for women. You had to be more tolerant or you could go a long time without getting laid.

Gawl watched Johnny Baggs, his bodyguard, Little Zippy and the girls. He felt isolated, powerless. Finished his pint and ordered another, not tasting the cider, thinking about the future, getting old, rotting in the flat, an easy target. Little Zippy wouldn't wind up like that — he hadn't much, but he had an apartment, friends who'd watch out for him, a boss who'd toss a hooker or old slapper like Alice/Annie to him every now and again if he could still get it up.

Gawl checked his t-shirt and jeans — untidy,

wrinkled, but no major stains. He swept his ginger/grey hair back with his right hand, smiled, picked up his pint and stepped across to where Johnny Baggs was entertaining the girls with a crude joke. He waited for the punchline, laughed lightly, then interrupted with a polite, "Good evening, Mr Baggs. May I treat you and yer friends t' a round?"

Johnny Baggs studied Gawl coolly, searching his memory for a name, then linking it to recent rumours — Gawl McCaskey, trouble-maker, woman-beater, double-crosser. Rumours, maybe true, maybe bullshit, but reason to be cautious. "Cheers," he nodded, "but we're fine. Can I buy you one?"

Gawl's smile spread pitifully. "No thanks, Mr Baggs. Are ye sure I can't get one for ye?" Johnny shook his head. Gawl gulped, feeling like he was four foot tall. He always went to pieces around men more powerful than him, men he needed, men who invariably rejected him flat. He tried thinking of something to say, to make Johnny Baggs laugh. Came up blank. "Good result for Millwall last week," he wheezed. Johnny was a season ticket holder.

"Fucking great result," Johnny smiled. "We're going up this year, no doubt about it, we'll finish champions."

"You're not talking football, are you?" one of the girls

pouted. "I can't stand football."

"Then we'd better talk about something else," Johnny laughed, winking at Gawl. "See you later, yeah?"

Gawl sighed, defeated. "Later." He nodded at Little Zippy and the girls, turned and left. Listened closely for sniggering but there wasn't any. They hadn't taken enough notice of him to make fun of him.

Gawl retreated to a corner of the bar, downed his pint quickly, ordered another and a shot of bourbon, angry, hating himself, wishing he had the nerve to take down that fucker Baggs and show him what sort of a man he really was. Why did he shrink this way? In a fight he was a force of fucking nature, fearless. But set him talking with Johnny Baggs, Weasel Coyle, Jimmy Burns or anyone of influence and he became a pathetic wreck.

His fingers tightened and his eyes darkened. Another shot, down in one, quick breaths, needing to bust out of here. He thought of starting a fight but that would ruin any chance he had of getting in good with Johnny Baggs. Looking round the bar, tense and twitchy, eyes strafing the regulars, the drunks, the gangsters, the girls, settling on...

Alice/Annie. Still alone, mooching over a half-pint, making it last, waiting for a knight in shining armour to sweep her away. Gawl grinned darkly, put his drink down, strolled over, stepped up beside her and ordered two pints, not asking if she wanted one. He shoved it at her and turned so he was sideways to her.

Alice/Annie stared at the pint, then at Gawl. "Thanks," she whispered, picking it up and drinking deeply.

"Finish it quick," Gawl grunted. "We'll stop at the offie on our way back."

"You're taking a lot for granted," Alice/Annie sniffed, acting the high-and-mighty. "What makes you think I'd leave here with a... a foul-smelling fuck like you?"

Gawl laughed, not offended, on solid turf with this level of scum. He leant in close and said, "If ye suck me off, I'll toss in a tenner on top of the drinks."

Alice/Annie almost threw her pint at him but her fingers wouldn't obey. They clutched the glass tight, as if it was the holy grail. Gawl saw her loathing and her desperation and he laughed again. Put a hand on her arse and squeezed. She saw that he was a violent man, in a violent mood, and knew she'd suffer if she left with him, maybe a light beating, maybe worse. She gazed around the bar, but there was nobody else she could rely on and she needed to be drunk, she'd been shaking all day, couldn't face the night sober.

"We'll have another one here," she said firmly, looking Gawl straight in the eye. For a moment he thought he'd miscalculated, that she was stronger than she appeared. But then her gaze dropped. "After that I'll come with you. And I'll want twenty to suck you, not ten."

Gawl laughed, ordered another round and rubbed his groin against her thigh, letting her feel his stiffness, fingers tightening on her arse, a rough promise of things to come. Alice/Annie made up her mind to get so drunk that she wouldn't feel the pain, wouldn't feel anything, wouldn't even be there really.

NINE

Big Sandy was, to his surprise, growing fond of Shula Schimmel. It had been years since he'd spent much time around a teenager. He'd forgotten what the world was like from their viewpoint, the excitement of it, the wonder, the incredible highs and woeful lows which only those caught between childhood and adulthood experienced so heartfully. Escorting Shula around, watching her gyrate in nightclubs, sharing a table with her and her friends in restaurants or cafés (she wouldn't let him sit at a table of his own, said he looked lonely), taking her shopping... It made him part of her teenage world, even if only vicariously.

It was a world Big Sandy barely knew. His daughter was a few years younger than Shula, but it had been a long time since she'd been part of his life — he had missed all but her youngest years. As for himself, he'd had to grow up quickly and secure a place for himself in adult society before he hit his teens.

His mother had been murdered when Big Sandy was eleven years old, slain in her bed by her lover, Davey Connors, a cruel man who regularly beat her and Sandy for most of the short but bitter month he lived with them. Sandy found her body when he returned from a pool hall one night, where he was already running errands for local gangsters. Walked in clutching a bag of sweet and sour chicken, Mum's favourite, eager to please, knowing she was having a tough time with her new man, not sure why she didn't kick the monster out, but sure she'd see sense eventually and get rid of him.

He called out, "Mum, I'm home. I brought Chinese." No answer. He took the bag to the kitchen, unpacked the boxes, took the lids off, set plates on the table, left the food steaming in the boxes, went looking for his mother. Found her in her bedroom, choked to death. Nobody ever found out why he did it — Connors vanished into the night. Friends of Sandy's mother searched for him for many months, keen to do unto him as he'd done to Nancy Mooney (although his mother never married, she'd given Big Sandy his father's surname), but they never found him and eventually abandoned the search.

Not Big Sandy. He'd been looking for Davey Connors all his life, always studying faces on the street, on the Tube, in pubs, the killer's features seared into the cells of his brain. Big Sandy would know him the second he saw him, no matter how much time might have changed him. Know him and kill him.

Big Sandy often thought of Nancy. He imagined her behind him every time he killed, perhaps the reason he took the deaths so hard, knowing she wouldn't approve. He dreamt of her often, and in his dreams she pleaded with him to stop killing, put his wicked ways behind him, embrace God while there was time to repent. But stopping wasn't an option. He had to continue, engulfed by evil, living in the darkness. Not only because that was all he'd ever known and all that his childhood had prepared him for, but because somewhere in that cesspit lurked the man who'd murdered his mother. Big Sandy believed he'd find him if he explored the darkness long enough, surrendering to it, even though he knew the cost — the sorrow of God, the denial of heaven, the eternal damnation of hell.

Big Sandy had discussed this often recently with the new priest in the church of his mother, the Church of Sacred Martyrs. He hadn't attended mass since her death, but he'd spent many long, quiet hours in the church, silent, not praying, seeing himself as God saw him, sometimes apologising, sometimes welling up with bitter tears. The priests would try talking with him, wishing he'd take them into his confidence, eager to ease his suffering. Big Sandy resisted, maintaining a lonely silence — until Fr Sebastian.

Big Sandy had seen the priest's true colours from the start, a weak man who intimately knew the contours of the vile, whose experience of wickedness wasn't limited to what he read in the bible or heard in the confessional. This was a man who wouldn't be distressed by anything he was told, a sad sinner who wouldn't dare judge another lest he be judged himself, a damned man with whom Big Sandy could talk openly, freely, exploratively.

They'd shared many troubling discussions in the months since, never in the confessional, always in the sacristy or Fr Sebastian's personal rooms in the house behind the church. Big Sandy hid nothing from the priest. He told him about his mother's murder, how Dave Bushinsky had taken the young Sandy Murphy under his wing, how he'd mushroomed during puberty and become a valuable tool, his path since then, the lives he'd taken. He knew it was dangerous, the priest under no obligation to keep Big Sandy's unofficial confessions secret, a weak junkie who might one day sell out the giant for a hit. But after so many years of silence, the need to confess was overpowering. Big Sandy had unburdened himself before, to Sapphire and a few other carefully chosen hookers, but that wasn't the same. They were good listeners but they weren't messengers of God, privy to the sacred secrets of the church — and as corrupt as Fr Sebastian was, a tarnished priest still knew more about sin, God and redemption than anybody else

Big Sandy dared raise such matters with.

"Of course you're not beyond redemption," Fr Sebastian snorted one October evening. They were sitting in the priest's bedroom, overlooking the shrub-lined avenue to the rear of the house. Shula was having dinner with her uncle and aunt tonight, Big Sandy surplus to requirements.

"But I've killed," Big Sandy said gruffly. "I'll kill again if I have to. I've no excuses. I do it of my own free will, for money. I don't repent. I –"

"There's the rub," Fr Sebastian cried excitedly, half-high on coke he'd scored from Clint Smith, working himself up into a religious fervour, always closer to God when he was flying high. "You *must* repent. The doors to the kingdom of heaven are always open to those who seek forgiveness. You admit your sins, but the truly evil of this world can't, they see themselves above the laws of God and man, accountable to no one. You know you're doing wrong. Take strength from that knowledge, repent, and the glory of the Lord God Almighty shall be yours."

Big Sandy smiled wryly. He could hear the coke in the priest's voice, see the fire twinkling in his dark green addict's eyes. "But I can't repent," he said plainly. "I'm not sorry. To repent in name only, to beg God's forgiveness without working for it... Wouldn't that be sinful too?"

"Of course," Fr Sebastian exclaimed, jumping to his feet. "That's not what I'm advocating. You must be truly sorry. Your plea for forgiveness must come from the heart, from the core of your being — your soul. It won't be easy but you *can* do it. Put violence behind you. Leave this city and your circle of damned friends. Devote the rest of your life to charitable work and prayer. Nothing's worse than hell. Redemption doesn't come easy, not for the likes of us, but the struggle is nothing compared to the torment we'll endure if we fail, if we don't earn God's love, if we wind up roasting in the flames of hell."

"I know," Big Sandy said lowly. "But how can I be what I'm not? *You* can't do it, Father. What makes you think *I* can?"

"I'm different," Fr Sebastian said, pacing to the window, fingers twitching, an addict's hollow honesty. "My corruption is weakness — yours is strength. I'm evil because I haven't the strength to fight my dark desires — you're evil because you are too strong to be genuinely afraid of yours. But it's much easier to find weakness within yourself than it is to find strength. There's hope for both of us – this is a world of hope – but your path to everlasting glory is simpler than mine."

"But your sins are less dreadful than mine," Big Sandy disagreed. "I kill people. You just get high."

Fr Sebastian wheeled around to argue with him, to tell him about the girls, his terrible lusts, the monster he'd set on three of his congregation... then paused. Big Sandy didn't know about the children or Gawl McCaskey. If Big Sandy knew that he was a paedophile, that he'd sicced Gawl McCaskey on frail old women to rob, terrorise and beat them, the priest's collar wouldn't protect him. The giant would show Fr Sebastian no mercy. There were limits to what even a hired killer like Sandy Murphy would accept.

"You have the blessing of a motive," Fr Sebastian muttered. "Your mother was butchered when you were a boy. You were reared on violence, claimed by it as a child. God understands that and will allow for it. Forsake the gangs. Renounce your evil ways. Repent. You *will* be saved."

Big Sandy shook his head slowly. "Repentance won't work," he grunted. "I can't believe God lets sinners off the hook just for saying sorry. What about an act of pure goodness or self-sacrifice?"

Fr Sebastian sighed and returned to the bed, sitting close to Big Sandy, feeling like a real father, wishing he was stronger, that he knew what to say to help. "You must put such thoughts behind you. We've discussed this before. Salvation lies in prayer, honesty, selflessness, putting God before –"

"That isn't enough," Big Sandy barked, face darkening. "My hands are stained with the blood of the innocent as well as the guilty. I have to wipe the slate clean, an act of purity, a moment of..." He grimaced and slapped the mattress with a massive paw — the bed shook hard. "I don't know what I can do, how a black-souled son-of-a-bitch like me can ever cleanse himself, but the answer isn't prayer. It has to be something greater, something glorious."

Fr Sebastian shrugged helplessly. "I could refer you to my superiors. They know more than I do. Perhaps they could help."

"No," Big Sandy said immediately.

"You should talk with them," Fr Sebastian persisted. "I'm a poor choice for a confessor. I know holy men, compassionate men, men who could –"

"Holy men can't save me," Big Sandy said, rising, downbeat. "They couldn't understand where I come from, how I live, the hell I'm in. You can, because you dwell there too." Big Sandy shook the priest's hand and gently pushed him back as he tried to get to his feet.

"Stay where you are, Father. I'll let myself out."

"You're sure?" Fr Sebastian asked, mind spinning.

"Yeah," Big Sandy said and retreated, leaving the priest to his high, thinking about God, the emptiness of the world, the promise of heaven, the impossibility of redemption for one so foul.

The next day, an early phone call from the Bush. "You don't have to worry about Shula any more."

"She's going home?" Big Sandy asked.

"No, she's staying, but she's enrolling in college, that was what she had to tell us last night. Night classes, then maybe a degree. She's here for good, getting an apartment of her own, so let her off."

"I can pick her up from her lessons if you want," Big Sandy said. "Or check in on her from time to time. Larry Drake's still hounding her."

"Don't worry about it," the Bush laughed. "She's got the measure of that dick. She won't waste herself on him."

"So what do you want me to do instead?" Big Sandy asked.

"You remember the Tynes?"

"The brother and sister."

"They've been calling Clint a lot, requesting backup. I've had others taking care of them but now you can do it for a while. You have Clint's number?"

"Yeah. And when I'm not looking after them?"

"Relax. Take it easy. I'll let you know when I need you."

The Bush hung up. Big Sandy was uneasy, brow furrowed, figuring, *Maybe I was getting too close to Shula, developing a thing for her. Maybe I'm just pissed because I won't see her any more.* But he wasn't convinced. This didn't feel that straightforward. He had a sense that something bad was going to happen. Big Sandy thought about his mother, shivered, almost crossed himself but didn't.

TEN

Clint surfed the Tube. Coming up the stairs from the Bakerloo line at Embankment, heading for the District and Circle, a strong gust of wind whipping through the tunnel as he rounded a corner, most passengers grimacing and pulling their coats tight around themselves, Clint spreading his arms, embracing the wind, grinning. Up the escalator and west for the hell of it, whistling softly. Changed carriages every time the train stopped. Spotted a small group in the third carriage, four guys and three girls, late teens, dressed for grunge, talking and laughing loudly, cans of beer and cider in a big plastic bag.

"Going somewhere special?" Clint asked, pulling up beside them, wrapping an arm around a support pole. They squinted at him suspiciously until he unzipped the cardigan he was wearing beneath his jacket to reveal a hint of brown paper. He gave the bag a soft rustle. "Want to arrive in style and take off like a comet?"

One of the girls laughed at Clint's patter. Two of the boys hushed her. Another turned to Clint, faux-cool. "What have you got and how much?"

"E's to please," Clint smirked. Quick calculation — what were the pills worth to the kids? Decided not to be greedy. "I could say fifteen, you could say five and we could haggle. But let's not waste time. Ten a pop."

The boy licked his lips and glanced at the others. One of the girls piped up with, "How do we know they're real?"

Clint reached into the bag, produced a small red pill, tossed it to the girl. "That one for free. The rest now twelve pounds each."

"You said ten," one of the boys growled as the girl popped the E and gripped the armrests of her seat.

"That was before we started talking quality control. My advice is to snap them up at twelve — once that beauty kicks in and your friend starts spacing, the price will rise and rise."

The five teens looked from Clint to the girl. She shrugged. "Nothing. I think he's trying to... Whoah!" Eyes widening, smiling feverishly, fingers digging into the arm rests.

"Thirteen," Clint said and hands disappeared into pockets, tens, fives and pound coins appearing like magic. One of the guys asked Clint if he wanted to come party with them — there would be lots more customers there. Clint declined. He had wanderlust and wanted to surf the trains, light up the night in a dozen different spots, not worried about making quick scores. Got off at Hammersmith, Picadilly line towards the West End, scored in the first carriage he tried.

Clint loved nights like this when he was master of his world, no trace of a stutter, slick and cool. A dangerous game playing the Tube, you never knew who was listening, who you were selling to, what could go wrong. He usually didn't take such risks. But excited tonight, needing the danger and thrill. One train after another, always on his feet, never pausing, north to Finsbury Park, south to Stockwell, north to King's Cross, Circle line all the way around to Embankment, where he caught the Bakerloo line back to Elephant & Castle, coming up for air, cash-heavy, striding like a god, elated, wanting the night to continue forever.

In an ideal world he would have trailed around after Shula. He'd eased off for a while when Big Sandy had been given the job of guarding her, but had resumed his shy pursuit when cousin Dave had pulled her guard after she'd decided to make London her home. Clint ecstatic when he heard the news. Growing bolder. He'd even approached her a few times recently and started conversations, not just about old movies but places in London that she might be interested in visiting, working up the courage to offer to be her guide one day.

But Shula had a class tonight. Finished by this time, but she always went back to her flat afterwards, to study and make a start on her homework assignments. She was surprisingly dedicated that way. Clint had followed her home a few times, trailing her from a distance, and stood across the road watching the light in her window until she turned it off and went to bed. But he couldn't afford to waste too much time doing that. Plus he worried that someone would notice and report him. Didn't want to have to explain to cousin Dave why he was shadowing the boss' sweet niece.

With no Shula to trail and dream of, he thought about hitting a massage parlour in Soho, but brave as the night had made him, he got cold feet when he considered that. He'd been unable to maintain an erection the last few times, a recurring problem that he'd always struggled with, viagra of no benefit when he'd tried it. One of the hookers had laughed at him and he'd left red with shame. The laughter echoed inside his head every time he contemplated a return.

Clint decided not to ruin the night by seeking the cold embrace of a whore. The pubs and clubs were another option. On a high, oozing confidence, he was certain he'd pull. Didn't see that as a betrayal of Shula. It would be different if (*when*) they were a couple, but he'd be a fool to limit himself when he hadn't even started to court her. The trouble was he'd failed with real women as well as hookers. Didn't dare chance it, not wanting the night to end on a sour note.

So he went where he knew he'd be welcome, where a friend would surely be glad to see him, to the lab and its constant prisoner, Dr Tony Phials.

Bragging of his exploits to Phials, emptying his pockets, showing him the money, describing the night's deals, dreaming aloud. "Enough nights like this, Dave will have to take me seriously. I'll be given more responsibility, more respect, then... Shula and America."

"I hope so," Phials said, smiling mechanically, wishing Clint had brought some hash. It was a lot easier to listen to the dealer when he was half-stoned.

"I could go now," Clint insisted. "More than seven grand in my bank account. I could cash in my shares with Dave, must be worth fifteen, maybe twenty thousand, maybe more."

"So why don't you?" Phials prodded him. "It's a good time of year, New York not too hot, not too cold. Twenty-five thousand sterling is, what, forty or more in dollars? You could go a long way on that."

"Without Shula?" Clint snorted.

"Maybe it would be easier to start without her. Move there by yourself. Get established. Come back for her when you're in a position to really wow her."

"I dunno," Clint said uneasily. "Nobody would know me. I don't have contacts. I wouldn't know who to trust."

"If I could get out of here and come with you, I could help," Phials said, trying to sound casual. He'd been dropping hints like this every time Clint called in, always apparently offhand. "I know people in New York. I could steer you right."

"You could give me their names and numbers," Clint suggested.

"No point," Phials smiled. "I've been away a long time. People move, change addresses and phones, especially in my line. I'd have to track them down."

Clint glanced at the doc, wondered if he could put direct questions to him, decided to go for it. "Tony..." Hesitant, a rare use of Phials' first name. "What are you working on? Why are you kept locked up?"

Phials hid a smile. He'd been waiting weeks for the kid to work up the nerve to ask. Shook his head mock-glumly. "I can't really talk about that."

"Oh. OK." Clint ready to drop the subject instantly.

"You could always ask your cousin," Phials said slyly, planting the seed. "It's probably not a problem, but you should clear it with him first."

"I might do that," Clint shrugged, acting like he didn't care. But Phials had seen interest flare in Clint's eyes. Clint would ask Bushinsky. He'd better. Phials would have wasted a hell of a lot of time on the dull little coward if he didn't. Not sure how he might be able to use Clint, but scenting possibilities in the weak but cunning young man.

October passing in a blur, Clint selling lots of E's, grass and coke, but most of it on the Tube or in pubs and clubs, one-off deals, not building a regular customer base like he'd planned. The money was good, but chump change to the Bush. Clint had been thinking a lot about what Dave had said the night of Shula's party, about contacts and Clint needing to get serious to get ahead. Clint was good at selling to students and clubbers, he could talk with them, joke with them, win their trust and make sales. But when it came to the rich people, the confident, the powerful and influential, he was lost. He didn't know how to handle them. And without them there could be no progress, no Shula, no America.

He'd made a half-hearted attempt to use Kevin and Tulip Tyne. The men who paid for their services were men of wealth and dark pleasures, in the market for all of Clint's goods. But they had their own established dealers. They saw Clint as a pimp, didn't take him seriously when he offered to meet their other needs too.

So Clint continued surfing the trains, hitting pubs, circling clubs, doing good business, making good money, but feeling stale, stuck in neutral, going nowhere fast. Until Larry Drake came to see him in a house of God.

The Church of Sacred Martyrs. Clint sat near the back, head bowed, waiting to be approached. Not a religious man, raised Protestant but hadn't been in any kind of chapel for years, until meeting Fr Sebastian in a pub some months earlier. Fr Sebastian had seen Clint touting for business. Once he'd checked every face in the pub to make sure nobody from his flock was present, he sidled up to the dealer and muttered, "I need grass, pills, coke if you have it." Clint on guard immediately, unaccustomed to being accosted directly. Then he saw the hunger in the stranger's eyes and relaxed. Sold him a couple of E's in the toilet, watched him pop them, curiously studying the pale-faced man in the shabby duffel coat, not making him for a priest but sensing something different about him.

The truth surfaced a week later when the man came to Clint again. The first time, Fr Sebastian had left his clerical collar at home, but this time he forgot and had to hurriedly stick it in a pocket. It fell out when he was paying Clint. His face ashen, putting it back quickly, leaving without the merchandise. Clint hurried after him, caught him at the end of the street, made him take the coke, assured him his secret was safe. "I ask no questions, tell no tales. I don't know your name and I won't look for it. You're safe with me. You can trust me."

And Fr Sebastian did come to trust Clint. So much so that within a fortnight he'd told Clint his name and where his church was, and even invited Clint to deal to him there, figuring it was safer than meeting him in public places.

On his second visit to the church, while he waited his turn for the confessional, Clint was gazing around, enjoying the peace and calm, when he had a crazy but brilliant thought — this would be a great place to deal! At first he dismissed the notion, sold the coke to Fr Sebastian, went home. But he kept coming back to the idea. He could force Fr Sebastian to let him use the church. It would be a safe haven — police didn't stake out churches. And if he was ever busted, he could cut a deal with the police by betraying the priest to them. They'd be much more interested in taking down a priest than a dealer.

Fr Sebastian savagely opposed the plan until Clint

threatened to cut off his supply and drop a few hints locally about the priest's fondness for nose candy. He agreed eventually, reluctantly, on the condition that Clint only sell to those the priest sent his way — he didn't want the dealer bringing trash into his church. It hadn't occured to Clint that the priest might know other junkies, that he would be prepared to send them to Clint. He couldn't believe his luck.

Clint agreed to Fr Sebastian's condition, let the priest supply him with a slim but steady stream of customers, told none of his own clients about the sweet set-up. But only for a few weeks. Once he'd established himself, he spread the word about his new base, telling some of cousin Dave's crew, paying them to send their select clients his way. He was able to charge more than normal, the novelty of the backdrop a turn-on for yuppies who could boast to their friends about scoring in a church.

The Sacred Martyrs was soon a roaring success, Clint dropping in three times a week, Mondays, Wednesdays and Fridays, between midday and three. The regular church-goers were surprised by the upturn in business, but they thought it was the appeal of Fr Sebastian, figuring he must be more charismatic than they'd assumed.

One Wednesday, while Clint sat soaking up the silence, a man genuflected at the end of Clint's pew then slid over to where Clint was waiting. When Clint looked up he saw Larry Drake.

"Luh-luh-luh-Larry?" Clint said stupidly, louder than he intended.

"Quiet," Drake hissed, then spared Clint a nervous grin. "I like your office. I heard you're selling good shit, blessed by the Pope himself."

"Not in puh-person," Clint grinned, "but he gave the shipment his huh-holy seal of approval. What are you looking for?"

Drake sniffed, trying to be casual. "Whatever."

"This a one-off duh-deal?"

"Depends on the quality and how quiet you can keep it."

"I can keep it real quiet," Clint said. "I can do you a good deal too – twenty percent duh-discount – *if...*"

"Go on."

"Lots of muh-money in showbusiness. You mix with celebrities, directors, pruh-producers and the rest. If you send some of them my way, I'll be generous, cut you a duh-discount every time."

"I scratch your back, you scratch mine," Drake chuckled. Every dealer he knew would sell their grandmother for the chance to tap into celeb money. He kept most of his contacts well away from his showbiz associates, but a guy with enough imagination to deal from a church might be worth introducing to certain people. "I'll test the shit and see if you can keep this under your hat. Later... yeah, maybe. What can you supply?"

"Anything," Cliff said confidently. "I always carry coke, grass, E's. If you want something else, let me know in advance. You have my nuh-number?"

"No."

Clint slipped a card to Drake — he'd printed off a load in a shopping mall a while back. Drake pocketed the card without looking. Clint gave the church a quick scan, to make sure nobody was watching. "What can I tuh-tempt you with?"

"Like I said, whatever you have. I'm stocking up for the weekend."

Clint searched through his pockets, produced a cigarette box full of E's, a thick stick of hash, two small baggies of coke. "That enough or do you want more?"

Drake's eyes lit up. "Fuck no, that's plenty." Snatching the gear from Clint, stashing it inside his jacket. "What do I owe you?"

"First batch on the huh-house," Clint said freely. He'd never given away that much before but Drake was a potential mother lode.

"You're sure?" Drake asked, surprised but not astonished.

"As long as you're on the level about recommending me to your friends."

"If the shit's good," Drake said, rising and clapping Clint lightly on the back, "you can consider it a deal."

Drake slid out, masking his face with the lapels of his jacket, walking fast. Clint leant back, smiling radiantly, wishing he could shout out loud with triumph, the tumblers of the future clicking into place. His shit *was* good. Drake *would* return and bring others. Nothing could stop him now. Yankee doodle Clint!

ELEVEN

Tulip lit a candle, stared into the heart of the flickering flame, pulled back slowly and crossed herself, praying silently. Kevin sat nearby, nervous, never comfortable in church even when he had nothing to hide from God, genuinely edgy now that he was engaged in unnatural acts with his sister. Not really convinced that God existed, but if he did and was watching...

Kevin kept trying to talk Tulip out of her visits to the Church of Sacred Martyrs, but she turned a deaf ear to his pleas and threats. She'd always been religious – talk of becoming a nun when she was seven or eight, though that soon passed – but now more than ever, now that she needed God more than before. Kevin had thought the stain of sexual sin would drive her from the church, but it had served only to strengthen her faith. Tulip believed her current pains were a test, and that only by remaining true to God could she come through them intact.

Watching her pray, Kevin felt guilt bubble up inside him. At moments like this he could see the truth — a sixteen year old girl turned into a drug addict and whored out by her perverted brother, victim of the monster he'd become, unwilling to break free because she loved him and feared for his life if she abandoned him. He wanted to release her, seek help, engage the monster within himself and defeat it. But he was too weak. He knew that once they left the sanctity of the church, the sick cravings would return and he'd succumb. His suffering was minor compared with Tulip's, but he *did* suffer. At times he even took comfort in his pain. If he could feel hurt, it proved he wasn't truly evil, didn't it?

Tulip crossed herself and rose, her auburn hair straggly and unhealthy in the dim light, looking fatter than she was, old, haggard — but still somehow innocent. "I want to make confession," she said.

Kevin stiffened. "Can't you confess privately to God?"

"I do that constantly," Tulip replied softly. "But I need to confess to a priest as well."

Kevin didn't like it – he knew she confessed *all* her sins – but at least Fr Sebastian would respect the privacy of the confessional, like his predecessor. Kevin still recalled the terror he'd experienced when Tulip first told him she'd confessed to a priest. Blind panic, jamming a bag with clothes, planning to flee London with Tulip, expecting the police to come crashing through the door. He only calmed down when Tulip explained that she'd confessed several times over the last three months — if the priest was going to break his solemn vows and inform on the Tynes, he would have done so long before now.

"What did he say when you told him about us?" Kevin screamed.

"I can't tell you," Tulip answered calmly. "That's between us and God."

Kevin threatened to stop her going to mass, yank her out of school, take her away from everyone she knew and everywhere she felt safe. It had no impact on her. She knew that he knew she wouldn't stand for such upheval, that she'd send him to prison before she'd let him come between her and God. Eventually his anger abated and he let her continue going to mass and confession.

Fresh fear when Fr Sebastian replaced Fr Andrew earlier in the year — new man, perhaps new rules. He begged Tulip not to confess to the incoming priest but she ignored him. Fr Sebastian wasn't as reserved as Fr Andrew had been. Whereas the previous priest had simply subjected Kevin to the cold shoulder and dirty looks, Fr Sebastian stormed over to him after hearing Tulip's confession, dragged him outside and throttled him, crying, "You demon! Demon! Demon!"

Fr Sebastian told Kevin never to return, vowed to kill him if he did. Kevin stumbled home, shaken, followed by a bemused Tulip. He said they weren't going back, the priest was a lunatic. She said he could abstain if he wished, but she wouldn't. He offered to take her to a different church but she said Sacred Martyrs had been their mother's church and it was now hers and she had no wish to change.

In the end Tulip got her way. Kevin avoided the church for many weeks, until Fr Sebastian issued him with a summons — the priest wanted to see him one evening on his own, not to tell Tulip. Kevin went, trembling, half-afraid the priest was planning to execute him. But Fr Sebastian only wanted to talk, hopeful of convincing Kevin to stop doing this to his sister. A long conversation, the first of many, in which the priest beseeched Kevin to confess to God and the police, to seek professional help and divine forgiveness. When his pleas fell on deaf ears, he asked Kevin to explain how he had come to this terrible place.

"It's not the money," Kevin insisted. "I couldn't care less about that. It's the thrill and the sexual release. I'm addicted."

He told the priest about his father's death two and a half years earlier, moving back into the family apartment to look after Tulip, nothing but her best interests at heart. For six months just brotherly love, helping her cope with her grief, caring for her, providing. Some time after her fourteenth birthday he began noticing her as a young woman, her body changing, maturing, developing. Tulip wasn't prudish around the apartment, Kevin often catching sight of her naked coming out of the bathroom, or of her breasts as she walked about in a loose robe. Nothing provocative in Tulip's flashes of flesh. She still thought of herself as a girl, Kevin her harmless brother, sexual attraction between them an impossibility.

Over the coming months Kevin would sometimes fantasize about his sister, but only hazily, the way he'd fix on any woman's face when he was masturbating. He harboured no dark desires, had no wish to interfere with her, didn't believe himself capable of genuine lust for Tulip.

"I'd had a few girlfriends before," he explained, "but sex never thrilled me the way it did other people. I was starting to think that maybe celibacy was more my line. Then I caught Tulip making love."

He'd returned home early one day with a headache, expecting Tulip to be at school. Entering their apartment, he heard the sounds of sex in her bedroom. Shocked, the first thing that crossed his mind was that she was being raped. The door was half-open. He almost barged in, but stopped when he realised her moans of pleasure meant she was a willing participant. He stood by the door uncertainly, worried about her, wondering if he should break it up. While he was debating what to do, he caught a whiff of marijuana. With a frown he leant forward and spotted the sexually engaged teenagers in Tulip's dressing table mirror.

And everything changed.

"The sight of her fucking..." Kevin's voice and eyes filled with wicked wonder. Fr Sebastian clocked the wonder and knew in that moment that Kevin Tyne was beyond salvation, his vice born of a genuinely twisted urge, no mere bad man, but one who was lost to his inner demons, truly warped.

Kevin said nothing to Tulip but obsessed about her for the next few weeks, masturbating frequently, feeding on the image of her with her boyfriend. Then the power of the image faded and needed to be refreshed. He started coming home early regularly, making up all manner of excuses, or telling Tulip that he would be working late then sneaking home at the normal time. But he didn't catch her at it again. Frustrated, he took a week off work and shadowed her when she was at school or hanging out with her friends. No joy, Tulip not even kissing or petting.

But she wasn't entirely clean. He saw her smoking

pot a few times and found a stash in her room. He remembered the smell in the air *that* day. Maybe the hash had lowered her inhibitions. Maybe drugs were his way in.

He confronted her one evening, said he'd been cleaning her room and had found the pot. Tulip wept, said all her friends were doing it, begged him not to tell anyone. He waved her worries away, said it was no big thing, he'd smoked when he was younger, still had the occasional spliff when he was feeling low. In fact, would she mind sharing a joint with him now?

Tulip was delighted that he wasn't judging her, even more delighted to share. They had an amazing night, smoking, talking, more honest with one another than they'd ever been. Kevin cried for the first time since they'd buried their father. Tulip held him and did what she could to comfort him.

The pot became a regular part of their evenings together, Kevin buying it now, feeding it to Tulip, laughing away her concerns when she worried about becoming addicted. Eventually he brought back some coke, giggled when she was shocked, told her not to be a square, made a joke of it. Careful not to use much himself, pretending to snort, pressing most of it on her.

A prolonged, determined campaign to addict her,

making light of Tulip's fears when she voiced them, treating her like a grown-up, saying this brought them closer together, writing sicknotes for her when she was too stoned to go to school, leaving her alone in the flat with grass and coke.

One night, when she was properly hooked and flying high, he told her that he'd caught her making love. She laughed and called him a voyeur. He smiled and asked her to tell him about her sexual history. There wasn't much to tell. She'd only had sex with one boy, four times. She regretted giving up her virginity, but it was too late to go back. She'd confessed the sin in church and had agreed with Fr Andrew that she wouldn't have sex again until she was married.

Over the next week Kevin raised the issue frequently when she was high and he was pretending to be, saying it was good to experiment, she should feel free to try it again. Tulip said she didn't want to. Kevin said she was letting her beliefs blind her to her true desires, that she secretly wished to have sex again, and should — it was wrong to suppress one's natural urges. One night, when her head was spinning and he was going on at her about doing what she pleased, Tulip laughed and said it was as if he actively wanted her to have sex. Kevin stared at her solemnly, heart thumping, then took the gamble and told her softly that he did, and more than that, he wanted to watch. "That night when you called me a voyeur — you were right."

Tulip incredulous. She thought he was joking, a sick joke, not funny, even when she was high. Distraught and disgusted when she realised he was earnest. Tears, screams, locking her door, wanting to leave, thinking he meant to rape her. Kevin was calm, soft, kept on talking, finding words instinctively, discovering eloquence in his unnatural lust. He convinced her that he would never touch her, he had no desire to have sex with her, she should pack her bags and leave if she ever thought that he did. Made her feel safe, talked most of her fears away, got her to open he door and sit down with him and discuss it rationally.

Tulip tried to reject the drugs the next night and the night after. She wanted to clear her head, think about the situation clearly. But she had the hunger now. She needed her fix. Kevin played on that. Came back from work with heroin, said that was all he'd been able to score. A lie – he'd had the heroin for weeks, had got his dealer to teach him how to use it – but Tulip believed him. Not knowing any better, she gave it a try, figuring it was OK to try anything once. Thought it was odd the next night when Kevin returned with the same story and more heroin. Stopped thinking after that. Hooked on a whole new world, carefully led into it by her artful, deceptive brother.

Once he had her trapped, Kevin admitted to fantasizing about her all the time. He faked tears, said he was vile, threatened to kill himself. Tulip was aghast — he mustn't think such things, suicide the greatest sin. But he was weak, he moaned, a fragile man, prey to the sickness. He'd go mad if they continued as they were, unable to stop dreaming about her. But if she had sex again – not with him! never with him! – but with her boyfriend, the same as before, and let Kevin watch... maybe that would cure him.

Tulip begged Kevin to seek help, God's or a counsellor's, but he wouldn't, he swore that he couldn't. Tulip was too young, too naïve and too high to see him for the liar that he was. When he grabbed a knife and cut into a wrist (not deeply, making it look worse than it was), her heart went out to him and she agreed to give him what he wanted, hoping and praying that it would satisfy him.

He made Tulip ring the boy that night, while she was stoned, and invite him over, knowing he had to strike while she was open to the idea. The boy came running, as any horny teenage boy would. Kevin hid, waited for them to start fucking, snuck back to the open bedroom door, watched as he had before, even better than the first time, his heart pounding, his cock hard, but not masturbating, saving that pleasure for the future.

Tulip had woken disgusted, ashamed, sobbing. He'd taken the day off work, wept with her, thanked her for saving him, fed her heroin and coke, convinced her to invite the boy back again that night.

A few days later the boy wasn't enough. He needed new flesh, a fresh thrill. He asked her to seduce one of her other friends. Tulip broke down, refused the drugs, told him this couldn't continue, it was immoral and ungodly. He'd expected this. Sat her down, brewed tea, wiped her tears away, kissed her demurely. When she recovered he produced a folder packed with documents, bank accounts, legal details. "Everything you'll need is here," he said evenly. "The lawyers will sort it out for you. There should be enough to live on for a long time. You'll have to go into care for a while, but –"

"What do you mean?" Tulip gasped. "What are you going to do?"

Kevin smiled softly. "I'm going to cure myself the only way I know how. You won't have to worry about me any more. I'm setting you free."

"*No!*" She believed he truly meant to kill himself.

Offered to bring a boy back like he wanted, but he shook his head, said it was wrong of him to have asked, easier to let go, for her to get on with life, not to worry about him any longer. Tulip got hysterical, clung to him, begged him to let her try. In the end Kevin *relented reluctantly*. Tulip went on the addle-headed prowl once he'd doped her up, found a boy from school, brought him home and let him fuck her while Kevin watched and masturbated. The seediness of it, the fact that this wasn't her boyfriend, that she was offering herself to someone she had no real attraction to, purely to sate her brother's inhuman appetites...

That excited him. Even before he came – harder than ever, so hard that he had to jam a hand into his mouth to stifle his gasps – he began to wonder what it would be like if he told her to bring back a stranger, some random guy from the street.

Tulip stepped out of the confessional, walked to a pew near the front of the church, genuflected, knelt, said her prayers. Fr Andrew used to make her say dozens of them – she'd be praying for hours after each confession – but Fr Sebastian limited Tulip's penance to a few Hail Mary's and Our Father's. The priest often pleaded with her to tell the police or social workers about her brother's abuse, or to come to him outside of the confessional, so that he could act on what she said. He was a broken, pitiful, weak man in most ways, but he had yet to break the sacred seal of the confessional and hoped that he never would — it was the last good thing in his life that he had to be proud of.

But Tulip refused to rat on her brother. To a large extent it was fear for his life — she knew he was an addict (if he hadn't been in the beginning, he certainly was now) and was sure he'd kill himself rather than be parted from her. Regardless of what he'd done to her, he was her brother and she wanted him to live. But shame was also a factor. Though she didn't mind admitting every act of indecency to Fr Sebastian and God – who forgave all sins – she cringed at the thought of confessing to anyone else.

Kevin studied Tulip as she prayed. He felt wretched, but passion was never far from the surface. Recalling the early months when watching had been enough, Tulip bringing home boys from school, having sex with them, quick and cold, Kevin getting off on the scene. He still fantasized about her bringing back a stranger but was worried that he couldn't control the situation. If a teenager caught him outside the room, trousers around his ankles, Kevin could threaten the boy — *you were doing wrong too*. An adult couldn't be so easily manipulated. A man could hurt or expose them. Kevin might never have moved up from friends of Tulip's if he hadn't been called in by her headmistress one day for a heart-to-heart.

The headmistress was concerned — vicious rumours were sweeping the school that Tulip was having intimate relations with a variety of boys. Not unheard of – girls sometimes went wild when puberty hit – but disturbing in Tulip, in all other respects a model student, a lovely girl, very quiet. Could this be a delayed reaction to her father's death and did Kevin want to avail of a psychiatrist who had assisted other pupils with similar problems?

He broke into a cold sweat. Forced a crooked smile. Asked if there was any proof that the rumours were true. The headmistress pursed her lips — no actual *proof*, but the rumours were widespread. Kevin said that he'd talk it over with Tulip and take it from there. The headmistress saw him out with a smile, telling him they could set this straight, to keep his chin up, it would all work out. Kevin smiling desperately, stomach sinking, sure that he had come to the abrupt end of his voyeuristic odyssey.

Tulip was relieved when he told her. She thought the nightmare was over. Said it was for the best, they could start afresh, put the sickness behind them. Kevin not so willing to let go. Considering options — teenagers from different schools? No, teen circles too tight, word might trickle back. Move from London, enrol Tulip at another school? No, similar rumours would kick in after a while and her teachers might get in touch with the old school. Send Tulip out clubbing or to the pubs to pull? No, too young, people might notice and alert the police. Get her to pick up strangers in a park? Too dangerous, no telling what calibre of man she might bring back, and again, people might take note.

Slowly ticking off the options, relinquishing the dream. Then — the obvious, the terrible, the logical. Prostitution. They could control their clients that way, visit them in hotels or their homes, build up a base of regular customers. Lots of research to find out how and where to advertise, how much to charge, how to avoid crossing the professionals. Eventually ready to chance it, Tulip hating him for what he wanted her to do, Kevin having to threaten suicide again until she gave in.

The first time Kevin hid in a wardrobe in a hotel room which they had set up. Tulip met the john in the lobby and brought him up. For Tulip — horrible, bestial, humiliating. For Kevin — nirvana, the illicitness of the arrangement adding to the natural taboos. Tulip threatened suicide afterwards, trying Kevin at his own game. He wept and said he'd do nothing to stop her but would kill himself too. He made a suicide pact with her, calling her bluff. It worked. She abandoned hope, accepted her fate, surrendered any last vestiges of her innocence, kept human and alive only by her love for God and belief in redemption. Kevin lost himself more and more to the voyeurism, until it was no longer enough, until he had to take it further and play a more active role in the show, getting more of a high from being by her side when she was fucked than Tulip ever got chasing the dragon. When they performed together he felt complete. In a sick, blasphemous way he felt closer to God.

Tulip crossed herself one last time, rose, genuflected, returned to Kevin's side. "I'm ready." Kevin stood and smiled shamefully, wrapped an arm around her and squeezed encouragingly. Stepped out into the aisle and walked with her to the exit. Spotted Clint Smith near the back, on one of his Friday sessions. Kevin thought it was disgraceful but he kept his opinions to himself. He needed Smith, the customers and drugs which he provided, Dave Bushinsky and his thugs. He kept his head low, marched Tulip out of the church, pretended not to see the dealer.

Wan October daylight, cleansing except for those

who could no longer be cleansed. Facing home, strolling slowly, arm in arm, Tulip distracted, Kevin gloomy, a pair of lost, lonely, drifting souls.

TWELVE

Gawl ran his bloodied knuckles under cold water and grimaced, wounds washing clean, rust-coloured water trickling down the drain, examining the cuts, one over the middle knuckle especially deep. Couldn't remember who the fight had been with or what it had been about. Couldn't even recall if he'd won or lost, or if it had just been one of those scraps where they knocked each other around then retired to the bar for a few more pints.

He dried his hands on a pair of Alex's knickers. *Alex*, not Alice/Annie. Sneering as he ran the damp cotton over his knuckles. He'd beaten her and she'd taken it, whimpering and drunk, then returned for more. Visited him on and off for two weeks, letting him do what he wanted as long as he provided booze. Hadn't seen her recently though. She must have found another mug, less violent than Gawl. Or else she was dead. He didn't care either way, a bit of hole always welcome but he wouldn't die without it.

Gawl tossed the knickers away and wandered through to his grotty living room, wincing, ribs aching, killing the pain with a glug of cider. Collapsing into a chair, he gazed moodily at the wall, then at the watch he'd stolen from some goon he'd kicked the shite out of the week before. Three-seventeen. He'd have to get a move on soon, but not to the pub. Gawl was on a mission, better things to do with his evenings than waste his time getting drunk.

The *mission* had fallen into his life on Wednesday, Gawl waiting in the Church of Sacred Martyrs, there to collect money which Fr Sebastian owed him. Keeping a curious eye on the young dealer near the back, Clint Smith, Fr Sebastian's go-to man. Gawl had thought about edging Smith out of the equation – supply the priest himself – but he worked for Dave Bushinsky and Gawl still clung to faint hopes of catching the Bush's eye at some stage. Even if that dream came to nothing, it was bad news to fuck with a man of the Bush's standing.

Idly watching Smith when Larry Drake walked in. Gawl recognised Drake, had seen him in newspapers and magazines, occasionally on TV in pubs. Came alert when Drake slid up to Smith. Saw Smith slip the actor a shit-load of gear, no money exchanging hands. When Drake left, Gawl followed, curiosity aroused. Gawl was sure Drake owned an expensive car or drove about in limos, but just as sure that the actor wasn't dumb enough to pull up at a small church in a flash car. Drake made a bee-line for the Elephant & Castle, lapels up, head low, not wanting to be ID'd while carrying enough shit to get an elephant high.

Drake got the Tube from the Elephant, changed at Embankment, District line to Fulham Broadway, short walk to his disappointingly ordinary apartment, Gawl hot on his heels, noting the address, retiring to a nearby café to order a coffee and mull this over. Figuring, *Must be thousands of junkie actors, nothing unusual in that, but how many walk into my life? Might be money here, an angle to be played*. He considered blackmail or burglary, but reckoned there was more to be made if he could strike a bargain with the actor. Gawl could act as a procurer – drugs, women, whatever – or protector, adept in both roles. The problem was how to get close to a man like Larry Drake. Gawl now knew where the actor lived, and that he liked to get high, but how to introduce himself and convince Drake to make use of him?

Thinking hard but getting nowhere, he finished his coffee and got ready to call it quits and go collect his cash from Fr Sebastian, when providence struck again. Larry Drake walked into the café, beaming at the waiter. "The usual, please."

The waiter beamed back. "Coming right up, Mr Drake."

Gawl hunched over his empty mug as Drake sat just two tables away from him and produced a showbusiness magazine, ruffling the pages, sighing happily. When the waiter came with the drink, Gawl eavesdropped.

"Busy day, Mr Drake?"

"Not too bad. Got off early for good behaviour." Dry laughter.

"Still shooting around Kennington?" the waiter asked.

"Yeah. Bloody location shoots are killers. Some bastard kept walking by today when we were trying to get a shot outside a restaurant, did it just to piss us off, laughing like an idiot."

"Did you get the shot in the end?"

"Nope. Trying again tomorrow. We're there till the weekend and the light wasn't right anyway."

"Any exciting plans for tonight?"

"You know me." Laughing knowingly. "Quiet night in."

Gawl ordered another coffee, sat sipping it slowly, trying not to stare at the actor, waiting for him to leave. When he did, Gawl rose and followed him back to his apartment, walking past as Drake entered. Stopped at the corner of the street, lingered a moment, decided he was too obvious here, crossed to a pub with a view of Drake's place. Gawl found a seat near the front window, settled down, watched.

Shortly before eight a car pulled up outside. Moments later the actor appeared, dressed to impress. Sat into the back and drove away into the night, Gawl watching silently, pondering. He went home early for once, sober, plotting.

Thursday morning, Gawl in fresh jeans, a jumper and overcoat, clean shaven, making a rare effort to look presentable. Brushed his hair into place as best he could, carefully combing ginger hairs over the grey. Paused in front of a mirror, studying his reflection and the jagged top of his stumpy left ear, the kind of mark people noticed and remembered. Gave up on his hair, ducked into the garish Elephant & Castle shopping centre – some genius had a brainwave years earlier and painted the fucking thing pink – and bought a loose wool cap which he could tug down over his ears, then strolled to Kennington in search of a TV crew.

He found them setting up cameras and lights outside a restaurant, the actors standing around and talking quietly, technicians busy. A small crowd of interested onlookers stood gathered nearby. Gawl joined them, staying near the back. A tedious business, equipment had to be carted all over the place, actors told where to stand, what to say, the different shots they were planning, make-up artists fussing around the actors, crew clearing out of the way, public asked for quiet. Then the big moment — Larry Drake and three others walk into scene, pause outside the door of the restaurant, have a short conversation and enter.

"Cut."

Applause from the crew as the actors re-emerged. Then they swept forward to move the cameras and lights, preparing the next shot, a close-up, actors huddled together, drinking and smoking while they waited, looking bored.

Some of the onlookers drifted away. Gawl drifted with them, took a left at the end of the street then leisurely circled back around, this time positioning himself clear of the crowd, alone, observing silently. Moved five more times over the course of the morning, not wanting to draw attention to himself by lingering in any spot too long.

Lunch break. Most of the crew filed into the restaurant. A couple of the actors joined them but Drake left with the director and a few others for a nearby pub. Gawl followed, keeping a safe distance, not entering until they were all seated and had ordered food and drinks, engaged in conversation, taking no notice of the other customers. Then he walked in casually, ordered a pint and pie, sat as close to their table as he could, ears sharp.

Lots of dull shop talk, jokes, the actors name-dropping, Drake mostly silent. He wasn't the star of the show, nobody here in awe of him, not giving it large like he did in public, saving his grand performances and stories for those who were easily impressed. Gawl tuned into a conversation between the director and one of his assistants. They were discussing the schedule for the rest of the week. They planned to wrap by three outside the restaurant, then transfer to Kennington Tube station to shoot a short scene. Friday they'd be filming around Waterloo all day, Saturday morning around Blackfriars, that afternoon at the Imperial War Museum. "Then back to the sanity of the studio," the director sighed.

Gawl stayed seated when the TV people left. He still had no idea how to wring money out of Larry Drake, but he was pleased with the way the morning had gone. He'd shadowed Drake professionally, aroused nobody's suspicions, got close to the actor during his personal time. If he could keep this up, hovering at the edges of Drake's world, fishing for titbits, something would surely present itself.

Gawl went for a walk after lunch. Returned to the restaurant as the crew was packing up and relocating to the Tube station. He cut ahead of them. Passed a homeless guy selling copies of the Big Issue. Flash of inspiration — he stopped, checked his wallet, bought nine copies and told Mr Big Issue to piss off. "It's not legal, re-selling them," the homeless guy protested. Gawl growled threateningly in response and Mr Big Issue quit while he was ahead.

Gawl found a spot near the station, started crying, "ISH-ooo! Get yer Big ISH-ooo!" Quietened down when the TV crew began to set up, careful not to annoy them. Silent while they were filming. Watched Drake do his stuff – he had to run out of the station, trip over a box, get up and run again – and bid goodbye to everyone when he was done, heading away before most of the others. One of the actors called out, asked what his plans were for the night. "Theatre," Drake shouted, sliding into a cab.

Gawl wondered whether or not to follow the actor. Decided he'd done enough for one day, struck for home, then the King's Head, his local on the Walworth Road, to get pleasantly drunk, feeling he'd earned it.

Friday brought more of the same. Even easier to spy on Drake and the film crew in the crush around Waterloo, invisible in the crowd. Missed him at lunch – he took a car up the West End – but picked him up again in the afternoon. Hit paydirt near the end of the day, as Drake was preparing to leave. One of the technicians asked if he wanted to come to a party tomorrow. "Can't," Drake said. "Hot date in the Groucho, then she wants to check out some dive called the Starsky & Hutch, a seventies disco I think."

"I've been there," the technician said. "A bit downmarket."

Drake laughed. "If it gets me in her pants, I don't care."

Gawl excited — a Saturday night disco, Drake most probably stoned (from what Gawl had seen, he hadn't yet dipped into the gear he'd bought in church), a chance to mingle with the actor, get talking to him, steer conversation around to Clint Smith, let it drop that he could get much better shit at a far more reasonable price, set Drake up with some pussy if his own bitch wasn't giving any, become his friend, his associate, his right-hand man.

Home, dreaming big. He hit the King's Head again, to find out more about the Starsky & Hutch, learnt it was over by the Borough. Then he struck east to find a pub where nobody knew him, where he could get drunk and fight without any comebacks, knowing he'd have to keep a clear head the next day.

Gawl caught up with the film crew again Saturday afternoon, outside the War Museum, watched for a few hours, then left for home at six, shortly after Drake had quit for the day, to ready himself for his big night out. Washing with cold water, shivering as he scrubbed clean, shaving again, careful not to nick himself, new clothes laid out on the bed, flares and a purple polo neck. Gawl tried them on, checked in the mirror — *ridiculous!* He decided to go in his regular clothes. He'd stick out more if he tried fitting in as one of the clubbers. Pulled on jeans and a jumper, back to the mirror — much better.

Nearly a quarter to eight. Figuring, *They'll have something to eat, a few drinks, won't leave for the club until eleven thirty, maybe later.* He planned to head over about half-ten, find the place, settle in, be there when they arrived.

Nervous, pacing the flat, checking the time every few minutes, running through plays in his head, how to introduce himself. Start by offering to buy Drake a drink? Say he recognised him from TV or act like he didn't know who he was? What if Drake refused Gawl's offer of a drink or told him to get lost? Come straight out and ask how Clint Smith was or retreat and try again another time?

No clear answers. He thought about calling it off and getting drunk. Crazy to think he could mix with the likes of Larry Drake. Out of his league, not even in the same game. Foolish to go after a legendary big score. He should be hitting the local pubs, making real contacts, not wasting his time on wild dreams.

Ten o'clock. Ten-fifteen. Ten-twenty. Ten-twenty-two.

"Fuck it!" Out the door, quick march along the landing, down the stairs, bus to the Borough, a pub, a shot of whiskey, a pint. Relaxxxxed. Asked the bargirl if she knew where the Starsky & Hutch was. She stared at him oddly – why was an old fart asking about the Starsky & Hutch? – but told him how to get there. He took his time finishing his pint then headed for the nightclub. Looked like a miserable dump from the outside, heavy security on the gates and doors, Gawl subjected to a rough search, bouncers eyeing him suspiciously before waving him through.

Inside — low ceiling, loud pumping music, girls in tight tops, short skirts, thigh-high boots, gyrating, sreaming along with the music. Boys in tight trousers, flowery shirts or loose cardigans, dancing moronically with the girls or sitting at the bar and taking in the floor show, getting drunk. Gawl pushed through and shouted his order at a pimply bartender, sipped at his piss-poor beer, watched the doors, waiting for Larry Drake.

Half eleven. Quarter to twelve. Midnight. Depression

setting in. A total waste of a night if the actor didn't show. Ogling the girls on the dance floor, half-thinking of making a move on them. Been a long time since he'd enjoyed a bit of snatch this fresh and presentable. They'd probably laugh him off, but nothing ventured... He'd give it another half hour. If Drake hadn't shown by then, Gawl would toss back a few shorts and strut his funky stuff, give these kids a taste of what the seventies had really been like, the genuine article.

At seventeen minutes past twelve, Larry Drake bopped into the club, a beautiful young woman on his arm, both giggling and wide-eyed from tequila slammers and a couple of E's. Drake led the girl straight to the dance floor, where he wrapped his arms around her and tried stealing a kiss. The girl laughed and pushed him away, dancing erratically. Drake swirled around her, waving his arms like an octopus, pressing up close every chance he got.

Gawl watched intently, ears thrumming from the music, broken lines of patter flashing through his thoughts. Most of his attention focused on Drake, no interest in the blonde teenager with the actor, dismissing her as a nameless bit of skirt, no idea she was Shula Schimmel, Dave Bushinsky's niece.

Drake and Shula spun off the dance floor and found

two chairs in a dark corner. Rocking as they sat, giggling, Drake clearing a space on the table they were sitting at, crouching over it, making two lines of coke, Shula watching uncertainly, Gawl incredulously — what sort of an arsehole did coke in the middle of a club, out in the open, where anyone could see?

Drake took out a fifty pound note, rolled it up theatrically, snorted half a line, transferred it to his other nostril, finished the line. Offered the rolled up note to Shula. She waved it away, but half-heartedly, woozy from the tequila and E's, not thinking clearly. Drake pressed the note upon her again, shouting something in her ear. This time she shrugged, glanced around nervously, leant over the table and attacked the coke, shivering as she sat up, panting heavily.

They took to the dance floor again, stumbling, almost falling over, out of their heads. Drake wrapped his arms around Shula and groped her breasts. She laughed. He tried to slide a hand up her skirt but she wasn't *that* stoned — slapped his hand away, shook a finger at him, *naughty-naughty!* Drake pulled a face then grabbed her tight, bounced up and down with her, Gawl watching, a plan half-forming. If anyone interfered with them – tried to grab the girl from Drake, or told them they had to leave – Gawl could step in, control the situation, ensure the pair enjoyed the rest of the night uninterrupted. Seeing himself coming to their rescue, Drake grateful, ordering a car to take them home, slipping his phone number to Gawl, telling him to give him a call, Gawl nodding politely, "Thank you, Mr Drake." "Hey, call me Larry."

After a couple of fast-paced songs, the pair retired to another table, did two more lines of coke, crooked lines this time, more coke than previously, neither of them able to finish, letting two nearby boys snort up the last of the coke, waving away their thanks. Sitting, gazing off into space, smiling dreamily. Gawl thought about approaching Drake but the actor was out of it, grinning blankly. He decided to wait, still hoping that someone would mess with Drake and his girl, affording Gawl the opportunity to flex his muscles and impress.

Later they returned to the dance floor, a slow shuffling dance even though the rhythm was fierce, both glassy-eyed, numb, Drake nuzzling the girl's neck and playing with her breasts, Shula taking no notice, her first time on coke, hardly aware of where she was or who she was with.

Another number started. Halfway through, Drake guided Shula towards the exit. Stoned as he was, he had plans for her and they didn't end here. Gawl saw that they were leaving. He thrust his pint away, lurched to his feet, started after them, pausing when they swayed, letting them get ahead, not wishing to barge up behind them.

Outside, past the bouncers, no cabs. Drake took a right turn, guiding Shula, muttering to her, laughing, Shula responding sluggishly. Gawl trailed them, alert. This was a dangerous area, dark alleys, not many people around. Drake and his girlfriend were easy targets. Gawl prayed for an attack. Thinking ahead — if they weren't attacked tonight, he could arrange a mugging another time, hire a couple of toughs to give Drake a going over, Gawl on hand to leap to the rescue.

Shula stumbled and yelped. Drake laughed, bent over, hands busy at her breasts, kissing her. Shula panting hard when she got to her feet. Drake tried sliding his hand up her dress again. Gawl heard a sharp, "No!" The girl gave Drake a push, staggered ahead on her own. Drake caught up with her, tried to kiss her. Shula stubbornly resisted. She pulled aside, doubled over, threw up. Drake glared at her, horny, interested only in fucking her, not caring what state she was in. He handed her a tissue to wipe around her mouth, the extent of his chivalry. Then it was back to mauling her as they walked, wearing her down.

Drake looking for a cab, desperately hailing each taxi that passed, even those already taken. Gawl drew gradually closer, planning to take firmer action, stand in the middle of the road and force a cab to stop, pull the passengers out if any were in it, cite this as an emergency, push in Drake and his girl, wink big, Drake tickled pink. Almost upon them, ready to do it, when...

A fucking cab stopped. The driver pulled over and rolled the window down. "Where you going, mate?"

"Fulham Broadway."

"Get in, I'll take ya."

Drake tried to drag Shula into the cab. She resisted, mumbling, just conscious enough to know she didn't want to go to this man's home with him. "Come on," Drake urged her, tugging hard. "You can sleep on the couch, or I can drop you off along the way, or —"

"No!" Shula shouted, shoving him away, weaving dangerously, almost falling over again. "Let me alone. Don't want to."

Drake lost his temper. "Get in the fucking cab or I'll leave you here."

"Don't care," Shula muttered, swaying, eyes swimming.

"Fuck you then," Drake roared. He jumped in the cab and slammed the door shut. "Drive on," he barked at the driver.

"What about the –"

"Fuck her. Drive." He thrust a tenner at the cabbie, who was worldly enough to accept it and keep his mouth shut. The cab pulled away from the kerb, stranding the girl.

Shula stared after the cab, slack-jawed, thinking it was a joke, that he'd stop and come back for her. When she realised he'd really left her, she slumped. Cursed beneath her breath, made obscene gestures, mumbled senselessly. Then shook her head, did a full circle – Gawl ducked back into the shadows so she wouldn't see him – and lurched ahead, the way she'd been going. Alone.

Gawl disgusted, not by Drake's behaviour but because he'd been cheated out of a golden opportunity to break the ice with the actor. Rage building, a whole night wasted, money down the drain, half-deaf from the fucking club, more sober than he could ever remember being on a Saturday night. About to wheel back to the Starsky and Hutch to get truly pissed. He stopped, sights fixing on the tottering Shula Schimmel as she staggered further away from the club, into darkness and a warren of threatening backstreets.

Gawl grinned bleakly and set off after the girl, large steps, cock hardening, determined to get something out of the night. Closed the gap, moving like a shark, dead eyes, all-driving hunger. Waited until Shula was at the mouth of a dark alley. Rushed her, grabbed her, hauled her off the main street, into blackness.

THIRTEEN

Big Sandy knew it was trouble when the phone rang at a quarter past ten. Not especially early, but everyone knew he liked to sleep in past midday on a Sunday and took a very dim view of being disturbed. Nobody dumb enough to piss off Big Sandy unless it was urgent. Groaning as he rose, head throbbing — he enjoyed his Saturday night piss-ups, a long-established tradition. Picked up with a grumpy but respectful, "Yeah?"

"I'm at Guy's Hospital. Get over here. Now." The Bush, furious.

"Which ward are –" Big Sandy began, but the Bush had already hung up. He set the phone down, scratching the stubble on his chin. He wanted to freshen up, shower and shave. But the Bush hadn't told him to shower and shave. He'd told him to get over to Guy's. *Now.* Big Sandy yawned, dressed, left his flat, stinking of beer and sweat.

He got a cab to Guy's and asked in reception for Dave Bushinsky. The receptionist gulped then gave him a room number and directions. Big Sandy strode through the corridors, wondering what was wrong, assuming one of the Bush's men had been hit, feeling like shit and wishing this could have happened twenty-four hours earlier.

The Bush waiting for him outside a private room, no bodyguards, not what Big Sandy had been expecting. "Boss," Big Sandy said cautiously, curiously. The Bush nodded stiffly then stepped aside and nudged the door of the room ajar. Big Sandy moved forward warily. Inside were a nurse, two middle-aged women he vaguely recognised as relatives of the Bush's, and Alice, the Bush's wife. The middle-aged women crying, Alice's face harsh and stained with dried tears, the nurse fussing over a patient in the bed. Big Sandy focused on the patient and his insides tightened, hangover forgotten in an instant. Shula Schimmel, looking like death, bruises, split lips, nightmarish rims around her eyes, shuddering, moaning.

Big Sandy fixed on Shula for several long seconds then closed the door gently and looked to the Bush for answers. "Larry Drake got her high and raped her. She was found in an alley, half-naked, unconscious, beaten."

"You're sure it was Drake?" Calm, saving his rage for later, when he could unleash it on a live target.

"She told me he was with her. Plied her with E's and coke. She doesn't remember the rape, thank God — the end of the night's a blank, maybe because of the drugs, maybe because of the blows to her head. They were at a club together. I checked with the bouncers – got them out of bed, *very* unhappy bunnies – and two of them recalled Drake leading her away."

"I told you not to trust him." Big Sandy bitter, a rare criticism of his boss.

"You want a fucking medal for being right?" the Bush hissed, face reddening. He took a step towards Big Sandy, then controlled himself. Deep breaths. Turned away, massaging the back of his neck, weary. "Find him. Break him. Kill him."

"You want in on it?"

"No. Alice needs me here."

"You have his address?"

The Bush passed a piece of paper to Big Sandy. "He won't be there, not after this. He must have been out of his fucking head to do something this crazy, but as soon as he comes to his senses he'll realise he's fucked. He'll run."

"I'll find him," Big Sandy said and the Bush saw the hatred in the giant's eyes, knew he could trust him to do the job right.

"I want this taken care of quick," the Bush said. "If he gets out of London it could be weeks – months – before we track him down." A pause. Looking to make sure they were alone. Lowering his voice. "Use the hounds."

Big Sandy stiffened. "I can find him without them."

"Yeah, but it's how I want it done. Fast Eddie will help." Big Sandy shrugged and turned to leave. The Bush called him back. "Sandy — make it painful."

Big Sandy didn't smile. "On that you can fucking rely."

The lab. Fast Eddie and Phials waiting for him, Fast Eddie nervous, Phials grim. The chemist spoke first. "Letting them out in the middle of the city is a bad idea. If they break loose…"

"Just get them ready," Big Sandy replied.

"I know Dave's upset, but if we wait for him to calm down, I'm sure —"

Big Sandy turned to Fast Eddie. "Can you prep them?"

"If I have to," Fast Eddie nodded, not liking it but knowing better than to argue with Big Sandy when his eyes were like this, flecks of fire amidst the grey.

"No," Phials grimaced. "I'll do it. It's crazy, but if you won't listen to sense…" He stormed ahead of them, muttering bleakly. Stopped when he reached the hidden door leading down to the cellar. Scoured the wall with his fingertips, searching for the secret panel. Slid it up and keyed in a five digit code. The wall opened, three sliding doors retracting one by one to reveal a steel door. Another code had to be keyed in for this, again five digits. When it slid back, a strong scent hit the three men — disinfectant and faeces. Big Sandy gagged, Fast Eddie flinched, Phials took no notice, accustomed to the stench.

The chemist's eyes glowed unnaturally in the cold neon light. He pressed ahead, leading the way. The cellar was a maze, stacked with boxes of chemicals, crates of guns, an illegal and valuable arsenal, reason enough for the secrecy, though not the primary reason — that lay further on.

The trio passed the crates and boxes, not glancing sideways or hesitating until they came to the cages. Four of them, one inhabitant per cage. The bars were thick steel. The floor, plates of steel. The hounds, each on a short chain in the centre of its cage, howling, snarling, snapping at the scent of humans in the air.

The Bush loved dogs. He'd been breeding and trading them all his life. But no pedigree poodles for him. He bred dogs to fight and hunt. For years he'd owned the toughest, meanest dogs in London, if not the whole country. He fought them regularly and they usually won, ripping out the throats of the competition, a nice little earner, the Bush's most prized possessions.

For some men the fights were not enough. They wanted more and were happy to pay big for even darker, twisted pleasures. The Bush saw an opening and set up the hunts deep in the countryside. He bought forested property which couldn't be traced back to him. Installed a shitload of video cameras. Had his team pick a homeless guy from the streets, a junkie without any friends, who wouldn't be missed. Set him loose in the forest then freed the hounds. They had been specially bred and trained. They hungered for blood and fresh flesh. They ran the junkie down and tore him apart. The Bush and a handful of carefully selected guests watched it all through the cameras, betting on how long the junkie would last once the hounds started after him.

The Bush didn't free the hounds often, no more than three or four times a year, always for a small, wealthy, appreciative audience. He made a sweet profit but not enough to justify the risk — he'd serve serious time if word of his games ever leaked. He kept the hounds because he needed the bloodshed, the betting on human life, the vicious thrill of the savage hunt. He had a hunger for the debased, and the hounds allowed him to channel and stay in control of his darker desires and needs.

Phials loved dogs too. It was how the pair's paths

originally crossed. A mutual acquaintance told Phials about the hounds and invited him to come see them in action. The Bush and Phials bonded. Phials wept with joy as he watched the dogs run down their prey. He had never seen anything so wretchedly beautiful.

To entertain himself during his incarceration, Phials had been experimenting with some of the Bush's prized hunters. He'd added chemicals to their genetic mix, curious to see what he could do with them, how far he could push them, keen to prove that he could triumph over any design of nature's.

The hounds in the cellar were the fiercest of their kind. Most hunting dogs were bred either for their speed or keen sense of smell. They weren't designed to fight. The hounds were different, larger than most, stockier, more like German Shepherds in appearance. Their fangs were long and thick, their eyes wide and crazed. Savage to begin with, under Phials' influence they had become creatures of pure, undiluted hate. The four that he kept at the lab were the most monstrous of the lot, victims and pioneers, the face of a ferocious future. The Bush delivered his meanest specimens to the lab and Phials drove them even further down the road of madness and bloodlust.

The Bush had never used the hounds in London.

They had only ever been unleashed in the safety of the forest, where no casual observer could see them hunt and kill. Releasing them on the streets of the nation's capital was a crazy, reckless gamble. But his niece had been raped and dumped in an alley. The Bush was in a crazy, reckless mood, and the men who served him knew better than to question the commands of their master.

Big Sandy studied the hounds as they spun in wild circles inside their cages, leaping at the bars, their large nostrils splayed wide, drooling, howling, snarling, snapping at the air. Their hair was caked with blood, vomit, shit. Phials' drugs had shortened their lives. They found it hard to digest food. They couldn't control their bodily functions. Their hearts beat too fast and they had trouble breathing. Phials expected these four to be dead within months. He didn't care. Nor did the Bush. Plenty of replacements on standby.

"How many of them are we taking?" Fast Eddie mumbled, squinting nervously, praying to God that Big Sandy didn't want to take them all.

"Could we handle one each?" Big Sandy asked.

"I wouldn't advise it," Phials said. "The pair of you *might* be able to control one between you..."

"Then we'll take that one," Big Sandy said, pointing

to a hound which had just pissed itself with excitement. "Get it ready."

Phials plucked a syringe from a rack on the wall and prepared it, fingers steady as they gripped the needle, features assertive. Fast Eddie produced a set of keys and unlocked the door of the cage. The hound retreated, growling gutturally. Phials stepped past Big Sandy and Fast Eddie, syringe held down by his side.

"Need a hand?" Big Sandy asked.

"No," Phials said softly. He opened the door and walked straight at the dog, head erect, empty left hand slowly rising, fingers fluttering, the hound's eyes locking on the chemist's dark, smooth palm. Big Sandy watched uncertainly. He hadn't seen Phials at work with the hounds before. He was worried, thought this would end in a bloodbath. Fast Eddie not flustered — he knew Phials was on solid ground.

The hound growled, pissed itself again, then leapt, fangs bared, powerful hind legs driving it forward at pace. Phials ducked and wrapped his arms around the dog, as if embracing a lover, hauling it upright. As the dog staggered around the cage on two legs, trying to make space to bite, Phials plunged the tip of his syringe into the beast's neck and pushed down the plunger with his thumb. The hound made a choking noise and stiffened. Its eyes closed and its jaw and limbs went slack. Phials gently laid the animal to rest on the floor then exited.

Fast Eddie took the syringe. Phials was shaking now, but only a slight tremor. Big Sandy stared at him, the first time he'd felt anything approaching admiration for the captive chemist, but tinged with pity, seeing what Phials could have been if he hadn't fallen victim to his addiction.

"He'll be out for ten minutes," Phials said. "Slip his harness on while he's unconscious."

"Will he be docile when he wakes?" Big Sandy asked.

Phials laughed. "For about five seconds." He turned to Fast Eddie and licked his lips. "Can I have one of the guys call for Clint while you're gone? Ask him to bring Tulip?"

"Sure," Fast Eddie smiled.

"How about some E's?"

Fast Eddie frowned. "I can't authorise that."

"Please..." Phials shaking bad now.

Fast Eddie took pity. "OK. But only enough to give you a mild buzz."

"A mild buzz is all this sad old buzzard longs for," Phials grinned, then drifted away, muttering over his shoulder, "Shout if you need me."

Big Sandy watched the chemist leave, still torn between admiration and pity. Then he put Phials from his thoughts and focused on the animal in the cage, hurrying to fetch its harness, conscious of the clock ticking, not wanting to be caught in the cage with the thing if it came back to life unharnessed.

Breaking into Larry Drake's apartment, Big Sandy alone, Fast Eddie in the van, the hound chained in the back. Quick exploration — clothes scattered across the floor of the bedroom, a wardrobe door half-open, space on a shelf where a travel bag might have been. The bird had flown.

Big Sandy hurried downstairs. A young man – one of Drake's neighbours – was in the corridor. He eyed Big Sandy suspiciously and started to ask a question. Big Sandy locked gazes. "You don't want to get involved." The young man flinched and made to withdraw. "Hey." Big Sandy spread the thumb and little finger of his left hand, closed the three middle fingers, lifted the hand to his ear and shook it. "You don't want to phone anybody either." The young man stared at the giant, gulped and nodded then shut his door hastily.

Big Sandy and Fast Eddie hustled the hound up the stairs. It was muzzled. The leash was a steel bar with a leather choker round the dog's neck. You could administer an electric shock by pressing a button on the leash's handle. Big Sandy had sneered when Fast Eddie pointed that out to him, didn't think he'd need it. By the time he'd got to the top of the stairs he'd already had to stun the beast four times. He was sweating, muscles strained, struggling to hold the powerful hound in check.

They hustled the hound to Drake's bedroom. Big Sandy grabbed a handful of clothes and stuffed them in the dog's face. Snorting, the hound tried to back away. Then it caught the smell of Larry Drake and stiffened, flashing on previous hunts, recalling past kills, adrenalin kicking in, pressing its snout deep into the clothes, inhaling, slavering, locking on to the scent.

Big Sandy let the hound get a long whiff of the clothes, then crashed down the stairs with the dog, Fast Eddie following. The hound stopped on the pavement, sniffing wildly, passersby staring with shock and distaste at the filthy creature and its handlers.

"Does Drake have a car?" Fast Eddie asked.

"No. Banned for three years for drunk driving."

"I didn't know that."

"The Bush kept it quiet."

"What if he got a cab?"

"He wouldn't have — afraid he'd be traced."

"But if he did?"

Big Sandy shrugged. "Then we drag this fucker round London till he catches the bastard's scent."

Fast Eddie nodded wearily. It wouldn't be the first wild goose chase he'd been on. No point complaining, he was paid good money to take whatever shit the Bush threw his way. Besides, anything was preferable to babysitting Phials.

The hound was drifting off to the left when it changed its mind and spun right, picking up speed, lunging along awkwardly. Big Sandy and Fast Eddie panted as they kept up, Big Sandy keeping a firm grip on the hound's leash, ignoring the startled stares of the people they passed. Fast Eddie said a quick prayer that they didn't run into any cops but Big Sandy didn't pray — didn't believe God heeded the prayers of the damned.

The hound led them steadily east, snout to the pavement, cutting a path through the Sunday strollers and shoppers, everyone ogling the bizarre trio. Big Sandy hated drawing so much attention. If they caught up with Drake and the hound was linked to his death afterwards, Big Sandy and Fast Eddie were screwed. Too many witnesses would have seen them with the dog. There were limits to the number of people that even someone like the Bush could buy off.

They cut through Harrington Gardens, past the Harrington Hall Hotel where Big Sandy had first met Shula. Anger flared fresh in him and he urged the hound on, thinking viciously of Larry Drake and the torment he'd put him through before killing him.

Angling south down Sloane Avenue, then further south towards the river, Big Sandy trying to guess where the hound was leading them, how Drake would have run. The actor had skirted local Tube stations, Fulham Broadway, West Brompton, Earl's Court. In Drake's position Big Sandy would have hopped on a train, got out of the city ASAP. But Big Sandy wasn't a public figure, likely to be recognised wherever he went. And Drake didn't know about the hounds, how easy it was for them to track him. He tried to think like Drake — anxious, desperate, panicked, eager to hole-up, get his head straight, formulate a plan. Couldn't check into a hotel. Had to be a friend's house, someone he could trust, close enough to get to on foot.

Halfway down a residential street, the hound stopped outside a house and threw itself manically at the front door. Big Sandy stunned it several times until it went limp. Then he handed control of the hound to Fast Eddie, put his shoulder to the door, counted to three, and slammed it. He slammed again. Again. The fourth time it cracked. Big Sandy kicked in the door and hurried through, Fast Eddie and the hound crowding in after him. Stairs. Doors. Apartments. Big Sandy stepped aside and nodded Fast Eddie forward. Fast Eddie stepped past, struggling with the hound as it whined with excitement and hunger, scrabbling towards the stairs.

Fast Eddie checked with Big Sandy to see how he wanted to play it. Big Sandy closed the front door, stared up the stairs, waved Fast Eddie on. The hound lunged up the steps, dragging Fast Eddie with it, Big Sandy taking the steps three at a time after them. Left at the top, past two doors. The hound stopped at the third door and went insane, jumping at the handle, trying to bark, eyes wild. Fast Eddie tugged back the dog, teeth gritted, fingers slipping on the leash, cursing. Big Sandy ignored his partner's struggles, stepped up to the door, kicked it open.

A living room. A woman and Larry Drake. Drake crying, the woman trying to comfort him. They leapt to their feet when Big Sandy burst in. Drake screamed. The woman rushed Big Sandy. Drake darted for the window. Big Sandy slapped the woman aside. The hound dived for her but Fast Eddie dragged it back. Big Sandy caught Drake and hurled him face-first into the wall. The actor slumped to the floor, groaning. The woman got back on her feet and rushed Big Sandy, shrieking. Big Sandy caught the woman by the throat, silencing her. He leant forward and hissed, "He raped a girl."

"No," she gasped. "Not Larry... he told me..."

Big Sandy, soft but firm, "I don't want to kill you, but I will if you fuck with us." The woman went cataleptic with fear. "Take me to the bathroom." She didn't respond. Big Sandy snarled, "*Now,*" and released her.

The woman stumbled backwards, rubbing her throat, weeping. Big Sandy took a calculated step towards her. She moaned and led him to the bathroom, trembling wildly. The hound was over Drake, keeping him on the floor, Fast Eddie letting the muzzled beast worry the actor. Big Sandy checked inside the bathroom door for a key. He took it out and shoved the woman in. "You'll hear us leaving. Don't make any noise until we're gone." She started to protest. He silenced her with a finger. "Don't push me." Seeing murder in his eyes, she nodded obediently, terrified.

Big Sandy locked the door and turned on Larry Drake. The actor was squealing, trying to slap the hound away, scratched and bleeding from the dog's claws. "Pull it off," Big Sandy grunted, cracking his knuckles. Fast Eddie gripped the leash tight and hauled the hound away. The hound didn't want to retreat, remembering previous kills, the taste of human blood and flesh. It lashed out at Fast Eddie, straining against the hold of the choker.

"I didn't rape her!" Drake yelled, pressing his hands together, praying to Big Sandy to spare him, face distorted with dread, eyes swamped with tears. "I only heard... about it... this morning. I swear I didn't –"

A snapping sound — the hound's choker. It broke free and hurled itself at Larry Drake. Drake screamed. Big Sandy started forward to pull the hound off. Then he paused. He'd had an idea. He knew he might end up regretting it, but he wanted Drake to know real fear and agony before he died. Before he could talk himself out of it, he leant down and undid the clasp at the back of the hound's muzzle, then pulled it free.

"Are you fucking crazy?" Fast Eddie shrieked.

"It's not interested in us," Big Sandy smiled humourlessly, watching as the hound tore into Drake, the actor already bleeding and whimpering. His screams rose sharply, then died away to a gurgled groan as the hound attacked his mouth, as if kissing him. Drake fought back, but the hound ignored the feeble blows and dug in. Big Sandy watched solemnly, passionlessly, as it readjusted and fastened on Drake's throat, biting through flesh and cartilage, blood gushing from the wounds, soaking the hound's face, Drake's body thrashing.

He didn't last long. Within a minute he'd stopped shaking, eyes fixed on an indeterminate point in space, limbs relaxing as he surrendered to death. The hound carried on biting, clawing, chewing, snuffling like a boar in search of truffles.

Big Sandy moved to the front door and checked the hall outside. Nobody had come to investigate, neighbours either out shopping, sleeping off hangovers, or too wary to show any interest.

Big Sandy closed the door then emptied the contents of Drake's bag over the floor, making sure there was nothing there to tie him to Dave Bushinsky or Shula Schimmel. He thought about the woman in the bathroom. Drake must have told her about the Bush and his niece. She could identify Fast Eddie and himself.

They had to kill her.

He felt sick as he recalled his mother, walking in as an eleven year old to find her dead on her bed. He hated killing women, especially when they were innocent. But Drake had involved her. She could bring them all down, him, Fast Eddie, the Bush. He had no choice.

Big Sandy focused on the hound. It was moving slower now, almost sated, whining softly. He picked up the choker and examined it — no good any more. He was still holding the muzzle. He turned to Fast Eddie. "Get the van. Park outside. I'll slip this on when it finishes with Drake. We'll bundle it down the the stairs, drive it back to the lab."

"You're sure you'll be OK here with that thing?" Fast Eddie asked.

"On a full stomach it should be easy to handle."

"And the woman?"

"I'll deal with her while you're gone. We'll bring the bodies with us."

"We're not gonna leave them here?"

"Can't. It'll be obvious they've been mauled by a dog. People saw us on the streets with the hound. We have to dispose of the corpses. I'd like to send in a team to clean up but there won't be time, we made a lot of noise, the cops won't be far behind us."

"They could come while I'm gone for the van," Fast Eddie noted.

"All the more reason to get a fucking move on," Big Sandy huffed.

Fast Eddie blanched, nodded, made sure his clothes weren't bloodstained, then left to fetch the van. Big Sandy spent another minute studying the hound as it fed on the remains of Larry Drake. His eyes were almost as lifeless as the actor's and his hangover had kicked in again. He felt absolutely wretched, but he knew that he would soon feel even worse. Leaving the hound to mop up the scraps, Big Sandy set down the muzzle, cracked his knuckles and turned to face the bathroom door. A pause. A long, agonised breath.

He started forward.

FOURTEEN

Halloween horror at White Hart Lane. Clint sat with cousin Dave in the South Stand, watching Spurs lose 3-1 to Birmingham in a Worthington Cup game, home fans screaming abuse, everyone disgusted except Dave Bushinsky who seemed delighted by the poor quality of football on display.

The Bush a life-long Tottenham Hotspur fan. A regular since he was a boy, when he used to cycle to home games with his grandfather. Travelled a lot around the country in his teens and twenties to follow them on the road. Now he tended to go to home games only, and not even all of those – a busy man – but his love for the club was as strong as ever.

Clint had been doubly horrified when the news broke about Shula. First, he was honestly devastated. It tore him up inside when he heard the sickening news. He wanted to rush to her side, profess his love for her, tell her this changed nothing, offer to do anything he could to help ease her pain. Since he couldn't do that – it would look strange, him turning up out of the blue to proclaim his love for her – he turned his thoughts towards punishment. He would find the one responsible for hurting her, track him down, torture him, kill him, deliver his head on a plate to her. But Big Sandy beat him to the punch, and therein lay the source of the second horror.

Larry fucking Drake.

Clint had sold Drake the drugs that he'd used to get Shula high. The guilt of that was bad enough, but if cousin Dave found out it could be the end of the line for him. Dave might view him as an accomplice, wonder if Clint had known what Drake was planning. Especially if someone had spotted Clint outside the Groucho, earlier that night.

Clint hadn't known about Drake when he'd trailed Shula to the Groucho. He just wanted to see where she was going for dinner, who she was dining with. A shock when he spotted her meeting up with the actor. Miserable as he watched Drake kiss her cheeks, seeing his dreams go up in flames, no way of competing with a celebrity. He had planned to follow Shula around for the rest of the night but he abandoned those plans immediately. Depressed, he'd wandered away and spent the night surfing the Tube, but only occasionally dealing, spending most of the time staring off into space, feeling like a groom who'd been jilted on the altar.

Cousin Dave might not see it that way. If he learnt that Clint had supplied Drake with the drugs, and that he was present when Drake linked up with Shula, he might think that Clint had served up his niece to the scumbag. Clint would have a hard time defending his case if Big Sandy and the hounds were sicced on him. From what he heard on the rumour mill, Drake had barely even had time to scream.

He'd barely slept the next few nights, waiting for Big Sandy to break down his door, for the nightmare to claim him as it had claimed Larry Drake. But to his relief the weekend passed, then Monday and Tuesday, with no mention of it, no summons, no sign of the giant or the hounds. He started to sleep soundly again.

Now that he was free to focus on Shula again, he made plans to visit her, not right away, but soon, when she was over the worst of it. Maybe this would turn out to be a blessing in diguise. The rape changed nothing as far as he was concerned. He still loved her, still wanted her. She would see that in his eyes, feel grateful for it, come to see him as a man she could depend upon, one who would overlook what had been done to her, who could love her purely, in a way that many men maybe no longer could.

As Clint recovered from his shock, outraged disbelief that Drake had raped her gave way to a different kind of anger as he realised that with Drake dead, his dream of selling to the stars was in tatters and he was back where he started. He came to hate the actor even more than he already did, furious at him for getting Clint so close to the real action, only to leave him stranded.

Clint tried putting the Drake business behind him but he couldn't. The bitterness wouldn't go away. America had seemed so close, almost within reach. He'd thought a lot about what Phials had said, about setting up base there before trying to win Shula's heart, and it made sense. If Drake had come through for him, he could have made the move, established himself in New York, returned for Shula within a few years when she still young and unattached. Now he was back to looking at things long-term, and who knew what would happen with Shula while he was labouring away with all the other dreamers.

He found it hard to return to penny-ante deals. He made the rounds as before but he had no enthusiasm for it now, poor sales, no satisfaction in those he made, obsessing about Drake and his cronies, the money and contacts he could have made with the actor's assistance. Depression setting in hard. Couldn't turn to drink or drugs like most people, since he had no stomach for them. Feeling his life was a waste, precious years slipping by, Shula moving out of his sightline, America dwindling in the distance.

He fell to thinking about Tony Phials and what he might be working on in the lab. Phials was now his only decent contact, his one hope of making it big and hitting America in style. Involved in something major, something he couldn't tell Clint about. He'd told Clint to ask cousin Dave — if Dave OK'd it, Phials would talk. Clint curious, wondering if there was an angle for him in this.

On Thursday he dropped by the office. Dave was in a meeting but could see him later. Clint went for a long lunch, returned in the afternoon. Dave grim-faced. Clint asked about Shula, trying not to appear too concerned, not wanting to betray his feelings for her.

"She's as well as can be expected," Dave sighed, his standard answer. "Her mother flew over on Monday and has been taking care of her. She's hoping to take her back to Switzerland soon, if that's what Shula wants. I'm hoping Alice goes with them. I'm getting nothing but grief from her at home."

"Why?" Clint asked. "It wasn't yuh-your fuh-fault." Inwardly thinking, *More my fault than yours*.

Dave laughed sharply. "Try telling the women that. Whenever anything like this happens, we're supposed to know about it in advance. Alice is of the opinion that I should have guessed what was on that bastard Drake's mind and moved to stop him before he had a chance to hurt Shula."

"Do you think she'll return to Switzerland?" Clint asked.

"I don't know," Dave said. "I don't think she knows either. Still in pain, still in shock. I think she'd be better off there, but I'll support her if she wants to stay."

Clint wasn't sure if he wanted her to leave or not. He'd miss her if she went, but maybe she'd be safer there. She lived in a small town, much quieter than London, fewer men to pester her, less competition for Clint when the time came to go a-courting.

Dave stretched, yawned and changed the subject. "So what can I do for you, cousin, or did you just come to offer your sympathy?"

"Mostly that," Clint lied. "It was a tragedy. Shula didn't deserve it. Anything I can do to help..."

Dave raised an eyebrow. He almost said, *And just what the fuck could you do, cousin, and so late in the day?* But he didn't. The kid was only trying to help.

Clint caught the Bush's unvoiced thought and blushed. He almost lost his nerve, but he knew that if he didn't ask now, he never would, so he muttered miserably, "I also wanted to ask about Ph-ph-ph-Phials."

"The good doctor." Dave was surprised but pleased. Fast Eddie had reported to him about Clint and his sessions with Phials. Dave had been brooding over what to do about it, wondering if he could use Clint to slip inside the chemist's defences, whether it would be better to direct Clint or let their friendship develop naturally.

"I've been wuh-wondering..." Clint halted, not sure how to phrase his question.

"...why I keep him locked up?" Dave prompted.

"Yeah."

"Have you asked him?"

"Yeah."

"What did he say?"

Clint shrugged. "Not muh-much. I think he's working on something buh-buh-big and he can't talk about it. He said I should ask you — said he cuh-could discuss it with me if yuh-yuh-yuh-you gave me the all-clear."

Dave's eyes narrowed. Phials was testing him. If he came straight out and told Clint why the chemist was so valuable, Phials would swiftly distance himself from Clint, as he had from Dave's other envoys. He had to play this cagily, keep Clint close, but not so close that Phials would think he was a plant.

"You doing anything next Tuesday?" Dave asked.

"No."

"Want to come to a football match?"

"Spurs?" Clint blinked, bewildered. Dave had never taken him to a game before.

"Yeah, Worthington Cup, what used to be called the League Cup. We're playing Birmingham, the night before Halloween."

"Should win," Clint noted. He didn't know much about football, but he knew Spurs were in the Premiership, Birmingham the division below.

Dave snorted. "We'll see. Coming?"

Clint smiled uncertainly. "Sure."

"My place, six o'clock, and be on time — traffic's a nightmare."

They got to White Hart Lane early. Passed kids trick or treating, clad as skeletons, witches, ghosts. Nobody in fancy dress inside the stadium, everybody sombre, in no mood to party, the air thick with self-doubt. Dave had three season tickets — he usually brought a couple of friends or business associates to the games. The seats were in the South Stand Upper, towards the centre. Not the best view. He could have got premium seats in the West Stand, or a director's box, but his grandfather had been a South Stand die-hard and Dave was sentimental where his beloved Spurs were concerned.

Dave knew Clint was a football novice, so he filled him in on the recent history of Tottenham Hotspur while they were waiting for kick-off. "We've had a shit decade, bad managers, poor signings, nowhere in the league. Won the Worthington Cup the season before last, but that's it as far as silverware goes — and the Worthington Cup's more commonly known as the Worthless Cup, doesn't mean a thing. The fans blame the chairman and manager. The former, Alan Sugar, hasn't invested enough money in the club as far as the fans are concerned, while George Graham used to manage Arsenal, our arch rivals. Most Spurs fans would resent him even if we were doing well — since we're not, they hate his guts, but Sugar's even more, for hiring him in the first place."

The teams ran out. Half-hearted applause, the stadium far from full, the Birmingham fans making more noise than the home crowd, the Spurs players looking edgy.

The boos started when Birmingham scored their first goal. "Sugar out! Sugar out!" When they scored their second, most fans were standing, screaming, all their hatred directed at the chairman, abusive, vulgar, demonic. When the visitors got a third, the abuse intensified, calls for Sugar's head, venomous chants, Birmingham fans laughing, Spurs players demoralised. Clint listened to the furious fans around him — Sugar had to go, he was clueless, tight, money had to be pumped into the club, Sugar not the man for the job. Some criticised Graham and the players – a few even claimed it was the fault of the fickle fans – but most agreed that Sugar was the source of their sorrows.

Dave Bushinsky was also listening to the fans — and he was smiling.

The game ended 3-1, Spurs booed off the pitch, screams for Alan Sugar's resignation, hundreds of hardcore fans remaining after the game to protest, singing loudly, "We want our Tottenham back!" Police moved in to disperse them. An ugly end to an ugly night.

Dave was upbeat for the first time since what had happened to Shula, whistling as they slipped through the departing fans, as happy as if Spurs had won, leading the way to a pub called the Victoria, ordering a pint for himself and a bottle of beer for Clint, finding a free table in a room out back, nobody to eavesdrop, saluting Clint with his pint, "Bottoms up!"

"Cheers." Clint looked at his cousin quizzically. "Why aren't you pissed-off? Your team just got huh-hammered."

"Humiliating, wasn't it?" Dave laughed. "I've seen some terrible games at the Lane and endured some woeful results. This ranks with the lowest of them."

"It doesn't bother you?" Clint frowned.

"I'm ecstatic." Dave gulped his beer, drained a third of it, remembered he was driving, eased up. "We've all got dreams," he said, eyes on his beer, voice low, having decided over the weekend how to play the Clint card. "You know I've been distancing myself from my less legal operations lately, concentrating on my legitimate business interests."

"Yeah..." Clint was nervous, wondering if his cousin was about to announce his retirement from the narcotics industry, flashing on a horrible image of himself out of work, standing in a dole queue.

Dave sighed. "It's the wise play. I've put in my time, taken more than my fair share of risks, made the fortune I set out to. Now I want to enjoy it. Time to kick back, leave the dirty work to the young and hungry, get out before I become a victim of my own success. It's not an easy thing to do but I think I can pull it off."

There was a meditative silence, Dave still staring at his beer. Clint felt his cousin was waiting for him to say something. Chipped in with a weak, "That's guh-good, isn't it?"

"Yes." Dave looked up. "But at the same time it doesn't excite me. I don't want to be a dull businessman, cocooned in an office, bored out of my skull. I need a challenge, something to get passionate about. I have the hounds of course, the hunts and fights, but those are occasional pleasures. I've been thinking about it for a long time and the one thing that gets me going... what I'd really love..."

Dave stopped. Sipped at his beer. Glanced around the pub at a handful of disgruntled Spurs fans moaning about the match. Dave grinned when he saw them, then faced his young cousin. "Sugar's going to sell his controlling interest in the club before the end of the season. I have this from an excellent source. He's had enough of the abuse and ingratitude. He's been a success at everything he's turned his hand to, except football. He's ready to cut his losses. He's history."

Clint nodded, wondering where the hell his cousin was going with this and what – if anything – it had to do with Tony Phials. Dave noted Clint's confusion and said softly, "I want to buy out Alan Sugar's shares."

Clint blinked dumbly. "Oh." Couldn't think of anything else to say.

"I want to run Tottenham Hotspur," Dave continued, in case Clint hadn't grasped the full extent of what he was saying. "Sugar's the majority shareholder. When he sells, the buyer will replace him as chairman. I'd control the club. I think I'd be a natural. I know the fans because I'm one of them. I think the way they do, want what they want. I'd have Graham out within a week. Bring in someone we love – Glenn Hoddle maybe – and start re-building bridges between the club and the fans. We could be great again, we could build a winning team, we..."

Dave realised he was rambling. Cut himself short. Started over, Clint listening in a daze, still not sure what to make of this — was his cousin lining him up for a role at White Hart Lane?

"I've been making enquiries, putting out feelers. Sugar knows I'm interested. He's not keen to sell to me – he knows about my background – but he also knows about my love for the club, and if I can put up the money and convince him I want what's best for Tottenham Hotspur, that I have the savvy and people to take the club forward, he might accept my offer."

"That's... nice," Clint said weakly.

Dave grimaced. "Yes. *Nice*. Except do you know how much it costs to buy a Premiership club?" He rubbed his fingers together. "A team doing well, riding high in the league... forget about it, they're the province of PLCs, multinational corporations, TV conglomerates. But Spurs are small fish at the moment, much as it pains me to admit it as a fan. Sugar's shares won't come cheap, but I think he can be bought out for twenty million, give or take."

Clint whistled appreciatively, sitting to attention. "You have that muh-much?"

Dave laughed curtly. "Not in ready cash."

"But you can raise it?"

Dave hesitated. "Maybe. It depends." Looked Clint straight in the eye. "On our good friend Tony Phials."

Clint felt the world dissolving around him. Dave talking twenty million pounds, Dave talking Tony Phials, Dave talking *Clint*. Ears pricked when Dave continued, absorbing every word, forgetting Larry Drake and TV stars and selling a shitload of coke, dreaming now of a slice of twenty million.

"Phials is a genius — that's old news. What's new is that he's working on a drug which will knock everything else out of the ring. I can't tell you much about it, but I can tell you this, I have contacts in New York, L.A., Moscow, Tokyo – all across the globe – waiting to dump more money on me than you could dream of once I phone to say that I have the formula." He paused, his expression darkening. "But I can't do that until Phials cracks it, and so far, apparently, he hasn't."

Clint frowned. "He's still working on it?"

"Yes."

"Can't he tell you when he expects to have it ready?"

Dave sneered. "This is an experimental drug, nobody's ever seen anything like it, you can't put a time limit on something like that. But if he doesn't pull it off soon, Sugar will sell his shares elsewhere and I'll be stuck with a shitload of cash and nothing to do with it."

"You could always buy another club," Clint suggested. "Millwall?"

"Those hooligans?" Dave snorted. "I want the team I've supported all my life, the team my grandfather supported. I want the super Spurs and I'm determined to have them." Dave toyed with his glass. This was the delicate part. He had to be careful. "I think Phials is lying. I think he's perfected the drug but is holding back the formula."

Clint's eyes widened. "To sell it to somebody else?"

"No. I think he's afraid I'll kill him." Dave pushed his glass away then pulled it back. "When we start producing the drug, we'll control the supply. We'll be the only manufacturers, distributing it through contacts of our choosing. That's why our foreign friends are prepared to shower me with so much cash up front, for exclusive national rights. It's a complex beast, maybe the most intricate chemical compound anyone's ever seen. It won't be easy for others to decode its secrets, it'll take months, maybe years. Eventually some clever fuck will find a way to copy it — they always do — but until that happens we can charge what we like. Which makes Phials something of a liability."

"How so?" Clint asked.

"If he escaped, he could find a backer and go into opposition. The security at the lab is first rate but nothing's foolproof. There's only one way to make sure Phials doesn't spill his secrets — kill him."

Dave looked deep into Clint's eyes and saw the cowardice there, the weakness, the reluctance to be associated with violence. He realised his cousin didn't want to hear the truth, so he fed him a soothing lie instead. "Of course we wouldn't do that — he's too valuable to us, there's no telling what he might come up with next — but Phials doesn't trust us and there's nothing we can do to convince him."

"I could try," Clint said. "Tell him you don't mean him any harm. He might believe me."

Dave shook his head. "Don't even mention it. Just talking about it would drive him further into his shell."

"Then what do you want me to do?" Clint asked, sure Dave wasn't telling him all this just to pass the time.

Dave sniffed. "I think Phials cracked the formula a month or two ago — he's slowed down during that time, not as manic as he was when he started working on the drug — but I can't be certain. If I knew for definite, I could wring it out of him, send Big Sandy in, tighten the screws, get him to spill, make it sweet with him afterwards. But if I come down hard on him and he *hasn't* developed the drug, I risk isolating him forever. He might never trust me again."

"You want me to be a spy," Clint said quietly, finally clicking to his cousin's scheme. "Ask him about his work, try and trick the truth out of him."

"That's the long and the short of it," Dave agreed. "I doubt he'll say anything to you, but it might slip out when he's high, while you're chatting, if he thinks he has nothing to fear. If it does, and you report it to me, then — cousin — you'll be part of the biggest drugs deal in history."

"How much?" Clint croaked greedily. "How much for *me?*"

Dave shrugged. "How much do you need? A million? Two?" He smiled and lifted his glass. "It's yours for the asking once my buy-out of Spurs goes through." Clinked his glass against Clint's bottle. "*LeChayim.*"

"*LeChayim,*" Clint muttered weakly, returning the toast, staring ahead dazedly, *two million* ricocheting through his thoughts, head filling with dreams of Shula and America, loyalty to Phials not an issue — he'd sell out his own mother for that much.

november 2000

FIFTEEN

"Forgive me Father for I have sinned. It has been six days since my last confession and these are my sins."

Fr Sebastian listened impatiently while Mrs Brady reeled off a list of *sins*, including laughing at a rude joke, cursing twice, and falling asleep one night before she'd said her prayers. He asked if she was truly sorry. She was. He told her to say three Hail Mary's and two Our Father's, sent her away with God's blessing, bored, nervous, horny.

He hadn't seen or heard from Gawl in more than a fortnight. The priest didn't know where the Scot was based. Didn't dare ask around in case anyone connected him with the thug. He'd visited a few local pubs, hunting for Gawl, without any luck. Getting desperate — he'd come to rely on Gawl, needed his contacts, the safe brothels, the young girls. Fantasizing late at night. Masturbating over a stash of obscene magazines. Not enough. The priest's perverse hunger increasing with every celibate hour that passed, Clint Smith's drugs dulling his senses to the worst of the pain, but not entirely, drugs never enough to satisfy Fr Sebastian when the need was fierce inside him.

The door to the confessional opened. His hopes flared, as they did every time the door opened, but then a shadow slipped in, too small. Hope dying, misery setting in, until the confessee spoke and he placed the voice — Tulip Tyne. His breath caught as she said, "Forgive me Father for I have sinned." Tulip's sins as predictable as Mrs Brady's, but far darker and more intriguing for a man of Sebastian Parry's persuasions.

He tried driving the dark thoughts from his mind as Tulip unburdened herself. This was the one line he had never crossed. He'd forced himself upon choirgirls in the past but he'd never taken advantage of his position as God's Earthly confessor. But he'd rarely been this desperate before and never this isolated.

His heart was beating so hard, he didn't hear her when she finished confessing. Face pressed into his hands, willing his desires to pass, praying to God for strength. Tulip paused uncertainly, waiting for him to respond. Then, quietly, she said, "Fr Sebastian?"

He lowered his hands. His eyes opened. He sighed. "Sorry, my child." Pulling himself up straight, granting absolution, figuring, *I can always absolve her again, and if God hasn't forgiven me for my previous sins, one more can't hurt.*

When Tulip left to make her peace with God, Fr Sebastian slipped out of the confessional and looked for Kevin Tyne. Spotted him near the back of the church and started towards him. An elderly man shuffled to his feet and halted the priest. "Are you hearing confessions now, Father?"

"In a couple of minutes," Fr Sebastian smiled, helped the gentleman back into his seat, hurried down the aisle, trying not to appear too anxious.

Kevin was brooding about work, sick of London Underground. Pondering his options. Quit and look for work as a temp? Go on night courses, brush up on his computer skills, wait for something decent to come his way? Main problem — whatever sort of job he landed, he'd have to be close to Tulip. Job satisfaction a very distant second behind his need to be within walking distance of his sister.

Kevin was surprised when Fr Sebastian slid in beside him. He braced himself for a lecture. But the priest didn't say anything, just sat beside Kevin, looking like the world was about to end, breathing raggedly.

"Fr Sebastian? Are you OK?" Kevin concerned — the priest looked like he was on the verge of a heart attack.

Fr Sebastian glanced at him sideways, trembling. "This is a terrible world," he croaked. "We have so much to be ashamed of." He stared at his fingers, dancing feverishly on his knees, and willed them together — if he could join them in prayer, perhaps he could beg God for the strength to deny himself this illicit, inhuman pleasure. But his hands remained apart and instead he stuttered the words of damnation. "Huh-huh-how much... fuh-for your suh-suh-suh-sister?"

Kevin stared at the priest, bemused. He thought it was a barbed query, the precursor to a condemning sermon. "That's none of..." he began to retort. Stopped when he saw the priest's eyes, full of wicked yearning. Realised what he was being asked. Shocked, he couldn't respond.

"I'll pay whatever you ask," Fr Sebastian snarled.

"She's not a whore," Kevin said numbly. "I don't rent her out."

"I know." Fr Sebastian smiled weakly. "I understand. You must watch. I accept that. I'll play along. But please, how much?"

Kevin shook his head. "I can't. Tulip wouldn't, not with a priest."

"She does what you tell her."

"It would ruin her."

"No." Fr Sebastian firm. "*We* are the ruined ones. Tulip is pure. The likes of you and I can sully her but we can't ruin her."

"I..." Kevin gulped, flashing on a picture of Tulip and the priest. Something new. A fresh taboo. "Five hundred pounds."

"I don't have that much. But I can get it." Fr Sebastian ready to pay whatever it took.

"Let me know when you've got the money," Kevin said evenly.

"No!" Fr Sebastian grabbed Kevin's wrist, squeezed sharply. "I can't wait. It must be now, this afternoon. I need..."

Kevin saw the desperation in the priest's expression and grew strong on it. "How much can you pay up front?"

"Two, maybe two-fifty. I'll have to check."

"Get it. And another five hundred by the end of the week." Fr Sebastian nodded eagerly, too horny to haggle. Rose to fetch the money. Kevin stopped him. "You know where we live?"

Fr Sebastian paused, then chuckled self-deprecatingly. "No."

"Long Lane, in the Borough."

"I don't know it. Still new to the area. But I'm sure I can find it."

Kevin smiled snidely. "I'm sure too. Get the money. I'll have the address ready for you when you return."

Scribbling down the address while the priest hurried through the church to his home at the rear. Studying

Tulip as she knelt and prayed, wondering how she'd react, deciding not to tell her until they left the church, maybe not until Fr Sebastian turned up on their doorstep. She couldn't argue with him if she didn't know about it in advance, and she'd be so stunned when the priest stepped in and dropped his pants, she'd probably accede without a murmur. Even so, he'd make sure she was high when Fr Sebastian arrived. Clint Smith's finest. Take her as far as she'd ever been, make sure her moral barriers were at their lowest.

Guilt wormed through Kevin's mind — soiling his sister's relationship with her priest, perhaps robbing her of her faith — but guilt was nothing new and had never held him in check before. Besides, it would be for the best if he could destroy her faith. One less place for her to turn if Kevin's hold over her ever wavered, making her solely dependant on him, supplanting God and his priests as the only man in her world. Kevin her lover, her religion, her life, her all — as she was his.

SIXTEEN

Getting drunk. Fighting furiously. He took a bad beating in West Ham, almost kicked to death by a group of skinheads he'd insulted, recovering in his bed for three days, surviving on water and cider, wishing he was dead.

How fucking jinxed was he! Of all the women Larry Drake could have been making a move on, why did it have to be Dave Bushinsky's niece? Gawl not worried about being connected to the rape – the Bush thought Drake did it, ran him down and killed him, end of story – just disgusted that he'd lost his meal ticket. It was typical of his current run of luck. Everything he touched turned to shit. Maybe London wasn't right for him. Recalling his last stay, decades before, bumming around, petty jobs here and there, having to flee when he killed a woman, number three of eight, but one of only two he hadn't planned. She'd wound him up and he'd snapped. Not like most of his kills, where he staked out his prey and targeted someone he had no connection to. He'd had to run like a dog, scared, vulnerable, directionless. Now here he was, back in London and suffering again. Maybe this city just didn't like him. Might be better to get the hell out, try Cardiff or Dublin. Never did like the fucking English.

Slowly recovering from his beating. A wash, shave,

crawling down to the café for some food, throwing up in the toilet before he finished, making himself eat everything on the plate, getting sick again, buying bread, biscuits, jam and coffee in the 7-11 across the road, stumbling back to his flat, sleeping off the rest of the day, guzzling the food when he woke, keeping it down, feeling better, halfway human.

Another day indoors recovering, staring at the walls, eating, drinking, wounds healing. Examining his body. He was going soft. He'd never worked out – gyms were for fags – labouring on building-sites kept him trim. But it had been a long time since his last bout on the sites. He was fattening out, biceps not as taut as they'd once been. His brute force was all he had going for him. He couldn't afford to soften up. He'd have to return to the sites soon if he didn't catch a break, get back into shape, stay strong.

Gawl hit the King's Head and sipped beer slowly, feeling sorry for himself, considering the future. Didn't want to quit London. Deep down he knew the city wasn't the problem. He'd been sinking lower and lower, getting old, losing his hunger and nerve, looking for a cushy number to see him through his final years. He'd abandoned too many cities prematurely. Old and experienced enough to know he was running out of options, a change of venue not the answer, needing to take control of his destiny now, while he still could.

He rolled out of the King's Head before eleven and headed home, lying in bed in the dark, still thinking, determined not to sleep until an answer presented itself. Getting nowhere with the gangs. His best half-hope of making a big score – Larry Drake – had been butchered for a crime of Gawl's. That left Fr Sebastian and his coterie of miserable old widows. How many more could he target before they were linked to the Church of Sacred Martyrs? Not many. And what good were they to him anyway? Loose change. Beer money.

Thinking of Fr Sebastian, his thoughts turned to the dealer he'd spotted in the church, Larry Drake's connection, Clint Smith. Gawl's eyes narrowed in the dark. Smith had looked like a weak man, most of his clients of the nondescript variety, some of them lowlife dole queue scum. But Drake had come to him. Other actors might too. Maybe Smith was worth Gawl's time. Stake him out, see who else visited him, latch on to another minor celeb, take care not to rape their girlfriend this time and queer the deal for himself.

A long shot – Smith didn't look like the sort who had TV stars lining up around the block – but it was all Gawl had. The dealer was a regular in the church, simple to stake out. Maybe trail him around, find out where else he dealt, get close to him as he had to Drake, find a way to use him. If that failed...

Fuck it. He'd spent too long brooding on his failures. Time to think positively. Smith the ticket. He'd already led Gawl to one potential goldmine. He could – *would* – lead him to another.

Gawl finished off the bottle of cider by his bedside, settled back and waited for sleep to claim him, inviting dreams of Clint Smith, major drug deals, a rose-tinted old age — instead dreaming of the past, men he'd broken, women he'd raped and murdered. He smiled in his sleep. *Good times*.

SEVENTEEN

Big Sandy and Fast Eddie on the beach at Margate, a strange-looking couple, trying to blow off hangovers. Grey skies, drizzle, beach deserted except for the two men reclining in deckchairs, staring moodily out over the churning sea, hair and faces slick with rain, both silent.

They'd left London shortly after killing Drake and the woman. Lots of media interest, the police having to put on a good show, searching hard for the bodies, looking for scapegoats. The Bush slipped the pair some cash and told them they wouldn't have to go into exile for long, just a few weeks, as long as nobody came forward to connect them with the blood in the apartment and the disappearances.

He knew it was madness, but Big Sandy called Sapphire on his first morning in Margate and told her to come to him. Shaking bad. He hadn't been able to sleep. The murder of Drake didn't bother him – that bastard had it coming and Big Sandy just wished that he could bring him back to life and kill him again – but the woman had done nothing wrong except offer harbour to a friend. Her face haunted him. What he had done to her haunted him. He needed release.

Sapphire had been careful. Three trains instead of a car, the last a tiny local service, virtually nobody on board, as sure as she could be that she hadn't been followed. Big Sandy and Fast Eddie were sharing a room – safer that way if anyone came after them – but Fast Eddie made himself scarce and booked a single room that night. If he disapproved of Big Sandy's visitor, he kept his opinion to himself. Killing was hard, even for men accustomed to it. Sometimes you needed to reach out for help and take a risk. Fast Eddie respected Big Sandy enough to allow him that gamble. If it went wrong, he'd share the blame and consequences with his old friend.

Big Sandy had broken down almost as soon as he was alone with Sapphire, not needing to get drunk this time, the guilt and shame having built in him all the way down from London. She held him tight, stroked him calmingly, soothed him as best she could, granted absolution. She'd already heard about Larry Drake, but hadn't linked his disappearance with Big Sandy. Thrilled to have the inside scoop on the notorious story. Appalled because she feared that this time Big Sandy had gone too far. Drake was a small time celeb, but a public figure nonetheless, and she wasn't sure Big Sandy's crew could make this one go away. The press would keep investigating. People would talk. The police wouldn't let it drop. Scared of being linked to it, of being seen as a liability, of being quietly eliminated by another of the Bush's men if he found out that she'd been here.

Sapphire gloomy the next day, getting ready to leave. Big Sandy read her mood and tried to dispel her fears. "Fast Eddie won't say anything about you being here. He knows you can be trusted. It won't be the first time we've kept secrets from Dave. When you're in our position, you look out for one another."

"Thanks," Sapphire smiled.

Big Sandy ran a finger down her cheek and sighed. "Still, I shouldn't have summoned you."

Sapphire shook her head. "You needed me."

"Yeah. But sometimes it's wiser not to act on your needs." He scowled. "I don't think anyone will try to trace me through you. The cops probably won't get that far, and I'm pretty sure Drake didn't have any contacts who cared enough about him to come in search of revenge. But if I'm wrong... if men like me and Fast Eddie track you down and ask if you know where I am... tell them."

Sapphire stared at him. "I wouldn't do that."

"You would," he said sternly. "You *will*. If they get that far, they'll push all the way. You won't be doing me any favours if you try to protect me. You'll just end up dead like..." He didn't need to finish the sentence.

"Sandy," she whispered, eyes filling with tears.

"No need for that," he said gruffly. "Like I said, I doubt it will happen. But if it does, give me up, tell them everything you know, save yourself." He didn't add, *if you can*, not wanting to scare her any more than he already had.

Margate dead in October and November. Big Sandy lonely after Sapphire had gone. Not much to talk about with Fast Eddie, neither a man of many words. Fast Eddie went off with women most nights and got drunk, but Big Sandy kept a low profile — inclined to talk too much when he was with a woman or half-cut. That was fine if the woman was Sapphire or one of her girls, dangerous if it was some stranger.

Unable to bear the boredom, he'd gone drinking last night. Fast Eddie stayed with him to keep an eye on him. An enjoyable night, the pair remembering the past and discussing old friends and acquaintances, but both men hungover this morning. Fast Eddie had suggested a beach cure, the cold wind blowing in off the sea the perfect pick-me-up. It had worked, though as Big Sandy staggered back to their hotel, shivering, he wondered if the cure might not be worse than the curse.

That night, having finally warmed up, he went to

another pub with Fast Eddie, this time just for a bite to eat and one or two pints. While he was nursing his second and final drink, his mobile rang. Thought it would be the Bush summoning them home or telling them they had to flee, but it was Julius Scott. "Hi Julius," he said, shuffling away from Fast Eddie so he could talk privately.

"Hello Sandy. Is this a good time?"

"Sure. Got some hot tips for me?"

"A couple of crackers."

Julius Scott was Big Sandy's investments manager. Eight years earlier his ten-year-old daughter had been kidnapped and held for ransom. Julius called the police. They advised him to pay. The kidnappers took the cash then sent him one of his daughter's fingers and demanded more money. Julius turned to Dave Bushinsky. The Bush set Big Sandy on the case. It took him fourteen hours to track down the kidnappers. Three Brixton boys, small-time amateurs. Big Sandy knocked out the trio and carried the girl downstairs to her father. Started back up to finish the job. Julius said, "I want to watch." Big Sandy said, "No you don't." Julius said, "I need to be sure." Big Sandy said, "I'll fetch you when I'm done." Upstairs he tore the kidnappers to pieces, then brought Julius up. Julius vomited, wept, thanked Big Sandy for sparing him the sight of the actual killing. Big

Sandy sent him away, thinking that was the end of their relationship.

Three weeks later, Julius Scott on the phone, saying he had some market tips for Big Sandy if he had cash to invest. Big Sandy not that bothered – he'd never been interested in money – but then he thought about Megan and Amelie. He sent most of his earnings their way, but never felt as if he was sending enough. If he could make a little more, maybe set up a trust fund for the girl...

Big Sandy discussed it with the Bush. Dave thought it was a good idea. He had been handling Big Sandy's affairs but was happy to turn the purse strings over to Julius, figuring he could keep an eye on things and make some investments of his own if Julius proved himself a sound guide. Big Sandy had been an active, albeit slightly bewildered investor since then. As well as being able to bump up his payments to Megan, according to Julius he was now worth more than three hundred thousand pounds. That would take Amelie far in life, and it didn't matter to Big Sandy that she would probably never be told where the windfall had come from.

"We took some losses recently," Julius said, "but I'm sure we can recoup them. I want to transfer..."

He droned on, Big Sandy only half listening. At the end, when Julius asked if he had Big Sandy's approval to sell off stock, transfer funds and buy new shares, Big Sandy said, as he always did, "Sounds good to me." He'd tried convincing Julius to do as he pleased – he didn't have to ask Big Sandy's permission every time a deal presented itself – but Julius believed in keeping him fully informed.

When Big Sandy hung up, Fast Eddie asked who'd called. "My stockbroker."

"Of course it was," Fast Eddie snorted. "It's OK if you don't want to tell me. No need to lie about it."

Big Sandy smiled, took a sip of his beer, thought about Sapphire and wished he could go home. Then thought about Megan and Amelie, smile fading, knowing he could never return to the place that in an ideal world he *would* have called home.

EIGHTEEN

Phials lined up his shot, sunk the black, grinned at Clint, who sighed and handed over a twenty. Phials wouldn't play pool unless there was money riding on it. The size of the stake didn't matter – he'd play for a pound if that was all Clint had on him – as long as money was involved. Said pool was like poker, meaningless if played purely for fun. "Want to go again?"

"Maybe later." Clint drifted round the table, troubled. Phials watched him out of the corner of his eye. Clint had been moody the last few times he'd come, working up to something. Phials was anxious to get the talks underway but knew he couldn't rush it, Clint liable to flee if he got scared.

"Go to see Shula yet?" Phials asked.

"No."

"You should. She'd appreciate it."

"Maybe tomorrow." Clint shifty. He'd wanted to go every day but hadn't been able to find the nerve.

"Want to watch a movie?" Phials tried.

"No, I'm not in..." Clint stopped, cleared his throat then came out with it in a rush. "I asked Duh-Dave about... yuh-you know."

Phials forced a puzzled expression, then snapped his fingers. "Oh, my work. What did he say? Is it OK for me to fill you in on all the grisly details?"

"Not really." Clint licked his lips, trying to play it artfully, Phials almost feeling pity for the clumsy fool. "He told me you were wuh-working on something buh-big, but he wouldn't go into specifics."

"Did he say how big?" Phials asked softly.

"Said it would revoluh-luh-lutionise the industry."

"That's for sure." Phials cocked an eyebrow at Clint, playing the question for laughs. "He say anything about me taking my sweet goddamn time?"

"Yeah," Clint chuckled. "But he said it's an experimental drug, a bruh-bruh- breakthrough. Said you can't ruh-rush genius."

"Very understanding of him," Phials said softly. "But not the impression he's given me." Phials started racking up balls. "He keeps pressing me for results. First time he's ever done that. Like he can't wait, needs the shit *now*."

"Maybe he th-th-thinks you're holding buh-buh-back on him," Clint said, blushing, heart pounding.

Phials paused, surprised by how bluntly Clint had come out with that. "Holding back? Why should I?"

"I dunno," Clint said quietly. "Maybe buh-because you're afruh-afruh-afraid of him?"

Phials finished racking up the balls, broke, played the next shot, then another, choosing his words carefully, pleased that Clint had come so directly to the point. "Did Dave say he'd cut you a deal?"

"Duh-duh-duh-*deal*?" Clint laughed shrilly. "Wh-wh-what kind of —"

"Don't bullshit me," Phials interrupted. "I like you because you speak the truth. If you start lying, I'll have to ask you to leave." Clint gulped and glanced around the room uneasily, afraid he'd say the wrong thing and that cousin Dave would hear about it. Phials saw what was worrying him and calmed Clint with a smile. "Nobody can hear us. Surveillance has always been a sideline of mine. I sweep my quarters every week."

"I didn't know that."

"I'm a man of many talents. You're free to speak. So speak."

Clint gulped again then spat it out. "Dave thinks you know how to make the drug. He asked me to find out."

"Did you get fifteen pieces of silver up front or do you collect all thirty upon delivery?"

"It's not like that," Clint said hastily. "Dave needs the money. He... I can't say tuh-too much about it, but he has a big duh-duh-deal going down. If you know, you should tell him. This is the key time. You can ask for whatever you want and he'll have to guh-give it to you."

"What did *you* ask for, Clint?" Playing pool, focused

on the balls.

Clint wondered how much he should reveal. Thought about lying but didn't think he could fool Phials. "He promised me a million, maybe tuh-tuh-tuh-two."

Phials whistled. "A considerable amount by anyone's standards."

"Yeah," Clint beamed.

Phials laid down his cue, turned to face Clint. "It's chickenfeed. This product is like no other. I'm flying with the gods on this one. If I pull it off, it will change the world. And the secret will hold. I told Dave I didn't think anyone would crack the formula for a couple of years, but that was a conservative estimate. The profit will run into *billions*. If you could deliver that formula – not just to Dave, but to any established businessman – you could cut yourself in for a percentage. Instead you're willing to settle for a couple of million which your cousin would probably gyp you out of anyway. My guess, you'd be lucky to score a hundred thousand — more likely to wind up like me, with a bullet between the eyes."

"Nuh-nuh-nuh-no," Clint gasped. "Dave wuh-won't kuh-kill you. He nuh-nuh-nuh-needs you too muh-muh-muh-much."

"All he needs is the formula," Phials disagreed. "Of course the formula doesn't exist yet, because I haven't finished working on it. But if it did... and if you were to betray me to your cousin for the possibility – the *possibility* – of a measly two million... you'd be an asshole, Clint, an even bigger one than your cousin thought you were when he sent you here to pump me for info."

Phials leant over the table, potted the black, then scattered the rest of the balls with his cue. "I want you to go now."

"OK," Clint sighed, slouching towards the door.

"Clint," Phials called him back. "I'm not banishing you. We're still friends. Just don't ask me about this again. Let your cousin hire somebody else to do his dirty work."

"OK," Clint said quietly and exited quickly.

Phials stared at the pool table in silence, wondering if he'd played the hand the right way, if Clint would heed his warning and not discuss the mystery drug again, or if he'd get to thinking about the billions on offer, pick up on Phials' not-so-subtle messages – *your cousin will cheat you... you can sell the formula to one of his competitors* – and come back looking to play. He offered up a quick prayer. *Please, gods, let the boy be greedy. Let him be brave. Give him the strength to turn on his cousin. Help the poor fool set me free.*

*

Clint hurried down the stairs, some thug he didn't know trotting by his side to let him out, Fast Eddie still in hiding after the murder of Larry Drake. Flushed and confused, he stumbled out into the night, feeling like a failure, cursing himself, an idiot to think he could squeeze the truth out of Phials, he should stick to what he knew — dealing. Forget Shula, America, the millions, the... billions...

Walking up Walworth Road, slowing, thinking about what Phials had said. No drug could be worth *billions*. The chemist had to be exaggerating. Then again, if cousin Dave was willing to pay Clint a couple of million just to find out if Phials had cracked the formula, there must be a huge amount at stake.

If cousin Dave was willing.

Clint gave serious thought to that as he wound his way through the streets to the Borough. Two million a lot of cash, even to someone like Dave Bushinsky, even on a deal this big. Why give Clint two when he could give him one? Why one when Clint would settle gladly for half of that? Why half a million when...

Coming down to chump change, a bone for a dumb, faithful dog. Recalling what Phials had said about established businessmen and percentages. His meaning clear — cut a deal but cut Dave out. Did Clint have the balls to doublecross his cousin? Even if he did, who could he take this to? He knew nobody apart from Dave who operated at that level. Best to forget about it. Besides, he hadn't been able to get Phials to talk. The chemist was cagy. There was nothing Clint could do to loosen Phials' tongue. If he was a woman, maybe he could fuck the doc and trick him into some giveaway pillow talk.

Clint smiled at the absurd thought. Stopped dead when he realised it wasn't so absurd. He stood stiff as a corpse on Borough High Street, mind flying with the germ of an idea, seeing a way to maybe get Phials to talk, spill his guts, tell Clint anything he wanted to know. Risky, could backfire badly, but if it worked…

He relaxed and headed home. Fished out his mobile, checked for Kevin Tyne's number, upping the ante, scared but thrilled, getting in the ring with the big boys.

NINETEEN

Tulip had been giving Kevin the ice treatment since Fr Sebastian made his first visit (he'd been back twice already). Wouldn't talk to him, wouldn't cook for him, stayed in her bedroom ignoring him, watched TV silently when he dragged her out. He'd tried discussing it with her — he lied and said that Parry had threatened to blackmail them — but she wouldn't engage, trembling if he touched her, rosary beads gripped tight, lips moving wordlessly as she prayed. Kevin thought (hoped) she might stop going to church, but she hadn't abandoned the Sacred Martyrs, though she was avoiding the confessional, offering up her own penance, unable or unwilling to deal with Fr Sebastian as a man of God any more.

The easy solution — cancel the priest's visits. The first time had been exciting, the shock value adding to the customary buzz that Kevin experienced when watching his sister have sex. But Parry was all too human and pitiful when naked, weeping as he made love. Kevin would be glad to see the back of him.

The problem — Tulip might think he was caving in, banning Parry to please her. Might get it into her head that if the silent treatment worked once, it could work again. A slippery slope.

Kevin found Tulip in her room reading a Maeve

Binchy novel. He rapped on the door. Smiled the smile he'd been smiling incessantly of late, acting as if all was normal between them. "Clint's coming."

Tulip didn't look up. "Is he bringing drugs or someone new for me to fuck?"

Kevin's smile slipped. He sat at the foot of the bed and reached out to massage Tulip's insteps the way she liked. She pulled her feet clear. Kevin laid his hands in his lap. "We can't go on like this." She glanced at him over the top of her book. "I didn't invite Fr Sebastian here."

"But you let him in."

"He said he'd expose us!" Kevin getting indignant. He'd repeated the lie so many times, he was almost beginning to believe it. "He knows all about us. Whose fault is that? Not mine."

"He wouldn't reveal what I told him in the confessional," Tulip said.

"Grow up," Kevin snorted. "You think he'll fuck you but he won't rat on you? Parry's a junkie and a paedophile. He'd do anything to get his own way."

"Not that," Tulip disagreed softly. "Sex is a disease with him, he can't resist it. But he respects the sanctity of the church, the word of God."

"So you want me to tell him to get lost?" Kevin challenged her. "You want to chance it? You know I'm finished if I'm arrested. Even if I could take being separated from you – which I couldn't – jail would destroy me. If Parry blows the whistle on us, I'll –"

"– kill yourself," Tulip finished, almost sneering.

Kevin went rigid. His threats of suicide were the only real hold he had over her. If she lost interest in his life, he couldn't keep her. He had to do something. Nip her insurrection in the bud before everything was ruined. "I could... ask Clint... for help."

"What could Clint do about it?" Tulip frowned.

"Get somebody to have a word in Fr Sebastian's ear. Big Sandy maybe. Warn him what will happen if he tells anyone about us."

"I don't want to hurt him," Tulip said quickly and Kevin saw his way out, his sister's concern for others her downfall.

"I don't either." Kevin sighed mock morosely. "But it's the only way. We can threaten him but I don't think that will work. Maybe Big Sandy could, you know, silence him."

Tulip's eyes widened. "No!"

"But if it's the only –"

"No." She closed her book. "No, Kevin." Softer this time.

"I can't think of any other way to stop him."

"We'll plead," Tulip said. "I'll pray with him and ask him to beg God for strength."

"You think that will work?" Kevin sceptical.

"Prayer can move mountains," Tulip smiled. "Maybe not right away, but if we keep trying, keep praying…"

"And in the meantime?" Kevin pressed. "The silent treatment's driving me crazy." Pouting, making her feel as though she was in the wrong.

"I'm sorry," Tulip said. "I won't do it again." She offered him her foot. He made a show of turning his head away and ignoring it, then smiled, took the foot and began to massage her instep, Tulip smiling crookedly, Kevin peaceful inside, deciding to limit the priest's visits then cut him out completely, their world restored to normal, all wrongs set right.

Watching soaps with Clint, Tulip guzzling crisps and Pepsi Max, Clint making small talk, edgy, Kevin wondering what the dealer was leading up to. They'd had little to do with Clint outside of the appointments that he arranged. Kevin didn't trust the thin man with the devious eyes, but at least Clint had shown no interest in Tulip, one of the few men Kevin felt it was safe for her to be around.

"Any breaks pluh-planned for the wuh-wuh-wuh-winter?" Clint asked during an advert for ski holidays.

"I want to go to Italy," Tulip responded. "Kevin won't

take me."

"I never said that," Kevin objected.

"You did," she smirked. "You said there were too many horny Italians there."

Kevin smiled awkwardly. "I didn't know you were serious. I can arrange a holiday if you really want to go."

Tulip shrugged and faced the TV again.

Clint cleared his throat, started to say something, stopped. Kevin getting annoyed — he hated all this beating around the bush. Thought of asking Clint why he was here, but Clint was the sort who ran if confronted. Instead he sat back, watched soaps, waited.

The next advert. Clint cleared his throat again. Got it out this time. "Phials hasn't cuh-cuh-cuh-contacted you any tuh-time lately, huh-has he?"

Kevin shook his head. "He doesn't have our number. He always books through you. That's the arrangement."

"Good." Clint chewed his lower lip.

"Are you accusing us of operating behind your back?" Kevin snapped.

"No. That never crossed my mind. I... I need to ask a fuh-fuh-fuh-favour."

"Oh?" Kevin on guard instantly.

"Fast Eh-Eddie's away for a while. Security at the luh-luh-lab isn't as tuh-tight without him. I want you to tuh-

tuh-tuh-take these with you next time you guh- guh-go." Clint produced three small pouches. Kevin stared at them suspiciously.

"What's in them?" Kevin asked.

"Some cuh-coke. A few E's. Two baggies for him, one for yuh-you."

"We can pay for our goods," Kevin growled. "We don't need to trade favours for them. And Phials isn't allowed drugs."

"I know." Clint smiled jaggedly. "It's no big deal if you say nuh-no. I just feel suh-sorry for the poor buh-buh-buh-bastard. He luh-loves to get high. Can't with Fuh-Fuh-Fast Eddie watching over him all the time. Though I'd guh-give him a suh-suh-surprise while Fast Eddie was away. That's all."

"And if the drugs were found on us?" Kevin snorted.

"Suh-suh-suh-say it's for yuh-yourselves. The guh-guh-guys on the door won't know any duh-duh-duh-different."

"I don't want to do it," Tulip said. "Drugs are bad. People die taking drugs."

Clint gawped. "But yuh-yuh-yuh-*you*..."

"I'm an addict," Tulip said sadly. "I don't want to become a supplier too. I can live with hurting myself but I won't harm others."

"I'm sure Clint's products are safe," Kevin murmured, staring at the pouches, trying to figure this out. Clint wasn't the sort to spring a surprise for the sake of it. There had to be more than he was telling them. Kevin curious. "We'd just have to smuggle in the drugs?"

"Kevin!" Tulip squealed.

He silenced her with a wave of a hand.

"Nuh-nuh-not quite." Clint grinned nervously. "I wuh-want to stuh-stuh-stuh-stay. While yuh-yuh-you and Ph-Ph-Ph-Phials..."

Kevin's features hardened and he got ready to kick Clint out.

"No," Clint yelped, reading Kevin's expression. "It's not th-th-th-that. I'm not interested in suh-sex. I need to ask Phials something when he's ruh-ruh-relaxed. Cuh-catch him with his guard down."

Kevin softened. "I see. You want us to loosen him up for you."

"Yeah." Clint smiled shakily.

"What makes you think we'd do that?" Kevin asked coolly. "We like Tony."

"Fuh-fuh-five hundred pounds," Clint said softly. "Just to sneak in the drugs and say yuh-yuh-yes when Phials asks if I can stuh-stuh-stuh-stay."

"And if he doesn't ask you to stay?"

Clint grinned. "Leave that to muh-me. Five hundred pounds — nuh-nice holiday money. And a baggie for yourselves tuh-too."

"It's wrong," Tulip said.

"Everything we do is wrong," Kevin retorted, mulling it over, reluctant to turn down free cash and drugs. "What if Phials OD's?"

"He wuh-won't. It's guh-guh-guh-good shit."

"A thousand," Kevin said.

Clint smiled. "Five huh-hundred. Not worth any muh-more than that."

"A thousand," Kevin reiterated. "Five hundred each. We stand to lose a lot more if the drugs are discovered on us and we're banned from seeing him again."

Clint mulled it over. Nodded. "OK. Fuh-five up front, the ruh-ruh-rest after."

Kevin rubbed his fingers together. Clint dug out an envelope and passed it across with the baggies. Kevin counted and beamed. "A pleasure doing business with you." The men shook hands. Tulip looked on sourly, started to object again, then focused on the baggies and licked her lips. She wan't due a hit, but seeing the baggies, knowing what was inside, the craving grew within her and she couldn't resist. She reached out with trembling fingers, took a pouch from Kevin, and the deal was truly sealed.

TWENTY

Gawl observing Clint in church as he struck his measly deals. Hopes sinking — all of Clint's customers were low-lifes, handing over tattered notes, shaking until they got their hands on the merchandise, hurrying out to shoot up, desperate, addicted, worthless. No TV stars, no pop stars, nobody who even looked like they held down a steady job. Starting to lose interest in the dealer, but nothing better to do with his time, so he endured.

He renewed contact with Fr Sebastian. The priest loathe to let Gawl back into his life. Didn't have the money he owed, said he'd spent it on girls when Gawl left him in the lurch. Gawl laughed. Told Fr Sebastian to forget the money. Asked if he wanted Gawl to line him up with new girls. The priest said he'd made his own arrangements in Gawl's absence and could get along nicely without him. Gawl didn't like that but he didn't object, told Fr Sebastian he'd be here when the priest needed him. Left troubled, wondering who'd supplanted him as the priest's pussy supplier. Clint Smith? If so, the dealer's days were numbered. Gawl needed Fr Sebastian. Not prepared to sit back and let Clint steal his kiddie-fucking cash cow.

Keeping a watch on Fr Sebastian in the evenings. Hanging around outside the church, following the priest whenever he left, skulking around the neighbourhood after him. Harmless house calls – old ladies, potential targets for Gawl if nothing better presented itself – until one afternoon he scurried out, collar hidden, shaking nervously, hunger in his eyes and stride. Gawl had seen the priest like this before. Grinned and tracked him, getting close, knowing Fr Sebastian wouldn't notice a bomb going off the way he was. Followed him to a flat in Long Lane. A plump, pretty, sad girl opened the door and admitted the priest. Gawl recognised her. He'd seen her in church several times, always with a slightly older man.

So that's where Fr Sebastian had found his pussy. Gawl chuckled to himself on the landing. The sly bastard had preyed on one of his flock. Probably invited himself round on an innocent pretext, then slipped it to her. No problem breaking this up — just threaten to tell the older guy (probably her brother, too young to be her father) what the priest was up to.

Gawl waited. The priest normally finished in a quarter of an hour. He laughed softly when he saw the door opening twelve minutes later, Fr Sebastian practically floating through, much lighter now he'd shot his load. The laughter stopped when a man closed the door after the priest and Gawl glimpsed the girl's companion, the guy who was probably her brother.

What the fuck?

Wondering if he'd read the situation wrong, if this had been a normal house call. But there was no mistaking Fr Sebastian's sexual relief. Only answer — the brother must be in on it. Maybe not a relative at all. A pimp? Didn't matter. Just made Gawl's job a bit harder.

Fr Sebastian pressed a button for the lift. Gawl hurried down the stairs. Got to the ground floor first. Grabbed the priest as he stepped out. Hurled him against the wall. Fr Sebastian thought he was being mugged. "Take my wallet. Take my watch. Please don't hurt me."

"Quiet," Gawl hissed.

Fr Sebastian's eyes widened. "*Gawl?*"

"Now I know where ye get yer pussy, Father." Giggling as Fr Sebastian's face whitened. "A nice wee girl. Is she tight enough for ye?"

"She's... she's not... she's just..."

"Shut up," Gawl snapped. Leant in close, breathing in the priest's face. "If ye come back here again, I'll kill her. From now on ye fuck where I tell ye t' fuck. I'll arrange all the girls ye want, young and eager, just like before, right? Just gi'e me the nod when ye're horny and I'll fix ye up."

"I... I don't..."

"D' ye want me t' kill her?" Gawl growled. "D' ye want me t' cut her tits off and slice her face open and –"

"No!" Fr Sebastian cried.

"Then don't go back." Gawl released the priest, brushed him down, kissed his forehead and winked. "Normal service has been resumed."

TWENTY-ONE

Another dull, lonely night in Margate. Fast Eddie struck lucky with a young, good-looking but obese Spanish woman on a tour of the UK, vanished with her early, leaving Big Sandy to sit alone and brood. He missed London, a city boy, lost out here in no man's land. Read the papers every day, thumbed through a couple of novels, but no real interest in books. He'd spent the last few nights reading random passages from a Gideon's bible. Sitting in his tiny room, studying God's words, thinking about the life he'd led, the sins he'd committed, the blood on his hands, the impossibility of redemption, spirits sinking lower than ever.

He wanted to phone the Bush to ask when he could return. Didn't. The Bush had said he'd get in touch when it was safe. Big Sandy experienced enough to know that you didn't pester Dave Bushinsky.

He went for a long walk but was still back at the boarding house before eleven. He hoped Fast Eddie would have finished with his Spaniard and returned, so he'd have someone to talk with. But Fast Eddie was still on the job. Big Sandy figured he'd probably stay at her place. He picked up the bible then laid it down again. Not tonight, already depressed, the bible would just make matters worse.

He showered, water tepid, never hot here. Stayed immersed in the spray a long time, sandy hair plastered to his skull, eyes shut, thrum of the water drowning out all other sounds, thinking about Larry Drake and the woman. How the hound had stripped Drake's flesh from his bones, the terror in the woman's face when he'd opened the bathroom door and she realised she was damned.

Big Sandy had led a clean life on many counts. He'd never knowingly slept with another man's woman, avoided drugs, was respectful to the elderly, provided for his family. Wouldn't matter much when stacked against his guilty count – murder, violence, burglary, extortion – but Big Sandy was proud of his few virtues. Men in his line were not obliged to respect any of God's laws, so it pleased Big Sandy that he hadn't given in to the legions of temptations that he was faced with every day. Of course pride was another sin...

With a sigh he stepped out of the shower, dried himself, went to bed early. Lay still, willing sleep to claim him, but it was a couple of hours before he drifted off. A troubled sleep when it came, dreaming about his mother and finding her butchered. Davey Connors was there in the dream, standing over her corpse, grinning, a knife in one hand. He lunged and Big Sandy woke sweating.

Heart beating, he stared at the ceiling. Looked over. Fast Eddie hadn't come back. He checked the bedside clock. 3:57. He groaned, remembering the dream, knowing he wouldn't sleep again tonight, shivering, wishing he had Sapphire to hold and comfort him.

"I can't take this," he whispered. He needed something to take his mind off murder and bloodshed, to stop him thinking about the corpses in his life, the stains on his hands and soul. Work normally kept the dark thoughts at bay, but now that he was stranded here, he had to find some other distraction. But what? Margate a place with few options. What if he got out of here for a while, took to the road, nothing to do with work, but...

Big Sandy smiled in the darkness and mouthed the word, "Amelie." And though he still couldn't sleep after that, the smile stayed with him as he stretched out, put the grim dream behind him and started making plans.

TWENTY-TWO

Friday evening, hanging out with Phials, watching *Carlito's Way*, one of Clint's favourites. Phials talked over the movie, as he often did — the makers got this right, that wrong, this actor would never pass for a goodfella, that actor looked mob born and bred. Sometimes the narration irritated Clint but more often than not he welcomed it, valuable tips for when he went Stateside.

"*A favour will kill you faster than a bullet,*" Phials chuckled as the credits rolled. "True words, my friend. But a world without favours would be hell indeed." Licked his lips and winked at Clint. "Speaking of which..."

Clint calm. He'd been waiting for this, several visits now without Phials asking for Tulip, afraid the doc had gone cool on her. He tried to act the same as normal. "You wuh-want me to see if the Tuh-Tynes are free?"

"Would you?" Phials smiling, running a hand over his jaw, checking whether or not he needed to shave.

Clint phoned Kevin. A short conversation, Clint speaking out of earshot of Phials, yes they were free, yes they'd bring the drugs, no they wouldn't mention Clint if they were rumbled by the guards. He faced Phials, grinning nervously, willing everything to go right. "I'll hit the ruh-road when they cuh-cuh-cuh-come."

Phials shrugged, studying himself in the reflection of

the TV, his robe creased and stained, picking at it, wondering if it was worth changing into another.

"Mind if I ask you a quh-quh-quh-question?" Clint trying hard not to stutter. Phials knew he only stuttered when he was nervous — might wonder what he had to be nervous about.

"Ask away," Phials said, too concerned with his appearance to note Clint's nervousness.

"With the Tuh-Tynes... Kevin wuh-wuh-watching... what's the attraction?"

Phials chuckled. "Voyeurism's a kick. I used to enjoy watching others have sex at orgies, but it's only since I started with Tulip and Kevin that I realised what a buzz you can get from being watched." Looked around. "Ever tried it?"

"No." Clint laughed sheepishly. "A bit exotic fuh-for my tastes."

"You don't talk much about your sex life," Phials noted.

"Not much to tuh-talk about," Clint answered softly. He forced a bright smile. "I'm pretty nuh-normal in the sex department. A puh-puh-puh-pilgrim."

"Heh. I thought you were about to say a puh-puh-puh-penguin." Phials snorted.

Clint chuckled, though he reddened too. He didn't like it when people mocked his stutter. He pressed ahead as casually as possible. "I've been th-th-th-thinking that I might try suh-suh-something like what you have going with the Tynes."

"With Shula?" Phials asked.

"Of course not," Clint growled. "I'd never drag her into something like that. Shula's a luh-lady. I meant with suh-someone else, muh-muh-maybe a couple like Kevin and Tuh-Tulip."

"You should," Phials beamed. "Try everything once, man. Hell, I experimented with every kind of fetish you can think of, and probably a few you can't. It's easier when you're stoned – life's a lot simpler when you're high – but even straight it's worth messing about a bit."

"I dunno," Clint muttered. "I think I'd huh-have to be huh-high to perform under th-th-th-those sort of cuh-conditions."

"Well, you're Mr Connections. If *you* can't get high when you want, who can?"

"I suh-suppose." Clint pulled a bashful expression, wanting Phials to make the offer without Clint having to ask, more natural that way. Chanting inside his head, *Ask me. Ask me. Ask me.*

Phials stared at Clint, sensing a new need in him, taking a while to click to what it was. Then, seeing the young man's blush, he thought he knew. "Wanna stay and join in, Clint?"

Clint licked his lips, acting uncertain, and mumbled, "I cuh-cuh-couldn't."

"Of course you could," Phials laughed. "The more the merrier."

"But wh-where would I fuh-fuh-fit in?"

"I'm sure we could find a space for you," Phials smirked. "You can observe with Kevin if you want or take a more hands-on approach. Your call."

"Kuh-kuh-kuh-Kevin wouldn't luh-like it," Clint said dubiously.

"Actually I think he'd get off on it," Phials mused, dark brown eyes distant. "It's what he's been leading up to, only I don't think he's realised yet — to be watched while he watches. It's the natural next step. He might object, but secretly he wants it. He'll accept you if we push him."

"Muh-muh-maybe another nuh-night," Clint said, not having to fake the hesitancy, having second thoughts, half-wishing Phials would bar him, looking for a way out even while he was desperately plotting a way in.

"If not tonight, then when?" Phials smiled warmly but unevenly, nerves of his own to contend with. This would bring them closer together, make it easier for Phials to manipulate Clint. "You have to seize the moment, live life to the fullest. We could all be dead tomorrow."

"I guh-guh-guh-guess." Clint took a deep breath, half real, half fake. "But I cuh-cuh-can't do this struh-struh-struh-straight. I've nuh-nothing on me, but I'm suh-sure Kevin and Tulip could ruh-rustle up something." Pulled out his mobile. Paused. "Yuh-yuh-you want anything?"

Phials' mouth went dry. "I thought you needed to OK anything like that with Eddie or Dave."

"I do. Buh-but Eddie isn't here and the nuh-nuh-nuh-new guys aren't as th-th-th-thorough."

"You think Kevin and Tulip could smuggle something in?" Hope blinding Phials to the obviousness of the set-up, hunger winning out over his intellect.

"Wuh-wuh-worth a truh-try. Of course they muh-mightn't have anything on them, or they mightn't want to sh-sh-share, or they muh-might be stuh-stopped coming in, but if we duh-don't ask…"

He phoned a dummy number, moved to the far side of the bedroom, conducted a muffled one-way conversation, Phials rigid on the bed, trying to remember his last real high, excitement flooding his system.

Clint turned off his mobile, pocketed it, faced Phials glumly – Phials' stomach dropped – then grinned. "They have coke and E's. They'll do their best to smuggle them in." Stutter disappearing, eyes bright, locked on to his course, no turning back, in command now. Phials panted like a happy puppy, imagining the buzz, already feeling it. Clint watched smugly, thinking, *Who's the dumb, exploitable asshole now?*

TWENTY-THREE

Tulip was unhappy about the drugs, but otherwise she was more cooperative than she'd been in a long time. By no stretch of the imagination upbeat – she never looked forward to their appointments – but resigned. After several visits, Fr Sebastian had stopped coming. Kevin not sure what had happened – the priest avoided him in church, ashamed, afraid – but quick to make the most of the unexpected windfall. He told Tulip he'd had words with Fr Sebastian, told him never to return. Tulip relieved, hugging Kevin, kissing him the way sisters all over the world innocently kissed their brothers, insisting they go for a celebratory meal, thanking him over and over, Kevin acting nonchalent, no big deal, he lived to serve.

Nervous as they approached the lab, the small pouches hidden in Tulip's curly auburn hair, tied in with tiny pieces of thread, invisible to the eye. Fast Eddie sometimes combed through her hair. If the guards did that, they'd discover the drugs. Tulip had a story prepared – drugs for another customer – but she wasn't a good liar, especially when she was high, as she was was now, smiling crookedly.

Opening the large outer door, sliding it shut behind them, pressing the button, waiting for the inner door to open. Kevin didn't recognise the guard. He forced a smile as he stepped forward and spread his arms. "Fast Eddie's night off?"

"He's away," the guard grunted, patting Kevin down, a careful job but not as probing as Fast Eddie. "Holidays."

"Home or abroad?" Kevin asked, Tulip's turn to be searched, tense as the guard ran his hands up her body and over her shoulders — relaxing as his fingers slid down her back, not touching her hair.

"Don't know," the guard said. He stepped aside and nodded at a security camera. The door closed. He turned away from the Tynes. "Follow me."

Through the lab, up the stairs to Phials' room. The chemist opened the door quickly when they knocked, breathless, eyes alight, ushering them in without even an hello, slamming the door on the bemused guard. "Did you bring the gear?" Snapping, anxious, more interested in the drugs than Tulip. Clint watched, alert, smiling, smug.

Kevin reached into Tulip's hair and pulled the baggies free. Phials went limp. Stared at the pouches, tears in his eyes. "How much?" Willing to pay whatever they asked.

Kevin glanced at Clint, tempted to make him pay for his own drugs. Decided not to be greedy. "No charge." He handed the baggies to Phials.

Phials too stoked to thank him. He yanked the

pouches open, shut his eyes in delight, hurried to the dressing table, popped a couple of E's and began making lines of coke. About to snort the first line when he remembered his manners. Smiled at his guests. "Ladies first," he said, offering Tulip a rolled up note.

Tulip leant forward and inhaled deeply, expertly. The more she took, the less real it seemed. Kevin was worried she might OD but he didn't want to start an argument with her, not when she was high, no telling how she would react.

Phials offered the note to Kevin and Clint. Both men shook their heads. Phials was so excited, he forgot that Clint was the one who'd originally requested the drugs. "All the more for me," he murmured, thinking, *Don't blow it all tonight. Save some. Make it last.* Knowing he wouldn't heed his good advice, never able to call time when he went on a binge.

Phials leant over the dressing table. One line up his left nostril, one up his right. Pinching his nose tight, quivering with ecstasy, head filling with lights, grinning at Tulip, more beautiful than ever. "We're going to do some godalmighty fucking tonight," he whispered, moving towards her. "Wait till you see me hard on coke. I can keep it up all night."

Tulip smiled shakily and let her eyes roll towards the

ceiling, zoning out as Phials groped her. With the help of the coke she imagined herself elsewhere. Anywhere.

Kevin began unbuttoning his trousers. Stopped when he spotted Clint gesturing furiously at him. Remembered the script. Coughed and spoke loudly. "Time for you to leave, Clint."

Clint came back with, "Tony suh-said I could stay."

Kevin frowned ridiculously, a lousy actor, but Phials too far gone to notice. "We're not into group sex. Please leave."

"Tony?" Clint said. Phials didn't hear him. "Tony!"

Phials looked up, dazed. Waved absentmindedly at Kevin. "Let him stay. I'll pay extra. Get high. Get laid. Get happy."

Kevin swung in close to Clint. "What do we do now?"

"Whatever you normally do," Clint replied, watching as Phials simultaneously popped an E and rolled Tulip's jumper up. He had no interest in the glimpse of naked flesh, focused purely on Phials.

Kevin was watching Clint intently. If Clint made a move on Tulip, he'd have him thrown out. But he saw that Clint had eyes only for the chemist. He relaxed and spun away, circled the pair on the bed, losing himself to the passion.

Clint kept to the background at first, a neutral observer, no excitement as Phials stripped Tulip and mounted her, mild distaste at the sight of Kevin jerking off, nothing more. Phials as wild and persistent on the drugs as he'd claimed, a variety of positions, breaking only to make swift attacks on the coke and E's.

As Phials got higher and wilder, Clint realised he'd have to get closer to the action to interrogate the chemist, and quickly, before he went comatose — Clint now wished he hadn't added so many E's to the pouch. He slipped up beside the bed. Kevin paused when he saw Clint zeroing in, but relaxed when Clint patted his groin and winked — no erection.

Clint tapped Phials on the shoulder. "Mind if I join in?" Phials laughed with horny delight. Arched upwards to kiss Clint. Clint saw the kiss coming, ducked it – *not* part of his plan! – laughed and snuggled up to Tulip, cuddling her, running his hands over her, kissing her shoulder, putting on a show for Phials. Leaning over the table, he pretended to snort some coke. Phials cooed. Clint picked up a couple of E's and put them between Tulip's lips. She started to swallow. "No," he whispered. "Not for you — for Tony. Pass them to him." Tulip didn't like letting the pills go, but she did as ordered, kissing Phials, letting him take the E's from her with his tongue, Phials almost choking on the pills.

Clint decided it was time to act. He was half-naked,

sweating, making grinding motions against Tulip, cackling hysterically whenever Phials laughed. Pretending to snort more coke, he collapsed across the bed. Nudged Phials. "Is this great shit or what?"

"A1," Phials giggled.

"Bet it's better than the shit you're working on — the miracle drug."

"Never," Phials howled. "My shit's the best in the world."

"I can't wait to try it," Clint said. "When do you think you'll have it ready?" Phials mumbled something incoherent. "If we had it now, imagine the crazy shit we could get up to," Clint pressed. Phials moaned, thrusting into Tulip, barely hearing what Clint was saying. "If you've cracked the formula, why not cook some up? Or tell me where it is and I can get one of the others to prepare it for us."

Phials paused as Clint's words sunk in, self-protection mechanism kicking in. "What?" Shaking his head, trying to focus.

"Have you cracked the formula?" Clint grinned, unaware that Phials had clicked back into place, writing the chemist off as just another junkie who'd reveal his darkest sexual fantasy when high, no idea that users of Phials' stature existed, men with secrets so dark that they'd never reveal them, no matter how wasted they got.

Phials stared hard at Clint, mind clearing, seeing the fix now, Kevin and Tulip in on it, Clint planning to pump him dry and serve his head up to Dave Bushinsky on a coke-lined silver platter. A great rage built in the usually timid man. "You... fucking... bastard."

Clit smiled nervously, getting the sense that he'd lost his grip on the situation. "Hey, doc, I was just –"

"*Fucker!*" Phials screamed, wrapping his fingers around Clint's throat, fingers slipping, chasing him from the bed, erection wilting, scrambling after Clint. "Kill you! I'll kill you all! Fuckers!" Grabbed a paperweight off the dressing table and lobbed it at Kevin. It sailed wide, smashed into the wall, knocked a small hole in the plaster. Kevin panicking, imagining the damage it would have done if it had connected with his head.

"Tony! Calm down! This isn't..." Clint stopped abruptly as Phials whirled on him and lunged for his throat again. He slapped the chemist's hands away but suddenly the tall black man was over him, pinning Clint to the floor, screaming incoherently, spitting on Clint, unconsciously urinating on him.

Kevin Tyne grabbed his trousers and ran for the door, calling for Tulip. But the stoned Tulip only giggled and asked, "Is he going to kill Clint?" Kevin stopped, saw Phials choking Clint, Clint's eyes bulging, tongue sticking out. Ready to flee and leave Clint – his own fucking fault – but then Tulip knelt beside Phials to take a closer look. Kevin couldn't leave his sister — Phials might kill her too. He cursed and dived after her, pulled her away. Phials thought he was being attacked. He lashed out at Kevin and slipped off of Clint. Clint sat up, gasping, terrified. Phials came at him again. Clint kicked him away, shrieking. Phials shook his head, woozy. Clint kicked him again, between the eyes.

Kevin grabbed Tulip, thrust clothes at her, threw her towards the door. Clint stumbled after them. Phials groaned and grabbed for his ankle. Clint kicked him again, then stamped on the chemist's hand. Phials howled. Clint ran.

Tulip fumbled with the door. Kevin shoved her aside, yanked the door open, hurled Tulip through. He followed, Clint just behind. Phials was on his knees now, crawling after them, snarling, urinating, moaning. Kevin slammed the door shut, struggled into his clothes, barking at Tulip to get dressed. The door started to open. He put his shoulder against it and shoved hard, knocked Phials back to the floor. Shut the door again. Grabbed Tulip and Clint – both stunned, helpless – and herded them towards the stairs, past the startled guard who'd come to investigate.

"What the fuck?" the guard shouted.

"He lost his head!" Kevin screamed. "He tried to kill us! I think he's high!"

"Fuck." The guard whitened — his number one priority, make sure Tony Phials didn't have access to hard drugs. His head on the block if the Bush heard about this. "Get out of here," he snapped, hurrying up the stairs. "I'll take care of Phials. And hey!" he shouted after them. "Not a fucking word about this to anyone."

Kevin nodded fearfully, paused and watched the guard collide with Phials at the top of the stairs and wrestle him to the floor, Phials screaming bloody murder. Then he ran with Tulip and Clint through the lab, panting, heart racing, cursing himself for letting Clint talk him into this, half-afraid Phials would overpower the guard, catch up with them and slaughter them all, praying to God to save them, promising him anything in exchange for their safety, even vowing to stop abusing his sister if they made it out of here alive — *that* afraid.

TWENTY-FOUR

Gawl watched Clint Smith make his regular Friday deals in the Church of Sacred Martyrs. Depressed again. Fr Sebastian was back in his pocket, Gawl setting him up with girls when his needs grew too strong for him to contain, taking all the money the priest could raise, setting up another burglary — he'd squeezed more names out of the priest and had cased their houses, but pretty sure it would be peanuts no matter which of the old cows he hit. Drinking more than ever, most nights too drunk even to fight, waking in alleys outside pubs, crawling home, shivering, stinking, head pounding.

Not sure why he was bothering with Smith. The young dealer was small-time. No profit in him for Gawl. But he'd got into the habit of shadowing Smith, and without fail he found himself at each of Smith's church sessions, regardless of how hungover he was, sometimes trailing him as he did business on the Tube or in clubs. At least when he was following Smith he felt like he had some kind of a purpose.

His last customer of the day attended to, Smith rose and slipped into the confessional, Gawl figuring, *Fr Sebastian must be planning to get high. He'll be looking for company tonight. Better make sure I'm available.*

Gawl followed Smith as he left the church. Fr Sebastian

would need time to beg God for strength, before giving in to his demons and looking for Gawl. A few hours at least to kill. Better to spend them trailing Smith than sitting in the church waiting for the priest to summon him.

Smith led Gawl to the Elephant & Castle, then up the Walworth Road and off it into a cul-de-sac. Gawl figured he was visiting friends. About to depart when he saw Smith slide open a door fronting a decrepit garage. Gawl frowned as Smith disappeared from sight, wondering what he was up to and what lay behind the door. Scanned the rest of the cul-de-sac — mostly abandoned shells. He strode to one of the houses opposite the garage and checked the door, rotten, loosely hinged, easy to break down. Gawl loitered a while, wary of observers. Seeing nobody, he put his shoulder to the door and knocked it open, swinging it closed again as soon as he was inside. Made his way to the front room, squatted inside the window and trained his sights on the apparently disused garage.

Hours passed, the sun dropped, street lamps came on. No sign of Clint Smith. Gawl thought about Fr Sebastian, alone, horny, anxious. He should go see to his meal ticket, keep him happy, keep the money rolling in. But his curiosity had been aroused. What could be keeping Smith so long?

Getting cold inside the dark, deserted room. Gawl

losing interest, not just in the surveillance but in Clint Smith full stop. The dealer not worth his time and effort. Sick of London and ill-founded dreams. Making plans — hit one of Fr Sebastian's flock, maybe rape and kill the bitch while he was at it, blow London.

He'd almost made up his mind to leave when Kevin and Tulip Tyne walked up to the door of the garage and slid it open. Gawl watched slack-jawed — he knew nothing of Smith's connection to the Tynes and couldn't understand why they were here at the same time as the dealer. Forgot all about Fr Sebastian and leaving, immune to the cold, eyes harsh in the darkness.

Keeping a lonely vigil, but alert and curious now. Trying to imagine what lay behind the peeling, cracked garage door, something strong enough to draw both a small-time dealer and a whore and her brother/pimp. Some kind of underground club? A brothel? But then where were all the clients?

All of a sudden the door was yanked open and Smith and the Tynes spilled out, faces twisted with panic, running, stumbling. The girl fell and cried out. She was half-naked. Her brother picked her up and thrust a jumper at her. As she wriggled into it, he turned on Smith and shouted at him. Gawl didn't catch all the words but picked out a few choice curses. Smith yelled back, pale and shaking as he buttoned up his trousers.

Kevin Tyne started to close the garage door. Paused. Stuck his head inside. Drew back looking more terrified than before. Yelled something that sounded like, "Files!" Grabbed his sister and ran, Clint Smith hot on their heels, overtaking them at the corner of the cul-de-sac, all three swiftly vanishing from sight.

As Gawl stared, wide-eyed, a large naked black man stumbled out into the street, bellowing wildly, shaking his arms, head whiplashing left and right, high or crazy or both. Three men hurried out of the garage and surrounded the black man, tried to shepherd him back inside. He roared at them. Attacked one. They knocked him to the ground. The one he'd attacked pulled a gun. Another barked a command at him, protectively stepping in front of the black guy. The man who'd drawn the weapon glared at his colleague then put the gun away. All three bent and picked up the lunatic. His legs and arms thrashed wildly but they hustled him inside, the one at the rear pausing to slide the door shut. The last of the action, the cul-de-sac ghostly quiet after that.

Gawl in the shadows of the house, trembling with confusion and excitement, sensing something in the brewing, no idea what the fuck it might be, just that it smelled *BIG*.

TWENTY-FIVE

Big Sandy sitting in the back of a van, keeping a close eye on the road outside. He could see out through the darkened windows but nobody passing could see in. He'd been here a couple of hours. Wasn't comfortable being in position such a long time but didn't want to lose his parking spot. It was almost right in front of the house. Originally he'd planned to drive around, maybe get something to eat, but when he saw the space he couldn't resist.

Fast Eddie didn't know where he was or what he was doing. Big Sandy had hired the van and told Fast Eddie only that he was going for a drive. Fast Eddie wanted to come, eager to escape Margate for a day. Started to argue when Big Sandy refused. Then he caught Big Sandy's expression and realised this wasn't a joy ride. The giant had business in mind. Fast Eddie had no idea what it might be, but if Big Sandy didn't want to tell him, that was fine. Fast Eddie knew better than to stick his nose into the big man's affairs.

Big Sandy had spent nearly two hours driving to Hastings. Several years since he'd last swung by this way, respecting the promise he had made. If he'd been recalled to London, he would have dismissed the temptation and kept his distance. But the idea had lodged in his brain and, as the days dragged on, it became an irresistable summons. Finally, several days after that sleepless night, he caved in.

Megan was at work. Big Sandy knew that she worked for a travel firm. He also knew she'd been dating her boss for the last couple of years. He was fine with that. It had been a long time since he'd had any claim over her. He hoped her lover treated her well. According to the reports he'd received from the investigator he'd hired to keep an eye on her, the guy was solid, a divorced father of three who ran a legit ship and had never been in trouble.

Big Sandy hadn't come to see Megan. He'd felt close to her once, but not so close that he was distraught when their paths diverged. No, he was here to see Megan's daughter Amelie. *His* daughter.

A young man when he'd sired his only child. Megan had been on the scene for several months. They got on well, had a fun time together, but neither would have described it as a serious relationship. A faulty condom changed that. Big Sandy remembered Megan telling him. She wasn't sure how he'd react. Said straight up that she was keeping the baby. Big Sandy said he wanted it too. Telling the truth, even though he'd never thought about parenthood before.

They spent more time together and Big Sandy helped her prepare for the birth, but Megan only moved in with him a few months after Amelie was born, when she got sick of the constant arguments with her mother, who loved the baby but didn't want to be directly involved in raising the child. Megan uneasy at first. Big Sandy gave her lots of space and time. Eventually she settled in and they lived for nearly eighteen months as a normal couple.

That was easily the sweetest time of Big Sandy's life. He looked back on those days with fondness and thought of them often. A big smile every morning when he woke up and remembered he was a father and went to feed Amelie and change her and play with her. A big smile every night when he came home, loving it when she cried out with happiness and wrapped her tiny arms around one of his huge hands, swinging from him, barely bigger than a teddy bear.

Big Sandy hoped it could be like that forever. He knew Megan didn't love him but she was satisfied with him. He provided for them, was gentle with her, treated her with respect. Hopeful that she would stay, that he could be there all through Amelie's childhood, a loving, attentive father. And maybe it would have worked out that way if not for Jackie Greaves.

Jackie Greaves one of the Bush's rivals. A big, brutal

man, almost as big and brutal as Big Sandy. Nicknamed after the Spurs legend, Jimmy Greaves, because his old man once played in the same team as him, before Greaves went pro. Jackie Sr never stopped talking about that, which earned him the nickname, which Jackie Jr inherited. Jackie and the Bush had been friends when they were younger, went to Spurs games together if the Bush's grandfather was absent. But both men were determined to rule the roost when they got older. They'd been sparring for years.

Jackie decided to make a power play. Tried to wipe out the Bush and his closest allies in one fell sweep. Big Sandy one of the names on their list. A team hit him at home in the dead of night, while others were carrying out similar attacks across London. Word leaked just before the raids commenced. Hasty calls to anyone in the firing line. Most of the targets fled their homes or defended them if they had weapons and were confident. The Bush tried to call Big Sandy but Megan took the phone off the hook every night before going to bed, in case it woke Amelie.

Three men broke into their flat. Tried to pick the lock, failed, so smashed in a window. That woke Big Sandy. He reacted swiftly. Tackled them in the living room. They had guns, but it was dark and Big Sandy knew the room, didn't need the light, grappled with them, disarmed them, lashed into them.

Megan saw a lot of it, screaming, holding Amelie in her arms, trying to get past them. Big Sandy roared at her to stay where she was. Disabled the intruders. Megan saw blood. One man's head caved in. One man's throat slashed open. Ran while Big Sandy was moving in to finish off the third. She never returned.

Of course she'd known that Big Sandy worked for Dave Bushinsky. She wasn't naive. She accepted the manner of his business. But she hadn't figured on it spilling into their home life. Never assumed it could get that dirty, that bloody. Determined never to expose herself or her child to it again.

When Jackie Greaves had been taken care of, Big Sandy tried to mend fences, but didn't beg her to come back. He understood why she had run, why she wanted nothing to do with him now. In a way he had anticipated this all along, certain that a man with his history could never enjoy a normal life, sure that the good times would be ripped away from him. In his own mind he didn't deserve happiness, so he didn't complain when Megan vowed to sic the police on him if he ever came near her and their baby again.

Big Sandy let her flee London but kept tabs on her.

When she stopped running, he sent word that he would respect her privacy, but asked if he could contribute financially, to ensure that Amelie wanted for nothing. Megan rebuffed him at first, but it was hard bringing up a daughter by herself, so in the end she accepted his offer of help. She thought he would try to use it as a wedge to force himself back into their lives, but he never did.

He had kept sending money in the years since, and had built up a hefty trust fund for Amelie with the help of Julius Scott. But he'd had no further contact with his one-time girlfriend or the daughter he loved. He'd regularly staked them out in the early years, wanting to watch over them, to see his girl growing up. But he always came away feeling morose, so in time he stopped doing even that.

He wasn't sure why he had decided to check on them now, after such a long absence. Maybe it was just that he had time on his hands and was bored. But Big Sandy thought there was more to it. His recent interactions with unfortunate girls – Shula Schimmel and Tulip Tyne – had set him thinking about Amelie, who was a bit younger than either of those but in the same teenage territory. He'd started wondering if there might be a Larry Drake or Kevin Tyne lurking in the shadows of Amelie's life. According to the reports he still received, there wasn't, but sometimes you saw something in a person's eyes that you couldn't see in a photo. Sometimes a scared look told you more than an investigator ever could.

So here he was, in the back of a van, waiting. Amelie should be home from school soon. She was old enough to let herself in and out of the house. Hastings was a quiet town, Megan felt safe there and Amelie was a sensible girl. She'd been letting her daughter walk to and from school by herself for a couple of years.

A schoolgirl came sloping along, dragging a bag. Big Sandy leant forward, but saw almost immediately that it wasn't Amelie, too pale, the wrong colour hair. He stayed leaning forward, figuring if one kid had passed, it wouldn't be long until more came his way. But for ten minutes he saw no one. He started to think about after-school activities. Maybe Amelie had stayed on for music lessons or sports. He checked his watch. Megan due home in half an hour, maybe a little more. He'd leave before she came back, in case she got curious about the van parked so closer to their house. Megan was sharp, always had been.

As he was resigning himself to a wasted journey, Amelie appeared. She was with another girl and a boy. Chatting and laughing. Big Sandy stared. She was taller than he'd expected. She got that from him. Not a stunner, but a nice-looking girl. She got her looks from her mother.

The kids stopped close to the van. Big Sandy could hear them talking about school and homework and what they were going to watch on the telly that night. Then the boy reached across, grabbed the back of Amelie's bra and snapped it. She yelled at him and threw a punch at his head, but she was laughing. The boy and the other girl laughed too and carried on. Amelie waved after them, smiling. Then she turned her back on her unseen father and walked up the path to her house.

Big Sandy watched until she closed the door. Then he leant back and sighed. Unknown to himself, he was smiling, and the smile was the same as the girl's. She'd looked happy. The reports had indicated as much, but he was glad he'd come. He could rest easier after seeing her. Probably wouldn't feel the need to check on her again in person for a long time after this.

He frowned as he thought about the boy, the way he'd snapped her bra. Almost certainly harmless fun, but he'd ask the investigator to keep an eye on things, dig into the boy's background, make sure he wasn't a threat. Over the top, but Big Sandy didn't care, not when his little girl was involved.

One last look at the house, then Big Sandy moved up front and set off on the drive back to Margate, thoughtful as he went, sad but happy at the same time.

Four days later, having breakfast in a pub, the best thing about Margate in November. Good grub but Fast Eddie was sour and barely tasted the food. Nothing to do with Big Sandy's mystery trip. His Spaniard had hung about longer than expected. Fast Eddie had started to consider the pair of them an item. Thinking about taking her back to London with him. Then, earlier in the week, she did a runner, took his wallet, rings and watch while he was showering. Fast Eddie was all for setting off after her and strangling her. Big Sandy talked him out of it — they were here to keep a low profile, all was fair in love and war, etc. Secretly chuckling at Fast Eddie's fall from grace but he kept a straight face.

Big Sandy's mobile rang as they were returning to their hotel. He checked the incoming number in the corridor, then opened the door of their room and answered as he stepped in, "Yeah?" Listened carefully. "Yeah." Pause. "Thanks." End of call.

Fast Eddie stared at him hopefully. Big Sandy looked back blankly, then burst into a rare open grin. "We're going home."

Fast Eddie punched the air. "Thank fuck."

Big Sandy smiled and packed, thinking sadly of Amelie and how much he missed her, but also of Sapphire and how sweet it would be to seek the solace of her embrace once again.

TWENTY-SIX

Clint at his lowest ever. Glumly surfing the Tube, making hardly any sales, too despondent to care. He'd blown it. Stepped in with the big boys — first round knockout. Dreams blown. America blown. The chance to whisk Shula away into the sunset blown. Only comfort, there had been no comebacks from cousin Dave, so Phials mustn't have reported him and the guards must have kept word of the fuckaroo to themselves.

Clint disgusted. How had he made such a pig's ear of it? Thought Phials would be easy to play, get him high, blow him wide. Junkies by nature self-destructive. Phials should have spilled his secrets and told Clint everything. But he didn't.

Clint hadn't been back to the lab. No contact with Phials or the Tynes. Last sight of the brother and sister, they were fleeing up the Walworth Road, Kevin screaming bloody murder, never phone them again, they were through with Clint fucking Smith, long may he roast in the fires of Hell. So he'd lost the Tynes as well as Phials, on the back of losing Larry Drake. All his decent contacts wiped clean in the space of a few numbing weeks. Imagining Dave's contempt when he found out. Any plans to bump Clint up the ladder aborted. Might even cut him out of the organisation entirely, Clint too much of a liability. Dole queue or a dead end job. A nobody for life. No way of enticing Shula or striking out for the States.

The train came to a stop. Clint took no notice of the station name. Didn't even know what line he was on. Three boys got on his carriage, late teens, goths. Sat close to Clint. Talk of music, girls, movies, beer. Clint leant across. "You guys want to score?" Pulling the zipper of his jacket down, showing them the top of a baggie sticking out of an inner pocket. The goths stared hard at Clint, suspicious. "It's OK," he assured them. "Good shit, good price. I can let you have –"

"Fuck off," one of the goths snarled.

Clint withdrew without argument. Not sure what he'd said wrong or why they didn't trust him. Par for the current course. Couldn't even get the basics right any more, blowing the bread and butter deals. If this kept up he wouldn't be able to make this month's rent. He'd have to dip into his savings or ask cousin Dave for a handout. Determined it wouldn't come to that — he'd quit the apartment and skip London before degrading himself to that extent.

Clint stumbled out of the carriage at the next stop, feeling the eyes of the three goths hot on his back. Listlessly shuffled along with the crowd, wandered the station until he came to another line, waited for a train, got on, sat down and brooded, waiting for clients to magically appear and give him loads of money, knowing it didn't work that way, unable to bring himself to care.

Close behind Clint in the station — Gawl McCaskey. Sometimes so near he could hear Clint breathe. He'd been following the demoralised dealer everywhere since the mysterious night at the garage, and he was the reason the goths had been wary. They'd seen the bulky, unkempt, dangerous-looking man hovering a few seats along from Clint, made the connection between the pair, wary of it, fearing some kind of trap. Clint would have known he was being followed any other time – Gawl going to no pains to disguise his presence – but his depression was all-consuming, his senses turned inward in self-pity, seeing nothing but the scraps of his future drifting past.

TWENTY-SEVEN

Kevin still seething about the Smith/Phials fuck-up. He knew deep down it was his own fault for agreeing to sneak in the drugs and letting Clint stay while they got it on with Phials, but he couldn't admit that. Laid all the blame at Clint's doorstep, raged about him to Tulip, breakfast, lunch, dinner, as they watched TV, Tulip listening without interest, tired of the tirade.

They'd had appointments planned for Saturday and Sunday. Kevin cancelled them, partly because of his hasty promise to God as they'd fled the lab, but mostly because he was too agitated to focus on sex. Spending a quiet weekend with Tulip, their first free weekend in a long while, enjoying the peace, rage gradually abating, going on long walks together, checking out the London Eye on Saturday evening and Sunday morning, Tulip contrasting the night and day crowds. A movie up Leicester Square after Sunday lunch, mingling with the tourists, strolling around Soho and Covent Garden. The mood spoilt only when Kevin started in on another Clint Smith hate rant.

Tulip much more relaxed when there were no appointments looming, clutching Kevin warmly as they walked, telling him jokes, discussing his work and his alternatives if he quit. A different girl this weekend —

normal. Kevin loved her this way. He wanted her to be like this all the time. Considered putting the sex behind them forever, honouring his promise to God. Imagining Tulip's face if he told her there'd be no more appointments, the love she'd shower on him, the joy and happiness they'd share. Almost believing he could go without the voyeurism. Almost telling her the nightmares were over.

But Monday came. Tuesday. Wednesday. Long hours at London Bridge, angry customers, uncaring staff, a job he hated. The only way he could get through the drab days was by dreaming of Tulip. But the dreams not enough. She sensed the need growing in him. Tried to distract him. Asked him to take her out for meals. Talked incessantly about books she'd read and shows she'd seen. Said she was going to stay off the drugs, determined to get clean and match Kevin's sacrifice if he was willing to go cold turkey. Kevin grunted, touched by the offer, knowing it would be even harder for her to get straight than it would be for him, since she had a real, physical addiction. He wanted to meet her halfway and lead them both out of the wretched wilderness of his making. But in his mind's eye seeing her naked, writhing on a bed, growing hard on the image, needing more.

At work on Thursday his mobile rang. Martin Laskey.

"What do you want?" Kevin asked sharply. He'd told Laskey last time that they wouldn't be doing any future business with him, Laskey too rough with Tulip.

"I wanted to know if you were free," Laskey said smoothly.

"Not for you," Kevin snapped.

"Hey," Laskey laughed, "let's be friends. I was a bit forward before, but we had fun in the end, didn't we?"

"You hurt Tulip," Kevin said.

"So I squeezed a bit harder than I should," Laskey chuckled. "I paid a bonus, didn't I? And I promised I wouldn't hurt her again. Can you come tonight? I'll make it worth your while."

"I'm not sure." Nervous about going to Laskey's alone. Thinking about Dave Bushinsky and his heavies, how he needed Clint to set up protection. About to turn Laskey down when he remembered he had a number for the giant, Big Sandy. He'd given it to Kevin on their way home from Laskey's. "Let me ring you back," Kevin said, severing the connection, checking his watch, more than an hour till lunch. He wanted to slip away early but Dan Bowen had been on his back all week, riding Kevin hard. He'd have to wait.

The second the minute hand hit twelve, Kevin hurried home. Tulip called hello to him from the TV room when she heard him enter, but he only grunted and made for his phone book, skimming the pages until he found Big Sandy's number under M for Murphy. Tulip wandered out and watched him as he dialled, seeing the hunger in his eyes, sadness filling her soul.

The phone rang five times. Six. Seven. Then a heavy voice, "Yeah?"

"Sandy Murphy?"

"Yeah?" Cautious.

"This is Kevin Tyne. I was wondering if you could escort us tonight?"

A pause. "Clint normally arranges that."

Kevin started to tell him about his fall out with Clint. Stopped, not sure what codes these people operated by, figuring solidarity might be an issue with them, if you insult one you insult all. Safer not to mention his bust-up with Clint. "I tried calling him but I couldn't get through."

Another pause. Then, "What time?"

"I'll call you back and let you know."

Hanging up, beaming, digging out Laskey's number, thinking, *Fuck Clint Smith!* He caught Tulip's eye and smiled at her. "Better make yourself beautiful. We have an appointment tonight."

Tulip stared at her brother coldly, then turned her back on him and returned to the TV room, tears trickling down her cheeks, heading for her stash. Kevin didn't notice. He was entirely focused on the phone and making arrangements, promise to God forgotten, quiet contentment of the past week forgotten, thinking about the sex, trembling with the neediness of unnatural lust.

TWENTY-EIGHT

A week solid shadowing Clint Smith, staying off the drink except for a few pints on his way home at night, shaving daily, washing regularly, darkness behind him, a point to his life. Not sure what secrets were hidden behind the door of the garage – he'd been back a few times, no signs of life – but sensing promise, maybe a big score, maybe a steady earner. But definitely *something*.

Disappointed that Smith hadn't returned to the garage, but certain that in time he would. Smith looked like Gawl had felt a week ago, low, empty, suicidal. As Gawl knew from first-hand experience, you couldn't live indefinitely in that bleak place. Whatever mysteries the garage held, they were more important to Smith than anything else in his life. He'd have to return to them, move on in search of new dreams, or kill himself. Gawl confident Smith wouldn't move on or slit his throat — too weak a man. That left the garage, a humble return, tail between his legs.

Gawl not sure how he could get close to Smith, to find out who the black guy was, where Smith stood in relation to the Tynes, or what the purpose of the garage was. But an opportunity would surely present itself. He just had to follow Clint long enough and doggedly enough, and eventually the chance to squeeze himself into the dejected dealer's life would arise. When it did, he'd seize it, and he knew – deep down, on the level of animal instinct, he *knew* – life would never be the same for him again. Or for Clint Smith. Or for any of them.

TWENTY-NINE

Big Sandy sat in the TV room with Tulip watching soaps. Kevin had been kept late at work by his boss but hadn't had time to alert Big Sandy. When he'd arrived at the flat, Tulip had told him he could go away and return in a couple of hours if he liked, but he said he'd wait for Kevin. Patience one of Big Sandy's virtues.

He'd only been back in London since Monday, but Margate already seemed like a faraway dream. He'd celebrated his return with a rare booze-up, followed by a trip to Sapphire's. No weeping this time, no confessions, just a long night of love-making, laughing about how dull Margate was, catching up with Sapphire's more recent news. Lying awake beside her after she'd fallen asleep, imagining a life with her. Unlike Megan, she could accept him for what he was. No surprises for Sapphire — she knew him at his worst and most vulnerable. It might be a good life. She didn't trick much any more. He was sure it wouldn't be a loss for her if she had to give it up. Make an honest woman of her. Grow old together. He'd finally drifted off, thinking of the pair of them sitting in some room or other in the future, peaceful, sharing a warm, knowing smile. But he said nothing of it when they got up in the morning. Seemed like a childish dream when he was sober. He left feeling sheepish.

In the soap, a teenage boy and girl were having an argument. That reminded Big Sandy of his daughter and the kid who'd snapped her bra. He glanced at Tulip, chewed his lip a while, then said softly, "Can I ask you something?"

Tulip looked up, surprised. "Of course. What?"

"If a boy snaps a girl's bra, and she hits him when he does it, but laughs at the same time... what does that mean?"

"Depends," Tulip sniffed. "Maybe he has a crush on her and is trying to catch her attention. Or maybe she has a crush on him, and he knows, but isn't interested, and is teasing her. Or maybe they're just friends and it doesn't mean anything."

Big Sandy thought that over. He appreciated the feedback and cast an eye over Tulip, paying closer attention to her than he had before. She was nervous, worried about the night ahead, fingering her rosary beads while she watched TV. During a break, Big Sandy decided to ask her about that. "Are those fashion accessories?" Tulip stared at him uncertainly. "The beads. Are they only for show?"

"Oh no," Tulip said quickly, clutching them to her chest.

"You're religious?"

She nodded imperceptibly and looked at him. "You?"

He smiled. "In my line of work it doesn't pay to think of God too much."

"I would have thought people in your line of work needed to think of God more than most," Tulip said.

"How so?" Big Sandy frowned.

"You need him more."

Big Sandy's frown deepened. He thought she was criticising him. "People in your line of work need him too," he retorted.

"It's not a line of work for me," Tulip answered softly, "but yes, I *do* need him. That's why I pray so much, begging for forgiveness and understanding."

Big Sandy sat up, taking even more of an interest. "If you feel that way about it, why…?" He left the indiscreet question hanging.

"We don't all have the freedom of choice," Tulip said. "Some of us do what we have to, what we must."

"I don't agree with that," Big Sandy grunted. "We make our own choices. Some have easier choices to make than others, but nobody's locked on a single course, not unless they choose to be."

"You don't believe in fate?"

"No."

"I'm not sure I do either," Tulip said, "but sometimes it seems that everything is destined, that all our choices have been taken away, except for those which will damn us — and those are no real choices at all."

Big Sandy scratched the back of his left hand with his right, thinking about that. "So why do you do it?" he asked, genuinely interested this time.

"I have my reasons," Tulip answered cryptically.

"Does your brother force you?"

"Not directly."

Big Sandy's face darkened. "Does he hurt you?"

"No."

"But he's the one who arranges these *events*? They're his idea?"

Tulip didn't answer. She switched channels, distracted, rubbed an arm, needing a fix. Big Sandy studied her intently, the first time he'd taken real notice of her, having previously dismissed her as a young, conscienceless whore. Now seeing the lines around her eyes, the nervous tic at the edges of her lips, her fingers white on the rosary beads. Comparing her with Amelie, feeling sorry for her, imagining how much it would hurt if he found his daughter in this situation. Wanting to know more about her. Trying to think of a way to draw her back into conversation.

"What church do you go to?"

"The Church of Sacred Martyrs. It's over in –"

"I know it," Big Sandy interrupted. "I go there too."

"You go to mass?" Tulip blinked, turning away from the TV, eyeing the giant dubiously.

"Not to mass." Big Sandy grinned bleakly. "I'm no hypocrite. But I drop in to think sometimes, to look inside myself and wonder what God makes of me. I talk with the priest sometimes. He tries to –"

"You know Fr Sebastian?" Tulip snapped, heart jumping, seeing a chance to find out if the priest was as respectful of his confessional vows as she believed.

"Yeah."

"He hears my confession." Watching closely.

"You confess?" Big Sandy taken aback.

"I'm a sinner," Tulip said. "Of course I confess."

"But..." Big Sandy scratched an ear. "If you feel that way, why do you do this?"

"As I said, we don't all have the freedom of choice."

Big Sandy leant forward curiously. "Do you think God forgives your sins?"

"Of course."

"But if you're not truly sorry..."

"I *am* sorry," Tulip said stiffly.

"But you know you'll do it again," Big Sandy pressed.

"I pray to him that I won't, that I'll be delivered from..." Stopped short of incriminating Kevin outright.

"Prayers won't get you anywhere," Big Sandy snorted.

"Maybe not," Tulip said. "But they're all some of us have."

Big Sandy laughed out loud. Tulip looked hurt. She thought he was laughing at her. Big Sandy saw this and raised his hands apologetically. "No offence. I was just thinking that you're a strange one."

"How so?" Tulip asked coolly.

"Well, you talk like a nun but you…" He coughed, embarrassed.

"…fuck like a slut?" Tulip finished bitterly, foul language her way of hurting Kevin when she wanted to, automatically using it on Big Sandy too.

"That doesn't suit you," Big Sandy admonished her.

"Hookers are supposed to talk dirty," Tulip pouted.

"Do you think of yourself as a prostitute?"

She looked away. Whispered, "No."

"Then don't act like one. At least not when you don't have to."

Tulip squinted at the huge man in the chair, confused. "You talk funny too," she said. "Not like I expect a gangster to talk."

Big Sandy chuckled. "Is that what you think I am?"

"Well, aren't you?"

"Not really." Big Sandy never thought of himself that

way. Dave Bushinsky was a gangster. Big Sandy was just a hired hand.

Tulip shuffled closer to him. "Do you go to confession?" she asked.

"No."

"Why not?"

"I don't have the right."

"Everybody has the right to confess."

"I think those of us who deliberately ignore God's laws have no right to appeal to him when it suits us."

"You think *I* shouldn't go either?"

Big Sandy smiled warmly. "I don't think selling your body counts as a great sin, though I'm sure lots of holy Joes wouldn't agree with me." They shared a laugh, then Big Sandy's features darkened. "My sins run deeper than yours. I hurt people. God has compassion for those who cheapen themselves but do no harm. By the same measure I believe he has none for those who injure others, destroying where he has created."

"But if they see the error of their ways, stop and confess..."

"Some can redeem themselves," Big Sandy nodded. "But there are those whose souls are blackened, whose hands are stained with blood, who..." He stopped, coughed, afraid he was giving too much away.

Tulip studied her bodyguard, his broad, plain face, his sandy hair, his scarred hands. She tried to imagine the life he'd lived, the terrible things he might have done. "I think you're wrong," she said. "I think God forgives all sins if the will to be forgiven is strong enough."

"What about atonement?" Big Sandy countered. "If you were a priest, what penance would you set a man who'd murdered for money, who..." Cutting himself short again, figuring, *Not with Sapphire. Have to be careful. Can't trust this girl.*

"All sins can be atoned for," Tulip insisted. "I'm not sure what a killer would have to do to make his peace with God, but I'm sure he could."

"You believe in absolute redemption?"

"Yes."

"No matter what a man has done?"

"Yes."

Big Sandy reached across and touched the girl's chin lightly, lovingly. Tulip didn't pull away. She could see he wasn't a man who would take advantage of a child. "It's a wonderful world if you're right," Big Sandy said softly. Released her and added morosely, "But I don't think you are."

After that they waited in silence for Kevin to return.

THIRTY

Another stale Friday at the Church of Sacred Martyrs, Clint slumped on a pew near the back, listlessly making deals with his regulars. A grey November day outside. Clint's shoulders wet from the rain, he hadn't bothered with an umbrella. Not caring if he caught a cold, not caring about anything.

Dave had phoned earlier in the week (Tuesday? Wednesday?) to ask about Phials. "Time isn't on my side," he'd snapped. "I need to launch my bid for Sugar's shares *now*. Are you getting anywhere with Phials?"

Clint thought about lying or concealing the truth. Lacked the heart to. "Not ruh-ruh-really," he sighed. "I made a few quh-queries but he's not tuh-tuh-talking. Clams up tight whenever I raise the suh-subject." Careful to phrase his response in the present tense, making it seem like they were still friends.

"I didn't think you'd crack him," Dave grunted. "I'll send some men in to sniff around — he might have the formula stashed somewhere. If not, I'll ask him one last time if he's playing straight with me. If he sticks to his story I'll have to come down hard and keep my fingers crossed that he's been lying. In the meantime, keep asking on the off-chance."

Clint replaying the conversation, miserably fixating

on, *I didn't think you'd crack him.* Cousin Dave anticipating Clint's failure. Clint no longer even able to console himself with the thought that he'd fucked up gloriously. He'd simply been playing along to sad, pathetic form.

A girl slid up next to Clint, distracting him, Tess something-or-other. Seventeen or eighteen, thin, small sharp eyes, long untidy hair, a pinched unattractive face, deep frown lines around her mouth and eyes, looked like she never smiled. A dedicated junkie but only an occasional client of Clint's. She usually scored from one of the neighbourhood's cheaper dealers, only coming to Clint when she managed to save up for a decent fix. Tried to smile as she cuddled up to him, trembling, even wetter than Clint, brushing hair out of her eyes. "All right?"

Clint nodded wearily. "What do you want?"

Tess twitched. "I need some smack."

"I'm out. Coke, E's, grass, that's it."

"Coke then." Shaking bad now.

Clint reached inside his jacket. Paused. "Money first."

Tess stopped shaking. "I don't have any."

Clint took his hand away. "You think this is the NHS?"

"I can pay you next week."

"Get the fuck out of here." Not needing this, life bad enough as it was without needle whores trying to stiff him.

"Come on," Tess moaned, clutching his right hand, squeezing hard. "You know I'm good for it. I'll pay you Monday, I swear, but I need it now, I –"

"Fuck." Clint freed his hand. "Off."

Tess stared at him dully. She hadn't really expected him to give her anything on tab, but nothing to lose by trying. Emotionlessly kicked into her next strategy. "I'll blow you, fuck you, let you do whatever you want. I can do it here." Started to go down on her knees.

Clint pushed her away with disgust. "Just leave," he snarled.

"Come on," Tess pleaded, trying the smile again. "I'll do you good, let you fuck me up the arse, anything, as many times as you can come."

Clint sneered at the girl. Even if he wasn't a sexual failure, he wouldn't have anything to do with this skinny, ugly bitch. "You think I'm hard-up? You think I'd put my dick in diseased scum like you?" Tess stared back wordlessly. "Get the fuck out of here. Go blow your usual dealer. Maybe he'll –"

"I can't," Tess cried, her voice rising. "Tel was busted and I can't find Sammy. I think he's dead. You're the only –"

"Shut up," Clint snapped, digging her in the ribs with an elbow, seeing heads near the front of the church turning. "Keep quiet or I walk." Tess pressed a finger to her lips, tears streaming from her eyes, Clint unmoved. He checked his watch. "I'll be here another hour. Hit the streets. Get some money. Come back and I'll –"

"I don't have any money," Tess moaned.

"Sell your snatch to guys who are less demanding than me. Try the shops on the Walworth Road and offer discount blow jobs. I'm sure you'll find *someone* prepared to pay for the privilege. Come back when you have a few quid."

Tess started to rise. Stopped as a wave of sickness slammed her hard. Sat again. "I need it now." More tears, more shaking. "I'll do whatever you want later, but I need a hit first. Please, I'm begging you, we're in church, please, just –"

"Nothing for nothing." Clint was losing patience fast. "You think I've nothing better to do than argue with junkie whores? Fuck off. Get money. Come back when you can afford it." Tess opened her mouth to argue. "One more word and I won't give you the shit even if you get the cash together."

Tess' mouth closed, her eyes hardened, the tears vanished, her upper lip curled like a gorgon's. "Prick," she muttered. "All the fucking same." Shaking, she began to rise again. Stopped again. Stared at Clint.

Smiled and sat. He sighed and made to slide away from her. "I'll scream rape."

Clint paused. "What?"

"Rape." Her eyes cold but cunning. She raised her short skirt, gripped the fabric of her knickers and tugged — they ripped and she slid them down over her knees.

"Guh-guh-get the fuck out of huh-here," Clint sniffed uneasily.

Tess dragged the back of her left hand across her lips, smearing the thin line of lipstick she'd been wearing. Cheeks stained with tears from earlier. She looked a fright, like someone who'd been attacked.

"Nuh-nuh-nobody will buh-believe you." Clint sweating, studying the heads in the pews in front. Nobody was looking at him, but if the girl started screaming...

"Of course they will," Tess leered, sensing Clint's uncertainty. "If I scream, the others will rush back here to help me. They'll call the cops. If you stay, the cops will find the drugs on you, so you'll have to run and that'll make you look guilty." Grinning at her slyness and the hold she had over him. It wouldn't have worked with Tel or Sammy. They carried blades and would have slit her throat. But Clint was weak. He'd cave in. Stunned that she hadn't realised this before.

"Luh-luh-luh-listen," Clint said nervously. "I huh-have some huh-huh-heroin at home. Get some muh-money, come back, and I cuh-cuh-cuh-can —"

"Give me the coke and E's," Tess said calmly, "or I'll scream that you stuck your fingers up my cunt."

Clint started shaking worse than Tess, his spirit crushed, a total failure, feeling the walls of his life giving way, the roof crashing down, not just not one of the big boys, but a jerk who could be held to ransom by a scuzzy junkie, knowing it was all downhill from here, if she got away with it once she'd do it again, and tell her whorish junkie friends. They'd target him too and that would be the real end of him.

One last fumble for dignity, returning her threat with one of his own. "I'll kuh-kuh-kill you if you truh-try this. You muh-might get away with it in huh-huh-huh-here, but I'll cuh-catch up with you outside and —"

"Just give me the gear you feeble little prick," Tess snarled, ruthless in victory, her eyes bright, truly powerful for the first time in her life.

Clint collapsed. He reached into his jacket, handed over a baggie of coke then a handful of E's. He would have given it all to her if she'd asked — he didn't care anymore, he was finished, what did it matter — but she was too needy to be greedy, only concerned with getting high quickly, stopping the shakes, dealing with her present hunger. Later, when she had time to think, she'd return, look for more, push him further. But for now a baggie and a handful of pills would suffice.

"You're a prince," she snickered, kissing his cheek, Clint numb, staring at the altar, Christ hanging from the cross, thinking. *You had it fucking easy.*

Tess rose, pulled her knickers up, slipped the drugs into her handbag, tossed Clint a brisk, "See ya later, alligator!" and hurried for the exit, eager to get home, lock herself in, get high, chill out, savour the first victory of a life full of failures and setbacks.

Clint sat comatose, retreating further inside himself, wanting to cry but unable to find tears, hating himself, hating the world, hating life, wishing he was dead, wishing he had the courage to kill himself, knowing he didn't, looking ahead to a slow fall from… not grace… *mediocrity*, a slow fall from mediocrity into the pit of despair and utter hopelessness, fed upon by ravenous junkies, stripped clean until he became a blight on cousin Dave's good name, the Bush forced to despatch a man like Big Sandy to put a bullet through Clint's brain. Death the only thing he had to look forward to now.

Then, in his bleakest moment, when all had been lost, a hand gripped Clint's arm and squeezed sharply.

Wincing, he looked up and found himself staring into the face of a demonic guardian angel.

"On yer fucking feet," Gawl McCaskey snarled. "Ye're not gonna let the bitch get away wi' shite like that."

Clint stared at the stranger, his hard scarred face, mangled left ear, tightly cropped ginger/grey hair, steely blue eyes. "Who –"

"No time," Gawl snapped, yanking Clint to his feet and dragging him out of the pew. "We have t' stop her *now* or ye're fucked."

"How do yuh-yuh-you know about –"

"I was listening." Dragging Clint towards the exit. "Waiting to see Fr Seb. Saw you dealing. Pulled in closer, interested. I heard what the wee cunt said. Who the fuck does she think she is?"

Through the doors, looking for Tess, spotting her shuffling away from the church. Gawl pushed Clint ahead of him. Clint stumbled, head spinning. Turned to face the stranger. "Who the fuh-fuh-fuck are you? What duh-duh-duh-do –"

"No time," Gawl snarled, leaning in close, his breath foul in Clint's face. "I'll tell ye later. Right now ye have about a minute t' fix this. Ye have to catch that bitch, get yer dope back, teach her she cannae fuck wi' Clint fucking Smith."

"Huh-huh-how do you know muh-muh-my –"

"Don't argue," Gawl barked and shoved Clint ahead of him again. This time Clint didn't stop. He reeled forward, eyes locking on Tess, lumbering after her, Gawl close behind, urging him on, prodding him to make him go faster, Clint feeling like he was dreaming.

They caught up with Tess, fell in line a few paces behind. Tess didn't see them. Clint reached to grab her. Gawl stopped him. Shook his head. Mouthed the words, "Not yet." They slowed and dropped back, keeping a safe distance, Gawl studying the streets and buildings, Clint operating in a daze. As they approached a packed car park near the bottom of East Street, Gawl slapped Clint on the back, moved to one side, waited until the girl was walking past the cars, then darted forward, grabbed her, stuck a hand over her mouth, hauled her over the low bars of the car park, dragged her in between a cluster of cars and slammed her down on the ground hard, so she gasped for breath. Clint watched, stunned, then stepped over the bars and drifted across to where the stranger had the girl pinned.

"Get down, ye arsehole, before someone sees!"

Clint dropped to his knees. Tess struggled. Gawl released her mouth, then slapped her brutally, knocking her head sideways. "Thought ye could fuck wi' Clint

Smith, did ye?" he snarled, then punched her in the stomach. Tess' eyes shot wide, pain flaring, unable to breathe, terrified, but still clutching her purse, not prepared to abandon the drugs without a fight. "Get over here," Gawl grunted at Clint. He crawled across. "Look at this bitch," Gawl laughed, grabbing her cheeks and pinching them together. "Thinks she's lady fucking cool." Slapped her again, her eyelids fluttering, limbs spasming. Gawl snatched her purse from her fluttering fingers and gave it to Clint. "Take what's yers." Clint nodded weakly, opened the purse, rooted through. "Not like that," Gawl groaned. He grabbed the purse from Clint, upended it and shook it empty, then tossed it away. Clint spotted his baggie and pills among the mess of tissues and condoms. Scrambled for them and pocketed them. Tess moaned loudly. Gawl seized her by her throat and shook.

"OK," Clint wheezed. "I've guh-guh-got everything. Let's guh-guh-guh-go."

"Not so fucking fast," Gawl growled. "Kick her a few times first."

Clint blinked. "What?"

"Kick her. In the ribs." Gawl stood, keeping his head ducked, and demonstrated. Tess cried out with pain and threw up.

"Why?" Clint asked, genuinely confused.

"T' prove ye have power over her," Gawl said. "T' show her who's boss. T' make sure she never tries shit like this wi' ye again."

"But if someone spots us…" Clint looking around, worried.

"Fucking do it," Gawl snapped, grabbing the back of Clint's neck and squeezing hard. Clint yelped, then kicked out automatically. His foot struck Tess in the thigh and she shied away from him. "Good," Gawl murmured, not letting go. "Now a bit higher."

Clint kicked again, this time connecting with her stomach. To his shock he found himself grinning when she groaned. Without needing to be prompted, he kicked her again. And again. Losing himself to the moment, snarling, laying into her, paying her back not just for what she had done, but for what had happened with Phials and all the others over the years.

Gawl let go of the younger man's neck and watched with satisfaction as he struck the whimpering whore over and over. He thought about letting Clint go on until bones snapped, until blood pumped from her lips. But murder might be a step too far for the dealer. Gawl wanting to draw him in, not frighten him off.

"Enough," Gawl said, touching Clint's shoulder lightly.

Clint stopped and leant back against a car, dizzy-headed, smile fading. Fear crept back in. What would happen when she told the police? She knew his name. There was blood on his shoes. Probably security cameras around the car park. He started to shake, bravery deserting him.

"Don't worry," Gawl chuckled, reading Clint's mind. Pulled a knife and set it against the girl's throat. Waited for her eyes to swim back into focus, then made a shallow nick. She whimpered with pain and terror. "Ye say a word about this t' anyone," Gawl said softly, "and ye know what'll happen, don't ye?" He kneed the girl in the ribs when she didn't respond. "Don't ye!"

"Yes," she whimpered, curling up, sobbing, shivering, cold, wet, hollow.

"Women," Gawl laughed, clapping Clint on the back and guiding him out of the car park. "Ye just have t' know how t' treat 'em." Clint grinned weakly, pulling his jacket tight around himself, starting to shiver with aftershock. "C'mon," Gawl said, picking up the pace, hurrying Clint along.

"Wh-wh-wh-where are we guh-going?" Clint wheezed.

"A pub of course," Gawl snorted. "T' celebrate."

"Celebrate wh-wh-wh-what?"

"The death of a coward," Gawl laughed, "and the

birth of a fucking *man*."

Clint thought about that as they walked, then gazed up into the rough blue eyes of his grotesque saviour — and smiled.

THIRTY-ONE

Fucking Dan Bowen, making him work on a Saturday. Kevin had come *this* close to taking a pop at the little tyrant and bowing out on a bloody high. Only thing stopping him — without Clint's contacts, he and Tulip had to scout for new clients and rebuild their customer base. That would take time, and money wouldn't be as plentiful as it had been. He needed the job to tide them over. But once they'd re-established themselves, that was it, he'd quit in the middle of a shift, wait until it was really busy and some of the staff were out sick or on holidays, tell Bowen to go fuck himself and drop him in the shit.

Grinning at the thought as he trailed home, a grey Saturday, rain holding over from the day before. Maybe he'd tell Big Sandy that Bowen had been bothering them, set the giant on his case, see how Bowen dealt with that!

Thoughts turning away from Dan Bowen and towards Tulip as he swung on to Long Lane. Nothing planned for tonight but he'd get on the phone when he was home, make a few calls, try to arrange an appointment. Thursday with Laskey had been great, a forceful reminder of what Kevin had been missing, confirmation that he couldn't survive without the sexual element, needing his voyeurism more than a drug, on a high afterwards, oblivious to everything, including Tulip's distress.

Thinking of her tears as he rode the lift up to their apartment. She'd wept until she fell asleep, and again Friday morning. He'd stayed home with her for an hour, comforting her, going to work late (the reason Brown hit him with the Saturday shit), but his words had no effect. Tulip begged him to stop, set her free, seek help. He lied and said he'd consider it, but he knew she'd seen through him. He couldn't and wouldn't stop, not as long as he could get away with it.

Opening the door he heard voices, soft murmurs coming from Tulip's bedroom. There was someone with her. Kevin rushed to the door and barged in, thinking that Laskey or one of their other clients had found out where they lived. Stopped short when he saw a teenage girl on the bed with Tulip, the pair sitting cross-legged and talking. The girls stared at Kevin, Tulip hostile, the other girl curious.

"Hi," Kevin said weakly. "I heard you talking. I... I don't believe I know your friend?"

"This is Rita," Tulip said archly. "We went to school together."

Kevin smiled and nodded at the girl. She nodded shortly, squinting at him suspiciously. Kevin's stomach dropped. Had Tulip told her friend about them? He started to panic. Maintained his shaky smile. Not sure what to do.

"Rita will be leaving soon," Tulip said and gestured for him to get out.

Kevin half-waved to Rita, turned, closed the door, staggered to the TV room. If she'd told, that would be the end of him. He could control his sister, keep her quiet and compliant, but he couldn't do anything about her friend. If Tulip had told, Kevin knew it was over, Rita would talk to her friends, parents, teachers, police. They'd come for him, take Tulip away, lock him up.

His first instinct was to grab a knife from the kitchen, kill Rita, dump the body somewhere far from the apartment. Dismissing the thought almost as soon as it formed. He wasn't a man of violence, and even if he could bring himself to commit murder, Tulip would turn him in, he couldn't push her *that* far.

His next instinct, pack a bag quickly, as soon as Rita left, and get the hell out, don't tell Tulip where they were going, head for the countryside, somewhere far from London, rural, an old cottage, no telephone.

He heard the door of Tulip's room opening. The girls walked to the front door. Stood there a moment, talking, Kevin straining his ears. Heard Rita say, "Let me know," and Tulip reply, "I will." The door opened, closed. Tulip drifted into the TV room, arms crossed, looking distant. "How was work?"

Kevin opened his mouth to roar. Controlled his temper. Shrugged shakily. "The usual." Tried thinking of some similar conversational line. Couldn't. Came straight to the point but phrased his question casually. "Who was that?"

"I told you — Rita. We were at school together."

"I haven't seen her before."

"We talk on the phone, meet up occasionally when you're at work."

"How occasionally?"

"Not often."

"Here?"

"Usually at her place or a park or café."

Kevin trembled. "You go out when I'm at work?"

"Sometimes." Tulip stared at him oddly. "You didn't think I stayed in *all* the time, did you? Or only went out when I had to go shopping?"

That was exactly what Kevin thought but he didn't say so. "How many other friends do you have?" he asked instead.

"Not many," Tulip replied glumly. "Most of my old friends are still at school. Those who aren't tend to hang out with the people they go drinking and clubbing with.

It's hard to stay friends with people when you're not socialising with them."

"Why was Rita here today?"

"I asked her to come."

"Why?"

Tulip hesitated. "That's none of your business."

"I think it is," Kevin growled. "This is my apartment. I pay the bills. I want to know what she was doing here."

"It's my apartment too," Tulip said softly. "It was mine before it was yours. You left to get your own place."

"And came back to look after you when Dad died," Kevin reminded her, phrasing it softly, lovingly. "Why was she here, Tulip?"

Tulip crossed to the couch, sat, turned on the TV. "We were just talking."

"What about?"

"Girl talk."

"Did you tell her about us? Our appointments?"

Tulip gawped. "Are you crazy? You think I'd tell Rita – *anyone* – that I'm a junkie and a whore, that my brother watches me have sex and masturbates?"

Kevin relaxed. "I thought you might –"

"What we do is disgusting," Tulip interrupted ferociously. "I wouldn't dare tell anyone."

"You tell Fr Sebastian," Kevin reminded her.

"That's different. When I confess, I'm not speaking to him, I'm speaking to God." She turned off the TV and got to her feet.

"Where are you going?" Kevin asked.

"My room. I don't want to be with you right now."

Kevin half-rose to stop her. Sat again, letting her go, best not to upset her any further, give her a few hours to herself, let her calm down. Relieved she hadn't told her friend about them but still worried. He didn't want Tulip to have friends. Friends were dangerous. Thinking hard about how to get her away from Rita and any others and make her his alone, so he could keep her.

THIRTY-TWO

Gawl McCaskey, king of the fucking world! Quaffing champagne in Brown's in Shoreditch, Clint footing the bill, watching strippers gyrate on stage. Each girl circulated prior to going on, collecting a pound from everyone in the club, Clint tossing fivers to those he especially approved of, high on sex and champagne, bleary-eyed, grinning drowsily, hugging Gawl, blurting out every few minutes, "I can't believe we *did* that!" Gawl smiling condescendingly, the dealer getting on his nerves.

Ten pounds for a personal lap-dance in the back, twenty if you wanted two girls at the same time. Clint mad for it, dragging Gawl back with him, drooling as they went through their mechanical routines, Gawl as bored as the strippers but faking enthusiasm, cracking dirty jokes, making crude comments. The only time he put his foot down was when Clint wanted a black stripper. "I don't have anything to do with darkies," Gawl snarled and stormed off to the bar. Clint blinked dumbly, grinned apologetically at the stripper, paid her, then went after Gawl and bought more champagne, not commenting on his new friend's racist streak.

Gawl still couldn't believe how perfectly everything had worked out. Being there when the girl blackmailed Clint, seizing the moment, dragging Clint after her, the dealer amazed and gratified when Gawl showed him that he didn't have to be anyone's whipping horse, trailing after Gawl like a puppy. Even in Gawl's wildest fantasies it had never played out so smoothly. This morning Clint Smith didn't know who Gawl McCaskey was — now Clint hung on his every word.

They'd ducked into a local pub after the incident in the car park, Gawl forcing a few shots down Clint despite his protests, to keep him on a high. When he saw Clint's face turning a green shade, he switched to beer and slowed down. It was over the beer that Gawl told Clint his name and how he came to be in the church. "I know Fr Seb. I set him up with girls."

"I thought priests were celibate."

Gawl almost choked on his laughter. "Ye think a fucker who'll snort any shit ye gi'e him stops there? Does he fuck. *You* get him high, *I* get him laid."

"How do you know that I deal to him?"

"He talks, I listen. I watch too, always good t' know what people are up t'. I saw ye weeks ago in the church. Enquired after ye, thought ye might be a cop, out t' bust the horny fucker. When I learnt who ye were, I relaxed, but kept an eye open, worried ye might attract trouble. That's why I was eavesdropping. When I heard that wee bitch trying t' make shite of ye, I couldn't let her away with it. That would have been bad for you, and what's bad for you is bad for Fr Seb, and what's bad for Fr Seb is bad for me."

"So you didn't leap to my rescue out of the goodness of your heart."

"Did I fuck," Gawl laughed. "Always look out for number one. If ye can help others, fine, but first help yerself."

A few more pints, Gawl telling Clint about his past, presenting himself as a man of the world who'd seen and done it all, who had no time for the trappings of wealth. "Beer and pussy are all a man needs." Not mentioning that fighting was essential too, didn't want to give Clint the impression that he was overly violent.

When Clint was grinning drunkenly, Gawl led him to Brown's. Clint had been there a few times before but not often, no interest in the strippers, just in dealing, and strip joints not the best places to deal, most of the clients fixed on the women, sharp-eyed bouncers ready to bust you if they caught you working. Tonight was different. Feeling powerful after putting the would-be blackmailer in her place, he also felt horny. Wolf-whistled when he walked in and saw a half-naked girl on the small stage, twirling round a pole. Gawl steered him to the front, pushing others out of the way, ignoring their angry grunts. While Clint gawped, Gawl went to the bar and ordered pints. The champagne came later, when it was Clint's turn to buy. Gawl didn't like champagne – a woman's drink – but acted as if he did, let Clint spend big, toasting the young dealer, laughing as they quaffed, Clint getting seriously drunk, Gawl staying in control.

After several private dances and way too much champagne, Clint staggered off to the toilets to throw up. Gawl gazed around the club while Clint was absent, figuring his next play, wanting to keep the night alive, cement his friendship with Clint. Hit on the solution without too much hassle — get Clint laid.

He caught Clint as he was weaving back to the bar to order another bottle of champagne. Spun him towards the exit. "Where we going?" Clint mumbled.

"A place where we won't just have t' look," Gawl laughed.

Taking Clint on a long walk, the night air good for him, clearing his head. He got sick again, puked against a wall, groaned miserably when he was finished. Gawl spotted an off-licence, left Clint leaning against the wall, went and bought two cans of cider. Made Clint drink, even though he choked on his first mouthful. Poured it down him to line his stomach and keep him going for another few hours.

There were a number of local brothels Gawl could

have taken Clint to, but he led him to Susy-Lee's on the far side of Whitechapel, one of Fr Sebastian's favourite spots, the girls not as young as the priest liked, but willing to experiment. Susy-Lee herself was there to greet them, a gargantuan ex-hooker. Like many fat women, her smile was beautiful. "Who's your friend?" she asked as Gawl sat Clint in a chair. He was staring about uncertainly at the adverts for sun beds, manicures, facials and massages, not sure in his drunken state if this was a knocking shop or a legitimate beauty parlour.

"His name's Clint," Gawl said. "He wants a good time."

"Who doesn't?" Susy-Lee laughed. "Anything special?"

"No." Gawl lowered his voice, making sure Clint couldn't hear. "Just make sure he gets his fucking hole. I don't want him coming away dissatisfied, right?"

"I'll set one of my best girls on it," Susy-Lee said. "What's he drinking?"

Gawl studied Clint. His head was bobbing left and right, eyelids drooping, stomach heaving every time he breathed. "Just bring him some water." He saw Susy-Lee's frown. "Don't piss yerself. I'll tell him it's vodka and ye can charge him full whack."

"You're a gentleman, Mr McCaskey," Susy-Lee smiled and went to fill a shot glass with tap water.

Clint lost his nerve when the pretty, thin, black-haired

girl took his hands and tried pulling him to his feet. Remembering the last few times he'd tried to have sex, the failures. Mumbled something about having to go home. Gawl tried to laugh away his fears and force him to go with the girl.

"You don't understand," Clint whined. "I can't." Tears came to his eyes and Gawl realised what the problem was.

"Problems down below?" Gawl chuckled. "We've all had 'em. Can't let that stop ye."

"But..." Clint thumbed away tears, still hesitating.

Gawl hissed, "Remember earlier. Things are different now. Ye're strong, not weak. Women will do what ye tell 'em t'. Doesn't matter what happened before. Ye're a new man now. Ye don't take shit from anyone."

Clint's eyes cleared slightly. His jaw firmed. He nodded and went with her.

Gawl waiting for Clint in the lounge when he came back. "What was that like?"

"Brilliant," Clint mumbled, meaning it, no trouble this time, failures forgotten, a man once more. But his eyelids were heavy — he was ready for bed now.

Gawl took money from him to pay Susy-Lee for the drinks, asked her to arrange for a taxi, and rode home to Clint's with him. Clint fell asleep in the taxi and didn't wake when they got out, so Gawl had to drag him up the stairs, fish for the keys in his pocket, carry him into his flat and put him to bed, laying a bowl on the floor beside him, not bothering to undress him, Clint's clothes filthy and stinking, so what did it matter if he puked all over them.

Clint seen to, Gawl opened the front door to leave. Paused and thought about what Clint would feel like in the morning. He grinned sadistically — the hangover would serve the little whinger right. His grin turned thoughtful. If Gawl stayed, he could nurse Clint through the worst of his suffering, help clean up the mess, provide him with drinks – warm water and milk – cook for him in the afternoon, get painkillers if he didn't have any in stock. More importantly, as Clint's head cleared, be on hand to persuade him they'd done nothing wrong, the bitch had it coming, she wouldn't tell anyone, make sure he didn't panic and flee London ahead of an imagined posse, remind him that he was strong.

Gawl closed the door from the inside and went in search of blankets. Found some in a closet. Took them into the TV room, covered the couch with them, undressed and slipped beneath, naked, warm, happy. Lying in the darkness, planning the day ahead, how he'd nurse Clint through it and get him ready for another night on the town, smiling as he thought of his new role in life, *Florence fucking Nightingale!*

THIRTY-THREE

The lab, early afternoon, Big Sandy in the control centre with three technicians, all in plain clothes, chatting quietly to one another. The control centre was a large room near the rear of the building, connected to all the cameras and security devices in the lab, operatives constantly monitor-ing the situation, making sure everything ran smoothly, keeping watch on the hounds, observing Phials and his staff at work. There were a few blind spots — sectors in the basement, the sauna, Phials' bedroom and primary work station (an office come mini-lab where he did most of his formulating) — but not many. The Bush had tried installing hidden cameras in Phials' living and working quarters several times but the chemist always rooted them out, the equal of all the Bush's experts.

Big Sandy's mobile was in his left hand, tiny between his chunky fingers, waiting for Fast Eddie to contact him when Phials left his bedroom. The chemist a late starter, not shuffling down to work until two or three p.m. most days. No telling how long he'd work for when he rose, it could be an hour, six, twelve — no set pattern.

The mobile finally rang. "Yeah?"

"He's locked himself in his office and is hard at it," Fast Eddie said.

Big Sandy nodded curtly at the technicians. They stopped chattering and followed him through the corridors to Tony Phials' bedroom. This wasn't just where Phials slept. He spent most of his time here when not at work, watching TV, reading, writing. He kept a daily journal in a drawer near his bed, poems, stories, reminiscences. Fast Eddie had photographed much of the journal for the Bush to have examined, in case the entries were some form of code, but there was nothing cryptographic about them, just the scribbles of a bored man trying to fill the long hours between work and sleep.

The walls of Phials' bedroom were lined with stacked bookshelves and it was to these that the technicians beelined, spreading out wordlessly, each taking a section, working methodically from bottom to top, left to right, removing one book at a time, slowly riffling the pages, checking each page for notes or marks, then examining the spines and covers. When satisfied that no secrets were hidden within a book, they'd replace it exactly as it had stood and move on to the book next to it. Each man wore thin transparent gloves and a mask, careful not to even breathe on the books in case they left any kind of evidence.

They'd been working on the books for four days, Big Sandy standing guard, in touch with Fast Eddie, ready to move them out at a second's notice if he got word that Phials was returning. Big Sandy knew they were searching for a secret formula which the Bush thought Phials was keeping from him, but he wasn't sure what the formula was for. Guessed it was some new type of drug, but he didn't much care, not his business.

As disinterested as Big Sandy was, he paid absolute attention to the technicians while they worked. The Bush had been very clear about that. The formula was of the utmost importance to Dave Bushinsky and he didn't trust anyone who might be in a position to exploit it. "Watch them like a hawk," he'd told Big Sandy. "If they write anything down, take it from them before they leave. If they photograph something, grab their cameras. If they spend longer looking at one particular book than another, take it from them, put it back on its shelf, get them out of there and call me immediately."

Before the technicians hit the books, the Bush had sent in surveillance experts to scour the room for hidden panels or caches. They'd examined the bed, pillows, wardrobes, drawers, floorboards, TV, CD player, ceiling, window ledges, bath, sink, shower, working slowly and deliberately, Big Sandy watching over them. That had taken almost a week — nothing to report. At night, while Phials slept, a second team worked in his office, presided over by another of the Bush's most trusted men. Big Sandy hadn't asked how they were progressing, but he imagined they'd enjoyed no more luck than his own agents. The Bush would have called off the search here if he'd found what he was after there.

Three hours and thirty-eight minutes into the latest search, Big Sandy's phone rang, Phials on his way up. Big Sandy ushered out the technicians without any fuss and they returned to the control centre, where they'd wait in case Phials went back to work later, the technicians talking softly among themselves, Big Sandy sitting silently nearby, inhumanly patient, an unfeeling machine when he was working.

While Big Sandy and the technicians were taking up their accustomed positions in the control centre, Tony Phials entered his room and closed the door, leaving Fast Eddie to stand watch outside. He took off his clothes, walked through to his *en suite* and showered. Drying himself, he returned, naked, and drifted by the bookshelves where the scientists had been working, casting a cold eye over the books, cautious in case the Bush had installed another camera recently. The Bush's men were good – damn good – but Phials was a paranoid genius with an eye for the tiniest giveaway details, such as a pillow not lying precisely the way he'd arranged it, the remote control for the TV resting on the dressing table at a sixty-eight degree angle to the TV set when he'd clearly left it at sixty-six degrees, and books standing a few millimetres further in or out than they had been when he last scanned the shelves.

Phials knew what was happening. Bushinsky was losing patience. He needed the formula, believed Phials had perfected and stashed it, had sent in his goons to try to locate it. That was the first stage and it didn't bother Phials, let them search, they were doing no harm and they wouldn't find anything. It was the second stage – when they'd found nothing and Bushinsky had to decide whether to accept Phials at his word or increase the pressure on him – that freaked the lab-bound doctor. Because as thorough a job as Bushinsky's men were doing on Phials' living quarters, come the second stage they'd do just as thorough a job on *him*.

THIRTY-FOUR

Clint a man reborn, and loving it. A string of brothels this last fortnight, hungry for sex as he had never been before, feeling powerful, but also feeling that he had to keep proving to himself that he had changed, that he was a man who could do anything, that he wasn't the timid dealer he had once been. Always accompanied by Gawl. Hanging out with the Scot almost as intoxicating as rolling naked with the hookers. Clint had never had a friend like this. Gawl listened, understood, advised, cared. There were no barriers between them, the rough Scot like a father to Clint, closer to the young dealer than his real father had ever been.

He'd told Gawl about Shula. Gawl had flinched when he'd mentioned her name but Clint hadn't noticed. Gawl unusually quiet while Clint was raving about her, talking about his plans to win her heart, cursing the name of Larry Drake. He hadn't been to see her yet. He asked Gawl if he thought he should pay a visit. "I'd leave it a while," Gawl said, smiling sickly. "She's still probably upset about it. Gi'e her some time t' recover. Not the sort of thing a wee girl bounces back from quickly."

They'd meet most afternoons in a pub, have a few

beers, talk about their lives, their dreams, football, women, the news of the day. Some evenings Clint had to leave early to deal – he was spending more than usual, and didn't like digging into his savings too much – but they'd meet again later, have a few more drinks, move on to a strip joint or brothel, Gawl introducing the currently insatiable Clint to a variety of hookers, Clint not feeling the least bit unfaithful to Shula — he would never cheat on her if they became a couple, but to him there was no conflict in spreading himself around while he was single. At the end of the night Clint might do some more dealing or they'd hit another pub or club, then stagger home late to sleep it off. They usually went their separate ways but occasionally Gawl slept on Clint's couch. Clint had stayed at Gawl's one night when he'd got drunk in the King's Head, but Gawl's flat was a tip and he was in no hurry to spend another night there.

"Why don't you find a decent place to live?" Clint asked, a couple of days after his night in Gawl's. "Somewhere with hot water and heaters that work?"

"Luxuries make a man soft," Gawl laughed, then shrugged. "I don't plan t' grow auld there, but it'll do for the time being. I don't have the money t' rent and I can't be arsed looking for some flash squat with mod cons."

"I could cover your first month's rent," Clint said.

"Loan you enough to bide you over till you get back on your feet."

"I'm on my fucking feet," Gawl growled. "I don't need charity."

"I'm not suggesting a handout," Clint said quickly. "It'd be a loan. You could pay me back when you can afford it."

"And when would that be?" Gawl enquired sarcastically.

"Well... whenever you get a job."

They were drinking in a pub overlooking the Thames. Gawl paused at that point and gazed moodily over the brownish water of the river. "What d' ye think I've done t' get by all these years?" he asked softly.

"I don't know." Clint smiled. "Interior decorator?"

Gawl laughed. "Aye." Grew serious. "I did what I had t'. A lot of years on building sites and roads, breaking my back. When I wanted an easier ride, I stole."

"You're a thief?" Clint wasn't surprised.

"I've been one," Gawl corrected him. "I'm not at the moment. Wouldn't be living in the shit-hole that I am if I was stealing." Mixing truth with lies, wanting Clint to know parts of his life but not the whole.

"Why did you stop?" Clint asked.

"Got sick of prison. Spent some of my best years

there. Decided I didn't want t' die in a cell. I'm not saying I reformed – did I fuck – but I'm not that good a thief, always getting caught, no future in it. I never did find anything in life that I was much good at." Winked. "Except fucking and drinking."

"Here's to fucking and drinking," Clint cheered, downing the rest of his pint. All the beer was sickening him – waking with a hangover most mornings, stomach churning, mouth desert dry – but he wouldn't admit that. Besides, the hangovers and dodgy stomach were a small price to pay for what Gawl had brought into his life, self-confidence, friendship, strength. Clint was back to his slick best, making good money whenever he set his mind to it. Nervous in the Church of Sacred Martyrs that first Monday, but no sign of Tess, no police. Plain sailing after that.

It didn't take Clint long to tell Gawl of his American dreams, hitting New York in style, living as a gangster in a mansion, mounds of money, sending home for Shula. Gawl didn't laugh, only listened carefully, nodding thoughtfully. "How d' ye plan to finance the move?" he asked one night, as they caught a cab home.

"That's what I'm working on," Clint giggled then frowned. "*Was* working on. I knew a guy, thought I could use him. Things went to shit. Don't know what I'm going to do now. But something will come along."

Gawl knew Clint was talking about the garage and the black guy, but he said nothing, let it drop. A few nights later he steered talk round to America again. Told Clint of his own experiences there, how hard it was for a nobody, the brick walls he'd run into. "New York's teeming with muscle and dealers. What use would they have for the likes of ye and me?"

"You're thinking of going?" Clint asked, surprised.

"Half-thinking," Gawl chuckled. "Ye've got me excited, the way ye're always talking about it. I'm a bit long in the tooth t' be heading off on an adventure, but maybe one last trip before I retire disgracefully..."

Clint excited, discussing it with him the next few nights, eager to persuade Gawl to join him, certain he could make it if he had a partner. Clint waxed lyrical about women, money, the lifestyle. Gawl reminded him of their low position on the totem pole, constantly throwing their lack of cash and influence into Clint's face, waiting for him to start talking about the garage.

And eventually Clint told Gawl about Tony Phials, his meeting with cousin Dave, the promise of a couple of million if he could deliver the formula that Phials was working on, getting Phials high and trying to coax an answer out of him (he didn't mention Kevin and Tulip, and Gawl pretended not to know about them), Phials thwarting him, running him off, end of the dream.

"Not necessarily," Gawl disagreed, trying to figure out an angle, dreaming of what he could do with a slice of two million pounds. "The way ye tell it, ye're the only friend Phials has. Prison's a lonely place, ye take any friends ye can. He's mad at ye now but in time he might mellow, forget and forgive, accept ye back."

"It'll be too late," Clint sighed. "I've been reading the sports pages since Dave told me of his dream to buy Tottenham Hotspur. All the pundits agree that Sugar's going to sell soon."

"Fuck Spurs," Gawl snorted. "Fucking kikes, he's better off without 'em. When the dust settles he'll still want t' cut a deal with Phials and he'll find something else t' spend the money on."

"I don't think so," Clint said. "He plans to put Phials under pressure. If Phials *has* cracked the formula, he'll spill his guts. If he hasn't, he probably never will once Dave's interrogators are done with him. Dave knows this will be his last chance to pressure Phials if he goes down that route, which is why he hasn't set his team loose on the doc yet, hoping to get the formula some other way. But time's running out. He'll have to act soon if he wants Spurs, and he *does.*"

"Then ye have t' get yer arse in gear quick," Gawl

hissed. "Phone Phials. Drop in on him. Get back in his life. Get him talking. Try pumping him full of shit again — just because it failed once doesn't mean it'll fail twice."

"No," Clint said, shaking his head. "Best to forget about Tony Phials. I'm doing well dealing. I'd be making a fortune if I spent more time at it and stopped blowing my profits on women and champagne. Maybe you could work with me, be my back-up. If things go well I can tell Dave about you, he'll maybe give us more work, push some bigger deals our way. The reason he keeps me at this level is that he thinks I'm weak, and I guess in the past I have been. But with you I'm strong. Together we could make a real go of it."

"Maybe," Gawl muttered. A month or two earlier he'd have jumped at that chance. But he had the scent of a killing, the lab, Phials, millions. Hard to settle for peanuts when there were diamonds dangling almost within reach.

Clint didn't register Gawl's discontent. He only saw the pair of them working as a team, Gawl by his side protecting him, the two growing strong as one, Gawl needing him as much as he needed Gawl, never imagining that Gawl might see him as Clint saw Tony Phials, a pawn to be manipulated, a means to a personal ends, expendable. Intoxicated by the promise of his friendship with Gawl, blind to the very real dangers of it.

THIRTY-FIVE

Shopping with Tulip up Oxford Street, giving her a free head, telling her to buy what she liked, make-believe it was her birthday, not worry about the cost. She was suspicious – what was he after? – but soon forgot her suspicions in the shops and jewellery stores, trying on audacious outfits, Kevin beaming, checking out rare gem stones, grimacing good-naturedly. They returned home laden with bags, Tulip rushing straight to her bedroom to try on her new clothes and trinkets, Kevin collapsing on the couch in the TV room, calculating the cost of the shopping spree, trying not to wince.

He felt the extravagance was warranted, trying to buy Tulip's loyalty. If he kept her distracted – gave her everything she wanted in the way of material goods – he hoped to keep her happy. He'd been taking her for granted, not spoiling her, little wonder she'd turned to her friends for support.

Not naive enough to think the clothes and jewels would win her round entirely. A good start, nothing more. He'd have to pamper her, dazzle her with gifts, treats, surprises. A holiday would be good, somewhere sunny, a fortnight without any appointments. On reflection, maybe just a week, didn't think he could last a fortnight. Or perhaps they could arrange an appointment or two while on vacation, combine pleasure with need. Maybe Tulip would enjoy their liaisons if they were part of a laidback holiday. He knew in his heart she wouldn't – the scenic settings wouldn't alter the perverse nature of their relationship – but it was an idea.

A new apartment was another idea. Move out of London, away from Tulip's friends, somewhere pleasant, open fields, a more relaxed way of life. A new start would be beneficial for both of them and might serve to bring them even closer together. Without friends to meet with when Kevin was at work, Tulip would be desperate for his company, delighted to see him when he returned home.

The problem was money. He only realised how far off being able to afford a new start they were when he began checking into the possibility of selling up. He'd spent a lot of his recent free time on the phone to estate agents, sounding them out. Their apartment was well located but it was part of a council block. Also it needed a lot of work, and if he couldn't pay for the repairs (he couldn't) the new owner would have to foot the bill, which meant lowering the price further. He could definitely sell, but what could he buy with the profits? And how long could they survive on them?

Brooding about their lack of funds as he stretched

out on the couch, a headache building, trying to think of a way to generate more money. Surest way — pimp out Tulip, set her to work as a prostitute, take himself out of the sexual equation. But that was a non-starter. She wouldn't do it and he couldn't do it to her even if she would.

Perhaps they could schedule more appointments, try to cram as many into each week as they could, maybe do more than one a night, set up day appointments too. He could quit work if they were pulling three or four appointments a day. Save. Invest wisely. Move in a year or two when they were financially comfortable.

But could he hold on to Tulip that long? And would she tolerate three or four men a day? And how would he pay for holidays and gifts in the meantime? Groaning, rolling off the couch, heading for the medicine cabinet. Tulip came swanning out of her bedroom, twirling in a new dress — a week's wages. "What do you think?"

"Beautiful," he smiled weakly then hurried to the bathroom, popped pills, thought about his bank balance and how much today's shopping spree had eaten into it. Popped more pills, headache flaring.

THIRTY-SIX

"Have you ever killed a man?"

Gawl leant back on the couch in Clint's TV room and sighed. He'd been expecting the question, Clint building up to it for days. Nearly three weeks since Gawl injected himself into Clint Smith's life and made a man of the dealer. Three weeks of taking him to pubs, strippers, brothels, listening to him babble on about himself, pretending to be his friend. At first he'd found Clint almost impossible to tolerate – he despised weakness, and Clint was weak in every department – but his feelings had changed over the course of their conversations and boozing/screwing sessions. He still looked down upon the young man, but Clint was in awe of Gawl and idolised him, and Gawl was starting to get off on that. He'd never been hero-worshipped before. It pleased him to have Clint listen intently to his every utterance, attaching weight to what he said, respectful, obedient, trying to ape Gawl's gestures and expressions. He knew it was bullshit – the same nobody he'd been three weeks before, and no amount of wide-eyed wonder would change that – but fun to see himself through Clint's eyes, a man of importance, an authority on most issues, strong, confident, afraid of nothing.

Careful not to reveal too much about himself. Clint knew he could be fierce but he didn't know he was brutal. Gawl painted himself as a man of honour, merciless when he needed to be, but benevolent most of the time, peaceful unless provoked. All lies, but Gawl had to win Clint's trust and dependance, and the world for Clint was like the movies — gangsters were men of honour, with codes and ethics. That delusion helped Gawl manipulate him, so it had to be maintained.

At the same time he'd had to fill Clint in on parts of his violent past, so Clint would believe he was a man of action, a master of any situation. He'd gradually fed Clint relevant but edited facts, said he'd worked as a thief, done some mob work in the States, a few bank jobs, protection, served as a hired heavy in the UK, Europe, Australia. Mixing truth with lies, giving the impression that he'd moved around so much because he didn't enjoy being tied down, never mentioning the fact that he'd been run out of most places, that none of his bosses trusted him, that he'd always been hired for one-off jobs and rarely used again by his employers.

Gawl almost shat a brick when Clint brought up Shula Schimmel. He had been toying with the idea of mentioning that he'd recently raped a woman — given Clint's antics in the brothels, Gawl thought maybe that would impress him. Relieved that he'd thought better of it. A sleepless night worrying that Clint might somehow trace the rape back to him, that he might be setting himself up for his own downfall. But that was crazy. Nothing to tie him to what had happened. As long as he kept his mouth shut, Clint would never know. He pressed on as planned, kept talk of Shula to a minimum, changed the subject whenever Clint raised it, just not too obviously.

All the time trying to get Clint to talk about Phials and the lab, unable to let go of his dream of millions, sure there must be a way to crack the chemist. He'd suggested visiting the lab with Clint, having a go at torture before the Bush's men set to work on Phials, but Clint explained about Fast Eddie, the other guards, the security cameras. He didn't like discussing Phials – old news as far as he was concerned – and he kept steering talk away from him.

Earlier that night he'd asked about Gawl's name. Gawl admitted it was an invention, a derivation of Charles de Gaulle, while McCaskey was simply a name he liked. Said he'd had to change his name several times over the decades. Refused to reveal his real name, what Clint didn't know couldn't hurt him. That was when Clint came out with, "Have you ever killed a man?"

Gawl had anticipated the question and spent a lot of time preparing his answer. He fixed his pale blue eyes on Clint and said softly, "What do ye think?"

Clint gulped. Smiled shakily. "I think you probably have."

Gawl nodded sombrely. "More than one."

Clint held his smile. "Many?"

"A few." Gawl cracked his knuckles and adopted a faraway gaze. "I've killed for a variety of reasons. Self-defence. Because I was paid. Once, when I was young, I killed a man in a drunken brawl. I'm not proud of my record, but I never killed for kicks."

"And those you killed deserved to die?"

"Except for the guy in the fight, yeah."

"No women or children?"

Gawl rolled his head aside to hide a facial tic. "Of course not."

Lie heaped upon mistruth piled upon fantasy. Gawl an addicted killer, a ghoul who preyed on the weak. No children – they didn't interest him – but women? Oh yes. A couple of men in fights or the line of work. But mainly women. Eight of them. His slaughtered beauties.

The first in Glasgow, when he was a teenager. A tramp. Found her lying in the gutter, drunk, groaning. Nobody about. He rolled her for loose change, then, hands trembling, he choked her. He didn't mean to kill her. He kept expecting his fingers to part and slip away. But they locked together, throttling her, tightening further as she shook and wheezed and finally went still. Stayed closed long after she was dead, Gawl staring into her blank, open eyes, wondering if she was really dead or unconscious. Ran when he realised he'd killed her, from the corpse, the gutter, the alley, Glasgow. Terrified that he'd be caught and locked away for life. Hadn't killed again for several years, thinking a lot about it, coming to terms with the beast inside himself, controlling it, planning for the future.

Since then he'd killed seven times, different types of women, different cities. Careful to space them out, leaving long gaps between each murder, varying his routine, never choosing two who looked alike or killing them the same way. Most of them strangers, either women who knew him vaguely or not at all.

In an ideal world Gawl would have killed many more. Nothing fed his fires as much as taking a life. Strong as a god afterward, skin buzzing with electric elation. He'd have slaughtered one a week if possible but he knew he wasn't smart enough to beat the odds. He had to keep a tight rein on his hunger or fall victim to it. He'd be caught if he killed indiscriminately, locked away where there were no women, perhaps for life. Gawl didn't mind jail, not when he had the thought of freedom to look forward to, but if he'd been sent down for twenty years, thirty, life... insanity would have followed. The beast had to be fed. It could tolerate long intervals between feedings, but not decades. Gawl recognised this and allowed for it, planning his murders around the demands of his inner demon.

The beast hadn't mellowed with age. As hungry and demanding as ever. Gawl didn't know how many more lives he'd claim before death took him. If he stuck to his previous patterns, only one or two. Or perhaps the beast would demand a burst of chaos before the end, send him on a killing spree while he was still able, go out on a high, run the number up to fifteen, twenty, more. Gawl was hoping for a long, pampered retirement, but if the beast called for a murderous finale, so be it.

Gawl studied Clint, drinking a can of beer. Satisfied that Gawl was a conscientious killer, he'd moved on and was waffling again, talking of expanding with Gawl's help. Gawl smiled as he considered Clint's reaction if Gawl told him the truth about himself, that he was a serial killer, and by the way he'd raped the woman Clint claimed to love. Clint lived in a fantasy world. What a shock he'd get if Gawl opened his eyes to how the world really was. Would he run to cousin Dave for help? The police? Or would he take matters into his own hands? Gawl laughed as he pictured Clint coming at him with his puny fists, kicking and shrieking.

"What's funny?" Clint asked, gazing blearily at Gawl over the top of his can.

"Private joke," Gawl grunted and leant forward curiously, dragging talk back to murder. "Would *you* ever kill a man?"

Clint smiled nervously. "Only if I had to."

"But ye could if pushed?"

"I don't know. Maybe."

"If ye want t' make it t' the top the hard way — peddling drugs, dealing with the scum of the earth — ye'll have t' kill sooner or later. It goes with the territory."

"I guess." Clint looked unhappy.

"Of course if ye had a few million t' play with, ye could hire someone else t' do yer dirty work for ye..."

Sinking back in his chair, leaving Clint to muse about that, turning his own thoughts loose, lingering on the faces of the women he'd killed, remembering their death cries and shakes, smiling at the memories. Smile widening — looking ahead to a warm, crimson future.

december 2000

THIRTY-SEVEN

A taxi pulled up outside the lab and Dave Bushinsky stepped out, face as dark as the early December sky. From the other side Big Sandy emerged, yawning and stretching. It was afternoon but he'd been out late the night before with the Tynes. Unshaven and unwashed, as ordered. Dressed in black denim. Knuckles lightly smeared with vaseline to highlight his scars. The Bush stood aside while Big Sandy opened the outer door of the lab and pressed the button for the inner door. When that opened, both men entered, Fast Eddie closing the two open doors before following them into the lab.

"Where is he?" the Bush asked.

"At work."

"Take us."

Fast Eddie led the way to Tony Phials' office, standard sized, windows covered with posters and charts to block the view from outside. This was where he did most of his thinking. He'd never before been disturbed here, everyone in the lab under strict instructions to leave him alone when his brain was whirring.

The search of his quarters had yielded no results. No slips of paper, no secret codes, no hidden formulas. The search had concluded the night before, Wednesday. As soon as the Bush got the negative word, he phoned Big Sandy and told him the plan for Thursday. In a rush — if he was to buy into Spurs, it was now or never.

"You wait out here," the Bush told Fast Eddie, then rapped on the door and entered before Phials had a chance to respond.

The chemist's eyes widened with fear when he saw Dave Bushinsky and Big Sandy step into his office, then narrowed with relief. The Bush wouldn't place himself at the site of anything unpleasant. Phials had nothing to worry about — yet.

"Gentlemen," he welcomed them, shaking hands with the Bush, ignoring Big Sandy, who'd closed the door and was standing to attention in front of it. "I hope this is a social visit."

"I'm afraid not," the Bush said, taking a seat, smoothing out the creases in his trousers as he sat. Glanced at Phials seriously. "We need to talk."

Phials nodded and sat opposite his benefactor and captor. "So talk."

"The formula — I need it now."

Phials shrugged. "I'm doing my best."

"Are you?"

Steadily, "Yes."

The Bush looked away and muttered, "That might

not be good enough."

Phials sucked on his teeth. "Care to tell me what the rush is? When I started on this, I told you it would take time, I couldn't guarantee results, certainly couldn't commit to a deadline. You were fine with that."

"The situation has changed."

"In what way?"

The Bush smiled rufully. "You'd laugh if I told you." He looked at Phials semi-pleadingly. "I need this, Tony. I must have it. Now."

"But it isn't ready."

"Are you sure?"

"Why would I withhold it from you?"

The Bush maintained eye contact. "You know how valuable you are to me. I wouldn't sacrifice our friendship, even for something this big. There will be other drugs, other deals, more money to be made. I'm not going to cut off the neck of the goose that lays the golden eggs."

"I never assumed you would," Phials lied, playing it smooth, heart racing.

"You've no reason to be afraid of me, Tony."

"I'm not." Teeth chattering.

The Bush broke eye contact, gazed around the office. "How close do you think you are to cracking it?"

"It could be weeks, months, years." The Bush glanced at him sharply. Phials licked his lips hastily and grinned sickly. "More likely weeks or months."

The Bush grunted. "I wish I could believe you."

"I've never given you reason not to."

"Perhaps. Perhaps not." The Bush turned slowly until he was looking at Big Sandy, who stood impassively, staring at Phials. The chemist studied the giant of a man, his cold eyes, his scarred knuckles. Big Sandy looked more surly than usual — Julius had been chasing him about investments, and dealing with figures always put him in a foul mood. But Phials knew nothing about that. He thought Big Sandy was pissed at *him*.

"I swear," he mumbled, "if I could hand it to you right now, I would. I'd never cross you, I'm not dumb, I know the punishments if I tried to screw you. You've been good to me, afforded me sanctuary when everybody else turned me away, weaned me off the drugs, protected me from myself. Don't do this to me, Dave."

"Do what?" the Bush asked softly.

Phials shook his head. He couldn't answer.

The Bush leant across and gripped Phials' knee. "I have to know," he said. "I have to be sure."

Phials laughed chokingly. "Give me a polygraph test."

"You know how to fool the machines. You told me that

you did it before."

Phials winced, recalling his previous boasts. He should have kept his big mouth shut. "So what do we do?" he croaked. "How do I make you believe?"

"Deliver the formula."

"And if I can't?"

The Bush held his knee a moment longer then released it. "You have a week. Sandy, what day is it?"

"Thursday."

"Thursday," the Bush repeated thoughtfully as if making a spur of the moment decision. "I'll give you until Friday week. Nobody will interfere with you until then. On Friday morning Sandy will return and ask if you have anything for me. I hope you can tell him that you do."

The Bush stood and made for the door, not a hundred percent sure that he was playing this the right way, but needing the formula, the money, the means to buy the club he loved. If it blew up in his face, he'd accept the consequences. But he couldn't stand by idly, do nothing and just let the dream die.

Big Sandy opened the door for his boss and let him march out. Started to follow. Paused, turned back towards Phials and walked over, three giant strides. Phials stared at him, trembling. Big Sandy stuck out a hand. Phials didn't respond, so Big Sandy picked up the chemist's hand, smothered it with a massive paw and lightly crushed it, making Phials grimace, careful not to crack any bones. He let go and stepped back. "Best of luck, doc." A calculated pause. "See you soon."

Big Sandy exited and closed the door. The Bush was waiting outside. "You did it like I told you?"

"Yeah."

The two men returned to the taxi and went about their business. Tony Phials sat shaking in the lab for hours, not moving from his chair, eyes filled with tears, flashing forward to Friday week, imagining Big Sandy's hands at work, already feeling the pain. Finally snapped out of his self-pity, turned his thoughts inwards and put his brain to work, searching for a way out of the hell which awaited him.

THIRTY-EIGHT

Clint in a pub with Gawl, late Thursday, when his mobile rang. He switched it off without checking the incoming number and ordered another round. He was telling Gawl about Shula again, describing her to the uncomfortable Scot, talking about his plans to woo and win her. Gawl saying little, trying without success to change the subject. Hoping Clint never worked up the nerve to go see her, as he was threatening to do. Nightmarish visions of Clint sitting down with her, talk turning to the rape, Shula saying it hadn't been Larry Drake, instead some large guy with a Scottish accent and half a left ear, Clint stumbling to Dave Bushinsky to spill what he knew, the Bush's men coming for Gawl, his friendship with Clint the worst mistake he ever made. He was playing with fire. Afraid whenever the Shula subject came up that it was going to burn him to the bone.

Clint staggered home at two in the morning, drunk and happy, fell asleep on top of his bedsheets fully dressed. Slept until eleven, dreaming about Shula. In his dreams he overcame his shyness and went to see her, found out she was as keen on him as he was on her, flew off into an American sunset with her on his arm.

He woke with a splitting headache, and that was

when the smile disappeared and the dreams were temporarily shelved. Crawled to the toilet, hung his head over the rim, waited to see if he was going to be sick. When he didn't throw up, he stood, unzipped and pissed. Ransacked the medicine cabinet for aspirin. Downed a handful of pills with a glass of water. Back to bed, groaning, closed the curtains to shut out the dim light. Saw his mobile on the floor. Slowly stooped, picked it up, turned it on. Undressed and slid beneath the covers. Willed himself back to the refuge of sleep and the alluring world of Shula Schimmel. Then the mobile rang. He wanted to ignore it but thought it might be Gawl. Answered feebly, "Yeah?"

"Clint, it's Tony. Tony Phials."

A moment of stunned relief. Then he sat up sharply and his head exploded. Shut his eyes against the pain, fought it back, muttered into the phone, "Yuh-yeah?"

"How have you been?" Phials asked lightly.

"What do you wuh-want?" Clint groaned, in no mood for small talk.

"I'd like to see you. I need some grass. Maybe a hit of the Tynes too if they haven't run for the hills after last time."

Clint blinked at the phone, trying to piece an answer together.

"Clint? Are you there?"

"Yeah." Checked his watch but the numbers were blurred. "I'll cuh-come later."

"What time?"

"Later," Clint snapped.

"Don't forget the –"

He cut Phials off. Dropped the mobile. Lowered himself back, stared at the ceiling, feeling horrible. Ran the short conversation through his throbbing brain again. Smiled briefly as he realised this meant he was back in with Phials. Gawl would be pleased. Then he closed his eyes, focused on his breathing, waiting for the pills to kick in and the pain to recede, not prepared to move for anyone or anything until he felt at least halfway human again.

Early afternoon. The lab. Sitting with Phials in his bedroom, the chemist edgy, distracted, hadn't touched the grass which Clint had brought, playing with a can of Pepsi, picking at the ring-pull. Clint not sure what to say. Finally decided to try an apology. "I'm sorry for what huh-happened... you know... buh-buh-before."

Phials waved it away. "Have you spoken with the Tynes?"

"No. Kevin made it cluh-clear he didn't want to suh-see me again."

"I miss Tulip," Phials sighed and sat up straight, dark brown eyes clearing, coming to the point at last, his final gamble, all or nothing. "Your cousin came to visit me yesterday. I'm working to a deadline now. If I don't come up with the goods by next Friday, he throws me to the lions."

"Think you have a ch-ch-ch-chance?"

A sudden snap as Phials yanked the ring-pull off. He filled two glasses which were standing nearby, disposed of the can, handed one glass to Clint, saluted him. "Bottoms up."

"Cheers."

Both men drank. Phials drained his Pepsi in one quick gulp and spoke while Clint was still drinking. "I developed the drug months ago. I tested it on some bums off the street — Fast Eddie hauled them in for me. I gave them an overdose when I was done, to hide the evidence, but I clocked the results before I killed them. It works."

Clint spluttered a mouthful of Pepsi over his trousers and the floor. Gawped at Phials, astonished. "Wh-wh-wh-why are you tuh-telling —"

"It's a magnificent concoction," Phials interrupted softly. "I don't know what it will come to be known as, but I self-indulgently call it Baby P. Ten years from now we'll be a society of junkies, everyone will be doing it. It'll change the world completely."

"I don't understand. It's just a druh-drug. How —"

"Baby P produces a mild high," Phials continued. "I'm sure stronger versions will be manufactured later, but in its current form it produces nothing more than a pleasant buzz. No hallucinations, paranoia, queasiness or the sweats, just a long-lasting, relaxing high. That's not what makes it special." Phials chuckled. "How many genuine addicts do you know?"

"Loads," Clint said numbly.

"I doubt it." The chemist pursed his lips. "When you reduce it to the purest definition of the word, there aren't that many true addicts in the world, people who can't survive without their daily fix. Lots who need it bad, but very few who can't be rehabilitated. Baby P will change that."

"How?" Clint gasped, eyes alight. "Is it muh-more addictive than other drugs?"

"Not particularly," Phials sniffed. "Even if it was, we'd still only be able to sell to the converted, those who are looking for kicks. Baby P is the greatest drug ever because it's parasitic. That's how we'll convert those who don't want to party."

Clint frowned. "I duh-don't understand."

"It's destructive," Phials said softly. "The first hit you take, it starts to attack your system. It can't do much damage that first time, not unless you go crazy and hoover up a shitload of it, but by the third or fourth toke, you're fucked. Your body goes into meltdown. Death assured within forty-eight hours and there's fuck all any known doctor will be able to do to help."

Clint's jaw actually dropped. "What are you talking about? How's that going to change the world? Where will kuh-kuh-kuh-killing off our customers get us?"

"Nowhere," Phials giggled. "That's why we won't kill them off."

"But you just said –"

"Doctors won't be able to help," Phials interrupted sweetly. "Medicines won't help. Only one thing will keep the body ticking over. More that that, it will keep the user hale and hearty, in perfect health for as many years as they would have had even if they'd never taken the drug. Can you guess what that is, Clint?"

Clint shook his head. Then it clicked. "*Baby P,*" he wheezed.

Phials' smile grew legs and sprinted. "Correct," he crowed. "The poison is the cure. As long as you keep taking it, you'll be fine. Mildly high all the time, but hell, I think that'll be an improvement for most people."

"They wuh-won't take it," Clint mumbled. "Once word spreads and they know what it duh-does..."

"That's certainly a problem," Phials said, faking a troubled look. "I've never had much to do with the supply side of things, but I think the maufacturers will adopt a unique approach with Baby P. It's tasteless, odourless, it can be added to any food or drink and nobody will know. I reckon they'll cook up mountain-loads of the shit on various continents, then mix it in with every type of foodstuff they can lay their hands on, cereal, milk, flour, burgers, beer... maybe even Pepsi."

Clint flinched, glanced at his drink, looked up in a panic.

"Don't worry," Phials grinned. "As I said, one hit won't kill you, but even so I've not fed you any. I didn't want to cook it up, not with the Bush's men on the prowl, couldn't risk them finding it.

"Imagine, Clint, Baby P shipped out *en masse*, tens, maybe hundreds of million of people infected at the same time. Four or five bowls of cereal, cans of beer or servings of rice and they're ours for life. No choice but to pay up when we stop pumping it out for free and put the drug on the open market, hooked for as long as they live. Governments will go wild, there'll be the biggest public backlash ever, but we'll have them by the balls, they'll have to play along, they'll need us more than we need them, because if they stop us producing Baby P, everyone dies."

Clint's eyes grew round, seeing the true horror of it now, awed and appalled in equal measures. Phials watched the tumblers clicking inside the dealer's brain. He was smiling like a caterpillar. He knew he had Clint hooked, just as his monstrous Baby would hook so many others when it was unleashed on the world.

"If you're wondering why I'm telling you this," Phials said after a carefully judged pause, "it's because the information is worthless to you."

Clint blinked. "Huh?"

"You can't use it against me."

"I could tuh-tell Dave."

"To what end?"

"He pruh-promised me a sh-sh-sh-share. A muh-million pounds. Maybe two."

"I remember," Phials snorted. "Now you can see that what I said at the time was true — two million's peanuts for a wonder drug like this. But that's irrelevant, since you no longer have a stake to sell."

"How do you fuh-figure that?" Clint asked stiffly.

"The deadline," Phials reminded him. "Your only hope of getting in on the deal was to find out if I was hiding the formula from your cousin. He didn't want to threaten me in case it distracted me from my work, so he sent you to trick the truth out of me. For that he *might* have rewarded you. But now the threat's been made. The torturers stand poised. You could tell him what you know, but you'd only be saving him a few days. How much do you think he'll pay for that? How much is a week worth to any man, no matter how rich he might be? Knowing Dave as I do, I think he might toss you a few thousand to be kind."

"So you're telling me this just to spite me," Clint hissed, shaking with cold rage. "You're paying me back for what I duh-did with the Tynes." He stood and spat. "Fuck you tuh-too, doc. At least *I* won't be duh-dead this time next week."

"I don't want to die," Phials said quickly, grabbing Clint's sleeve. "But I *will* be executed, whatever way I play it. Exclusivity is essential if Baby P is to hold its value. Once Dave has the formula, he won't risk letting me fall into a competitor's hands." Clint stared at him suspiciously. Phials let go and lowered his gaze. "I didn't bring you here to mock you. I want to cut a deal."

Clint sat slowly, eyes tightening, brain churning. "What kind of a deal?"

"Freedom for the formula."

"You want me to put in a good word for you with Dave?" Clint frowned.

"No, you idiot," Phials snapped. "I want you to break me out."

Clint stared, slackjawed.

"I have contacts in the States," Phials said quickly. "If you get me out, we can sell the formula ourselves, split the profit fifty-fifty. We won't make the billions we could if we were manufacturing it, but we'll be able to demand way more than your cousin was going to pay. Fifty million dollars, maybe more. This is your chance to hit New York in style, as a man of substance. How'd you like to burn a trail through the Big Apple with twenty-five big ones in your back pocket? And a reputation second to none — Clint Smith, the man who delivered Baby P to the world. How do you think Shula Schimmel would view your advances then?"

"You're insane," Clint croaked.

"I'm a visionary."

"Cross cuh-cousin Dave — are you out of your fuh-fucking mind?"

"This may come as news to you, but your cousin's small shit, Clint. A big fish in London but a minnow elsewhere. Baby P would change that, but he's got no God-given right to it. If you get me out of here and we cut a deal with the right people, he won't be able to touch us. We'll be sharks."

"Even if I wuh-wanted to..." Clint muttered. "The security here..."

"It won't be easy. I know it's difficult. But they won't be expecting it. They don't suspect you. We have a week to work on a plan."

"If it wuh-went wrong..."

"Then you stand to lose everything. But think of your dreams of Shula and the States, weigh the possible losses against the potential gains. This is your title shot. Have you the balls to step into the ring and put your money where your mouth is?"

Clint said nothing. He was staring off into space, thinking about twenty-five million dollars, impossible to imagine so much cash. The world would be his. No way he could spend that much in one lifetime. He could gamble, invest, spread it about, do whatever the hell he wished.

"Go think it over," Phials said. He took Clint's elbow and guided him to the door. "Run it through the old brain cells. Sleep on it. Just remember the deadline, and that an offer like this will never come your way again."

Clint nodded and let himself out. He stood panting on the other side of the door, white-faced, head whirling. Fast Eddie stared at him. Clint shook himself and pushed on, thoughts spinning, mind afire, thinking *The Godfather*, thinking *Escape From Alcatraz*, thinking Shula Schimmel. Also thinking about the cost of failure, torment at the hands of cousin Dave's thugs, strung up alongside Phials, maybe fed to the hounds. Terrifying thoughts. But... twenty-five *million*...

On his way to the Church of Sacred Martyrs, having ducked home to get his wares, no reason not to keep his Friday clinic, wanting to stay busy, hoping that if he distracted himself he might find it easier to think clearly. Arriving late, he nodded apologies to his regulars, made himself comfortable, got on with business. Level-headed, the usual patter, whispering professionally as he dealt, no giveaway signs that his brain was shooting off in twenty-five million different directions all at once.

Towards the end Gawl stumbled into the church, looking rough. He waited for the last of Clint's customers to leave, then slid in beside the dealer. "How's the head?" he groaned.

"Fine," Clint answered softly. Studying Gawl, calculating. If he was going to bust Phials out, he'd need help. But could he trust the Scot? Did Gawl really have what it took? He'd changed Clint's life, and Clint wanted to cut him in for a slice of the action, but was he the right man for a challenge this size?

Clint was considering whether or not to mention his visit to the lab when Kevin and Tulip Tyne entered and passed them by. Gawl dug Clint in the ribs and nodded at the girl. "A tasty piece, right? I wouldn't mind a crack at a bird like that."

"Tulip Tyne," Clint said.

"Ye know her?"

"Yes. I could introduce you, but it would cost."

"She's on the game?" Gawl feigned astonishment.

"In a way." Clint thought again of telling Gawl about Baby P, then decided against it, wanting to mull it over before committing. He stood. "I fancy a pint."

"Will ye tell me about the girl?" Gawl asked.

"Yes. In the pub." Walked out of the church, confused, afraid, looking nothing like a man who held the future of the world in the palm of his hand.

In the pub with Gawl, drinking slowly, not much of a thirst, weighing up all of his options. Gawl unaware of the young dealer's state of mind as they discussed the Tynes. Clint told him about their sexual games — Gawl fascinated. Clint told him about their relationship with Phials — Gawl wondered if there was an angle.

Clint didn't mention his visit to the lab, but by the

end of the night he'd made up his mind. He didn't want to hit Gawl with this while he was inebriated. Wait for morning, take his proposal to Gawl, see what his friend had to say about it when they were sober and thinking straight.

Rolling out of a pub shortly after midnight, dizzy from beer and shorts, but not drunk, careful not to drink too much and spill the beans before he was ready. Gawl asked if he wanted to head to a club. Clint declined. Gawl's head still tender from the previous night's pub crawl, so he didn't argue. A cab home, drop Gawl off, on to Clint's flat. Clint fished out his mobile when he was indoors. Dialled the lab. One of Phials' minders answered. Clint asked for the doc. Moments later he was on the phone. "Yes?"

"I want to put Baby to bed," Clint giggled.

"Are you drunk?"

"No, just tipsy."

"Tipsy's not bad but sober's better. Phone again in the morning when your head is all the way clear. Or better still, drop in and see me."

"I will," Clint promised and cut the connection.

Clint didn't think he'd sleep, but he did, and his dreams were the sweetest ever. Got dressed in the morning and walked to Gawl's, roused him at what, for the Scot, was an ungodly hour. Gawl standing in the doorway, a sore head, scowling.

"Tony Phials contacted me yesterday and asked me to visit him at the lab."

Gawl's scowl disappeared and he stepped aside, inviting Clint in, the pact not yet struck but both men already smiling, the dangerous deal done in all but deed.

THIRTY-NINE

Nothing was going right for Kevin. Looking to make more appointments but finding it difficult to hang on to regular customers, never mind make new connections, many of his contacts out of town or low on funds or just not keen at the moment. Then Tulip caught a cold and was confined to bed for a few days, weak when she was recovering, not fit for anything.

Dan Bowen giving him grief at work. Kevin took some sick time off to look after Tulip, which irked his boss. Making Kevin work weekends and nights, threatening him with dismissal if he refused.

Gas bill. Electricity bill. *Medicine* (including real medicine for once) for Tulip. Kevin's dreams of moving to the countryside swiftly evaporating, wondering if he'd have to sell the apartment and move to an even smaller, less attractive flat. Savings dwindling, little coming in, Kevin growing desperate.

So when Clint surprisingly rang him on Saturday evening, Kevin didn't hang up immediately or chew him out. Instead he listened, grunting occasionally, as Clint apologised for the Phials cock-up then told him about a friend who'd like to try the sister and brother partnership. He couldn't afford to pay as much as Phials, but

Clint would consider this a favour and do all he could to repay Kevin and Tulip any way possible, set them up with a string of wealthy clients if Kevin could see his way clear to do business with him again.

"Well?" Clint asked at the end after several seconds of silence.

"Where?" Kevin asked.

"Your place."

"No. We never entertain here. We always go to the client."

"I know, but that won't work this time."

"Why not?"

"He has a wife, so he can't do it at home."

"Then let him hire a hotel room."

"He can book a room if you insist, but that will have to come out of the money he's paying, so you'll have to do it for even less. If you're OK with that, it makes no difference to me."

Kevin thought about that, then thought about his bank balance. Wanted to let the customer come to them, but wary of going down that route and attracting the attention of their neighbours. "He can deduct fifty for the hotel room."

"That might not be enough," Clint said.

"It will have to be. Book a room and let me know."

Then Kevin hung up and went to tell Tulip. She wouldn't like it. She'd probably pretend to still be sick. But they needed the money. And Kevin had the familiar itch that always demanded to be scratched. He'd persuade her.

FORTY

Gawl spent Saturday quizzing Clint about the lab. How many cameras and where? How many guards and where? How many windows and where? Were they wired? Any roof entrances? Was there a garden out back where Phials could go for fresh air? Any way into the cellar from outside?

Not keen on the idea of breaking out the chemist — too much could go wrong. But he agreed with Phials that Clint could expect nothing more than loose change if he went to his cousin with this now. Trying to figure another way for them to make a profit. He considered tipping off one of the Bush's competitors, selling the location of the lab to them, leaving them to do the dirty work. But how to get their story taken seriously? Clint had no samples of the supposed wonder drug, and neither man could expect to be taken at his word.

"We need the formula," Gawl grunted. "Get Phials t' write it down. We can slip something into his grass, finish him off, take the formula, sell it ourselves."

"Kill him?" Clint didn't like the sound of that. "He's my friend."

"Don't talk shite. He's an ally or an obstacle, but he's no fucking friend. If we get the formula, we won't need him. A lot simpler that way."

"But he won't give it to us," Clint argued. "Even if he did, who could we sell it to? He has contacts in the States. Who do we have?"

"We could sell it t' yer cousin," Gawl suggested.

"He'd kill us," Clint sniffed. "Even if he agreed a deal, we'd only get a couple of million tops. Phials is promising us twenty-five million dollars, maybe more."

"A fair chunk," Gawl chuckled. His eyes narrowed. "Maybe too much."

Clint frowned. "How can it be too bloody much?"

"Two million's a reasonable sum t' people like yer cousin. Fifty's a different story. Ye don't dole out that sort of money unless ye absolutely have t'. I'd rather a guaranteed million than a pie-in-the-sky twenty-five."

But he had to agree that the chances of Phials handing them the formula while he remained imprisoned were slim. So he put his doubts about the aftermath aside and focused on the possibility of freeing the chemist.

"It's not a real prison," he mused. "He isn't under lock and key in a cell. The lab isn't a fortress. We could knock through a wall or the roof, go in with a team, shoot down anyone who got in our way, frogmarch him out."

"But where do we get the team?" Clint asked.

"Exactly." Gawl sipped from a bottle of cider, trying

to think leisurely, letting ideas come freely. "We can't hire the fucking A-Team. If we do this, we do it by ourselves, maybe one or two others, though I don't like the idea of involving anybody else, too many opportunities for a double-cross."

And assuming they freed him, where would they stash him? How would they get him out of the country?

"Why not hide him here?" Clint asked.

"We probably won't be able t' do this anonymously," Gawl explained. "We'll be seen, identified, pursued."

"But nobody knows where you live, do they?"

"A few do."

"So we find a hotel or boarding house."

"Ye think yer cousin won't check every hotel and boarding house in London?"

"He can't check them *all*," Clint chuckled.

"He fucking can," Gawl snorted. "He'll put out descriptions of us. Set a reward that'll have yer own fucking mother sniffing around after ye, eager t' turn ye in. Don't be under any fucking delusions, we're putting our heads on the block. If we do this, we have t' plan for every possible hitch. We'll need a place t' hide, maybe for months until the heat dies down. Phials will need drugs during that time. We'll need food, drink, other supplies. But we'll all be housebound, unable t' go out."

"We need a safe haven," Clint mused. "Somebody working with us but who isn't part of the break-out, who can house us and shop for us."

"And smuggle us out when it's time," Gawl nodded.

Clint didn't have to think long about that. "It's obvious," he grinned. "Father Sebastian. He's tied to both of us but nobody knows. He could put us up behind the church. Nobody would suspect a priest. It's perfect."

"Could we trust the wee fucker?" Gawl growled. "He hates my guts. By selling us out t' the Bush, he could get rid of us both and make a powerful friend at the same time, line his pockets with cash…"

"He wouldn't dare," Clint said confidently. "We'd tell Dave about his fondness for little girls. He knows Dave wouldn't stand for that."

"And if he calls our bluff?"

"He won't."

Gawl pulled a face. "Remember what I said, we have t' plan for every hitch. What if he decided t' go t' the Bush, gamble on us not living long enough to talk?" Gawl scratched his chin hard. "Father Seb's a good idea but we'd need some form of insurance, something t' tie him tight t' us."

"Like what?"

"I don't know," Gawl sighed.

And the discussions continued.

*

Later in the day, making some progress but not much. Gawl could get his hands on guns, maybe some explosives, but guns no good unless they could get inside the lab, and neither of them knew anything about dynamite. Clint suggested bringing in an expert, to which Gawl said, "Ye know any explosives experts?"

"No."

"Me neither. So shut the fuck up."

Getting snappier as the day wore on, racking his brains, coming up blank. Trying to keep it simple, at a level he could deal with. Most direct method — kick down the door, storm the lab, drag Phials out. But the door couldn't be kicked down, it was too sturdy. Clint could buzz to be admitted, Gawl could wait outside, rush in after him, open fire. But security always tight at the lab, no chances taken, Phials usually never permitted anywhere near the door when it was open.

"What if we drugged the guards?" Clint said. "Phials could cook something up to knock them unconscious. Then he could simply open the door himself and walk straight out."

"If he could do that, he'd have done it by now and wouldn't have come begging for help. They probably eat at different times, never all together, or they test the food or some shit like that."

"What if I went in by myself, smuggled a couple of guns in, and Phials and I shot our way out?"

"How would ye smuggle the guns in? Stick 'em up yer arse?"

"There must be some way," Clint pouted.

"If we had state of the art guns, which we could disassemble and reassemble, aye, it'd be child's play. But we'll be looking at rusty auld revolvers because that's all we know how t' get our hands on."

"What if I set a fire? We could sneak out in the confusion."

"Is there a sprinkler system?"

"Yes, but I could fiddle with it, disable it."

"Any idea how ye'd do that?"

"No. But what if I set a monstrous fire that the sprinklers couldn't cope with?"

"How d' ye plan on getting out of there ahead of the flames?"

Hitting a brick wall whichever way they ran at it. Finally, in the evening, frustrated, Gawl suggested they head to a pub. "Let's get rat-arsed. Genius might strike while we're drunk or hungover."

"I doubt it," Clint said miserably. "I'd rather keep a

clear head."

"We're going mad in here. Let's go out for a few pints at least."

"You can if you want. I'm staying."

"Ye've got t' learn t' relax," Gawl grunted. "If ye can't see a thing from the front, ye have t' come at it from the side. We need t' unwind, have a few beers, get laid, give our brains a..."

He stopped, flashing on an image of Tulip and Kevin Tyne in the church the day before, Clint telling him about their double act. He'd thought a lot about them that night, hot for the girl but no interest in her brother. Talk of Baby P and Phials had driven them from his mind, but now he returned to the brother and sister act, something about the pair niggling away deep in his brain.

"How often do the Tynes visit Phials?"

Clint shrugged. "Kevin and Tulip? They haven't been since our bust-up."

"But when they *were* visiting — how often?"

"Maybe a couple of times a week, depending on how horny Phials was."

"What's security like when they visit?"

"The same as always, except when Fast Eddie was away, looser then, which is how I smuggled in the drugs."

"How many guards on the door when they enter?"

"Usually just Fast Eddie."

"And if he's not there?"

"Somebody else. Maybe a couple."

"The rest of the guards?"

"In the games room or the control centre or on patrol. Why?"

Gawl shook his head. "Just thinking out loud." Matching the Tynes to Tony Phials, then matching them to Father Sebastian. An idea germinating, only the ghost of one, but his instinct was to run with it. "I want t' check out the Tynes."

Clint blinked, bewildered. "Now?"

"Aye, if they'll see me."

"Don't you think we should –"

"Like I told ye," Gawl cut in, "we need t' relax. Ye can sit here and stew if ye like, but I plan t' get laid."

"So let's go to a brothel. I haven't spoken with Kevin since –"

"Clint." Steady. Steely. "D' ye trust me?"

Clint stared back uncertainly. "Yuh-yes."

"Then don't ask questions. Get on the phone t' Kevin Tyne. Arrange a meeting. Apologise for what happened with Phials. Beg for forgiveness. Make things right. Get me in, their gaff if ye can swing it, though we can go t' a hotel if not."

Clint nodded slowly. Got his mobile out. Paused. "You're not just going there to fuck the girl, are you? This ties in with Phials?"

"Aye."

"That's all I needed to know." Clint dialled Kevin's number, prepared to eat crow and say whatever he had to, trusting Gawl implicitly.

FORTY-ONE

Big Sandy dropped by the lab Sunday afternoon, strolled by Phials at work, smiled icily at the chemist and nodded. Phials shook, nodded back, scurried away quickly. Big Sandy's job to keep him scared, wind him up, crack him psychologically, save them the messy task of having to torture him. Big Sandy playing the part of the would-be torturer, though he wouldn't actually have much to do with it if they got that far. He was a brute force, a human wrecking ball. Phials' tormentor would be a man with smaller hands, more guile, an artist of infliction.

Checking with Fast Eddie, who was keeping a closer eye than usual on Phials, monitoring his behaviour. Fast Eddie said he hadn't been acting any differently, though he'd arranged a meeting with Clint Smith on Friday after a few weeks of no contact. Big Sandy saw nothing suspicious in that, Phials nervous, caught between a rock and a hard place, only natural that he'd seek the relief of his beloved weed.

"Maybe we should ban Clint till this is over," Fast Eddie suggested. "Increase the tension by denying him his regular hit."

Big Sandy considered that. "No. He might slit his

wrists if we push him too hard. Let Smith come."

"You think Phials knows the formula?" Fast Eddie asked.

"No idea or interest," Big Sandy sniffed.

"How long do you think he'll let this run if he does?" Fast Eddie persisted.

"Does it matter?"

"We've got a book going. The pot goes to the guy who calls it closest."

"I'd never bet on a man's life," Big Sandy said stiffly. Squinted and thought about it. "But I'd say he'll run it to the wire, even to the first stages of torture. If he's kept the formula to himself this long, he's not going to give it up cheaply. He'll only spill once he realises the Bush is prepared to ride him all the way."

"So you reckon he'll crack during the first hour of torture?"

"Yeah."

"Put money on it?"

Big Sandy shook his head. "Like I said, I don't bet on men's lives."

Thinking about Phials on and off for the rest of the day. Also thinking about God. Would he come to Phials in his hour of need? Murmur to him, as the Bush's man set to work, "This is it, Tony, enough's enough. You made a noble stand, now tell them what they want to know and spare yourself the rest." Big Sandy thought there were moments in everyone's life when an inner voice kicked in. Was that God whispering in your ear?

And what if Phials *couldn't* produce the formula? Would God reveal it to him at the last moment? Would God take pity on the chemist? Big Sandy didn't think so. God didn't work that way. Big Sandy didn't believe in miracles, only in God's good advice, which individuals were free to heed or ignore as they saw fit.

A quiet night in, watching TV, thinking about God and Phials, a difficult time getting to sleep. Still had the chemist in his thoughts the next morning, so he made his way to the Church of Sacred Martyrs to sit alone and brood. After a couple of hours of peaceful meditation he spotted Clint Smith entering. Smith slipped into the confessional, where Fr Sebastian was holding court, then to a pew near the back of the church. Big Sandy frowned. He'd never made Clint for a Christian. His frown darkened as he saw a teenage boy slide up to Clint, slip him money and take a baggie. The little bastard was dealing. The house of God, and he was treating it like a skanky pub.

Big Sandy filled with rage. Did Fr Sebastian know about this? Not knowing about the priest's unseemly habits, Big Sandy doubted it. Churches were a place of privacy, where people didn't interfere with those who wanted to pray quietly. That was why he felt comfortable coming here, knowing he wouldn't be bothered. He figured Smith was operating without Fr Sebastian's knowledge, no reason why the priest should have a clue what was going on, especially as he spent most of his time on this day of the week inside the confessional. Clint had seen a chance to manipulate the system and taken advantage of it, not caring that he was making a mockery of the church, flicking God the finger and demeaning his house on Earth. But Big Sandy *did* care.

Big Sandy rose, intent on storming to the back of the church, dragging Smith out, pummelling him to within an inch of his life, driving him off forever, putting the literal fear of God into him. Stopped when he saw a familiar couple enter — Kevin and Tulip Tyne. Sat again, not wanting to lay into Smith in front of Tulip, spare her the sight of violence. He watched Smith closely. Saw Kevin take a pew close to the dealer, waiting in line behind two junkies.

Tulip rose and headed for the altar. Spotted Big Sandy. With a surprised smile she genuflected then slid in beside him. "Hello."

"Hi," he grunted. "How are you?"

"OK." Tulip sounded downcast. She wasn't facing him directly, head tilted, jaw shaking lightly. Big Sandy reached across, gently took hold of her chin, turned her head around. Her left cheek was bruised, scratches on her neck.

"Kevin?" he asked quietly, releasing her.

"No." She looked over her shoulder, tears in her eyes. "A client. Clint sent him to us. He came on Saturday and again last night. He was fine the first time but last night he hurt me, didn't stop when we told him to."

"Why didn't you call me?"

"Too late by the time we realised he was a threat. I think Kevin wants to talk with you about it after he's done with Clint. It's good that you're here."

"A nice coincidence."

"Or God's handiwork."

"No," Big Sandy said softly. "If God was going to get involved, he'd have had me there when you were being hurt, so I could have stopped it."

"It's not that bad." Tulip smiled painfully, lightly touching the bruise.

Big Sandy glanced around. Kevin was next in line, waiting impatiently. Big Sandy noted Kevin's dark features and took a small measure of comfort from them. At least he wasn't a willing participant in his sister's beating.

"Does Smith deal here often?" Big Sandy asked.

"Every Monday, Wednesday and Friday."

Fr Sebastian's confessional days. Confirming what Big Sandy believed, that the priest was unaware of this, locked inside his box whenever Clint was in the church.

"Been doing it long?"

"A few months."

Big Sandy breathed out through his nostrils, angry. "He won't be doing it much longer."

"You won't...?" Tulip gasped, thinking he meant to kill the dealer.

"No." Big Sandy chuckled. "Just teach him a few harsh facts of life." Though if Smith hadn't been related to the Bush, he might have taken it a stage further.

Silence, Tulip praying, Big Sandy keeping an eye on Smith. He saw Kevin Tyne sit beside him, a brief, abrasive conversation, Kevin making sharp gestures with his hands, Smith nodding weakly. Smith thrust money and a baggie at Kevin. Kevin relaxed slightly and pocketed the cash and drugs, snapped something again. Smith nodded and offered Kevin his hand. Kevin ignored it, stood and marched away. Smith stared after him, then slid out of his pew and hurried from the church, ignoring his other clients. Big Sandy keen to follow, but Kevin was striding towards them and Tulip had said her brother wanted to speak with him. So he stayed seated and let the dealer pass unchallenged.

Kevin registered surprise when he saw Big Sandy sitting next to Tulip, then smiled and slipped in beside them. "I was going to phone you later."

"Tulip's been telling me."

"You saw what that bastard did?" Kevin snarled, wrapping a defensive arm around her. "He's an animal."

"Who was it?" Big Sandy asked.

"A guy called Gawl McCaskey. Scottish. Large, ugly bastard. Half his left ear is missing. Know him?"

"Heard of him." Eyes Burton had said something about McCaskey to the Bush, that he was looking for work. Hadn't recommended him, just told the Bush about him and left it at that.

"Somebody should teach that prick a lesson," Clint hissed.

"He couldn't have done it if you hadn't set him up with Tulip," Big Sandy retorted softly.

Kevin stiffened. "You're not going to do anything?"

Big Sandy sighed. "What did Smith have to say?"

"Full of apologies," Kevin snorted. "Tried to pay me off. Said he hadn't known McCaskey was violent. Promised he wouldn't send him our way again. But that's not enough. Somebody should do to him what he did to

Tulip. Animal!"

"I'll have a word," Big Sandy said. "Do you know where he lives?"

"No."

"I'll ask around, but it'll be next week before I can follow up." Under orders not to draw attention to himself until after Friday. "Will you need me any time soon?"

Kevin sighed. "I doubt it. I want to give Tulip a rest after what that bastard did. Besides, with her face like that..."

"You're all heart," Big Sandy said frostily. Smiled at Tulip. "You'll be OK?"

"Yes," she smiled back.

"Call me the next time you want to get into the ring with one of these beasts."

"I never want to get into the ring," Tulip said, glancing sharply at Kevin, then down at her crossed hands. Closed her eyes and prayed.

Big Sandy stood, nodded farewell to Kevin, let himself out. Checked for Smith in case he was hanging around but there was no sign of him. Clint Smith and Gawl McCaskey, two small, personal problems he'd have to deal with. Smith the more irritating of the two. A man who paid for the pleasure of a whore had a right to expect a certain leeway. McCaskey had overstepped the line by getting rough with Tulip, but it wasn't like he'd assaulted an innocent. A strongly worded warning not to do it again would suffice. But Smith, dealing in a church, spreading poison through the parish... that was a different matter. Smith deserved what Phials had coming, a shitload of pain. After the weekend, Big Sandy would see that he got it.

FORTY-TWO

Gawl was chuckling sadistically when he returned from his second visit to the Tynes late Sunday night. Told Clint to expect an angry phone call in the morning, maybe even a visit. Clint asked what had happened but Gawl wouldn't elaborate. Clint growing impatient. Gawl had said nothing about the break-out since going to see Kevin and Tulip for the first time on Saturday. He started to complain but Gawl silenced him by giving him instructions for Monday. "Go see Fr Seb when ye're at church. Tell him ye may need him t' put up a few friends and yerself for a while. Tell him t' stock up on supplies, stay in after dark, not t' be surprised if there's a knock on his door late one night."

"What if he wuh-won't do that?"

"Don't give him a choice. Tell him it's gonna happen and there's fuck all he can do t' stop it. Say ye don't want any trouble, just t' lie low a while. Don't say how long ye plan t' stay or what it's in connection with. And don't mention me."

"Will I tell him how many to expect?"

"No."

"Do *you* know how many?"

Gawl laughed. "I have a good idea." He moved on.

"Visit Phials after that. Tell him ye're working on a plan, so he doesn't get desperate and do something stupid. I don't know what night yet, probably Tuesday or Wednesday, don't want t' leave it till Thursday, that'd be cutting it too tight."

"And if he asks about the pluh-pluh-pluh-plan?"

"Say ye're still working on it. Tell him ye'll drop by t' discuss it with him in advance, once ye have it clear inside yer head." Gawl paused. "And ask him if he has any thoughts for getting Fast Eddie out of the way. I'd rather not have t' deal with him at the door."

Clint slept little that night, full of doubts and fears, worrying about the break-out, wondering what Gawl was planning, imagining all the things that could go wrong. Terrified, wanting to call the whole thing off, but the thought of twenty-five million dollars keeping him on track.

On Monday he turned up at the Church of Sacred Martyrs at the normal time. Headed straight for the confessional, where Fr Sebastian was waiting for heroin. "Bless me Father, for I bring sin. Want to shoot up?"

"You're late," Fr Sebastian snapped, sticking a hand over the top of the dividing wall, a gap of several inches between that and the ceiling.

"No I'm not," Clint chuckled. "The anticipation screws

up your sense of time."

Fr Sebastian grunted and tossed a wad of notes over to Clint. Clint tossed them back. A cautious pause, then Fr Sebastian said, "What do you want?"

"Sanctuary."

"Don't fuck me about," the priest snarled.

"I'm suh-serious. I'm going to need a safe hiding place soon, me and a few others. I was huh-hoping you'd be charitable enough to put us up in your –"

The money came flying back over the top of the divide. "No. I'll pay the way I always have."

Clint gently pushed the money back at the priest, standing on tip-toe to reach over. "This isn't a debate, Father. You do as I say or I stop dealing."

"I'll find another dealer. The streets are awash with scum."

"You'll hurt my fuh-feelings." Clint pressed his face close against the mesh. "We'll come at night, before the weekend. Be ruh-ready for us. Get in food and drink. Prepare beds. Make sure you're alone."

"I said I wouldn't –"

"I know about your fuh-fondness for young girls." The priest went quiet. "I've been waiting for the right opportunity to make use of that knowledge. This is the tuh-time. Welcome me and my friends and I'll forget about your other weakness."

Silence. Heavy breathing. Then, "How many of you?"

Clint smiled in the gloom. "Probably no more than six or seven. Maybe less."

"How long for?"

"I don't know."

"Who will you be hiding from?"

Clint rose without answering. "See you soon, Father. Keep a candle burning in the window." Slipped out before the priest could curse. Took his regular position near the back of the church, did some deals, pleased with himself for the way he'd handled Parry, growing in confidence, starting to believe in himself again, that he could pull this off, that the dream could become a reality. Then Kevin Tyne was beside him, face black with rage. "Don't ever send that fucker our way again."

Clint flinched, alarmed. "Kuh-kuh-kuh-Kevin. Wh-wh-what do —"

"That bastard hurt Tulip. He fucked her hard and slapped her around."

"Guh-guh-guh-Gawl?"

"You've some fucking nerve, sending an animal like him to us after what happened with Phials."

"I duh-duh-don't understand. I duh-didn't know."

"I won't let anyone hurt Tulip," Kevin seethed. "I'm

going to tell Big Sandy about the beast, send him round to fuck McCaskey up."

"No," Clint gasped. Stuck his hands in his pockets, grabbed cash and a baggie, shoved them at Kevin. "Here. Take it ah-ah-ah-all. I'm suh-suh-sorry. I wuh-wuh-wuh-wuh-wouldn't have suh-sent him if I'd known."

Kevin stared at the money and drugs, thought about throwing them back in Clint's face, then thought of all the treats he'd bought for Tulip recently. Pocketed the bribe, relaxing slightly. "You can't buy me off that cheaply," he huffed.

"I'm not truh-trying to. It's an apology."

"I don't want to see him again."

Clint nodded. "I'll tuh-tuh-tell him. But don't tuh-tell Big Sandy. No nuh-nuh-nuh-need to involve outsiders."

"We'll see," Kevin sneered.

Clint stuck out a hand in hope. Kevin ignored it and stormed up the aisle. Clint breathed a sigh of relief and got out quick. Wondering if Gawl's brutality had been calculated or just his natural way with women, if he really planned to use the Tynes to break Phials out or if he was just getting off on their weird sex act. Decided not to pursue the line of thought. He had to trust his partner, couldn't afford to have doubts. So he headed for the lab, walking fast, thinking of the day when he wouldn't have to sit and take shit from the likes of Kevin Tyne.

*

Fast Eddie on the door as usual. Clint wondered where he lived and if he ever took time off, always here except for that time when he'd had to flee London, Clint not sure but reckoning it must have been linked to the disappearance of Larry Drake. Decided to ask as they were walking up the stairs. "Are you a prisoner here tuh-too?"

Fast Eddie glanced at him. "Come again?"

"You always suh-seem to be on duty."

"It's my job," Fast Eddie said coolly.

"But surely you get the odd duh-day off? Don't you have a huh-home to go to?"

"Why are you asking?"

Clint shrugged. "Just curious."

"Don't worry about my personal life," Fast Eddie said. "It's none of your business."

"No need to buh-buh-buh-bite my huh-head off," Clint complained.

"I don't like people asking questions."

Clint pulled a face. "Fuh-fuh-forget I asked. Touchy fuh-fuh-fuh-fucker."

Phials greeted him off-handedly in his bedroom, suppressing his excitement. Waited for Fast Eddie to leave before pressing up close to Clint to whisper,

"What's the word?"

"We're wuh-working on it."

"*We?*"

"I can't do it alone."

"Who's your partner?"

"You don't know him."

"Can we trust him?"

"Yes." Clint paused, a thought striking him, amazed he hadn't considered it before. "But it'll muh-mean a three-way spluh-split."

Phials waved away the statement. "I'm not worried about shit like that. When does it happen?"

"I don't know, we're still fuh-finalising the plan." Thinking about the deal, calculating greedily. Until now he'd been planning to split twenty-five mill down the middle with Gawl. But if they divided the fifty three ways, he'd get close to seventeen million. If he could convince Phials to divide it up even further, and keep more for himself... "We muh-might have to involve a cuh-couple of others too, maybe split it fuh-five ways," Clint said slyly.

"I don't care about the fucking money." Phials' eyes wild with the promise of release and fear of failure. "How will you do it?"

"I cuh-can't tell you yet." Phials started to object.

"Don't worry, it's all in huh-huh-hand. I'll drop by again before it happens, tuh-tell you all about it then."

Phials relaxed. "Big Sandy was here yesterday, trying to freak me out. But I know their shit. I played mind games myself in the past. They won't break me that easily."

"My puh-partner would like some suh-samples of Baby P," Clint said, chancing his arm.

"No."

"It would muh-make it easier for us if we –"

"No samples. No copy of the formula. Only me." Phials tapped the side of his head. "With the secret in here, I'm worth the world to you. With the formula or a sample to work from, you might get ideas."

"You don't trust me?" Clint tried to sound wounded.

"Not as far as I could throw you," Phials laughed, then he stuck on a video and the pair settled back, pretending to watch it just in case Fast Eddie walked in and wondered what they were up to. Under the noise they talked about the drug, America, Phials' contacts, how he'd sell the formula. "They'll be queueing up for it," he predicted. "And they're sensible businessmen, they won't try to screw us. Getting out – of here and England – is the hard part. If we handle that cleanly, it's a downhill skate from there."

Clint asked about Fast Eddie, if he ever left the lab or

if there was some way to send him off on an errand. Phials said Fast Eddie was resident most of the time, but maybe he could distract him, set off an alarm in the basement just before Clint and his partner hit the lab. That sounded like a good idea to Clint, but he told him to think about it some more and see if he could come up with a better one.

Phials clasped Clint's hands tightly before he left, tears of gratitude in his eyes. "If we pull this off, we're made for life," he croaked.

"I know," Clint smiled.

"You really think you can get me out?"

"No sweat," Clint boasted, pretending he was the mastermind behind the plan. "Just work hard, make it look like you're desperately trying to perfect the formula, leave the rest to us." Opening the door, he called back to Phials so that Fast Eddie heard, "See you again in a duh-day or two, doc."

"Goodbye," Phials responded, smiling crookedly. "Good luck."

Down the stairs with Fast Eddie. Waiting at the front for the door to open — it didn't. He looked back. Fast Eddie standing by the wall, arms folded, staring at him. Clint started to sweat. Forced a faint smile. "Wh-wh-wh-what's up?"

"Phials say anything to you about what he's working on?"

Clint worked the flesh of his forehead into a frown. "No. Wh-wh-wh-why?"

"Nothing about Friday?"

"Fruh-fruh-fruh-*Friday?*"

Fast Eddie stared at him a couple of heartbeats longer. Shook his head. "No matter." He unfolded his arms and pressed a button in a panel in the wall. The door opened. Clint exited, half-waving. Fast Eddie didn't wave back. Clint hurried away from the lab, still sweating bad.

FORTY-THREE

Tulip had taken a long, hot bath and was on her way to her bedroom, drying her legs with a towel as she went. Kevin was waiting to get in the shower, and he could see the bruises and scratches where McCaskey had mauled her during their second appointment. Tulip hadn't said much since their session with the brute the night before, less upset than Kevin thought she'd be.

"Do you blame me?" he asked quietly, putting out a hand to stop her.

"For what?" Tulip sighed as she automatically glanced at his penis to make sure he wasn't aroused.

"McCaskey. What he did to you. I told him to stop but he ignored me. If Big Sandy had been there, I'd have sicced him on the bastard, but I'd have only aggravated the situation if I'd interfered myself."

"I don't blame you," Tulip said. Then, a few seconds later, "Not for *that*."

"Just for everything else," Kevin chuckled, trying to make a joke of it.

"Yes," Tulip said sombrely. She looked at him seriously. "Where does it end?"

"Where does what end?" Heart pounding, playing for time.

"We can't go on like this. I've taken more than I deserve – much more – because I love you and don't want to see you come to harm. But I can't do this forever." Tulip ran a finger over her wounds. "Set us free, Kevin. You should do it out of the goodness of your heart, but if you can't find any there, do it because it makes sense. If we continue, it's only a matter of time before somebody like Gawl McCaskey goes too far."

"That won't happen," Kevin said, shivering. "I tore Clint a new arsehole in the church today, told him never to set us up with McCaskey again. And I'll ensure Big Sandy is always with us going forward. I won't make any arrangements with new clients without him."

"That's just sidestepping the problem. One night a man will come who doesn't worry about Big Sandy, who won't care if he's killed, just as long as he can kill first."

"I won't let anyone harm you," Kevin promised, starting to cry. "I'd die myself before I'd let that happen."

"Maybe that's what you want," Tulip whispered, eyes locked on her brother's. "Maybe that's where all this ends for you, both of us butchered, together forever."

"No," Kevin moaned. He wrapped his arms around her and pulled her in close. Tulip didn't react. "Don't say such things. They're not true."

"Not yet," Tulip muttered.

"Never," Kevin swore. "I love you. I live for you. I don't want you to die."

"But if you couldn't have me? If I said I was leaving?"

"You know I couldn't go on without you," he wept.

"But could you bear to let *me* go on without *you*, or would you try to take me down with you rather than let me walk away?"

Kevin didn't answer. His eyes were blinded with tears and his throat had constricted to the point where he could hardly breathe.

Tulip pushed clear and wrapped the towel around herself. "We have to resolve this. Things have changed. We can't go on as we have been."

"What's changed?" he wheezed. "McCaskey? Is that what's bothering you? I swear, he'll never –"

The doorbell chimed, cutting him off. Tulip stared at Kevin as the chimes died away. She appeared to be on the verge of saying something, then smiled and shook her head. "It'll hold. Go see who's at the door."

She walked through to her bedroom, Kevin staring after her uncertainly. The doorbell chimed again. He cursed, then slipped on a robe and padded to the door. The bell chimed again. He looked out the peephole and saw a middle-aged woman in a dark coat. He didn't recognise her. He opened the door but kept it on the latch. "Yes?" he barked, thinking she was a Jehovah's Witness.

"Kevin Tyne?"

"Yes." More cautiously this time.

"I'm from social services. I'd like to talk with you about your sister."

Heart palpitations. Explosions inside his head.

"Mr Tyne?" His eyes swam back into focus. The woman was staring at him. "Are you all right?"

"Yes." Forcing a smile. "This isn't a good time. Could you come back –"

"I need to speak with you now," the woman said. "We've received a disturbing report which I must investigate immediately. I'll call the police if I have to, but –"

"No," Kevin cried, unlatching the door in a terrified hurry, opening it wide. "Please come in, I –"

Before he could finish, Gawl McCaskey stepped in front of the woman, put a hand on Kevin's chest and sent him tumbling. As Kevin sprawled across the floor, he saw McCaskey pass a baggie to the woman. She smiled grotesquely and Kevin saw rotten teeth, dark rims around her eyes, the hunger of a junkie in her smile. Disgusted at himself for letting such a cheap fake take him in.

"Get out," Kevin shouted as the woman scurried away and McCaskey closed the door. "Get out or I'll —"

McCaskey was across the room and over him in an instant. Grabbed Kevin's throat and half-hauled him to his knees. Kevin choked and slapped at the larger man's hands. McCaskey bent so his face was close to Kevin's. "I'm here for yer sister," he snarled. "No more hotels. Home visits from now on. And ye're gonna stay out of the room while I'm fucking her. Beat off in private, ye sick wee prick."

"I'll... kill... you," Kevin wheezed, face turning purple.

"Will ye fuck," McCaskey laughed, letting Kevin go. "Where is she?"

"No," Kevin croaked, eyes burning with hatred. "You can't have her after what you did last night. Get out or —"

McCaskey's right fist connected with Kevin's jaw. He flopped backwards, teeth smashing together, lips splitting, brain shaking in his skull. He blacked out for a second. When he recovered, McCaskey was standing over him, glaring coldly. "I'm off t' fuck yer sister. If ye're as wise as ye're yellow, ye'll stay well away."

McCaskey turned, paused, glanced down one last time. "If ye get any bright ideas, like phoning the cops or asking yer pal Big Sandy t' teach me a lesson, just bear in mind the amount of shite I can drop ye in, and what life in prison will be like for a sister-abusing fuck like yerself." Then he went striding through the flat, calling softly, "Come out, come out, wherever ye are."

The door of Tulip's bedroom opened. She caught sight of McCaskey advancing. Froze. Looked for Kevin. Saw him on the floor, bleeding, crying, trembling. Read the situation instantly. Calmly stepped back inside her room, McCaskey following eagerly, closing the door, blocking Kevin's view.

Kevin lay on the floor, weeping and shaking, listening to the muted sounds of McCaskey fucking Tulip. He wiped blood from his lips and tears from his eyes. Crazy thoughts of grabbing a knife from the kitchen and killing McCaskey. But he was weak, feeble, gutless. In the end he just lay where he was, moaning softly.

McCaskey was beaming when he walked out ten minutes later. "A grand wee fuck," he murmured. Kevin saw Tulip approach the door of her room. McCaskey didn't appear to have hurt her this time. The intruder stopped at the front door. Coughed to get Kevin's attention. "Ye won't get rid of me now that I have a taste for her. Best to accept that. I'll phone next time. If ye try anything clever, ye'll regret it." He saluted Kevin cynically, opened the door and exited.

Tulip stepped out of her room when she heard the front door close. She was naked, dark fingerprints on her shoulders where McCaskey had gripped her tight, but otherwise unharmed. She stared numbly at Kevin. He stared back, sobbing. Without saying anything, Tulip returned to the bathroom, where she ran another bath. Closed the door before getting in, cutting Kevin out, leaving him lying on the floor like a beaten dog, wretched, terrified, powerless, alone.

FORTY-FOUR

Gawl entered his shithole of a flat feeling like the master of the world. Everything falling into place, finally coming into his own after all these years, rising late in the day to snatch at greatness. His plan not yet fully formed, but confident he could manipulate all the pieces into place, just as he'd manipulated the Tynes.

Thinking about his three sessions with Kevin and Tulip as he sat on the edge of his bed and treated himself to a swig of cider. Saturday, more interested in the sex than in how the pair might fit in with the break-out. Kevin Tyne irritated him – a weak fool, dancing around like something out of a ballet, jerking off – but Tulip was fascinating, not drawn by her average looks but by her *innocence*. She was a multi-fuck whore but her eyes were pure, the eyes of a child unstained by the world. The paradox amused and excited Gawl, innocence and sluttishness a rare, intoxicating mix.

Sunday, after much thought, he decided to play rough, testing his theory that Kevin couldn't deal with violence, that he'd crumble when challenged. If he was to use the Tynes, he had to be sure he could bend them to his will. Their cooperation wasn't essential – he planned to use them without their knowledge – but he'd need them afterwards if he was to keep Fr Seb under his thumb. So he bullied them, tore into Tulip, slapped her around a bit, left his mark.

Monday, the clincher. Humiliate Kevin, threaten him, watch him break, make him servile. Gawl part of their lives now, a dark, hated but incontrovertible part. In Kevin's mind Gawl stood terrible and bleak, a monster to be feared and obeyed. In time Kevin would figure out a way to deal with Gawl – flee the city or hire someone to kill him – but he would have no time. Before he could think the matter through, he and Tulip would be submersed in Gawl's world, the world of the break-out. Gawl would keep them meek by keeping them off-balance. Throw them in deep and make himself their life buoy. They'd have to cling to him to survive and later he could shrug them loose when they were of no more value, just as he planned to shrug loose Phials and Fr Seb... and Clint if he had to.

Almost at the moment Gawl thought about Clint, there was a knock at his door and the dealer was there, entering in a huff, anxious, fidgeting. "Where the fuck have you been? I called round three times already. What's going on?"

"Sit down," Gawl smiled. "Get ye a drink?"

"Vodka," Clint sniffed, pulling his jacket tight around his frame. "It's freezing in here. Why don't you get an electric heater?"

"It'll be plenty hot in hell, so we'd best enjoy the cold while we can." Gawl tossed Clint a half full bottle of vodka, sat and had another swig of cider. Clint stayed on his feet. "I went t' see the Tynes," Gawl said.

Clint had been raising the bottle. Stopped. Lowered it. Stared at Gawl incredulously. "After all the fuh-fuss Kevin made? Are you muh-muh-mad?"

"They were delighted t' see me," Gawl laughed. "I'm growing on them."

"He'll set Big Sandy after you. If that buh-bastard gets involved..."

"Kevin won't be setting anyone after me," Gawl said softly. "Right now he's shitting his pants, and he won't start thinking till he stops shitting, and by then it'll be too late because we'll have made our move and he'll have t' play along."

"You're not making suh-sense," Clint frowned.

"We're gonna use the Tynes as a distraction t' help free Phials."

Clint put down the bottle of vodka and sat, no longer feeling the cold. "Why do you have to tuh-terrorise them? Surely we should get them on our good side if –"

"Did ye know about Fr Seb and Tulip?" Gawl cut in.

"What about them?"

"She was one of his little playthings."

Clint's eyes widened. "No."

"Don't act so shocked," Gawl snickered. "He's had younger than her, the horny auld goat."

"But he's her priest."

"Maybe he was trying t' bring God closer t' her," Gawl smirked, then grew serious. "We're gonna use Tulip t' keep Fr Seb in line, right? She'll be his piece of pussy while we're in hiding, when I can't set him up with whores. We can also use her t' threaten him with if we have t'."

"How?"

"Parry's a twisted fuck but he tries t' do the right thing. If I say I'll kill her if he doesn't play along, he'll do whatever the fuck we tell him t' save her life."

"But you wouldn't really kuk-kill her, would you?" Clint asked, shaken.

Gawl stared at him hard. "We're talking millions of pounds. I'd kill my own mother — if the bitch wasn't already dead — for that much money. Ye would too."

Clint forced an uncertain smile. "I suppose." He picked up the bottle of vodka and tossed back a shot. Shivered and grimaced. Looked at Gawl sideways. "Tell me about the pluh-pluh-pluh-plan now?"

Gawl smiled. "Aye." Leant forward. "There's still a few points I have t' get straight in my head – maybe ye can help me with 'em – but here's the start of it. We break him out t'morrow..."

FORTY-FIVE

Big Sandy called to the lab early, before eleven, intending to scare Phials awake. But when he arrived, Fast Eddie told him Phials was already up and playing host to Clint Smith. Big Sandy asked if Smith knew anything about the deadline. Fast Eddie said he'd quizzed the dealer yesterday and Clint was ignorant. Big Sandy tempted to take Smith to one side, explain a few religious facts of life to him, but he wasn't sure he could control his temper and he didn't want to do anything to jeopardise the Phials deal. Smith could wait until after the weekend.

He went looking for Gawl McCaskey. Tracked down Eyes Burton in a bookies in Balham and asked about the Scot. Eyes didn't know where McCaskey lived but thought it was around the Elephant & Castle. They'd worked on a job together in Australia many years before. Eyes didn't like McCaskey but said he had his crude uses and knew how to keep his mouth shut.

Big Sandy hit a few pubs around the Elephant. Several people knew McCaskey but nobody knew where he lived. The landlord in the King's Head, Paul, thought McCaskey was squatting in a flat on the Heygate but didn't know in which block. Said Big Sandy should come back later, Gawl was a regular, and even if he didn't turn up tonight, there'd be lots in the pub who knew him and might have a clearer idea of where he kipped. But Big Sandy not overly concerned, sure he'd catch up with McCaskey eventually, if not this week then later. Not a priority.

To the Borough next to check on Tulip. She was slow to answer the door. He thought she was out and was turning to leave when the door finally opened and she stood blinking at him. "Hey," he smiled. "Just wanted to see if you were OK."

"I'm fine." Tulip retreated. Big Sandy followed. In the light of the living room he caught a clearer look at her face. She'd been crying.

"Are you sure you're all right?"

"Yes."

"Kevin at work?"

"Yes."

Big Sandy sat, feeling awkward. He never knew what to do when a woman was crying, especially one as young as Tulip. If Megan had let him be a father to Amelie, he might have had more of an idea of what to say, but teenage girls were from a different universe as far as he was concerned. "I haven't caught up with

McCaskey yet," he grunted, bringing talk round to ground that felt solid, "but I've been running some checks. I'll find him soon."

"He came here last night," Tulip said softly.

Big Sandy stiffened. "Why didn't you call me?"

"He turned up unannounced. There was nothing we could do. I don't know how he found out where we live. Maybe Clint told him or maybe he followed us on Saturday or Sunday."

"Did he hurt you?"

"No. Just sex this time. But he's a bad man. When I look in his eyes..." She hesitated, then came out with it, voice hushed, fearful. "I see the devil." Big Sandy didn't laugh. Tulip looked up, fresh tears trickling down her cheeks. "I've seen a lot of wicked men since Kevin started..." Couldn't say it. "Gawl's different. Not just cruel, but really evil. I'm afraid of what he might do."

Big Sandy wanted to hug her but felt that would be overstepping the mark, worried she might think he was coming on to her. "Have you discussed this with Kevin?" he asked instead.

"He's as scared as I am. Last night..." She hesitated, then figured he knew so much already about them that there was no point holding back. "Gawl hit Kevin. Wouldn't allow him in while he had sex with me. It's the first time Kevin hasn't been present."

"Was it better or worse without him?" Big Sandy asked curiously.

"No difference. I never feel anything when it's happening. I blank out as much as I can. That's why I take the drugs."

Big Sandy bristled, wanting to protect Tulip, thinking about Amelie, imagining traces of his daughter in this scared, trapped girl. "I can move in for a few nights, be here if McCaskey comes again, stop this before it goes any further."

"He said he'd call ahead next time."

"You believe him?"

"Yes. Kevin wasn't terrified of him before. Now he is. Kevin doesn't run when he's afraid — he freezes. Gawl has Kevin under his thumb. Phoning before he comes will scare Kevin worse than just dropping in, so he'll phone."

"You seem to know a lot about him."

"It's all in his eyes."

Big Sandy nodded thoughtfully. "I'll speak with Kevin, tell him to call me the next time McCaskey's coming."

"You think you can stop him?"

"Yes." He gazed at her evenly. "But from what you've told me, I don't think a warning will suffice. I might have to go further."

Tulip held Big Sandy's gaze and said nothing. Acknowledgment in her eyes, and a silent plea, *Do whatever you have to.*

"Will Kevin be in tonight?" Big Sandy asked.

"Not for long. He's working late and we've an appointment at ten."

"I thought he said no more appointments until you'd recovered."

Tulip shrugged. "Kevin says lots of things. He phoned earlier. Clint has asked us to come to the lab. Kevin's eager to do it. I think he wants to prove to himself that he's still in control of the situation, even though he knows that he isn't."

Big Sandy wanted to tell Kevin to break the appointment, stay in and wait for McCaskey to call. But reluctant to interfere with Phials' schedule. It was good that Phials was enjoying his few pleasures before the day of reckoning — they might remind him what he stood to lose if he refused to cooperate with the Bush.

"I'll come round tomorrow," Big Sandy said, not wanting to abandon Tulip even with everything else that was going on, still thinking of Amelie and how horrible it would be if she was left friendless and hopeless in her darkest hour. "We'll sort this out. Tell Kevin to phone me if McCaskey calls in the meantime."

"I will." Tulip smiled, relieved. "I was going to fix lunch for myself — Kevin has to work through his break. Do you want some?"

Big Sandy started to say no then smiled and changed his mind. "Sure." Together they devoured a baguette filled with ham, lettuce, tomato, washed down with Pepsi Max. They didn't say much while they ate. Big Sandy asked if she wanted him to hang around when they were finished. She said it was OK, she could manage. He left, stooping low to clumsily kiss her cheek, and whispered, "Don't worry, it will all work out in the end."

"Of course," Tulip whispered back. "God takes care of all things in the end."

Strolling down Long Lane, disturbed by Tulip's tale of Gawl McCaskey, sorry he hadn't tried harder to track down the bastard, making up his mind to scour the Elephant & Castle for him tonight until he found out where McCaskey lived. Mulling over Tulip's last words. *God takes care of all things in the end.* Determined not to leave her fate in God's hands. Big Sandy didn't trust him.

FORTY-SIX

Clint couldn't sleep. Spent most of the night twisting beneath his bed sheets, sweating, thinking of all the things that could go wrong. Nightmares when he did drop off, jerking awake, heart beating fast in the darkness. He grabbed his phone several times to ring Gawl and call it off. Then he'd think about the money and set the phone back down. Torn between terror and greed.

He got up early, not long after seven, figuring it would be better to keep busy, maybe he wouldn't think about the break-out so much. But nothing could distract him. His hands were shaking. He vomited twice. It was useless. He couldn't go through with this. Picked up his phone, determined to ring Gawl this time. Gawl wouldn't like it, but Clint wouldn't let that stop him. He had to be firm. This was lunacy. Mad to think they could get away with it. To hell with the money. Not worth the risk. Nothing was worth...

He paused as a face flashed through his thoughts. Gulped. Made a snap decision and dialled the number before he could chicken out. Alice confused when she answered, not sure who he was until he reminded her. He could tell she was uncertain when he asked if he could visit, but he was her husband's cousin, so in the end she gave him permission, not wanting to offend family, even a distant and unloved relative like Clint.

He washed, showered, dressed in his finest clothes, then took them off and tried something less formal. Called for a taxi, not wanting to rely on public transport, concerned that the grime of the Tube might rub off on him.

Alice opened the door when he buzzed, let him in, kissed him on the cheek, took him through to the living room. Clint had only been here once before, back when he had first made contact with cousin Dave. He felt out of place but tried not to let it show. Said he'd love a cup of tea when Alice offered. Made small talk, struggling to think of things to say, stuttering quite badly. It took him an age, but finally he worked up to what he'd come here for and asked about Shula. He knew she had returned to them when she'd been released from hospital. Was she going to stay or return to Switzerland?

"She's going home," Alice sighed. "Later this week actually. She doesn't want to be in London any more. She quit her night classes. A pity, because I knew she enjoyed them. Maybe one day she'll..." Alice paused, realising that this was why Clint had come. He'd never struck her as an especially impressive young man. Shy and stumbling. And Dave spoke dismissively of him. But it would be rude to turn him away, and Shula had entertained so few visitors, not having made any real friends during her short stay in the city.

"Wait here," Alice said, getting up. "I'll see if Shula is in. She might want to chat with you."

Clint sipped his tea and stared at his feet while he was waiting. Almost bolted, but didn't want to look like even more of a fool. When he heard the door open, he was sure it was Alice come to tell him that Shula didn't want to see him. But when he looked up, cousin Dave's wife was nowhere to be seen. It was Shula Schimmel who'd entered. And she was smiling at him. Quizzically, sure, but it was still a smile, and Clint filled with warmth and hope.

"Clint. Hi," she said, crossing the room to sit close to him. "Long time no see."

"Yeah," Clint beamed then gulped. "I've muh-missed you."

She patted one of his hands and said politely, "I've missed you too."

Growing strong on that, he asked how she was, if she'd been out on the town recently, if she had any plans for what she was going to do when she returned to Switzerland. Growing less nervous as he went along, Shula answering pleasantly, not looking bored, laughing at one or two of his small jokes. They didn't talk about the rape. He wasn't dumb enough to bring that up.

"How about you?" Shula asked. "Have you been busy?"

"You know," Clint grinned. "Ducking and diving, wheeling and dealing." He cleared his throat. "Actually, things are going pretty wuh-well. I have a few deals lined up that might set me up nuh-nicely if they pan out the way I hope."

"I'll keep my fingers crossed for you," Shula said.

Clint licked his lips. "Yeah, I could be sitting swuh-sweet soon. Might muh-move to the States. It's always been a dream of mine."

"Yes," Shula nodded. "You mentioned that before."

Clint delighted that she remembered. It gave him the courage to go on. "I was thinking. If I fuh-find myself in Switzerland one day, would you muh-mind if I guh-guh-guh-gave you a call?"

"What would bring you to Switzerland?" Shula asked.

Clint wanted to say, *You*. But frightened of blowing it. "Oh, I don't know," he said softly. "I've always muh-meant to visit. It sounds lovely. It'd be nice to meet up with you if I'm there. I wuh-wouldn't take up much of your tuh-time."

"Don't be silly," Shula laughed. "I'd love to show you around. Give me plenty of warning before you come, so that I can clear my diary." She leant across to squeeze his hand. "And I'm not just saying that. I mean it."

Clint stared at his hand where she'd touched him. Then stared at her as she smiled at him earnestly. And he knew in that moment that he would find the courage to press on tonight. He wouldn't let fear turn him from his path. He would stand beside Gawl and do what was expected of him, no matter what. Not just for the money. For Shula and all the delights that he could read into her smile.

The warmth seeped from Clint's bones over the course of the day, especially when he went to visit Phials to tell him the plan and it began to get real. But he didn't truly start to waver until evening, when he got sick again and found himself shaking worse than ever. But by that time Gawl was there to talk him through his doubts, remind him of the prize, encourage him, stoke Clint's dreams. He probably would have bolted on the way to the lab without Gawl, despite what he had vowed earlier, caught a bus or taxi the hell out of there. But Gawl knew this and made the journey to the Walworth Road with him, driving there in a car he'd stolen earlier, parking in the street at the top of the cul-de-sac. He got out and waved Clint on. By then Clint had come too far to back down, so he staggered ahead, legs shaking, eyelids twitching, trying to focus on the money, Shula, America, anything except what was dead ahead of him.

Deep breaths at the outer door, fingers fumbling with the lock, five attempts to get the code right. Winced at the sound as the door slid open. Stepped forward into darkness, fighting back tears. More deep breaths. Slapped his face lightly to get some colour in his cheeks. Popped a strong mint, hoping the scent would mask the stench of fear. Pressed the button.

Fast Eddie opened the door. Clint entered and spread his arms, grinding his teeth so they wouldn't chatter while Fast Eddie was searching him. Fast Eddie did his usual thorough job, stepped back, closed the door. "You here for the show?"

"Wh-wh-wh-what shuh-show?"

"Kevin and Tulip are coming. Phials wants to show them the hounds."

"Oh." Clint smiled weakly. "He duh-did mention something about th-th-th-that." Stuttering worse than normal. Afraid Fast Eddie would notice. But he was already marching through the lab. Clint followed quietly, feeling nauseous.

"Enter," Phials called when Fast Eddie knocked on his door. He was lying on the bed in a robe, clipping his fingernails.

"Visitor for you," Fast Eddie grunted.

Phials turned his head and squinted. "Hello Clint. Come in, come in. Eddie!" Fast Eddie had been sliding out. He stopped and glanced at Phials. "We'll head down the cellar about ten to ten, to sedate a hound, OK?"

"Whatever."

"There'll be somebody on the door to let the Tynes in if they come?"

"Of course."

"Thank you."

Fast Eddie left. Clint sank to his haunches and dry heaved. Phials said nothing, went back to trimming his nails. Finally Clint stood, wiping his lips with a tissue, eyes filled with dread but also resolution. "You told him about the hounds?"

"Yes."

"He wasn't suspicious?"

"Not in the least. I said I wished to impress Tulip. He wasn't in favour of it, but he knows the Tynes can't afford to run around shooting off at the mouth. He agreed without a fuss."

Getting Fast Eddie down the cellar on a pretext, the solution they'd arrived at earlier in the day, when Clint had come to tell Phials about the plan. Phials' idea, once

Clint told him how they were going to use Kevin and Tulip. It would also provide the pair of them with weapons and allow them to be close to the front door when the shit went down. Gawl had cackled for five minutes when Clint reported back and told him about the new twist. Not annoyed that he hadn't thought of it himself. He didn't care where the ideas came from as long as they worked.

"Wanna watch a film?" Phials asked, finishing his nails and sitting up.

Clint stared at him with disbelief. "Are you crazy? We cuh-could be less than an hour away from having our bruh-bruh-brains blown out the back of our heads, and you want to wuh-watch a fucking fuh-fuh-fuh-film?"

"Relax," Phials cooed, switching on the TV. "If shit goes wrong, it goes wrong. Might as well enjoy the calm while we can." He pointed the remote control at the video recorder and hit play. A film came on and after a few seconds Clint realised it was *Escape From Alcatraz*. He started to laugh. Fell into a chair, crying with laughter, pointing at the screen, giggling uncontrollably. Phials smiled smugly. He'd anticipated Clint's fear and planned accordingly.

Clint less uptight after that. They went through the plan again, quietly, taking turns to tell it to each other, scrutinising it for any flaws. Neither spoke of what would happen later if they were successful, not looking any further ahead than the break-out, avoiding all long-term distractions and pitfalls.

Finally, at twelve minutes to ten by Clint's watch, Fast Eddie rapped on the door and stuck his head in. "Want to make a move, doc?"

"Certainly," Phials said. "Just let me slip on some clothes. It's cold in the cellar." The chemist pulled on a pair of trousers, a shirt, jumper, socks and shoes. No jacket — he didn't own any, had never needed one here.

Down the stairs, through the lab and secret passageway to the cellar, passing two armed guards near the front door, Clint deliberately not looking at them or at the security cameras overhead. Winding their way through the cellar, past boxes stacked with chemicals and guns, Clint's eyes watering, stomach clenching, bile rising. They arrived at the cages where the hounds were housed. At the sight and stench of them, Clint lurched aside and dry heaved, moaning with fear and pain. Fast Eddie glanced at him, surprised, then smiled, thinking it was a reaction to the hounds. "He'd never make a zoo-keeper," he chuckled.

"Mock not lest ye be mocked," Phials chided Fast Eddie, walking to the rack where the syringes were kept.

The hounds were howling and clawing at their chains, trying to break free.

"Which one do you want?" Fast Eddie asked.

"I'm not particular. You choose."

Fast Eddie studied the hounds. All four were spitting and snarling, one as savage as the next. He selected the smallest, opened the door and stepped aside. Phials entered the cage, got close, subdued the savage dog, patted it as it slumped at his feet. Clint thought he was crazy to risk a mauling with so much at stake, but Phials wanted to behave the way he normally did, didn't want Fast Eddie to get suspicious.

Fast Eddie closed the door as Phials came out. He turned to Clint, who stood pale-faced and shivering a few metres away. "Come on," Phials said, striding away from the cages, into the corridor, out of range of the security cameras. "I want to prepare for Tulip."

Fast Eddie trailed behind the chemist. "I still don't see how getting in that cage with the Tynes will impress the girl. You've got a funny sense of —"

Phials whirled, locked his left arm around Fast Eddie's head, sunk the tip of the syringe into the soft flesh behind his left ear, pushed hard on the plunger — he hadn't injected all of the fluid into the hound, saving some for Fast Eddie, just enough to knock him out cold.

Fast Eddie gasped with shock then elbowed Phials in the ribs and threw him off. His hand went for his gun. Clint jumped him before he drew, squealing with terror. Landed on his back, dragged him to the ground. Fast Eddie cursed, struggled with Clint, half-shrugged him off, then went limp, sighing helplessly, eyes rolling.

Clint slid off Fast Eddie, amazed it had worked. Phials staggered into him, groaning, massaging his ribs. He bent, reached inside Fast Eddie's jacket and took his pistol. Phials cocked the gun and handed it to Clint, then hurried to the nearby crates, scanning labels. Found one with a loose top, rooted around inside, came back with two pistols smaller than Fast Eddie's but just as effective, and clips for them. Loaded the pistols, stuck one into a pocket, spun the other on a finger like a cowboy. Winked at Clint. "Ready to rock 'n' roll?"

Clint stared at the gun in his hand. "Huh-how do I use it?"

"Just point and fire."

Clint looked down at Fast Eddie. "Is he duh-duh-duh-dead?"

"Just sleeping. He'll be fine when he wakes."

"Perhaps we should fuh-finish him off..."

"Do *you* want to fire a bullet through an unconscious man's brain?" Phials asked coolly. Clint thought about that and shook his head. "Neither do I." Phials pointed towards the exit. "Let's go. Kevin and Tulip will be here soon. We still have a shit-load to do." He held the gun down by his side and smoothed his hair back. "Hide your gun. Walk casually. There are cameras on the way out."

"What if they wonder where Fast Eddie is?"

"They'll think he's lagging behind or searching for something. We'll be out of here before they have time to investigate."

"But —"

"We'll die down here if we don't move fast," Phials snapped. Started for the exit at a forced but controlled pace. Clint took deep breaths, stepped over Fast Eddie, hid his gun, tried to look calm for the cameras, then shuffled after Phials.

FORTY-SEVEN

Kevin despondent when he arrived home. Hadn't slept the night before. Operating like a zombie at work, thoughts fixed on Gawl McCaskey and how the brute had disgraced him, reduced him to a wailing mess on his own floor. McCaskey had taken Tulip away from him, rid him of his self-respect and power. Hating McCaskey like he'd never hated before, but fearful too. He wanted to call Big Sandy, explain the situation, trust him to deal with their tormentor, but McCaskey had shaken his faith in their protector. In Kevin's mind McCaskey was an ogre, a mind-reader, a man of mystical powers. Ridiculous, but he couldn't shake the fantasy. Afraid to cross McCaskey, sure he'd sense any trap Kevin tried to lay, get the better of Big Sandy, come gunning for retribution.

When Clint rang and said that Phials had asked for the brother and sister, Kevin wasn't interested, he just wanted to crawl home after work, curl up in a ball and lick his wounds. But as Clint kept pestering him, Kevin started thinking about Tulip, the contempt in her eyes since McCaskey laid him low, the coldness in her touch. This could be where he lost her. McCaskey had come between them and that might be the excuse she needed to set herself free. Kevin couldn't let that happen. He had to get things back the way they were. Try thinking of a way to deal with McCaskey later. Tulip his first priority.

He agreed to the appointment, figuring he should carry on as normal, ignore the events of last night, pretend McCaskey didn't exist. Time was his enemy. He had to keep Tulip busy. He reminded Clint of Tulip's scratches and bruises, said Phials would have to be extra gentle. Clint said that was no problem, asked him to come at ten, to be punctual, Phials had a surprise arranged for Tulip and timing was important. Kevin wanted to know what the surprise was. Clint said that Phials hadn't told him. Kevin unhappy – surprises the last thing he needed – but he accepted the offer. Phoned Tulip and told her. She responded with a grunt. He said he'd have to work through lunch. Another grunt. End of conversation.

Home late. Dinner. A shower. Tulip already washed and dressed, sombre, quiet. As they were getting ready to leave, she looked at him. "I don't want to do this."

Kevin suppressed a shiver. "Why?"

"It's wrong. It's dangerous."

"We've been to the lab loads of times. Phials is safe. We can trust him."

"If you take me away from here now, and never make me do this again, I'll stay with you forever." Tulip's eyes were moist with unshed tears. She walked up to her brother and laid the back of her fingers across his cheek. "Do the right thing now, before it's too late. We can leave London, go wherever you want, set up home together. Accept this. Settle for it. I beg you."

Kevin gulped. Covered her small hand with his own. Shook his head sadly. "I know this McCaskey business has upset you – me too – but we can't let it tear us apart. We'll figure a way out of this mess. Running isn't the answer. We –"

Tulip jerked her hand free. "You're a fool." Not bitter, just making an observation.

He had no answer for that except, "Get your coat, it's cold out. And snort some coke before we go."

A cab to the Walworth Road, then a short walk to the lab. They said nothing during the ride or walk. Kevin was dreading the night ahead, wishing he'd turned Clint down. He couldn't get the thoughts of McCaskey out of his head and he was sure they would interfere with his performance. His penis was soft and cold, and he couldn't imagine it coming to life. He'd go through the motions, but he was dubious. Thinking, *What if I can't ever get hard again? What if his face is always there, mocking me, belittling me?* He quashed the crazy notions but they kept returning, stronger each time, his fears steadily multiplying.

The outer door of the lab was unlocked. He slid it open. Tulip whispered something. He thought she was speaking to him. Looked at her, smiling in the hope of a few kind words. Realised she was praying. Pouting, he angrily pressed the button of the main door and pulled her in close beside him.

The door opened. Two guards inside. Kevin recognised their faces but didn't know their names. He stepped in, Tulip just behind him, and spread his arms, neck stiff, head throbbing with anger and pain. One of the guards patted him down. The other was staring off into space, not paying attention, bored. The guard finished with Kevin and turned to Tulip. She was looing over her shoulder, frowning. "You next," the guard said.

Then a man burst through the outer door. Large, bulky, dark. He shoved Tulip at the guard. She collided with him and the pair fell to the floor, both crying out with surprise. Kevin froze, staring at Tulip on top of the guard. The other guard snapped out of his daze, snatched for his gun.

The intruder grabbed Kevin and turned him into a human shield.

Gunfire.

FORTY-EIGHT

Gawl on edge as Clint fumbled with the lock. Visions of the dealer losing his nerve and fleeing. Swearing to himself that he'd kill Clint on the spot if he did. But then the door opened, Clint slipped out of sight and Gawl relaxed — as much as he could. Waited a quarter of an hour, crouched in shadows, then slid across the street and into the house where he'd hid the first time he'd come here.

Focused on the lab as the minutes slowly ticked by. Replaying the scenario over and over, treating it as a memory of something that had already happened, robbing the future of much of its threat by placing it into a safe imagined past. Checked his gun, a piece of shit but it worked and it couldn't be traced. A long time since he'd shot anyone. Guns never his thing, too impersonal. He preferred to get up close when he fought. Dirtier, messier, riskier, but he didn't mind that.

The last few minutes the worst, sure the Tynes wouldn't come, that Clint would chicken out, that Phials had cracked and ratted them out, that it was a trap. Dying for a drink, wishing he'd brought a bottle along, just a quick shot to steady his nerves. Now that fear was gnawing at him, he was amazed Clint had made it so far. If Gawl was this afraid, what sort of petrifying panic was the cowardly Clint enduring? New respect for the dealer, though not much.

Checking his watch, glancing at the lab. Checking his watch, glancing at the lab. Checking his watch, glancing at...

There! Kevin and Tulip, glum as mourners at a wake. Gawl chuckled softly in the darkness. He knew why they were so miserable. He'd thought that he'd have to bully them into coming. Pleasantly surprised when Kevin responded positively to Clint's invitation.

As Kevin slid back the outer door of the lab, Gawl pulled on a balaclava and stood in the shadows, waiting, heart racing, watching as Kevin entered the outer rim of the lab *and didn't close the door!* Gawl hurried into the street and raced, delighted with this slice of good fortune. He'd planned on having to slide open the outer door, which would tip off the guards inside, give them time to free their weapons. Everything was playing into his hands but he warned himself not to get cocky, pride before a fall and all that shite.

Pausing at the open door, panting hard, trying to hear over the pounding of his heart. A heavy click. Streams of light. Gawl held his breath and crept forward.

Spotted Tulip just ahead of him in the gloom, blocking the entrance. Hesitated, unable to see past her. Tulip either heard or sensed him. Turned, frowning, peering into the darkness. Gawl almost ran. Then someone said, "You next."

And he exploded in a sudden burst of *action.* Darted forward. Propelled Tulip at a guard. They fell to the floor. Gawl's eyes like a camera lens, taking it all in, Kevin to his left, the guard on the floor trapped beneath Tulip, another guard a bit further ahead, nobody else.

The guard on his feet reached for his gun. Gawl flashed on grisly images, the guard shooting him, head exploding. He grabbed Kevin without thinking and fired around his shrieking human shield, blinking every time his finger squeezed on the trigger, retorts ringing sharply in his ears.

Kevin screamed and pissed himself — Gawl felt the spreading warmth on his thighs. The guard on his feet fired back. Gawl missed, the guard missed. Gawl kept firing, the guard kept firing. Gawl screaming wildly as he fired, the guard thin-lipped and professional.

Gawl clicked on empty. The guard paused, smiled, aimed. Gawl ducked behind Kevin, cursing, trying to reload. Kevin whined like a dog and pushed himself away. Gawl grabbed for Kevin, missed. Kevin hit the floor. The guard's grin spread. Adjusted his aim to shoot Gawl clean through the forehead.

Clint and Phials came spinning round a corner. The guard caught sight of them, assumed they were here to back him up. "I have him," he shouted. Clint and Phials raised their pistols at the same time. The guard's eyes widened. He swivelled. They fired. Bullets tore him apart, face shattering, heart and stomach punctured, sent flying backwards.

The guard on the floor pushed Tulip off and freed his gun. Fired at Kevin and Phials. Gawl still trying to reload. With another curse he reversed his grip and used the gun as a club. Dropped on the guard and pinned his gun hand with a knee. The guard roared at him. Gawl smashed the butt of his gun into the guard's face. Again. Breaking through nose, bone, eyes, the centre of the guard's face now a bloody, shredded hole. Blood pumping, soaking Gawl and Tulip. She lay sprawled next to the guard, staring into the nightmare remains of his face, too shocked and stoned to scream.

Clint and Phials raced across the room. "Come on," Clint yelled at Gawl, trying to drag him off the dead guard, Gawl still pounding away with his gun.

"Wait," Phials shouted, darting into one of the small rooms.

"Are you fucking crazy?" Clint shrieked. Phials ignored him. Clint stood, panting, looking around. Kevin, white-faced, the front of his trousers stained with urine, gawping at Gawl. Tulip, eyes fixed on the dead guard, lips parting and closing softly like a fish's. Gawl, soaked with blood, grinning, driving the butt of his gun through a pool of blood/flesh/bone, into the guard's brain.

Clint pointed his gun at the guard and shot him three times through the chest. Gawl whipped away from the guard and snarled at Clint, raising his gun to attack Clint as he'd attacked the guard, momentarily lost to the madness.

Clint saw murder in Gawl's eyes. Calmly levelled his gun at him, braver than he'd ever dreamt he might be. "Don't." Gawl hesitated. The shroud of hysteria lifted. His eyes cleared. Clint lowered his arm. "We have to get out of here."

Gawl nodded. "Where's Phials?"

"In one of the —"

Three guards appeared on the landing overhead and opened fire. Clint threw himself against the wall and returned their shots. Gawl finished reloading his gun, stepped up beside Clint and took aim. Phials reappeared carrying a large silver tin, saw what was happening, started shooting at the trio on the landing.

One of the guards took a bullet to the stomach and fell over the banister like a cowboy taking a fall in a movie. The others ducked low. Gawl grabbed Kevin, shoved him out into the street, picked up Tulip – still staring slackly at the guard's ruined face – and shouted to Clint and Phials, "Let's get the fuck out of here." Ran with Tulip, Clint and Phials backing out after him, keeping the guards at bay.

Gawl carried Tulip to the car, kicking Kevin ahead of him. Clint started after them. Stopped. Slid the outer door shut. Locked it. Grinned at Phials. "That'll slow them."

"Fucking A!" Phials laughed, delirious with freedom. He ran after Gawl, Clint following, feeling like a warrior.

Gawl pulled off his blood-soaked balaclava and tossed it away as he ran. Got to the car, dumped Tulip on the hood while he opened the doors. She finally screamed as she stared up at the dark night sky. Gawl flinched, then slapped her. No effect, so he slapped her again. This time the scream cut off abruptly, her eyes rolled and she slumped across the hood unconscious.

Kevin stared at Gawl slapping his sister and did nothing. He didn't understand what was happening. As Gawl bundled Tulip into the back seat, part of Kevin's brain roared at him to run, but he couldn't. He could only stand, staring, until Gawl thrust him into the car after Tulip.

Clint and Phials arrived, panting. Clint dove for the front passenger door. Phials stood by the car, wrestling with the top of the tin he'd risked his life for. "Get the fuck in," Gawl yelled as he sat behind the wheel and started the engine.

"Wait a minute," Phials yelled back. The top of the tin came off. He emptied half the contents over the ground, scattering a white, crystalline powder left and right, smearing it around with his feet.

"I'll fucking kill him if he doesn't get in," Gawl screamed at Clint.

"Tony! For fuck's sake! What are –"

Phials replaced the lid, threw the tin into the back seat, slid into the car, slammed the door shut, grinned at Clint. "The hounds."

Clint realised what Phials had done. He laughed. "Sweet!" He slapped Gawl's left arm. "Drive on, Jeeves."

Gawl jammed his foot down and concentrated on the road, Clint and Phials hooting jubilantly, Kevin shivering, Tulip unconscious, chaos behind them, the future dead ahead.

FORTY-NINE

Big Sandy was worried. He'd returned to the King's Head to search for Gawl McCaskey that evening. Though nobody seemed to be friends with McCaskey, many of the customers knew him by sight and a few told Big Sandy that they'd seen him with Clint Smith recently. That troubled him — what was McCaskey doing with the dealer? He finally got McCaskey's address from a woman called Alex who had nothing but bad things to say about him.

Big Sandy broke down the door when he got there and checked the apartment — a pigsty, filthy, freezing, stinking. McCaskey lived like an animal. Finding nothing of interest, Big Sandy sat on a creaking chair in the tiny living room, in darkness, waiting for McCaskey to return, trying to work out why the Scot's connection with Clint Smith made him feel so uneasy.

Then the call from the Bush came, telling Big Sandy to get his arse over to the lab ASA-fucking-P. The Bush even angrier than he'd been when Shula was raped.

The lab crawling with the Bush's men when Big Sandy arrived. Three corpses to the left of the door, covered by blankets. The floor and wall near the door were red with blood. Further in, Fast Eddie, slumped on a chair, eyes unfocused, guarded by Eyes Burton. Big Sandy stopped beside Eyes. "What happened?"

"A gang broke out Phials."

"They got away?"

"Clean as fuck."

"The corpses?"

"Ours."

"Fast Eddie?"

Eyes hesitated. "Phials knocked him out with the shit he uses on the hounds. We don't think he was part of the gang but the Bush told me to keep an eye on him, just to be safe."

Big Sandy walked on, guided by a technician, to the control centre, where the Bush was studying footage of the break-out, eyes clouded, teeth bared, cheeks quivering. Big Sandy stepped up beside him and stared at the screen. Clint Smith, Tony Phials and a man in a balaclava, firing at an overhead target. Kevin and Tulip Tyne close by, wild-eyed, stunned, terrified. On an adjacent screen, three guards, firing from the landing. One took a bullet and toppled forward.

Big Sandy watched the scene play out. The man in the balaclava shoved Kevin through the door, grabbed Tulip, rushed out with her. Phials and Clint backed out after him. The guards raced to the door, found it locked from the outside, spilled back into the lab, more joining them from upstairs, milling about like sheep, checking the dead, yelling questions, unable to believe what had happened.

"See what that little prick of a cousin has done to me?" the Bush whispered. "I take him in, give him a home, a job, a future. And you see what he's done?"

"The guy in the balaclava's Gawl McCaskey," Big Sandy said, bitter that he hadn't made the connection between the pair of them twenty-four hours earlier.

The Bush's head turned slowly. "Who?"

"Gawl McCaskey. He was sniffing around for work a while back."

The Bush nodded slowly, remembering. "How do you know?"

"He's been hanging out with Clint and he's involved with the Tynes. I was at his place, waiting for him, when you called."

"You knew this was going to happen?" the Bush barked.

"No. I was there to stop him bothering the Tynes."

"*Bothering* them?" The Bush snorted. "He was in league with them."

"No," Big Sandy said. "Play it again. Kevin and Tulip were as shocked as the guards. They weren't part of this. Clint and McCaskey used them."

"I'll kill them anyway."

Big Sandy said nothing, not the right time to plead Tulip's case.

The Bush turned to one of the technicians. "Rewind and start over."

This time Big Sandy saw the scene play out from the beginning, Clint and Phials heading for the cellar with Fast Eddie, footage of Phials sedating a hound, moving off-camera, Phials and Clint returning by themselves, the guards answering the door, Kevin and Tulip entering, McCaskey bursting in, the gunfight, Clint and Phials joining the action, Phials ducking into his work station for a tin, the three men shooting their way out. Big Sandy focused on Clint, nervous going down the cellar but remarkably cool when he reappeared, calming McCaskey, firing clean, in command. Big Sandy surprised by the dealer's newly discovered backbone.

"I've sent men to the Tynes' flat," the Bush said as Clint and Phials backed out of the lab on screen. "And Clint's. They won't go home, they're not that stupid, but they may have left some clues as to where they're headed."

"They might return to McCaskey's," Gawl muttered. "If he thinks we won't be able to tie him to the break-out, he might plan to hole-up there."

"Send somebody over." The Bush sat back, face darker than Big Sandy had ever seen it. "This means Phials has the formula. They wouldn't risk so much unless he could guarantee payment." He ran his hands through his jet black hair, then thoughtfully fingered the gold St Christopher medal hanging from his neck. "I need Phials alive. That formula means more to me than revenge."

Big Sandy nodded. "You think Clint and McCaskey are in this alone?"

"I don't care," the Bush grunted. "What the fuck does it matter?"

"If they're front men, you can get on the grapevine, find out who was backing them, maybe cut a deal for Phials' return. If they operated alone, they'll be harder to trace."

The Bush thought about that. Sighed miserably. "I'm not thinking clearly. I still can't believe Clint did this. Where the hell did he grow the balls?" He stared at Big Sandy as if he expected an answer, then looked away sourly. "I'll find out if they're connected. What else should we do?"

"Send descriptions to every hotel and boarding house that we can, post photos on the streets of the major towns and cities, offer a reward, have men at all the airports and ferries."

"What else?"

"They left on foot," Big Sandy said.

"So?"

"The hounds." The Bush's face lit up. Big Sandy spoke quickly before his boss got carried away. "They probably had a car waiting, but if the hounds can lead us to where they were parked, we can knock on doors, ask if anyone saw them, maybe get a make on the car."

"Yes." Rubbing his hands together. "Take the hounds to their homes too. They only had a few days to arrange this. They may not have had the resources to set up a safe haven outside London. They might be lying low somewhere local, waiting for the storm to die down. If they are, the hounds can track them. Take them and as many men as you need. You're in charge of the search. Do whatever you have to. Just remember, I want Phials alive."

"What about Clint?"

The Bush smiled at the screen as he hit the rewind button again. "Alive if possible, so I can kill him myself, but dead's fine too."

Big Sandy nodded and hurried to Phials' bedroom to grab some of his clothes – he picked the robe the chemist had been wearing earlier – then down to the cellar, taking three men from the crowd in the lab. All four hounds were alert and wild, howling at the men as they approached. Big Sandy didn't bother with the syringes, no time. Grabbed a harness and muzzle, walked to one of the cages, opened the door, stepped inside, waited for the hound to leap then punched it to the floor. The hound hit the ground with a stunned grunt. Big Sandy was on it like lightning. Slipped the muzzle on, bundled the hound out of the cage, turned him over to one of the incredulous guards. Grabbed another harness and muzzle, went to fetch hound number two.

When the pair of hounds were ready, the four men led them up through the lab, two per dog. Big Sandy's hound howled when it caught the scent of blood. Big Sandy hauled the dog away from the crimson pools, didn't want it locking on to the scent of the dead men. The guards followed with the other hound. On the pavement, Big Sandy grabbed the back of his hound's neck, then stuffed the balled-up robe into its face. The hound tried to back away, then fixed on the scent of Phials and growled eagerly. Big Sandy tossed the robe to the others, then gave his hound its head. The hound sniffed around, caught the scent of Phials, took off after him, Big Sandy striding fast behind.

The hound led Big Sandy to the mouth of the cul-de-sac, turned right, heading towards the Walworth Road. The other hound caught up, the guards struggling to control it. A few metres further on, the dogs came to a swath of white powder. They sniffed, inhaled grains, then stiffened, eyes widening. They started to choke and whine, then both went frantic, limbs spastic, collapsing, twitching, tearing free of their handlers. Within seconds they were coughing up blood and choking. Seconds later, dead.

The men stared at the dead hounds, then at the white substance. Big Sandy cursed silently then glanced around. This part of the street was bordered on one side by a furniture warehouse, on the other by offices, both buildings deserted this late. He picked up the nearest corpse and slung it over a shoulder. "Get the other one," he snapped, passing the guards, heading back to the lab, not looking forward to breaking the news to the Bush. It was going to be a long, horrible bitch of a night. Beginning to wish he'd stayed in Margate.

FIFTY

Clint sipped tea and gazed around the study at the others, Gawl, Kevin, Tulip, Phials and Fr Sebastian, all glum except Phials, who hadn't stopped grinning since Tuesday, forty hours of smiles and chuckles, even when he was sleeping. Kevin and Tulip clung to one another, wide-eyed, silent, scared. Gawl sat by the window, squinting through the material of the heavy curtains, cradling his gun in his lap. He hadn't washed since the break-out, still traces of blood on his face and hands. Phials was by the bookcase, reading a novel he'd picked out earlier. Fr Sebastian near the door, wringing his hands, blinking rapidly, in shock.

The priest went into meltdown when they turned up at his door on Tuesday, bloody, Kevin and Tulip in a daze, Phials punching the air with glee, Clint and Gawl packing guns. Hadn't even thought of turning them away, just ushered them in, speechless, bewildered. They'd sat up all night, too stoked to sleep, Gawl and Clint boasting about their exploits, Phials cackling dementedly, Kevin and Tulip shivering, hugging, crying, Fr Sebastian listening numbly to Gawl and Clint.

Towards dawn, Gawl and Clint ran out of words and

just sat, smiling, re-living the night inside their heads, neither able to fully believe it, wondering if this was part of a crazy dream. After half an hour of silence, Fr Sebastian said, "You can't stay here." Everybody looked at him as if he was mad, even the Tynes. "You killed people," he cried. "I can't grant refuge to killers. You have to leave. You can stay until morning, then you –"

Gawl pointed his gun at the priest, shutting him up. "Clint," he growled. "Explain it. I don't have the fucking patience."

"We've nowhere else to go," Clint said quietly. "This is the one place they'll never look. We're safe here. So are you."

"No," Fr Sebastian moaned. "This is a house of God. You can't –"

"If we leave, and we're caught, they'll trace us back to you," Clint said. Fr Sebastian stopped moaning. "You're in this now. What works for us works for you. We have to stay. It's best for all of us."

The priest said nothing for a long time after that. Mulled the situation over. He made breakfast for his guests, showed them where they'd be sleeping, watched as Gawl locked Kevin and Tulip into their bedroom, directed Phials to the bathroom – he wanted to shower – then returned with Gawl and Clint to the study. When the three were seated, he asked Clint how long they intended to stay. Gawl answered before Clint could. "Weeks, maybe longer, depending on how things pan out."

"How am I supposed to hide you?" Fr Sebastian complained. "I have a constant stream of visitors, parishioners, cleaning ladies, fellow clergymen."

"Not any more ye don't," Gawl grunted. "Tell 'em t' fuck off."

"I can't just –"

"Ye can," Gawl insisted.

Fr Sebastian's jaw firmed. "Don't push me too far, McCaskey."

"Why?" Gawl jeered. "What'll ye do?"

"You said a lot tonight when you were boasting. Told me about Tony Phials, that he's worth a lot of money, that you stole him from Dave Bushinsky. I know who the Bush is. I'm sure he'd reward me generously if I told him you were here."

"We'd tell him about your thing for little girls if you did," Clint snapped.

Fr Sebastian smiled witheringly. "I have a hold over you and you have a hold over me. But my hold is greater. You *might* tell the Bush about me, and he *might* act on that information. But if I *do* tell him about you, he most definitely *will* come after you and –"

"I'll kill Tulip Tyne," Gawl interrupted. Fr Sebastian stared. "If they come gunning for us, I'll kill her first."

"You can't frighten me with vacant threats," Fr Sebastian wheezed.

Gawl smiled coldly. "There's fuck all vacant about my threats. Why d' ye think I brought the Tynes here instead of shooting 'em and dumping their bodies on the way? If ye do anything t' fuck things up for us, I'll fuck things up for *them*. On the other hand," he added slyly, "if ye play along like a good wee boy, Tulip will be yer reward and ye can do what ye like with her."

"You're an animal," Fr Sebastian snarled.

"Aye," Gawl laughed. "But ye need young girls and I've brought one for ye. Cross us, she dies. Help us, ye can fuck her till yer dick drops off."

Fr Sebastian hadn't said much since. Wednesday passed quietly, Gawl and Clint dozed a lot, Phials joined them in the study and read, Gawl brought Tulip and Kevin down later. Everybody nervous and sullen, except Phials. To bed early, long hours of unbroken sleep, exhaustion overcoming fear.

Gawl and Clint more relaxed when they woke on Thursday, no sign that anyone had connected them with Fr Sebastian. Everything going according to plan. They ate a full breakfast, cracked jokes with Phials. Clint even tried striking up a conversation with Kevin and Tulip, but they were still too dazed to respond.

In the afternoon, as they all relaxed in the study and Clint sipped tea, Phials set down the book he'd been reading and coughed. "I know the last few days have passed in a rush, and we haven't had time to discuss our plans, but don't you guys think it's time we went over our getaway options?"

Gawl and Clint stared at Phials, then at each other. Clint looked pointedly at Fr Sebastian. "Father, would you mind taking Kevin and Tulip up to their room?"

The priest nodded sullenly and led the Tynes out. When they were alone, Gawl shook his head at Phials. "Don't talk in front of those three. The less they know about what we'll be getting up t', the better."

"OK," Phials smiled. "But now that we're alone, what's the plan?"

"We don't have one."

Phials frowned. "You're joking, right?"

"There wasn't time to think about it," Clint said softly. "We had to get you out and we had to do it fast. We could only afford to look ahead one step at a time."

Phials began to object. Stopped. Nodded respectfully. "No, you're right, getting me out was the priority and you did, and I thank you for that. But now that I'm free, what next? You must have some kind of an idea."

"That depends a lot on what kind of ideas *ye* have," Gawl said. "Clint told me ye've contacts in the States."

"Sure," Phials said, smiling crookedly, "but I can only get in touch with them when we reach America. I don't have up to date phone numbers, I haven't spoken to them in years, I'm not sure who I can trust, who's down on their luck and who's riding high. Once we hit New York, I can ask around, get the lie of the land. But I can't get us there. I thought you guys would handle that end of things."

"We will," Clint assured him. "But it's going to take a while. We –"

"Ye said ye had contacts," Gawl barked, silencing Clint. "Ye said breaking out was the hard part, that it was plain sailing after that."

"Once we cross the Atlantic," Phials insisted. "When we're Stateside I can sell the formula, we'll make a fortune, it'll be the good life. But I never said I could get us there. Clint?"

"That was the deal," Clint agreed quietly. "It's our job to get him to America. He kicks in with the formula after that."

Phials leant forward uneasily. "Are you saying you *can't* get me out?"

Gawl glared back aggressively. "Of course we can. It would've been a lot easier if we had someone at the other end putting up money, papers, arranging a safe hideout. But we'll manage by ourselves if we must. It'll just take a bit longer."

"So you have the situation in hand?" Phials asked dubiously.

"Aye," Gawl said. "Even if we had someone in the States, we couldn't go yet, the Bush'll have people everywhere looking for us. We'll stay here as long as we have t', wait for the Bush t' give up, then work something out. We can get false passports, steal a car, drive t' France, catch a flight west."

"How will you get the passports?" Phials pressed him.

"Don't worry," Gawl grunted. "We'll get them. In the meanwhile we might as well enjoy ourselves. We're gonna be locked up here a long time and it could get pretty boring, but it needn't be all doom and gloom. Clint, wanna make his day?"

"I dropped off a load of shit on Tuesday," Clint grinned. "Coke, E's, grass, even some heroin, enough to keep you and Tulip high for months."

"All right!" Phials beamed.

"Speaking of Tulip," Gawl added with a chuckle, "the Tynes aren't part of the team, they're gonna have t' pay their way. Any time ye want her, just ask."

Phials laughed softly. "You guys are great hosts." He licked his lips hungrily. "Could I have some of that stash now? I've been running on the rush of freedom since Tuesday, but that high's beginning to fade. I could do with a top-up."

"Go find Fr Seb," Gawl smiled. "He'll sort ye out." Gawl kept smiling while Phials rose and exited, but once the chemist was out of earshot, the smile vanished and he spun on Clint furiously. "That cunt has fuck all contacts in America."

"What do you mean?" Clint blinked.

"He bullshitted us. I saw it in his eyes. He just wants us t' get him the fuck out of here so he can ditch us and run for the fucking hills."

"Nuh-no," Clint frowned. "He needs us."

"T' get t' America, aye. After that..." Gawl shook his head, disgusted.

"He'll still need us," Clint insisted. "To protect him, make suh-sure he doesn't get screwed, keep him safe, see that the duh-deal goes down cleanly."

"What if there isn't any deal?" Gawl asked softly. "What if Baby P isn't ready, if he lied so that we'd sneak him out?"

Clink shook his head. "He knows we'd kuh-kill him if

he tried to cheat us."

"Maybe he figured he'd take his chances. Definitely dead if he stayed. At least out here he has a chance t' get away and give us the slip."

"He wouldn't do that," Clint croaked, but his voice lacked conviction.

Gawl strode to the door of the study, opened it a crack, looked out, closed it again. "What if we sold him back t' the Bush?" he whispered.

Clint stared at him with disbelief. "*What?*"

"The Bush is a businessman. He'd be mad as fuck, but if he could buy Phials back for a couple of million, with the promise of the formula..."

"But the formula's worth fuh-fifty million or more," Clint gasped.

"*If* Phials has cracked it. He might have bullshitted us."

"No," Clint said.

"Too many complications trying t' get him out of the country," Gawl muttered. "Simpler this way."

"No." Clint came to his feet, hands clenched into fists. "I want America. I want the fortune. I want..." Stopped short of saying *Shula*. "If we can't get him out, we'll suh-sell the formula here, but to some other dealer. *Not* to Dave. Dave would kill me rather than cuh-cut a deal with me."

"He's the only one we know who has that kind of money," Gawl said.

"And he's the only one who has ruh-reason to hate us, especially *me*." Clint was quivering. "We proceed as pluh-planned. It won't be easy, but we knew from the start it wouldn't be. This is no time to puh-panic."

"I'm not panicking," Gawl said calmly. He studied Clint's face, saw the dealer's determination, smiled. "But I guess ye're right. Best t' hold firm, thrash out a plan, pray that the drug's real, not make any silly mistakes." Clint relaxed and Gawl scratched his stomach. "Now, what about Tulip?"

"What about her?" Clint frowned.

"She's not just for Phials and Fr Seb. We can have a crack at her too."

Clint shook his head. "I cuh-couldn't."

"It's all right," Gawl chuckled. "I'll ban Kevin from the room."

"It's not that," Clint said. "I didn't mind the hookers. They were happy to take our money. Tulip's different. It wouldn't feel right."

Gawl shrugged. "Suit yerself. Ye don't mind if I take a turn though, d' ye?"

"No," Clint sighed, knowing there was no point taking a moral stand after all that they'd done, he'd sound like a hypocrite. "But no ruh-rough stuff. Kevin's docile, but if you hurt Tulip, he might fuh-fight back."

"I'll be gentle as a lamb," Gawl promised and slipped out, leaving Clint alone in the study, thinking about passports and plane tickets, beginning to wonder if they'd taken on more than they could handle, Tuesday's courage slowly deserting him, giving way to confusion and fear.

FIFTY-ONE

Kevin had been operating numbly since the events in the lab. An automaton, crushed, bewildered, lost. He retreated into a childish shell — matters would resolve themselves, problems would disappear, somebody would make everything right. He moved when ordered, ate when hungry, emptied his bladder, slept when tired. That was all.

Tulip was as helpless as Kevin, overwhelmed by the suddenness and brutality of what had happened. That first night she got high to numb herself to the shock, but the next afternoon she woke determined to seek help from less debasing quarters. Cutting down on her drugs intake – unable to abandon them instantly – she turned to God and threw herself into prayer. Late Wednesday and Thursday, when the church was deserted, she went there with Clint and prayed for hours, peaceful, quiet, finding strength in God. She would have liked Fr Sebastian to pray with her but he was ashamed of himself and avoided her as much as possible.

Fr Sebastian hadn't had sex with her yet but she knew it was only a matter of time before he succumbed to temptation. Phials and McCaskey had already taken advantage. McCaskey as rough as he'd been before, stroking her as tenderly as he could with his callused fingers, whispering to her of his past, his future, what he planned to do with his money.

Kevin was in the room when Phials made love to her but he took no part in it, staring off into space. Gawl made him sit outside. Kevin hadn't objected.

As Friday developed, Kevin slowly emerged from his haze. He found himself thinking clearly for the first time since the break-out, wondering what it had been in aid of (oblivious to all that Gawl and Clint had said), why they were hiding here, keeping him and Tulip captive. Looking around, he found himself alone in their bedroom with his sister. She was sitting by the window (Gawl had nailed it shut), staring through the curtains. Kevin rose sluggishly, walked across, touched her gently on the neck. "Hey," he croaked. "Are you OK?"

"Yes. And you?"

"I don't know." Kevin squatted. She put an arm around him absentmindedly. "What's happening? I blanked out for a while."

"You know where we are?"

"The Church of Sacred Martyrs."

"Remember what happened at the lab?"

He nodded. "But I don't understand it."

Tulip explained the situation quickly, quietly, about Phials and his new drug.

"But why are *we* here?" Kevin asked, still confused.

"They used us as a distraction."

"I get that. But why hold on to us? Why not leave us there?"

She smiled sadly. "They could be here a long time. They need something to keep boredom at bay. They have alcohol and drugs. And *me*."

Kevin recalled Phials and McCaskey visiting Tulip and winced. "We have to escape." He looked at her for reassurance, as if he might be crazy to even voice such an opinion. "Don't we?"

Tulip sighed. "We were at the lab when they freed Tony. We left with them. The men hunting them will think we were a willing part of it."

"We'll tell them the truth. They'll listen to reason. We'll lead them here."

"Getting away won't be easy."

"But we could do it," Kevin insisted, studying the glass in the window and the yard out back. They could break the glass, drop to the ground, cross the yard, scale the wall, flee through the alley which he could see on the other side.

"Maybe," Tulip agreed. "And maybe we could

convince Dave Bushinsky that we're innocent." She put both hands on Kevin's face, twisted his head around, locked gazes with him. "But what would happen next?"

"They'd come here, find Clint and the others, kill them."

"That doesn't bother you?"

"After what they did to us?" he snorted. "Do *you* care?"

Tulip hesitated. "Maybe not the others, but Fr Sebastian is being used like we are. He doesn't deserve to die."

"He can take his chances," Kevin snarled.

"What about us?" Tulip said. "Even if we can convince them we weren't part of the plan, we still know about it."

"So?"

"You don't kill four men in a church without attracting attention. There'll be public uproar if a priest is killed. An investigation. Dave Bushinsky won't talk. His killers won't talk. But you and I..."

"We won't talk either," Kevin huffed.

Tulip smiled thinly. "If you were Dave Bushinsky, would you take that chance or would you kill us along with the others, eliminating all the loose ends?"

Kevin nodded slowly. "So what do we do?" he asked, ceding authority to her.

"For now we have to play along," Tulip said softly.

"We're safe here. Maybe we can escape later, with the aid of Fr Sebastian. If the three of us can get away, we could go to the police, seek help and shelter."

Kevin stiffened automatically. "There must be some other way."

Tulip sighed. Even with their lives on the line he was desperate to maintain his hold over her. "There isn't," she said. "And bear in mind that you have more to lose than me."

"What do you mean?" Kevin frowned.

"If I'm here to keep the boys happy, I have a use, so they'll keep me alive. But you're not part of the sex deal any more. They don't need you, so what's to stop them killing you?" She got up, left the room and wandered downstairs, leaving Kevin alone, frozen by the window, struck dumb.

FIFTY-TWO

Gawl felt caged-in. Phials passed the time getting high, while Clint and Fr Sebastian had fear to distract them. But Gawl was sober and irritable. He wanted to get drunk, go on a bender, celebrate — but he had to stay focused, keep everything together. Afraid if he got drunk and blacked out that Clint might crumble and he'd awake to an empty house, all the others slipping free while he was comatose. Sex with Tulip helped distract him, but only temporarily.

Gawl didn't trust Phials. He was all smiles around the chemist, pumping him full of coke and grass, letting him ramble on, throwing in occasional probing questions, piecing together a picture of the chemist which was far from promising.

Phials a junkie who'd cheated a series of employers, on the run from several death threats. He'd found refuge in London when he was at his lowest, locked away from the world by a sly Dave Bushinsky. Most of his *contacts* were men who would kill him or sell him out for the rewards which had been posted since he went into hiding. Phials spoke of operating undercover, *Mysterious Doctor X*, but that was bullshit. Enough people knew of the wonder drug he was working on to be able to link it to him if it appeared on the market. He'd be a marked man the minute he started to tout Baby P around.

The mega bucks deal devaluing hourly. Even if Phials was serious about trying to sell the formula for fifty million — and Gawl didn't think he was — how could he? The more Gawl picked at it, the more the knot unravelled.

Getting out of England — how? He knew men who could provide them with fake passports, but the Bush would have posted a reward for information leading to their capture, and every one of those men would turn Gawl in for the cash.

Even if they escaped to the States, the Bush surely had allies in America. Photographs and descriptions would have been circulated. People looking for them in all the major cities. Never able to rest easy. And that was before he factored in those who hated and were already hunting for Phials.

If they hid safely, somewhere obscure, how would they negotiate a deal? And even if they weren't in hiding, Gawl didn't think they could pull off a coup this big. Too many sharks waiting to rip the novices to pieces.

And if, against all the impossibilities, they somehow negotiated a deal and got out of it alive, with a shit-load of money, how to invest and protect it? You couldn't just walk into a bank, dump millions of dollars in unmarked bills on the manager's desk and ask to open an account.

Gawl still thought they could make money from the chemist, but America was out. Fifty million dollars was out. They were cheap hoods. If they accepted their limits they might come out of this sweetly. If they set their sights higher, they'd come out of it dead.

By Saturday night Gawl had decided. They had to sell Phials – or the formula –to the Bush. He reckoned they could demand a couple of million, more than enough to suit his needs and see him nicely through retirement. Once he'd settled for the more attainable dream, he was still left with a variety of problems, such as what to do about the Tynes and Fr Seb, where to go after the deal, how to stash his cut, but they would be relatively easy to solve. Three key hurdles —

How to betray Phials without him clicking.

How to arrange the deal so he wouldn't get burnt.

And Clint.

Clint wouldn't go for this, no matter how Gawl laid it out. Gawl would have to find a way to drag him back to reality, remove the fifty million dollar option, leave him with no choice but to play along. If that didn't work and Clint still resisted... Cheat him? Dump him? Kill him?

Gawl considered.

FIFTY-THREE

The hunt was hot. All the Bush's resources dedicated towards finding Tony Phials and those who'd kidnapped him. Every airport and ferry in the UK covered, under guard twenty-four-seven. They'd collected footage from security cameras at most of the train stations in London, a team of men and women scrutinising the footage for traces of the fugitives. Men following EVERY train and bus route out of London, getting off at EVERY stop, quizzing guards, station personnel and taxi drivers. All of the Bush's contacts in the country notified, a reward of a million for the safe return of Tony Phials, half a million each for the return dead or alive of Clint Smith, Gawl McCaskey, Kevin and Tulip Tyne. Photos of Phials, Clint, Kevin and Tulip e-mailed, faxed, posted or hand-delivered to every city and many of the bigger towns, teams of freelance operatives driving around, flashing photos, the Bush covering everyone's travelling expenses.

The search was costing the Bush a fortune — he didn't care. His friends, family and troops thought he'd lost his marbles — he didn't care. All that mattered was finding Phials and the fuckers who'd helped him. He'd go bankrupt before he gave up the chase, blow everything on it, throw away the hard work of a lifetime if necessary, not content to let this one go.

Then, on Sunday, December 17th, a phone call from one of the Bush's moles at White Hart Lane. Alan Sugar was preparing a public announcement, declaring his intent to sell his controlling interest in Tottenham Hotspur. A deal likely to be agreed by the end of the week, a company called ENIC poised to buy him out. This was the Bush's final chance to push a claim. Could he come up with an offer by the end of the day?

The Bush at home when he received the call. Went wild. Thrashed the place. Alice and Shula fled. He stormed through the house, destroying anything he could lay his hands on, his bodyguards cowering outside. They phoned Big Sandy for his advice. He told them to let the Bush rage, keep out of his way, not to enter until summoned. They asked him to come and talk with the Bush. He laughed. "Do you think I'm crazy?"

The Bush stopped suddenly in the middle of taking an axe to an oil painting by Modigliani which he'd bought years earlier for seventeen thousand pounds, worth over a hundred grand now. Stared at the ripped canvas, then at the axe. Dropped it. Sank to the floor. Moaned. One last burst of fury, this time mental — he'd put in an offer for Sugar's shares even though he couldn't afford it, gamble on finding Phials before he had to pay, maybe tell his global contacts that the drug was ready, con them into putting up the stake money, buy into the club and hole-up at White Hart Lane in the hope that they'd never find him there.

The madness passed. He realised his plans were sunk. Spurs would never be his. Made a short apology to his dead grandfather. Set thoughts of the club behind him. Considered his recent actions. Smiled humourlessly at how much money he'd pissed away. Made a series of short calls, countermanding previous orders, freeing most of his people to return to their normal duties, drastically downscaling the search operation. Near the end of the calls he rang Big Sandy and told him to come a little later, he wanted to talk. Then he phoned Alice and tried explaining the situation to her — his most difficult task.

Big Sandy had been beating the streets since the break-out, grilling every friend and half-acquaintance of Smith and the Tynes. Not as gruelling as he thought it would be. Smith had dealt to lots of people but socialised with few of them, and the Tynes led quiet lives, hardly any friends to interview. Big Sandy found an address book in Tulip's room and phoned or visited all the contacts in it, but most were school friends who hadn't seen her since she left, and the couple who'd been in recent contact knew nothing of any break-out. They assumed she was at home, keeping her head down like usual.

Coming up blank on Smith and the Tynes, Big Sandy went hunting for Gawl McCaskey. No photos of the Scot, though they'd compiled a number of sketches from people who'd known him. The sketches differed wildly. In some he was lean, in others stout. He had grey hair, white hair, black hair, he was bald. He was tall, all who knew him agreed, but accounts put him between six foot and six foot eight. His eyes were blue/green/brown, his nose bent to the left, the right or was squashed like a boxer's. Everybody mentioned the missing upper half of his ear, but a few swore it was his right ear, not his left.

Big Sandy compiled a list of people outside London who'd known McCaskey in the past, getting names and phone numbers from Eyes Burton and others, phoning everyone he could, adding to his list whenever those he contacted passed on new names. McCaskey had travelled a lot and Big Sandy was soon logging calls to America, Australia, Europe, Russia. But the Scot had made no genuine friends that Big Sandy could find. Big Sandy told them about the reward and asked them to phone him if they heard from McCaskey. All said they would.

McCaskey troubled him. The man had all the substance of a ghost. He'd asked a lot of people if they had photos of him but nobody could find any. A few thought they might have old snaps lying around somewhere, and promised to look, but no comebacks yet. Prints had been taken from his apartment and were being checked against police records, but nobody had thought to do that until Thursday afternoon, by which time dozens of the Bush's men had been in and out, smearing prints, leaving their own. It would be a long, difficult process to isolate McCaskey's.

Big Sandy believed that McCaskey was the key. Smith would never have had the guts to instigate this. There might be someone behind McCaskey, the brains of the outfit, sheltering the kidnappers and planning for the future, but McCaskey was the catalyst. Piecing it together — Clint and McCaskey started hanging out a few weeks before the break-out. Big Sandy didn't know how they met, but they fell in together and bonded. When the Bush hit Phials with the ultimatum, Phials told Smith. Smith told McCaskey. McCaskey probably told someone with money and influence, who hit on the master plan of using a couple of amateurs to steal the Bush's pharmaceutical prize cow. No link between Smith and Mr X, but there must be one between Mr X and

McCaskey, most likely a guy the Scot once worked for. Trace McCaskey's past acquaintances and maybe Big Sandy would stumble across the mystery brains of the break-out.

He was doing this – phoning, asking questions, gathering names – when the Bush summoned him. Glad to hear sanity in the Bush's voice. He caught a cab. Noted the carnage when he entered – staff busy cleaning up the mess – but said nothing. Found the Bush in the kitchen, brooding over a mug of coffee. "Sugar's selling Spurs," he said as if announcing a death. "My chance to buy the club has come and gone."

Big Sandy took that in. "That mean you don't care any more about getting Phials back alive? He'll do dead?"

The Bush sighed. "No, I still want him alive. The money won't please me as much as it would have, but I'll find a use for it." His expression hardened. "But it does mean I now want Clint alive too. I want to make him suffer. Personally."

"Confident of finding him?"

The Bush nodded. "Now that time is no longer an issue, I'm sure we'll track them down. We can play it cute. I've already notified a lot of our people. We'll spread the word that the search is off. Admit defeat."

"But go on searching anyway?" Big Sandy guessed.

"Yes, but quietly. They'll think the heat is off, wait a bit longer, make their move, and we'll catch them." The Bush asked Big Sandy if he'd like anything to drink. Big Sandy accepted a beer, his first since Tuesday. "What have you been working on?" the Bush enquired. Big Sandy told him about his search for Gawl McCaskey. "Any leads?"

"Not yet. But he's the one. If we get him, we'll get them all."

"Think that he did this to me because I wouldn't give him a job?"

"No. He'd been asking all over for work, turned down by everyone. He just saw a good thing, persuaded somebody to back him, and went for it."

"I'm not so sure they had help," the Bush said. "If they'd had time to plan this properly, yes, they could have found people with the money and means to make it work. But it reeks of a rush job. I think they may have gone into it alone."

"Then who's hiding them?" Big Sandy snorted. "Who'll get them out of the country? Who'll sell the formula?"

"I know," the Bush laughed. "It's crazy. But wouldn't it be hilarious if they pulled this off without thinking ahead and are holed up somewhere, no idea what to do next, tearing their hair out?"

"It'd be brilliant," Big Sandy smiled. "But it couldn't happen. Nobody's *that* dumb."

FIFTY-FOUR

Clint frantic, toying with exit strategies all weekend. Monday morning, still didn't know how to work it. They had plenty of money — he'd transferred his savings in cash to the church before the break-out — and he and Gawl both knew people who could provide them with fake passports. But had to figure that the forgers would betray them for the reward that had surely been posted, or else demand a fortune for their services. One idea was to sneak out of the country — steal a yacht or hide in a truck bound for France, something like that — and find a forger in mainland Europe who hadn't heard about them. But that would take a lot of time, they'd be vulnerable, and Phials would have plenty of opportunities to give them the slip.

Worried about Phials, the doc doing too much coke and grass, stoned out of his skull, having frequent sex with Tulip, no apparent interest in their predicament. But Clint had caught Phials studying him slyly a couple of times, the doc's eyes focused. Clint thought he was putting on an act, assessing Clint and Gawl. If they came up short, maybe he'd formulate a plan of his own and ditch them.

He discussed it with Gawl, careful not to mention his suspicions about Phials. Gawl was already wary of the chemist and Clint didn't want him losing his cool. "Wuh-when do you think we should make our muh-muh-muh-move?"

"January or February," Gawl said. "We'll let Christmas pass, wait for bad weather – easier t' get about when everyone's stuck indoors – then slip away."

"You duh-don't think we should go earlier?"

Gawl squinted at him. "The plan was t' lay up here for a month or two."

"I know. Buh-but if we went now, we'd maybe catch them by surprise. They wuh-wouldn't be expecting it."

Gawl tilted his head warningly. "Don't lose yer nerve."

Clint bristled. "I'm nuh-not losing my nerve. I just th-th-th-think –"

"Don't think," Gawl barked. "Or if ye must, think about how we're gonna get passports and keep Phials under wraps when we're transporting him and what we'll do if his *contacts* turn out t' be bullshit."

Clint cringed then slunk away.

That evening, in the study, watching the news on a portable TV, eating corn flakes. Only idly interested until the sports section, when the big news of the day was announced, Alan Sugar selling his controlling shares in

Spurs. Clint thought of cousin Dave and the fit he must be throwing. Went looking for Gawl. Found him upstairs with Tulip, Kevin sitting outside their bedroom door, listening to them have sex, weeping. "You should steer clear while they're at it," Clint told him.

Kevin stared up at Clint through his tears. "Fuck off," he moaned.

"You're just tormenting yourself sitting here. You –"

"Fuck off!" Kevin snapped, louder this time, half getting to his feet.

"Easy," Clint said, stepping away. "Tell Gawl I want to see him when he's finished. I'll be in the living room."

Fr Sebastian was already there. He looked awful, pale, thin, trembling, unshaven. Clint tried to have a chat with him, but he ducked out, said he was heading back into the church, where he was spending most of his time, praying desperately for an end to this nightmare.

Clint poured himself a vodka and sipped slowly. Gawl entered, doing up his flies. "Ye wanted t' see me?"

"Newsflash," Clint smirked. "Alan Sugar's selling his shares in Spurs."

"That's no news," Gawl yawned.

"He's gone public, announced it to the media. They expect him to name a buyer by the end of the week."

Gawl sat, thinking about that. Studied Clint's smile.

"Why are ye so happy?"

"It means Dave's been cut out of the deal."

"So?"

"He wanted to sell Phials' formula to raise the money to finance the buy-out. Now that he can't, he won't be so all-fired-up to get Phials back."

"Phials is still worth millions t' him," Gawl said.

"Sure, but Dave wanted Spurs. Without the club, money's just money. He'd like more, the same as anyone else, but it's no longer essential."

"You think he'll turn round and let us have Phials?" Gawl asked sceptically.

"Of course not," Clint said. "But Phials isn't as valuable as he was. Dave won't chase us as hard as he would have if Spurs was still up for grabs."

Gawl scowled. "But it also means that if we try t' sell Phials t' him, we won't get as much as we could have a week ago."

Clint frowned. "We're taking him to America as planned."

"Aye. But if the worst came t' the worst and we couldn't get him out of the country and had t' cut a deal…"

"We'll cut it with somebody else," Clint said stiffly. "I already told you Dave would rather kill us than deal with us. Come on, have a drink, this is good news."

"Yeah," Gawl said. "I suppose ye're right." Taking the drink once Clint had poured a glass for him, saluting the dealer and smiling, Clint not noting the strained nature of the smile, unaware of the whirring cogs inside his partner's brain.

FIFTY-FIVE

Kevin sat in the hallway, crying with frustration, listening to Gawl McCaskey fuck Tulip. He wanted to charge in, attack McCaskey, kill him. But that was an idle dream. McCaskey would crush him without even shifting out of low gear.

Clint turned up in the middle of Kevin's torment and told him he shouldn't be sitting out here. Kevin told him to fuck off.

Picking apart their predicament as he waited for McCaskey to finish. Damned if they stayed, damned if they fled. Swaying continuously between their options. Wait, hope McCaskey and Clint got away with Phials and left the Tynes alive. Or attempt an escape and take their chances with Dave Bushinsky. Logcially it didn't look good either way. If they stayed, McCaskey would probably kill them, while if they escaped, Bushinsky would slaughter them once he got rid of McCaskey and Clint. No reason why either party should let them live and run the risk of having the Tynes come back to haunt them.

What if they escaped and avoided Bushinsky, got out of the country, holed up somewhere foreign? That seemed like their only real hope. But they had no money, no passports, not even spare clothes.

Clint had money. Kevin thought about stealing from the dealer. But even if he could, their passports were back in their apartment and Bushinsky's men would be keeping watch there. They might even have confiscated the passports to make sure Kevin and Tulip couldn't use them.

The door opened. McCaskey came out, flies undone, leering at Kevin. "She's a grand wee fuck." Kevin glared daggers. Told McCaskey that Clint wanted to see him. Hurried in to check on Tulip. She was dressing, eyes vacant.

"Did he hurt you?"

Tulip sighed. "No."

Kevin sat on the edge of the bed. Stared at his hands, twisted into feeble fists. "I'm sorry."

"You can't do anything about it. You could once. Not now." She sighed again. "It's Christmas this day week."

Kevin blinked. "Is it?"

"Today's the 18th."

He shrugged. "I've lost track of time. I suppose you're right."

"I've been thinking about our last Christmas with Mum and Dad. You came round, we had dinner, you and Dad got tipsy, we played charades."

Kevin chuckled. "It seems so long ago."

"I've never enjoyed Christmas since," Tulip said wistfully. "I recall that day, how happy we were, no idea it was our last Christmas as a family."

Kevin said nothing, ashamed to tell her that the last two yuletides, when he'd had her all to himself, had been his happiest ever.

Tulip finished dressing, walked around and crouched by his side. She took his hands. Gazed at him earnestly. "I don't want to spend Christmas here."

"Neither do I," he said, "but what choice do we have?"

"Christmas would be a good time to escape. The church will be packed on Christmas Eve. We can sneak through, shelter among the crowd, slip out with them when they're leaving, go to the police, tell them everything."

Kevin thought about it. Better than any plan he'd come up with. The only part he didn't like was going to the police. But since they had no passports or money, what were their alternatives? Besides, they didn't have to tell the police about their appointments. They could invent some story to explain how they'd got mixed up with the kidnappers, maybe persuade Fr Sebastian to accompany them and back up their version of events.

Tulip read Kevin's thoughts. Gripped his hands tighter,

hope growing in her heart. "You think it would work?"

"Maybe," he said hesitantly. "But we'd have to come up with something good to tell the police. We can't let them know how we came to be associated with Clint, Phials and McCaskey."

Tulip pouted. "We can't worry about that now."

"Our lives won't be worth anything if the police find out I've been acting as a pimp for my sister," Kevin said bluntly. He saw tears twinkling in Tulip's eyes. He kissed her forehead reassuringly. "It's a good idea. But we have to make sure we don't do anything stupid later. Getting out is the main thing, but holding on to our freedom if we escape is important too."

While they were discussing Tulip's plan, Fr Sebastian knocked on the door. Kevin welcomed him. "Glad to see you," he beamed, shaking the bemused priest's hand. "We were just talking about you."

"Really?" Fr Sebastian smiled crookedly.

"Any news, Father?" Tulip asked brightly.

"No." He stared at her, then at Kevin. He hadn't expected such a response. He wasn't sure how to react.

Kevin saw the confusion in the priest's eyes — then the lust. He pulled Tulip away. She frowned at him but he ignored her. "What can we do for you, Father?" he asked quietly, stepping between the priest and his sister.

"Just... calling to see... how you were," Fr Sebastian wheezed.

"No," Kevin said stiffly. "You weren't."

Behind him, Tulip's eyes widened. "Father!" she gasped.

Fr Sebastian's head dropped. "I'm sorry," he muttered. "But I've been locked up here like the rest of you. I have needs."

"You can't," Kevin snapped.

"But I... we did... before..."

"Before was before. Now you can't."

"But Gawl does. And Tony. Why not..."

Kevin took a step forward. Pressed his face close to the priest's. "Get out," he snarled, a hypocrite's moral outrage burning deep within him.

Fr Sebastian backpedalled. Hit the door with his shoulders. Scrabbled for the handle. Started to open it. Paused. "If I told Gawl and Clint, they'd make you let me," he said sulkingly.

"You won't tell them," Tulip said. She stepped up beside Kevin, eyes sad, heart heavy. "You aren't evil. Weak, yes, but not evil."

Fr Sebastian's eyes welled with tears. "I'm sorry," he cried, meaning it. "God forgive me." He threw the door open, lurched into the hallway, stumbling for the bathroom, hands over his mouth, bile frothing up his throat.

Kevin closed the door. When he turned, Tulip launched herself at him, wrapped her arms around him and wept, hugging him, thanking him. He stroked her hair, whispering kind words, loving her like a brother. When the tears passed they sat on the bed and she smiled gratefully. "Thank you," she said again.

"For what?"

"You could have let him have me."

"No. I can't do anything about the others but I can fight off Parry. That much at least I have the strength to do."

"But you didn't do it when he first came looking for me."

Kevin blushed. "That was different. Another time and place."

"But you could have let him have me again. It would have been simpler. And it would have made him easier to deal with if we're to include him in our plan. But you didn't. You stood up for me, no matter what the cost."

Kevin held a shaky smile. He hadn't thought of that. Instantly regretting his protective burst, wishing he'd let Parry have her.

Tulip didn't see that. She was still blinded by his temporary flash of chivalry. Clutching him close, she reached a snap decision. Moved away from him on the bed, placed her hands over her stomach, observed him seriously. "I have something to tell you. I've been trying to tell you for ages. Actually," she grinned guiltily, "I wasn't sure if I should. I thought about keeping it to myself."

"What are you talking about?" Kevin laughed.

"Remember when you walked in on me and Rita?"

"Your friend from school? Sure."

"She didn't come round just to talk. Rita works in a pharmacy. I was pretty sure but I wanted to be certain. She brought a kit and helped me with the test."

"Test?" Kevin frowned. "Are you ill?"

"No, silly." Tulip patted her stomach and smiled nervously. "I'm pregnant."

FIFTY-SIX

Gawl thinking hard about Phials, Clint, the Bush, Tottenham Hotspur, the future. Clint relieved that the situation was no longer infused with urgency. Gawl not so pleased. Urgency was good. Urgency created confusion. Urgency kept the price on Phials up Up UP! In a race against time they had the advantage over the Bush, he had to act swiftly, impulsively, without thinking everything through. On an even keel he could plot, out-think them, lay traps.

Mulling it over, Gawl made his way back to Tulip, hoping sex would help him focus — his thoughts often clarified in the afterglow. When he opened the door, Kevin was on the bed with his sister. She was crying. Kevin's face was red. "Lover's tiff?" Gawl grinned.

"Get out," Kevin shouted, leaping to his feet.

"What?" Gawl blinked with surprise.

Kevin took a couple of furious strides towards him, as if he meant to repel Gawl forcibly. Then he faltered, took in Gawl's size, smiled cringingly. Minced the rest of the way and whispered, "Tulip's sick. Not tonight, OK?"

"What's wrong with her?"

"I don't know. She's just sick."

"She looks fine t' me," Gawl laughed, pushing Kevin

aside.

Kevin sprang back, his face set again. "I'll scream if you go near her." Gawl choked with laughter at the feeble threat. Reached out to nudge Kevin aside. Kevin stood his ground. "I'll kick up the kind of fuss that attracts attention. I'll throw things through the window. You want the police to come?"

Gawl's expression darkened. "Don't fuck with me, Tyne. I'd kill ye before ye got yer second squeal out."

"Maybe, but how do you think Tulip would react? Think she'd sit there nice and quiet and let you have your way with her? Or would she go apeshit?" Gawl hesitated, not sure what to make of this new, confrontational Kevin Tyne. Kevin pressed home his advantage. "You need to give her a break. Come back tomorrow or the next day, when she feels better. Not now."

Gawl looked over Kevin's head. Tulip was still weeping. He relented. "If she needs anything, let me know, I'll send Fr Seb out t' get it."

"Thank you." Kevin led Gawl out and closed the door on him.

Gawl stood in the corridor, momentarily thrown. Then he shook his head and stormed downstairs to the kitchen, where he sat in darkness and thought alone, coldly, decisively.

Clint and Fr Sebastian came in while Gawl was thinking, for drinks and snacks. He ignored them, putting the pieces of his plan together, keeping it simple, easier to calculate all the angles and odds. Phials came in later, grinning twitchily, looking for drugs. "Not now," Gawl said.

"But I need my shit, man."

"We have t' start rationing. It won't last forever."

"I know, but a bit of grass, surely…"

Gawl opened his mouth to tell Phials to get lost. Instead found himself saying, "OK, but later, when Fr Seb's asleep, so that we don't have t' share with him."

"My man," Phials beamed, slapping Gawl's back, sauntering away.

Gawl took a long, ragged breath, the debate over, options eliminated, set for the showdown. Fear kicking in now that the safety net had been removed. No more procrastinating. Locked on course, fuck the risks.

Eleven thirty. Midnight. Half twelve. Gawl went on one of his regular patrols. Fr Seb asleep. The Tynes asleep. Back to the study. Phials fidgeting on the small foldaway cot which served as his bed in the tiny room connected to the study, originally a prayer chamber. Gawl kept the chemist confined here at night, while he and Clint bedded down in the study, one of them on watch at any given hour. Gawl stood in the darkness, listening to Clint's breathing. When he was sure the dealer was asleep, he padded across the room, nudged the door of the prayer chamber open and jerked his head at Phials. Phials rose and followed quickly.

Through the house, into the church. Dark, illuminated only by a few electronic candles and the occasional glowing halo. Gawl made for the altar. He'd been here earlier to stash the tools he'd need. Phials followed, whistling, unsuspecting.

Gawl dug a bag out from behind a curtain, along with a short length of rope. He handed the bag to Phials. "Hold that a minute." Phials took the bag, smiling. Then Gawl punched him. He dropped, still clutching the bag. Gawl was on him quick, jerking his hands up behind his back, the rope around his wrists, tying a hasty but firm knot. By the time Phials' head cleared his hands were bound and Gawl was working on his legs with another length of rope.

"What the fuck's going on?" Phials shouted.

"Not so loud," Gawl said.

"Fuck you! What's –"

Gawl covered Phials' mouth with a large hand. Opened the bag with his free hand. Dumped the contents on the altar — knives, a hammer, nails, a lighter, pliers, a blank notebook, three black pens. Phials took in the objects. Understood immediately. "No," he moaned into Gawl's calloused palm.

"Yes," Gawl grunted, taking his hand away. He reached into a pocket and produced a gag. "I don't want t' silence ye but I will if ye raise yer voice."

"This is madness," Phials croaked, fear hitting hard. "Why are you doing this? You'll fuck everything up. Clint –"

"Clint's a waste of space," Gawl cut in bluntly. "So am I. If ye didn't know that before we broke ye out, ye've put it t'gether by now. Ye know we're a pair of clowns. We haven't a chance in hell of getting ye out of England, never mind all the way t' New York. We wouldn't even be able t' begin t' put a fifty million dollar deal together."

"I'll handle the deal," Phials said quickly. "All you have to do is –"

"Please," Gawl winced, "no more bullshit. We both know yer only way out of this was to gi'e us the slip and shoot off on yer own, maybe toss us t' the Bush as a bone in the hope he'd be so busy ripping us apart that ye could disappear before he thought t' look for ye. It took me a while t' see it – I'm not the brightest bulb – but ye must've been wise t' it from the start. We were yer only way out of the lab, but this is as far as we can take ye."

"Gawl, you've got this all wrong, I never –"

Gawl slapped him quiet and picked up the notebook and a pen. "I want the formula. Write down everything we'll need, all the steps involved in its production. Leave nothing out. Don't play cute. I've a chemist lined up t' test it. He's not in yer league but he's got enough smarts t' follow clear instructions. We'll test it on junkies. If it works, we'll sell it t' the Bush. If it doesn't – if ye try t' pull a fast one – I'll cut yer nose off and there'll be no more snorting coke."

Phials trembled. "What happens to me in the meantime?"

"We keep ye here. Once the deal goes through, we leave ye. The Bush'll want ye and he'll pay more if ye're part of the deal. It'll mean going back t' the Lab but wouldn't ye rather be a prisoner than dead?"

"Not necessarily," Phials said bitterly.

Gawl laughed. "Oh, I think ye would. If not, just keep yer trap shut and ye'll be dead by dawn. Lots of pain first, but a guaranteed death at the end."

Phials wet his lips with his tongue, terrified. "How do I know you won't kill me once I've given you the formula?"

Gawl shrugged. "This is all about money. Ye're worth more t' me alive than dead. I don't know what the

Bush'll do with ye – he might kill ye himself – but that's a worry for another day."

Phials' brain exploding as he searched for a way out, figuring all the plays. Gawl let him think. He knew the chemist was screwed and the sooner Phials realised that, the easier he'd be to deal with. After a while Gawl picked up a small knife. "Do I have t' slice ye up a bit?"

"Dave won't cut a deal with you," Phials said as calmly as possible. "Let's talk about this. I can ring a few numbers in New York, set up some –"

Gawl clamped the gag over Phials' mouth, tied it in place, undid the front of the chemist's trousers and yanked them down, along with his boxer shorts. Grabbed the flesh of the chemist's scrotal sac, pulled it out tight, hacked at it with the knife, not the whole sac, just the flesh on the lowest underhang of his genitals. Phials writhed, screaming into the folds of his gag. Gawl had to sit on top of the chemist's chest, pinning him down, to finish the job, sawing through the last threads of flesh, tearing the strip loose, tossing it away. Blood oozed, but not uncontrollably, Gawl careful not to hit anything vital this early in the proceedings.

He waited for Phials' gagged screams to abate. Raised the knife to his lips and licked the blood off the blade. Phials went rigid. Gawl lowered the blade. He wasn't smiling. "Now ye know. I'm a fucking psychopath. I'll do things no one else would, not even Dave Bushinsky's torturers. Give me the formula."

He removed the gag.

Phials coughed up vomit and spit, gasping for breath, eyes bulging. Stared down at his blood-soaked groin and whined. Gawl leant in close and whispered, "Once I made a man eat his own bollocks."

Phials vomited some more then nodded weakly. "You'll have to free my hands."

"I'll handle the pen, just tell me what to write."

"Too complicated."

"Ye think I can't spell?"

Phials snarled at Gawl. "If you want me to do this, free my hands and give me a fucking pen. That's the only way it'll work."

Gawl studied Phials' expression for deceit. Found only a desperate desire to comply and avoid further torture. He loosened the knots binding Phials' hands, then passed the notebook and pen to him. Stood back, exchanging his small knife for a sturdier one, prepared for anything.

Phials rubbed his hands together, sullen, hateful. Flashed on a picture of him driving the tip of the pen into Gawl's neck. Almost went for it. But commonsense prevailed — a pen no match for a knife. Opened the notebook and started to write.

Phials wrote swiftly. It was the first time he'd committed the formula to paper but he had it set in his mind, every last ingredient and equation. Mentally running with escape plans while he was scribbling, not ready to admit defeat. He had to get to Clint, turn him on Gawl, get out of here with the dealer. He could manipulate Clint. A fool to think Gawl would be as easy to use. He should have done a runner long before this, taken his chances on the streets.

It took forty minutes to complete the formula. It ran to several pages, close to the genuine article – to even a trained eye it would look like the real thing – but riddled with a number of errors and omissions. The manufacturer would produce something approximating Baby P, a drug that would generate a pleasant high. But it wouldn't attack the inner organs the way Baby P would. A partial success, worth a nice bit on its own, but not the devastating, unbelievably valuable monster that he had the power to deliver. Designed to buy him time, so he could work on Clint.

"There," he snapped, thrusting the notebook at Gawl, spitting on it for dramatic effect. "I hope it brings you as much luck and joy as it's brought me."

Gawl flicked through the pages, studying the squiggles and equations. He didn't think for a second that this was the actual formula but acted as if he did. Smiled dumbly. "Ye made the right choice, doc. Would've been a shame t' lose yer nose." Slipped the notebook inside his jacket, like he believed the matter was done and dusted. "Now I'll tie yer hands again, free yer feet, grab one of Fr Seb's jackets, and we'll –"

"What do I need a jacket for?" Phials snapped.

"It's cold outside."

"Where are you taking me?"

"We have t' test it."

"But you said you had a chemist lined up to test it for you."

"Aye," Gawl lied, "but I can't leave ye here. Ye might have made a mistake that'll need tweaking. Easier t' bring ye with me than have t' return for ye."

"But it's a long, time-consuming process," Phials objected. "I doubt your associate will have all the ingredients required. Even if he has, it'll take the better part of a week to fix up a batch."

"That's OK," Gawl grinned. "He has a cellar. A bit more cramped than yer current room, and ye won't have the run of a house – ye'll have t' stay trussed up until we're done – but ye'll be safe there." His grin died. "And if ye did make a mistake – purely by accident, like – ye'll be close at hand t' fix it."

Phials stared into Gawl's eyes. No idea that Gawl was bluffing, that there was no chemist, no test, no cellar. Seeing only captivity, torture when Gawl found out he'd tricked him, being forced to cough up the genuine article. Spirits sinking. Simpler to spare himself the hassle and deliver the real thing now. Get into Gawl's good books, hope a chance to escape presented itself later.

"Give me the notebook," Phials said sourly as Gawl reached down to bind his hands again.

"Why?" Gawl asked mock-innocently. "Did ye forget something?"

"Just fucking give it to me!"

Gawl restrained his smile. Reached inside his jacket. Passed the notebook back to Phials. Phials scanned through the formula page by page, making alterations and insertions, spilling all his secrets. He started to cry, his only trump card exposed, negated, void. At the end of the day he'd be back where he started, a prisoner. Baby P would change the world, but Tony Phials would remain a slave, living out a dreary existence, his pleasures few and far between.

"There," Phials wept, sliding the notebook to Gawl when he was finished.

Gawl stared long and hard at Phials. Everything came down to this moment and whether or not he made the right call. If he got it right, a happy ending, riding off into the sunset, free to enjoy his fortune. If he called it wrong, temporary elation, then a furious Bush snapping at his heels, a fevered pursuit, capture, torture, death. Had Phials provided him with the real formula or was it another time-wasting gambit? Studying the chemist's tears, his self-pity, his desolation. Concluded — *It's real.*

"It's been a pleasure doing business with ye, doc," Gawl chuckled blackly, then pushed Phials on to his back and drove the tip of his knife deep into the chemist's unprotected stomach.

Phials gasped with pain and shock. His hands gripped Gawl's forearm. He tried pushing Gawl away. Gawl dug deeper with the knife, working it left and right. Phials coughed up blood. His strength deserted him. He pissed himself. His limbs shook. Blood oozed out over the blade and Gawl's hand. Gawl kept stabbing, doing it because he had to, Phials a liability now that Gawl had the formula. Easier to sell a notebook than a living person. Less complications. It would also put an end to Clint's American dreams — he'd have to deal with the cold hard facts now and follow Gawl's lead.

Phials died gurgling blood. A tragic end to what could

have been a brilliant career. Gawl didn't spare him a second thought. He knew nothing of the chemist's early promise, his youthful plans to cure cancer and make the world a better place, his gradual fall from grace and descent into disgrace. Wouldn't have cared if he'd known, hard luck stories didn't impress him.

Gawl fetched blankets, a mop, hot water, black plastic bags. Wrapped Phials in blankets and a couple of bags. Cleaned up the blood around the altar. Fetched a torch, gave the altar a quick once-over, returned to the corpse. He hadn't masked Phials' head. Now he did, carefully covering it with a towel, leaving the chemist's throat exposed. He slipped a bag under Phials' neck, then a second towel. Picked a knife with a sharp serrated edge. Got busy severing the head from the body.

Hard but fast work. Let the blood soak into the towel. Plugged the neck of the body with tissues and tea-towels, then covered it with a plastic bag. Shoved the body aside, made sure it wasn't leaking, then dragged it through to the closet under the stairs in the house. Returned to the church and checked the head. Most of the blood had drained off. Replaced the towel, left the head for ten minutes, then stuck it in a plastic bag, rolled the plastic tight around the head, then dumped it inside another bag. Dropped in the note he'd scrawled earlier, making sure it was on top of the bag with the head, where it would be instantly seen when the outer bag was unwrapped.

Gawl checked his watch — loads of time. He carried the notebook through to the kitchen and hid it behind the fridge. Took down a packet of biscuits. Chewed automatically, hands steady, heartbeat normal. No thrill in this murder, not like when he killed a woman. Just business.

Back to the church, pausing in the hallway of the priest's house, grabbing his coat and one of Fr Sebastian's hats and scarves. Covered as much of his face as he could. Hunched his shoulders, so he appeared much smaller. Shuffled into the church, grabbed the bag with the head, returned to the house and let himself out.

Walking quickly through the streets, he struck for a main road and caught a bus to the Elephant & Castle, just a few stops, but enough to throw off the Bush's dogs if they were set after his scent. From the Elephant he made his way to the lab. Dangerous — he would have preferred to post the head or dump it outside a pub, sure that word would trickle back to the Bush. But he wanted to get the head to the Bush quickly, tie up the deal ASAP. The reward worth the risk.

Gawl came at the lab from the maze of side-streets

to the east of the Walworth Road. Paused at the mouth of the cul-de-sac. It looked deserted. He hurried to the large garage door and laid the bag by the foot of it, where it was bound to attract attention, positioning it carefully so it wouldn't be mistaken for refuse which had blown against the door during the night.

Bag settled to his satisfaction, Gawl beat a hasty retreat, not looking back but listening closely, no sounds of pursuit. Smiling to himself beneath the cover of the scarf and hat. Walked to the Walworth Road, caught a bus, got off after several stops, took a different route back to the church. Chuckling as he pictured Clint's reaction when he woke him and broke the news, sorry he hadn't been able to hold on to Phials' head to dangle in front of the dealer, give him a *real* fucking shock!

FIFTY-SEVEN

Monday, searching for Gawl McCaskey, hitting the same pubs and cafés as before, flashing various artist's impressions of the Scot, making calls on his mobile as he roamed from one place to another, chatting with people who'd known McCaskey, old friends and enemies, building up as thorough a picture as possible. Beginning to feel like he knew McCaskey. A vile, violent nobody. In trouble most of his life, but he had a knack for survival. He'd spent time in jail but not as much as his crimes merited, and those he'd crossed – there were many – had never caught up with him. Always one step ahead, being able to make a swift getaway his sole gift.

Big Sandy returned to McCaskey's apartment in the evening, studying it in light of the new insights he had into the man's character, hoping to find a previously overlooked clue. He fingered clothes and bed sheets, tossed the drawers, wardrobe and cupboards, trying to think as McCaskey might have.

Nothing.

Two of the Bush's men standing guard. Another two in the Tynes' apartment. An almost certainly pointless watch, but best to cover the pads, just in case. Thinking about Kevin and Tulip, wondering if they were dead. He figured they were, innocents in the break-out, used by McCaskey and Smith, discarded when they were of no further worth. He didn't care about Kevin, but Tulip deserved better. One more reason to extract painful revenge on the kidnappers.

Midnight. Home to bed. A troubled sleep, tossing and turning. He hadn't slept properly since the break-out. Not sure why he was taking it to heart, this wasn't personal, just business. He'd stayed with Sapphire a couple of nights, telling her what was happening, calm in her arms. Wanted to go back tonight but reluctant to outstay his welcome. Sapphire was starting to act like a girlfriend. Getting snappy when it was all about him, not liking it if he just turned up when he needed her and then buggered off again.

He managed a grin despite everything else. He'd have to be careful or that might develop into a real relationship. Romance the last thing he was looking for, but men rarely had a say in such matters when a women made up her mind. Then he fell back to thoughts of Tulip, and the smile faded, not to return.

He was surprised but relieved when his phone rang in the early hours of Tuesday, welcoming any excuse to abandon his doomed attempts to fall asleep. "Yeah?" he muttered, answering the phone in the dark.

"It's me." Fast Eddie. Big Sandy hadn't seen him since the break-out. The Bush didn't blame Fast Eddie – nobody did – but Fast Eddie was ashamed of the way he'd let himself be duped and had kept a low profile, sticking to the lab, taking no active part in the hunt for Phials.

"What's up?" Big Sandy yawned.

"Come quick. We've had a delivery."

Fast Eddie rang off. Big Sandy frowned, wondering what the cryptic message meant. He got dressed and walked to the lab. The outer door was unlocked. Fast Eddie opened the inner door immediately when Big Sandy rang. He looked worried but excited. Headed straight for the secret door to the cellar, nodding at Big Sandy to follow. The cellar less cluttered than normal. The Bush had thought about shutting down the lab in the wake of the break-out, in case the kidnappers tipped off the police to make life uncomfortable for their pursuers. In the end he decided against closure, but most of the staff had been evacuated temporarily, and many of the crates in the cellar had been transported elsewhere. The two surviving hounds had been left where they were, the Bush keeping them in reserve in case the kidnappers needed to be tracked down.

Fast Eddie led Big Sandy to a table in the centre of the underground maze. A football-sized object rested on the table, wrapped in a black plastic bag. There was a hand printed note beside it. *We'll be in contact soon.* Fast Eddie unwrapped the bag. Big Sandy found himself staring into the vacant eyes of Tony Phials.

"When?" he croaked.

"We found it about a quarter of an hour before I phoned you. I checked the security tapes. It was dropped here two and a half hours before that. A large man, probably McCaskey, but his face was covered so we can't be sure."

"You phoned Dave?"

"Not yet. I wasn't sure if I should disturb him. Thought I'd check with you."

"He won't mind being disturbed for this." Big Sandy smiled grimly at the sad, bloody face of Tony Phials. "You made the wrong call, doc."

"You know what this means," Fast Eddie said softly. "They're still in London and they want to cut a deal."

"They must have squeezed the formula out of Phials before killing him," Big Sandy nodded, thinking it through. "Easier to sell the formula than Phials."

"But why come to us? Why try to sell it back to the man they stole it from?"

Big Sandy began to shake his head. Stopped and laughed. "The Bush called it right. He didn't think they had anyone behind them, that McCaskey and Smith set it up themselves. I didn't buy it, but that's the only explanation, they're a couple of dicks who don't know anyone else they can take this to."

"You think the Bush will do business with them?" Fast Eddie asked.

Big Sandy shrugged. "That's his decision, not mine." He covered the head with the bag and dug out his mobile. Told a groggy Dave Bushinsky the news. The Bush snapped out of grogginess fast, first incredulous, then uncertain. Said he'd be right over and not to do anything until he arrived.

"What about the hounds?" Fast Eddie asked when Big Sandy hung up. "If the guy who dropped off the head was McCaskey, we could set them on his trail."

Big Sandy thought about it. "No. He probably drove. Even if it was McCaskey and he came on foot, they might have more of that powder that Phials used on the other hounds. Best not to chance it. They're thinking straight right now. Later they might panic, make mistakes. That's when we'll hit them with the hounds."

Big Sandy looked over the note again. Fast Eddie read it beside him. "I hope the Bush doesn't cut a deal with the fuckers," he muttered sourly. "I want to be there when those sons of bitches are taken out." He rubbed the back of his head where he'd been sapped during the break-out.

"We'll play it like the Bush tells us," Big Sandy grunted, turning his back on the severed head and retracing his steps through the maze.

"Of course," Fast Eddie said, hurrying after him. "But if he decides to pay them off and settle for the formula..." Bothered by the thought that he might be cheated of revenge.

Big Sandy paused, thought about Clint Smith, how he'd screwed the Bush and cost him the chance to buy control of Spurs. He smiled reassuringly at Fast Eddie. "I don't think that will happen."

FIFTY-EIGHT

"– fuck! Oh fuck! Oh fuck! Oh fuck! Oh fuck! Oh fuck! Oh fuck! Oh –"

Clint staring blankly at the kitchen table, *Oh fuck!* riffing, as distraught as he'd ever been, wanting to get sick, unable to force up any vomit. Gawl sitting smugly close by. He'd told Clint about the murder. Took him to see the body when Clint didn't believe him. Guided the stunned dealer to the kitchen afterwards, sat with him, waiting for Clint's thoughts to clear.

"– fuck! Oh fuck! Oh fuck! Oh..."

Blinking, shaking his head, hoping this was a dream, that he could jolt himself awake. Staring at Gawl, his sneering smile. No dream. Phials dead. Fifty million dollars cut off at the neck. America dumped in black plastic bags beneath the stairs. Shula forever beyond his reach. Cousin Dave, the grand executioner, waiting in the wings to swoop down upon them.

"You buh-buh-bastard," Clint moaned. "You mad fuh-fucking bastard. You've ruined us."

"I've saved us," Gawl smirked.

"Dave will kuh-kuh-kill us. He knows we're in London. You slaughtered the one buh-bargaining chip we had.

We're fucked."

"He has to find us first," Gawl disagreed. "And Phials was never a bargaining chip, he was a fuck-us-over waiting t' happen. And like I said, I got the formula from him before I finished him off."

"How do you know it's ruh-real?" Clint snapped.

"I'm gambling that it is."

"And if you're wrong?"

Gawl shrugged. "Then ye're right, we're fucked."

Clint laughed hysterically. "We're fucked anyway. They'll track us down and kuh-kill us and..." He stopped. Frowned. "Where did you leave the head?"

"The lab."

"How'd you take it there?"

"I walked."

"What about the hounds?"

"I took them into consideration. I bused it some of the way there and back."

"Some of the way?" Clint snapped. "What if that wasn't enough?"

"It will be," Gawl grunted, then sat forward. "D' ye see that what I did was for the best?"

"Bollocks," Clint retorted. "*The best* would have been to stick to the pluh-plan and smuggle Phials out. *The best* would have been to sell the fuh-formula for millions of dollars and –"

"That was never gonna happen," Gawl interrupted. "Too much could have gone wrong. We were too inexperienced. Too dumb."

"I'm not dumb," Clint protested.

"Ye are," Gawl laughed. "But don't get the hump. I'm dumb too. We were smart enough t' bust Phials out, but not t' follow through, not unless we do it this way." Gawl grabbed Clint's hands, held them tight. "We have the formula. The Bush has the money t' pay for it. We sell it t' him for a million each – pounds, not dollars – and hit for Ibiza or Lanzarote, live stylish, live loud — *live!*"

"But I want New York," Clint groaned.

Gawl sighed. It was like talking to a child. "OK," he said. "Ye can take yer half and fuck off t' New York. A million will take ye a long way there. And ye'll have infamy on yer side too."

Clint blinked. "What are you talking about?"

"The Bush will manufacture and market Baby P. He'll be a legend. Ye can get in on some of that, publicise yerself up as the man who gave the world Baby P. Get yer story in early, before the shit hits the market, so people know ye're genuine. Ye'll have money and a reputation." He let go of Clint and beamed. "If that doesn't get ye up and running in the States, what fucking will?"

Clint dwelt on that a while. Still seething about the way Gawl had acted without consulting him, but forcing himself to focus on the positives. A million pounds *was* a shit-load of money, and he *could* talk up his involvement with the new drug set to sweep the world. Still in a good position to hit the ground running, make powerful alliances, then make a play for the heart of Shula Schimmel.

"What if Dave tuh-tells us to go fuck ourselves?" Clint asked.

"He's a businessman. Money comes first. He'll deal."

Clint unconvinced. "How are we going to approach him? Phone?"

Gawl shook his head. "He might be able t' pinpoint our position."

"It takes a few minutes to do that, doesn't it?"

"Technology these days..." Gawl sniffed. "Who fucking knows? We can't risk it."

"How then? Send Kevin or Fr Sebastian?"

"No. The Bush would squeeze our whereabouts out of them. One of us has t' go." Clint started to object loudly. Gawl silenced him with a gesture. "It'll be me."

"You're vuh-volunteering?" Clint was surprised.

"He hates me less than you," Gawl chuckled. "Plus I won't start stuttering like a retard if I get nervous."

"What about the formula? You'll leave it with me?"

"Will I fuck," Gawl snorted. "I've hidden it, and it stays hidden till the time comes t' hand it over."

"And how will we do that?"

"Once they give us the money, I'll tell 'em where it is."

Clint choked on a laugh. "It doesn't work that way. They'll want a trade-off, the money in exchange for the formula, a handover. Assuming you can convince them to accept the formula unseen and untested, without knowing if it works."

Gawl thought about that and nodded. "So what d' ye suggest?"

"We use the Tuh-Tynes or Fr Sebastian," Clint said. "Give the formula to one of them, have them at the meeting place but not standing with us. Once we get the cash, we walk and they step forward to hand over the formula."

Gawl considered that. "It can't be Fr Seb. We'll need t' stay here after the deal, get our shit sorted. Can't let them know we're in league with him."

"Kevin, then."

"What if they take him captive? They'd torture him and he'd tell 'em where we are. We'd have t' go on the run."

"Tulip?"

"They'd do the same t' her."

"Maybe not. Don't forget that Shula was raped recently. She was the same sort of age as Tulip. Dave might shy away from hurting a girl."

Gawl almost laughed out loud at that, but Clint would get shirty if he thought the Scot was making fun of his beloved. Would get a whole lot more than shirty if he knew that Gawl was laughing because he was the one who'd raped her. "There's no guarantee the Bush would see things that way," he said instead. "It's dangerous involving them, more factors t' calculate."

"It's still the best way," Clint insisted. "Worse case, if they doublecross us, they'll kill Tulip, not you or me. At least we'll have a chance to get away. And we'll have the money. We can use it to buy our way out of trouble."

"Thats true," Gawl grunted. "Ye're starting to talk me round."

"Of course there's no guarantee that Dave will duh-duh-deal with us in the first place," Clint added, doubts returning.

"He will," Gawl said confidently. "It makes no sense for him not t'. Now, let's talk about where we want this t' go down and how we break it t' the Tynes and what safe measures we can take. I want everything laid out nice and clear before I go visit the Bush and put my life on the fucking line."

FIFTY-NINE

Kevin told her she had to have an abortion. She refused. He reasoned. He pleaded. He threatened. Tulip refused. Life was sacred, a gift from God. If he tried to make her kill the baby growing inside her, she'd finish with him, run away, leave him to rot. It didn't matter that the child could be the offspring of any of the men she'd been having sex with, that the father was one of any number of sick, twisted paedophiles. This new life was hers to safeguard and she would not destroy it.

"What if it's Fr Sebastian's?" Kevin moaned. "What if it's McCaskey's?"

"I was pregnant before he had sex with me," Tulip replied. "I'm not sure how far advanced I am, but I think a couple of months at least."

"How did it happen?" Kevin cried. "We took so many precautions."

Tulip shrugged. "Condoms split. The pill isn't foolproof. Spermicides don't always work." She smiled through her tears. "Where God wishes to create life, he finds a way."

"This isn't the work of God," Kevin snarled. "It's an abomination."

"No," Tulip said calmly. "It's a child. *My* child. And I'm keeping it."

That was her line and she stuck to it. Kevin spent the rest of the night trying to wear her down, but she rejected all his arguments. She fell asleep fully dressed, face stained with tears, rosary beads clutched between her small pale fingers. Kevin sat beside her, unable to sleep, tormented. With no choice, he reluctantly accepted Tulip's decision and assessed where that left them.

Their tentative escape plan would have to be reworked. No way they could go to the police now. They'd find out Tulip was pregnant. Questions and examinations. They might worm the truth out of Tulip — in her state, there was no knowing what she might say. Jail for Kevin. Separation. Tulip would have a child of her own, grow up, turn her back on him.

If they escaped and didn't go to the police? Same problems as before – nowhere to go and no way for him to support Tulip – only more emphatic, since now he'd have two to hide, house, clothe and feed.

Frowning as he lingered on that thought. Two to support, a wife and child, the perfect family. Half-smiling in the gloom, imagining himself and Tulip with a child, rearing it, watching it grow. Picturing Tulip with a baby. She'd be a good mother, protective, understanding and…

Trembling at a terrible flash — *the baby could be my hold over her.* A secret they'd have to share. Tulip would need him to help bring up the baby. She might be able to muddle by on her own if she left him, but rearing a child would be hard. She'd *need* him. And if her loathing proved stronger than her need, he could use the baby against her. Threaten to report her to the authorities if she left him. They'd take the child away from her if they found out the full story, brand her an unfit mother. He could use her love for the baby against her, just as he'd used her love for him against her.

Running with the idea, excited, sensing new opportunities, playing with wicked thoughts. If the child was a girl he could watch her grow and mature, maybe mould her to his own warped desires as he'd moulded Tulip, ultimately replace Tulip with her. Sick thoughts. He cursed himself for thinking them as soon as they formed, but he didn't stop. Scheming in the dark, gazing at Tulip, at her stomach, figuring blasphemously, *Maybe this is a gift from God.*

Coming back to the impossibility of escape. On the run, pursued by McCaskey and Dave Bushinsky, unable to work without attracting attention, unable to support Tulip and her child. But if they didn't run, McCaskey and Clint would strike their deal and clear out, kill Kevin and

Tulip or leave them for Bushinsky. Damned either way. Unless…

Cold in the dark, but sweating as a crazy thought struck. *Unless I can cut myself in for a share of the profits.*

Clint knocked on their door early, before eight, asked them to come to the study. Kevin said they'd be down in ten minutes. Faced Tulip when they were alone. "I've decided. We'll keep the baby." Tulip stared at him uncertainly, then broke into a grin, relieved that she wouldn't have to argue any more. She leant over to hug him. He pulled back. "Do you trust me?"

Instantly wary. "Why?"

"The baby changes everything. We can't turn to the police now, not with you pregnant, too many questions, too many risks."

"But –" she started to object.

"No," he snapped. "We can't have it both ways. This baby complicates matters and we have to deal with those complications."

"What are you thinking?" Tulip asked suspiciously.

"We have to get in on the drugs deal. Make them include us in their plans. Take a cut of the money."

"Are you insane?" Tulip shrieked.

"It's the only way."

"What they're doing is wrong. Drugs ruin lives and destroy people, and this one is the worst ever. I know what it's like to be in that addictive grip. There's no way I'm going to –"

"This isn't the time to get moralistic," Kevin snarled. "If we get out of this mess alive, we'll have to lie low for a long time. I won't be able to work. You won't be able to draw child benefits. How do you plan to look after the baby?"

"There are charities..."

"I told you, we'll have to keep our heads down. We'll need money for lodgings, food, baby clothes, medicine, books, toys..."

"All right," Tulip sighed. "I understand. But even if we were to accept their blood money, why should they give us anything?"

"Let me worry about that," Kevin smiled. "I just wanted to make sure you knew what was happening, so you don't pipe up, horrified, when I start trying to muscle in on their action." He felt ridiculous talking like a movie gangster but he could think of no more suitable expression.

They headed downstairs. Clint, McCaskey and Fr Sebastian were in the study, no sign of Tony Phials. Clint and McCaskey were stiff with tension. Something had changed, Kevin sensed it immediately. Cautious as he sat with Tulip, waiting for them to speak.

A few seconds of edgy silence, broken bluntly by McCaskey. "I killed Phials in the church last night. Stabbed him t' death then cut off his head. The body's in the closet under the stairs if anyone doesn't believe me."

Kevin and Tulip gawped. Fr Sebastian turned white and blessed himself.

"The game's almost over," McCaskey continued. "In another few days we'll be gone and ye can get on with yer lives."

"Until Dave Bushinsky catches up with us," Kevin interjected bitterly.

"That's what we brought ye down t' talk about," McCaskey said. "Fr Seb's fine – nobody knows that we stayed here – but ye're in a different boat. We haven't talked much about what happens t' ye when we leave. Now's the time."

"We'll be clearing out," Clint said, "leaving England. We can take you with us and set you free abroad."

"But –" Gawl began, meaning to tell the Tynes they'd have to work for their freedom.

"Not good enough," Kevin interrupted, catching both Gawl and Clint off-guard. "We're not going to let you strand us in a foreign country. You dragged us into this, ruined our lives, set Dave Bushinsky on our backs. Now you want to abandon us and leave us to the wolves? No way."

"Ye don't have much fucking choice," Gawl growled, starting to rise. Clint laid a hand on the Scot's arm, nodded him back into his chair.

"You have a different idea?" Clint asked Kevin.

"Pay us," Kevin said quietly. "All I keep hearing is how much money the pair of you are going to make. Slide some of it our way. Set us up with a nest egg, so we can disappear and live in comfort like you."

"Why should we?" Clint asked.

"It would keep us sweet." Kevin forced a shaky smile. "We could make life difficult for you if we wanted. Much simpler to buy our compliance."

"How much were ye thinking?" Gawl asked.

Kevin wet his lips and croaked, "Five million?" Gawl burst out laughing. Clint smiled. Kevin fumed. "What's so crazy about that? You keep talking about fifty million. You wouldn't miss –"

"The plan's changed," Clint cut in. Gawl was still laughing. "We're selling the formula to Dave now."

"Dave?" Kevin frowned.

"Bushinsky."

"But he's the guy you stole it from."

"There were too many complications the other way," Clint said. "We're going for the easy money. It's safer but a lot less, a long way short of fifty million."

"How much?"

Clint looked to Gawl for guidance. The pair hadn't meant to reveal more than a shade of their plan to the Tynes, but they hadn't expected Kevin to ask for a pay-off. Gawl stopped laughing and leant forward, scratching his chin, studying Kevin. Decided to reel out some statistics. "We'll start the bidding at four million – pounds, not dollars – but settle for two."

"Jesus. That's a long way short."

"But it's real money," Gawl said. "The fifty mill was fantasy."

Kevin recalculated quickly. "OK. If you get four, we'll take a million. Three, we'll take three-quarters. Two, half a million."

"Fuck you," Clint exploded. "I'd rather –"

Gawl grabbed him and dragged him outside, smiling at Kevin, Tulip and a still-in-shock Fr Sebastian. "A moment t' ourselves, please." In the hall outside he shook Clint silent. "What the fuck are ye shouting about?"

"That little prick wants to take half a million off us," Clint yelped. "The nerve of the fucker! I say we take him into the chuch and finish him off like Phials."

Gawl shook his head wearily. "Don't ye see? He's playing into our hands. He wants t' get involved. I don't know why, but this is perfect. Now it'll be easy t' convince him t' hand over the formula."

"But at a price," Clint huffed. "Settling for a million was bad enough, but if I have to give a quarter to that scummy —"

"Who said anything about giving him money?"

Clint frowned. "*You* did."

Gawl shook his head. "I'll agree t' half a million but that doesn't mean I'll gi'e it t' him." Gawl lowered his voice. "We'll promise him all the money he wants. Use him and Tulip as planned. They'll play along, thinking they're part of the scam. When we get back here, we'll kill him, keep it all for ourselves."

Clint blinked at the obviousness of it. "What about Tulip?"

Gawl shrugged. "If she doesn't freak out, we'll let her live, maybe take her with us. I've grown fond of the wee bitch. Otherwise we kill her too."

Clint gulped. Thought it over. Nodded. "But we have to make it seem like he's forcing our hand. He'll smell a rat if we give in to his demands too easily."

"Agreed."

The pair returned to the study. Fr Sebastian was still

white-faced and trembling. Tulip was rubbing her stomach. Kevin was trying to look cool.

"A quarter of a million," Clint said stiffly as he and Gawl sat.

Kevin smiled witheringly. "We wouldn't last long on that."

"Three-fifty," Clint growled. "We have to arrange travel, passports, safe houses. That will all come out of our cut."

Kevin mulled it over. "And if you get the four million?"

"We'll give you six hundred and fifty thousand," Clint said. "If we get three, then half a mill."

"But ye'll have t' work for yer cut," Gawl said. "We're not gonna hand it over just because we like the look of ye. If ye want t' be part of this, ye have t' be a real part. Dig in with us. Run risks. Face the Bush."

"What are you talking about?"

"We got the formula for the drug from Phials before we killed him," Clint explained, as if he'd been an equal partner in the torture and execution. "We're going to arrange a deal and set up a swap, the cash for the formula. If you want a cut, you'll have to assist us with that."

"I'm not sure…" Kevin stalled.

"We'll be there too," Gawl said. "Ye'll be running no

greater risk than us. We can do it without ye, in which case ye get nothing. But we stand a better chance of pulling it off with ye, in which case ye get the price we've agreed."

While Kevin was thinking about that, Tulip spoke up suddenly. "What about Fr Sebastian?" All eyes turned on her. "He deserves to be included too."

"I want no part of this," Fr Sebastian squeaked. "I just want you out of here, so I can get back to normal."

"I like the cut of yer jib, Father," Gawl chuckled, then faced Kevin. "I'm gonna thrash out a deal with the Bush this afternoon. Are ye in or out?"

Kevin exhaled shallowly. He didn't like this, felt he was signing up for a ride he couldn't control. But it was the only way. If it worked, he'd have money, freedom, the baby, Tulip, everything. Staring straight at McCaskey, not blinking, he said, "We're in."

SIXTY

Gawl walked to the Elephant & Castle, caught a cab, gave the driver the address of the Bush's Whitechapel office, sat back and concentrated on his breathing as he drove to his date with destiny/death. Terrified but thrilled. It didn't have to be face-to-face, would have been safer to phone the Bush. But Gawl wanted to be there, to sit down with the gang boss as an equal, look him in the eye, show he had balls. A calculated risk – the Bush might flip and set his men on Gawl – but he was in the mood for risks.

Thinking about his life. A petty, wasteful, forgetful existence — except for the murders. Proud of the women he'd killed. They were his legacy, the mark he'd made on the world. Gloating, feeding off the memories, wondering if he'd meet them again in hell. Sure he was going there if it existed, not bothered, this world his only concern.

Looking ahead, he could go a long way on a million. Check into a hotel on a sunny sandy island, drink himself catatonic every night, pay beautiful hookers to pamper him. Gamble, but cautiously, careful not to blow everything. Tell tall tales in bars and clubs. Impress young gangsters and their girlfriends. Grow old and fat on the local cuisine. Die of a heart attack, smiling. Murder? Perhaps. But only if he could get away with it. Maybe take a holiday a couple of times a year, hit a city, butcher a prostitute, nobody cared about them. A wonderful, blood-soaked end to his career.

The taxi pulled up outside the Bush's office. Gawl checked his watch. A quarter past three. They'd spent most of the morning discussing the plan, Kevin asking lots of questions. He'd also raised the issue of passports. Gawl and Clint would be able to use theirs freely – if all went well, the Bush wouldn't track them out of the country – but the Tynes' were in their apartment. Gawl said he'd make the Bush hand them over with the money. Kevin said he'd better, vowed to queer the deal if he didn't see their passports first.

Gawl ready to go at midday. Clint told him to wait, the Bush's lunch hour could fall anywhere between twelve and three. Gawl impatient but he heeded Clint's advice, Clint the Bush expert. Going over the plan again and again. They were fixed on Wednesday for the handover, but couldn't decide on the location. They debated the merits and drawbacks of Tube stations, banks, airports, restaurants, parks, a crowded area or a deserted stretch. Safety uppermost in their thoughts. They'd been arguing for more than an hour when Tulip unexpectedly chipped in with, "What about the London Eye? Lots of people, so they can't start shooting. You can check out the scene from Westminster Bridge. Not easy to park a car, but plenty of taxis and buses go across the bridge, and Westminster and Waterloo station are nearby." They all stared at her, startled — then smiled.

Gawl stepped out of the cab. He was wearing one of Fr Seb's long jackets over his jumper and jeans, unbuttoned to make it easier for the Bush's men to search him. He wasn't carrying any weapons. He slicked his hair back, ran a finger over the top of his half-severed ear for good luck, entered the building.

The receptionist took no notice of him as he approached. She was on the phone and made him stand in silence for a couple of minutes before she hung up. Smiled thinly, dismissing him as a nobody with one quick glance. "Can I help you, sir?"

"I'd like t' see Mr Bushinsky."

"Do you have an appointment?"

"No."

"He's rather busy today, sir. May I take your name and a contact number?"

"I'm Gawl McCaskey."

"Could you spell…" She stopped and stared as the name hit her. He winked. "One… second please." Fumbling for an intercom button. A hushed conversation, eyes on Gawl the whole time. He stood rock solid, sweating but not fidgeting, gazing at her forehead, avoiding her eyes. The receptionist hung up and managed a weak smile. "Somebody will be here shortly to –"

One of the doors to the foyer burst open. Eyes Burton charged in. Made Gawl. Half drew his gun. Gawl spread his empty hands, keeping them far out from his sides. Eyes slid his gun back into its holster but kept his hand on it. "What the fuck are you doing here?" he wheezed.

"I want t' see the Bush."

Eyes blinked stupidly. Realised the receptionist was gawping at him. Coughed and pulled the door open. Gestured Gawl through. "Nobody comes in until we tell you," he grunted at the receptionist. "Close the office. Don't interrupt us."

Gawl stepped past Eyes into a long grey corridor. Eyes let the door close, grabbed Gawl and slammed him against the wall. Two more guards appeared and covered Eyes while he frisked the Scot. Satisfied that Gawl was clean, he stepped away and prodded Gawl ahead of him, down the corridor, up a flight of stairs, to where the Bush was waiting.

The Bush seated behind a long oak desk. Face neutral. Elbows resting lightly on the table. Fingers steepled. Prepared for anything. Studied Gawl curiously as Eyes herded him in, an ugly, scarred, brutish man. So this was the neanderthal who'd cheated him out of Phials, the wonder drug, Spurs. Hatred flared in his chest. He thrust it down — *Keep it for later.* Gawl sat and smiled shakily at the Bush. The Bush didn't smile back but said coolly, "A drink, Mr McCaskey?"

"Just water, thanks."

Eyes poured water into a white plastic cup from a cooler in the corner. Set the cup in front of Gawl. Looked to the Bush for orders. "Wait outside. You hear anything out of the ordinary, come in firing."

"Ye got the head?" Gawl asked as Eyes stepped out.

"What do you want?" the Bush tossed back, not in the mood for bullshit.

"I got the formula from Phials before I killed him," Gawl said.

"That was clever of you," the Bush sneered. "Did you test it?"

"No." He'd discussed with Clint whether he should lie or tell the truth. They decided on the truth, keep talks on the level from the start.

The Bush blinked. "Then how the fuck —"

"He was terrified. In pain. Facing worse. He thought I'd let him live if he gave me the formula. He knew what'd happen if he tried t' play me for a sap. It's real."

"You can't know that for sure."

"No. But I'm betting my life."

The Bush grunted, noting the sweat trickling down Gawl's cheeks, the shiver of his shoulders. "You brought the formula?"

Gawl chuckled sarcastically. "Aye. Why wouldn't I?"

The Bush tilted his head, acknowledging that it had been a dumb question. "So where is it?"

"Clint has it," Gawl lied. "If I'm not back by five, he disappears, sells it elsewhere, ye never see him again."

The Bush checked his watch. "That gives me more than an hour and a half to rip you apart and wring his hiding place out of you."

"Ye wouldn't break me that quickly," Gawl said.

"Want to bet?" Soft, menacing, reading Gawl, ready to sic Eyes and his other troops on him if he flinched in the face of the challenge.

Gawl grinned. "Wouldn't do ye any good anyway. Clint's gone walkabout till he hears from me. I've no idea where he is. Now, are we gonna do business or hurl threats at each other?"

The Bush settled back in his chair. Gawl hadn't crumbled. Prepared now to hear him out. "Tell me what you want."

Gawl leant forward, loving the feeling of being in control, on a par with Dave Bushinsky. "We could get more for the formula if we sold it on the open market."

"So why are you here?"

"Because the risk increases with the price. When we broke out Phials, we thought he could handle the sale, he told us he had contacts ready t' sweep in the minute he was on the loose. We trusted him and that was a mistake. We accepted that, discussed the situation, dealt with it."

"By cutting off his head."

Gawl shrugged. "He'd have fucked us over. I saw that after a few days." Played it bold. "Ye should've seen it too when ye had him under yer thumb."

"I had Phials in hand," the Bush growled. "It was that bastard Clint I trusted. He was my mistake, not Phials."

"Whatever. Point is, I did what you should have. I squeezed the formula out of Phials, then killed the fucker. I would've liked t' test it first but we lacked the resources. If we'd had more time, we could've set something up, but there's yer club t' consider, the super fucking Spurs."

The Bush stiffened. "Too late for that, or haven't you heard?"

"I heard Sugar's selling, but a buyer hasn't been announced yet."

"It will be soon." The Bush's mole had told him about ENIC.

"All the more reason t' hurry," Gawl smirked. "Deals can be bushwhacked at the last minute. If ye come in with a better offer, ye'll get yer club, no matter how late in the day it is."

"Sugar doesn't work that way," the Bush disagreed. "He's a man of his word. A week ago, if I'd had the capital, I could have hit him with an offer. Now..." He shook his head. "I've given up on that dream."

Gawl didn't like the sound of that, four million looking more and more out of their reach. Pressed ahead regardless. "Whether ye can buy the club or not, ye'd be crazy t' turn yer back on the fortune ye can make from the drug."

"Maybe money isn't that important to me," the Bush said softly, testing Gawl again. "Maybe I'd rather see you and Clint squirm."

Gawl smiled. "If that's the case, I'm fucked. That's a gamble I took coming in. But it'd make no sense.

Revenge is one thing, business another. Phials was nothing personal t' ye. What we did wasn't personal either, just business. Only a fool confuses one with the other, and I don't think ye're a fool."

"Indeed I'm not." The Bush impressed despite his loathing of the man. For a nobody, McCaskey was handling himself impeccably. The Bush decided to advance the discussion. "Tell me —" The phone on his desk buzzed. He snatched for it angrily. "I gave orders not to be disturbed!" On the point of slamming the phone down. The person on the other end spoke rapidly. The Bush frowned then sighed. "I forgot about her. No, let her stay. Get her something to drink. I'll be ready for her shortly." Replacing the phone gently, the Bush turned to Gawl again and said quietly, "How much do you want?"

"Four million," Gawl blurted.

"Not a hope," the Bush smiled, pleased that Gawl had set the bar so low — he'd been anticipating a ten million starting point. "I admire you for coming here, it shows you have a spine. But at the same time it's an admission that you have no one else to turn to. You want to grab some easy money and make a quick getaway. I could hold that over you and beat you down to chump change, but I don't want to belittle you. Name what you think is a fair price and I promise I won't gyp you."

Gawl wet his lips. "Two million, one for Clint, one for me."

The Bush nodded slowly. "When would you want it?"

"T'morrow."

"Too soon," the Bush demurred. "It takes time to –"

"Don't jerk my chain," Gawl snarled. "Two million t'morrow or no deal."

"Would I be expected to pay in advance?" the Bush asked softly.

"A straight swap," Gawl said gruffly. "I'll ring ye just before the meet, tell ye where t' send yer man. Tulip Tyne will be with us, hanging back. We'll withdraw when we've checked the cash and she'll come forward with the formula. Everyone goes home happy."

The Bush thought it over, playing with a pen that was lying on his table, imagining the scene, if he could send in a team at such short notice to take down the blackmailers. Gawl saw this in his eyes and said quietly, "Why risk it going wrong by trying t' screw us? A couple of million is nothing t' ye. All ye have t' do is give us the money and let us go. We haven't made any copies of the formula or kept pages t' ourselves, we won't come looking for more cash. A one-off deal, no fear of a fuck-up as long as we all play it square."

"What about the Tynes?" the Bush murmured. "What do they get?"

"Don't worry about that pair," Gawl said. "Toss their passports in with the money, then forget about 'em."

"You'll take care of them?"

"Aye."

"Like you took care of Tony Phials?"

Gawl looked away, fake bashful. The Bush thought some more, weighing up the pros and cons. He could probably arrange an ambush, even without much warning of where the swap would take place, come out with the formula and the money — but if it went wrong the formula could be lost or destroyed.

"You can't stay here if I pay you off," the Bush said and Gawl's eyes lit up as he realised he was close to pushing through the deal.

"I've no intention of staying," he grunted.

The Bush tapped the table with the pen. "I'll give you forty-eight hours to get out of the country and never come back. After that, all deals are off. I won't have you embarrass me on my own turf."

"That's fine by me," Gawl said. "I'm sick of this shitehole anyway."

"What if I test the formula and it doesn't work? Do I get a refund?"

Gawl and the Bush shared a laugh. "No refunds," Gawl chuckled. "But ye'll easily be able t' track me down. I won't be laying low – I want t' enjoy my money – so I won't be hard t' find."

"What if it works and I hunt for you anyway?"

Gawl shrugged. "Why would you? Only a petty man goes panting after a couple of million like a dog when he's just made tens of millions or more."

The Bush laughed. "I'm sorry I didn't hire you when you were looking for work. You'd have been a fine addition."

Gawl almost blushed. "So, are we agreed? We'll do the swap at midday, I'll ring half an hour before t' let ye know where. Aye?"

"Aye," the Bush smiled. "I'll send Big Sandy. Is that OK with you?"

"Whoever the fuck," Gawl sniffed.

The Bush set down his pen and sighed. "There's just one sticking point."

"What?" Gawl sweating afresh.

"Clint," the Bush said and his face twisted. "You said this wasn't personal and for the most part you're right. But with Clint it is. He's blood, I gave him his start and did my best to nurture him, yet he fucked me over. With you it was business – I was fair game – but with him it was an insult."

"He —" Gawl began.

"Don't interrupt," the Bush barked. The door to the office flew open. Fast Eddie appeared, gun in hand. The Bush waved him away then spoke softly. "Clint is part of the deal or there *is* no deal. Make sure he's with you when you collect the money. Big Sandy will subdue him and bring him to me with the formula."

"He's my partner," Gawl said, even softer than the Bush.

"I don't care. You I can deal with. Clint, never." The Bush watched Gawl as he turned the thought over, weighing betrayal against profit, blinking and shivering. The Bush grinned slyly. "Think of it this way. No Clint means no sharing. Two million for yourself, Mr McCaskey." He stood and walked to the door, to show Gawl out. "Take the idea away with you. Mull it over. If you don't ring me, I'll know you place friendship ahead of profit. I'll understand. I'll even admire you. That won't stop me hunting you down like —"

"I don't have t' take it away," Gawl cut the Bush short. "Ye can have yer answer now." He offered the Bush his hand and said emotionlessly, "It's a deal."

Down the stairs, along the grey corridor, Eyes Burton

behind him, Gawl fighting back a smirk, ecstatic, nothing could stop him now, he was going all the way. Sorry about Clint, but that was life. Never a real triumph without a sacrifice. He'd think of Clint occasionally when he was lying in the sun, sipping champagne, an actress or model blowing him in the open air. But not often.

Gawl smiled at the thought, then pushed the door to reception open and walked in on Shula Schimmel.

The Bush's niece was talking with the receptionist, telling her that she was going shopping with her uncle, he was taking her to her favourite stores as a treat before she returned home to Switzerland. She was standing half-turned to Gawl, who stopped as if he'd been struck. In his mind's eye she looked up, saw him, screamed. He tried to run. Eyes drew his gun and winged him. The Bush stormed in as Shula pointed at Gawl and cried, "That's the man who raped me!"

Cold sweat. Disbelief. Was this God paying him back for his years of cruelty? Had fate let him get this close to success, just to yank it away from him abruptly, spit in his eye and howl with laughter? A disgusting way to go. He felt sick. A second ago he was enjoying his highest high. Now he'd dropped lower than he would have thought possible. Game over. Gawl fucked.

Shula turned as he'd anticipated. Stared at him as

he'd known she would. He readied himself to run, feeling a twinge in his upper back where the bullet would catch him. But then...

Shula's gaze passed over him, clear and unknowing, and he realised — *She doesn't recognise me!*

Gawl stood, gaping, until Eyes nudged him. "Get a move on." Gawl looked back, blinked, then focused on Shula again. She was gazing around the office, no interest in the tall, broad, rough, ugly man in the doorway. She remembered almost nothing of the night she had been raped. She assumed like everybody else that it had been Larry Drake.

Gawl was in the clear. He walked to the door. Nodded politely to Shula as he passed her. She half-nodded back. He started to get a horn as he recalled the night he'd fucked her. Hurried past in case she noticed. Barged out of the office. Eyes said something but Gawl ignored him, strode away at top speed, grinning at his daring, his wit, his close escape, knowing now that nothing could come between him and his holy grail, lord of the world and all he surveyed. Thinking, *Fuck what they tell ye in the movies and books. Bad guys* do *come out tops!*

SIXTY-ONE

Big Sandy couldn't sleep. Didn't even try. Went to Sapphire's, not wanting to pester her, but unable to be by himself this night. A marathon three hours of lovemaking, slow, repetetive, lots of talk afterwards, mostly about Sapphire and her girls, letting her complain about them, tutting in all the right places, acting like a real boyfriend, wondering if this was the shape of things to come, both uneasy and intrigued if it was.

No mention of the swap tomorrow. He would never speak of something like that before the fact. Sapphire sensed the tension in him, assumed he had a hit lined up, didn't ask about it, pleased that he was showing so much of an interest in her, not sure if she wanted to take things further, torn between wanting him and knowing the complications he would bring into a relationship. Lay sprawled across his chest after sex, both of them halfdozing and thinking moodily about the future.

Earlier, in the Bush's office, Big Sandy had listened bemused as the Bush described his meeting with McCaskey, the deal they'd struck. A long silence at the end, the Bush awaiting his henchman's verdict, Big Sandy not speaking until he had it clear in his mind. "I could take men with me, let them sneak up, take Gawl and the rest of them, get the formula and keep the money."

The Bush shook his head. "Too many things could go wrong. I'm guessing they'll meet you in a place with lots of witnesses. I don't want to stage a gun fight in public. Besides, he came to bargain in good faith. He was open and honest. And he's giving us Clint."

"Still," Big Sandy rumbled, "two million…"

"A lot of money," the Bush agreed. "That's why I want this to go smooth. No traps, no surprises, no screw-ups. We do this right, we do it clean, we take the formula and Clint, we let the others go, we get stinking rich and live happily ever after."

"Except the Tynes." Big Sandy's face dark as he thought of Tulip suffering at the hands of Gawl McCaskey.

"Tell me if you don't want to do this," the Bush said quietly. "You're free to choose. But if you do it, you do it the way I tell you. The Tynes made their bed, let them lie in it. If you're not happy with that, I can send Eyes or Fast Eddie."

"What if they try to stiff us? What if there's no formula or it's a fake and they make off with the money, Clint as well as McCaskey?"

"That would be my concern, not yours. I agreed the

deal, so I'll bear the blame."

Big Sandy considered it, thinking he could maybe convince Tulip to come with him once he had the formula, get her away from McCaskey and her pimp of a brother. He'd grown fond of her. In a way she had taken the place of the daughter he'd lost. It was silly, he barely knew her, but he couldn't deny what he felt. He would do all that he could to help her. Within reason.

"You can get the money?" he asked.

"Yeah. I might come up short but McCaskey is hardly going to complain if I'm a couple of hundred grand shy. I doubt he'll even count it all."

"Can I pack a gun or do I go unarmed?"

"He didn't mention weapons, so take all you like. Just don't fire unless you have no other choice."

"And the passports for the Tynes?"

"They were in their apartment. I'm having them delivered."

Big Sandy nodded slowly. "I don't like it but I'll do it." He rose. "I'll pick up the money in the morning."

He walked away from his meeting with the Bush nursing a bad feeling and it got worse as the night wore on, but he couldn't put his finger on why he felt uneasy. Lying in the dark, Sapphire snoozing on his chest, one of his giant hands resting lightly on her back, trying to chase the feeling down to its source. The Bush impressed by McCaskey, prepared to do business with him. But Big Sandy didn't trust the Scot. Too quick to give up Clint. Greedy. A man like that would always look for more, a way to sell you out. Big Sandy worried that McCaskey would pass them a fake formula, or keep a copy and sell it to their rivals. The Bush had absolved Big Sandy of blame, but would he remember that if the deal went tits up?

Six o'clock. Seven. Eight. Sapphire stirred, rolled off, stumbled to the toilet. Big Sandy scratched his chest then went searching for his clothes. Sapphire found him tugging on his shoes when she returned. "Leaving?" she yawned.

"Work," he said, kissing her, slipping her all the money he had in his wallet.

She frowned at the bills. "That's too much."

"Keep it."

Sapphire stared at him, half-scared. "Are you in trouble?"

"No." Big Sandy smiled then frowned. "I don't think so." He kissed her again, let himself out, caught a cab to the office. Niggling worry rode with him all the way. He couldn't escape it.

Two of the Bush's bankers in the office, counting

notes, snapping elastic bands around them. A large pile on the Bush's desk. Big Sandy stared at it dully. He was sure that Julius Scott's eyes would have lit up if he'd been present — he wished that he could drop by the stockbroker's place, share the moment with him — but money had never excited Big Sandy, even hard, naked cash like this.

"You OK?" the Bush asked, gazing miserably at the notes being counted off, glum now that the time had come to part with them.

"Yeah," Big Sandy lied.

"Get any sleep last night?"

"No."

"Me neither." The Bush glanced at him and grimaced. "I wish I'd let you talk me out of this. I didn't know how many strings I'd have to pull to free up this much cash. I won't go under if I lose it, but I'll be a long time making it back."

"It's not too late to change your mind," Big Sandy said. "Send in snipers. Kill Clint and McCaskey. Take the formula, keep the money. Fuck the witnesses, they'll think someone's making a film."

The Bush laughed as the bankers completed their count. "One million, eight hundred and eighty-four thousand," one of them said.

"Close enough," the Bush grunted. "Stick it in the bags." Two thick black canvas bags lay on the floor close to the table.

"Any way of tracing the money?" Big Sandy asked.

"We noted a selection of random numbers," the Bush said.

"So you're not convinced of McCaskey's good intentions."

The Bush shrugged. "I think he'll play it square – as he put it – but why take chances? If he deals straight, I'll leave him alone to enjoy his reward. If not, it's comforting to know I can find him."

The bankers finished bagging the money and went about their business, asking no questions. The Bush hefted the bags. Sighed. "I thought two million would weigh more." Tossed a bag to Big Sandy, who caught it one-handed and set it down by his feet. The Bush tossed him the other bag.

"The passports?" Big Sandy asked.

The Bush rolled his eyes. "Almost forgot." Took them out of a drawer, handed them to Big Sandy, watched him slide them into one of the bags. "Still concerned about the Tynes?"

"About Tulip, yes."

The Bush cocked his head. "Soft on her?"

"I like her. She's a good kid. Only in this mess because of her brother."

"I don't care about the Tynes," the Bush said. "The formula and Clint will do nicely. Tell McCaskey he can release Kevin and Tulip. I won't bother them."

"Thanks." Big Sandy smiled, feeling a weight lift, but not entirely. Checking the time. Early, but he couldn't stay here, needed to be on the move. "I'm going."

"Where?" The Bush briefly nervous, imagining Big Sandy disappearing with the money, making a mug of him.

"I'll walk around, clear my head, come back for the bags and directions nearer the time. Don't want to sit here thinking about all the things that could go wrong."

The Bush nodded, dismissing his momentary lapse of faith, angry at himself for doubting Big Sandy. "You're lucky. I have to sit here, twiddle my thumbs and wait, in case they ring earlier than planned to throw us off guard." He laid a hand on Big Sandy's broad right arm. "Take the money with you. I'll call you on your mobile when I know where you have to go."

"You're sure?" Big Sandy asked.

"Yeah. If I can't trust you, who the hell can I trust? Ring me as soon as the transaction has been made, then bring the formula here. I want to make a copy before I send it to the lab."

Big Sandy stood outside the Bush's office a minute, feeling the weight of the bags, wondering what it would be like to have two million pounds. He laughed at himself — he wouldn't be able to spend it! He'd just turn it over to Julius Scott and let him invest it as he saw fit, pass the profits on to Amelie.

Big Sandy shook his head, unable to understand why people cared so much about things like this. Then he clutched the bags close and went for a walk, tuning out all other concerns, focusing solely on the deal.

SIXTY-TWO

Clint was sick during the night, total terror, even worse than the night before they broke out Phials. Then, nobody knew of their plans, their destiny was in their own hands. Now, the Bush forewarned, his troops maybe armed to the teeth and waiting for the word, walking into a lion's den. Gawl insisted they had nothing to fear, the Bush stood to benefit by playing on the level. Clint unconvinced. Almost bolted several times during the night.

But greed held him. So close to the million that could make him. How small and useless would he feel if he fled and the deal went ahead cleanly, leaving Gawl to reap it all? A close-run thing, but in the end he stayed, threw up some more and lay on his bed fully clothed, trembling, torn between the glory of the dream and the desolation of the nightmare.

Gawl slept close to Clint in the study, snoring. He'd tanked on vodka when he returned from the Bush's, relating the minutes of the meeting *ad nauseam*, more eloquent the drunker he got, rewriting the script, giving himself new, powerful, abundant lines. The only thing he didn't talk about was his deal with the Bush at the end. Even when he peaked early, moaning, head spinning, staggering for bed, he was alert enough not to hint at his betrayal of Clint.

Pre-dawn, Clint heard someone shuffling down the stairs to the kitchen. He went to investigate. Found Fr Sebastian sitting in the light of the open fridge, drinking milk, looking forlorn. "Muh-mind if I join you?" Clint said, sitting beside him, taking a can of Coke from the fridge.

"I'm terrified," Fr Sebastian croaked, shaking even worse than Clint.

"Why?" Clint frowned. "You've nothing to wuh-worry about. You don't have to fuh-fuh-face Big Sandy. They don't even know about yuh-you."

"Still," Fr Sebastian sighed. "This last week's been hell. It's coming to an end, and I should be pleased, but I can't shake the feeling that the worst is yet to come." He studied Clint in the cold light of the fridge. "You feel it too."

Clint looked away. "There's nuh-nothing to worry about," he muttered unconvincingly. "Everything's suh-set."

"Do you want to pray with me?" Fr Sebastian asked out of the blue.

Clint blinked. "What for?"

"Success. Luck. God's blessing. His forgiveness."

Clint smiled dismissively. "I don't believe in any of that."

"Then I pity you," Fr Sebastian said. "In all my fear, weakness and confusion I at least have God to turn to. How do *you* cope when the world becomes too overbearing and terror strikes you cold?"

Clint had no answer for that. He placed the can of Coke back in the fridge without opening it, glanced at Fr Sebastian and smiled. "Want to get high?"

Fr Sebastian shivered. "I thought Gawl had the drugs."

"I know where they are. I can get them. You game?"

"Yes," Fr Sebastian said eagerly, eyes widening hungrily.

Clint slipped through to the study, found the drugs behind a stack of books, returned to the kitchen with a small sample of coke for the priest, plenty of grass for both of them. Rolled joints while Fr Sebastian shot back the coke, passed one to the priest, one for himself. They smoked in silence, pungent smoke filling the kitchen, calm taking the place of panic, Clint not as mellow as Fr Sebastian but chilling nicely, fears receding.

"What will you do when this is over?" Clint asked as Fr Sebastian rolled the next set of joints.

"Carry on as normal," Fr Sebastian said.

"It won't be easy. You won't have me to supply you any more, or Gawl to set you up with girls."

"I'll survive," Fr Sebastian murmured. "I always

have." He sat back, lit up, blew smoke rings and observed them thoughtfully as they dispersed in the air. "I might clean up my act. I've tried before but always slipped back into my bad habits. Maybe it will be different this time. I've never been so close to hell, or to pure human evil. This has been an education and I hope to learn from it. Put the drugs and sex behind me, give myself over to God, seek help, fight long and hard to cleanse my soul and make amends for my sins."

"I wish you luck," Clint said and he meant it.

"I'd rather you prayed for me," Fr Sebastian responded.

"I can't do that," Clint said lowly.

Fr Sebastian smiled beatifically. "Then *I* shall pray for *you*, once I've finished praying for myself." He giggled ruefully. "Be warned, it might be some time before I get around to you."

They laughed, smiled, rolled more joints, reflected as they smoked.

Gawl stumbled into the kitchen at twenty past eight, made for the sink, stuck his head under the tap, poured on the cold, shivering and groaning. Clint and Fr Sebastian laughed. He came up half a minute later, sputtering, dripping. Grabbed a tea-towel and dried his face. Glared at the two men. "Why didn't ye stop me getting drunk?"

"How?" Clint retorted.

Gawl shut his eyes and took a deep breath. Faced the sink again. Vomited, a combination of the vodka and nerves, though Clint and Fr Sebastian thought it was just the vodka. Ran the tap again. Stuck his head back under. Felt better when he came up for air this time. Raided the bread bin. Munched one slice, two, three, four, five. Clint and Fr Sebastian watched and smoked.

Gawl's head cleared. He sniffed the marijuana. Whirled on Clint. "What the fuck are ye doing?"

Clint gawped. "Huh?"

Gawl slapped the joint from his fingers. "This is no fucking time t' get high."

"No," Clint smiled, "this is the *perfect* time to get high, just like last night was the perfect time for you to get drunk. You want me calm and sensible, don't you? In control, on top form?" He picked up the joint, re-lit it, stuck it back between his lips. "This is the only way I'll be like that. I'd be crapping my pants otherwise."

Gawl laughed at Clint's stoned honesty. "I guess a little grass can't do any harm at that," he conceded, inwardly adding, *Might as well go out on a high.*

Gawl ate more bread, brewed coffee, chewed

biscuits. Kevin and Tulip came down, Kevin shaking, Tulip downcast but calm. Clint saw the tremble in Kevin's hands. Offered him a joint. Kevin refused, he wanted to keep a clear head.

Fr Sebastian cooked breakfast, toast, pancakes, sausages, bacon, baked beans, scrambled eggs. They all ate, except Tulip, who said she had a stomach bug. Gawl made Clint and Fr Sebastian lay off the grass. He didn't want Clint *too* high. They didn't complain, happy with their lot. Clint talked about what he'd do with his money, New York, flash car, penthouse apartment, the finest suits he could find, an enormous diamond ring for when he proposed to Shula. Fr Sebastian spoke of transferring out of the parish, going abroad to work for the missions. Gawl laid out his life in the sun, a spot of gambling, a lot of women. Kevin didn't say much, muttered something about mainland Europe, maybe the Netherlands, living quietly. Tulip said nothing at all, only rubbed her stomach, worried about the ordeal to come, praying to God for guidance.

After breakfast Clint, Gawl and Kevin washed, shaved and dressed like three men preparing for interviews. Gawl sobering up, Clint buzzing along nicely, Kevin shaking constantly. Fr Sebastian and Tulip waited in the kitchen. Tulip wanted to ask the priest to hear her confession but she couldn't, remembering the times he'd lain with her, coming to her door a few nights before, weak and twisted. Fr Sebastian saw in her eyes how low he'd fallen. It depressed him, negated his high. Doubts returned. No longer sure he could find the strength to reform, turn his back on his vices, get out and get clean. Thinking about dealers he could take his trade to, brothels he could visit, girls he could corrupt.

Gawl returned to the kitchen first. Then Kevin. Clint last, looking dapper, hair gelled back, fingernails scrubbed clean, cheeks rosy where he'd slapped colour into them. Clint checked the time. Coming up to eleven. "When do we leave?" he asked breezily.

"Soon," Gawl said. "We'll take our time, do a bit of sightseeing, ring them on the way."

The three men and Tulip fetched their coats while Fr Sebastian remained in the kitchen. Gawl picked one of Fr Sebastian's long jackets plus a hat and scarf. They returned to the kitchen fully wrapped. "Will ye be all right by yerself, Father?" Gawl asked.

"Fine."

"We should be back by half twelve or one," Clint said.

"And if you're not?"

Clint and Gawl glanced at each other, Clint nervous, Gawl knowing. "Then you can start saying your pruh-

pruh-pruh-prayers for us," Clint half-laughed.

They filed through the kitchen, out the back door, then struck for Vauxhall, planning to wander around a while before making their way to Westminster Bridge. Gawl in front, Clint at the rear, the Tynes sandwiched in the middle, Tulip the only one not consumed by the iciness of fear and doubt, the only one completely resigned to whatever hand they were dealt.

SIXTY-THREE

Cold, grey, blustery. Kevin didn't notice. Oblivious to all but his terror and hope, playing out the dual scenarios over and over while they walked. In the first it was a trap, killed or captured, lives forfeited, pain, death. In the second they pulled it off, walked away wealthy, Kevin took Tulip to Europe, three hundred and fifty thousand pounds to fund their future, a home, a baby, Tulip growing ever more dependant on him. The lure of the second scenario balanced against the dread of the first, the scales level.

He kept close to Tulip, held her hand, squeezed occasionally, automatically, comfortingly. Tulip unaware of her brother's touch, praying, thinking about her baby, hoping the drugs hadn't harmed it, promising herself again that she would junk the junk ASAP, wondering what God had planned for her and her child. The outcome of the deal of no interest to her, little to choose between failure and success. If they died, God would take her and her unborn baby. If they came away with the money, she faced dilemma after dilemma, how to deal with Kevin, how to raise her child, how to survive alone if she abandoned her brother. She wanted to live but she didn't fear death. It would be simpler to die.

The streets adorned with Christmas decorations, lights, tinsel, Santa, baubles, Christmas trees. People out shopping for presents or cards. Yuletide songs spewing from millions of radios. Tulip the only one of the four who noted the festive trappings, the men all focused on the deal.

Past the Elephant & Castle and on to Vauxhall, discussing the plan, going over it one last time. A quick call to the Bush at eleven-thirty, then east to Westminster along the river, nobody talking now, stomachs tight, eyes watering in the wind. Gawl felt like puking from the vodka. Clint and Kevin felt like puking with fear. Tulip felt like puking because of her pregnancy.

They marched methodically until they were almost at Westminster Bridge Road. Gawl stopped them outside St Thomas' hospital. Kevin, Tulip and Clint sat on a bench, shivering in the cold. Gawl stayed on his feet. "I'm gonna check it out. I'll be ten minutes max. Any more than that, go back t' the church and wait." He set off. Paused. Looked back at Clint. "Make that fifteen minutes."

Kevin wrapped an arm around Tulip, hugged her close. "It'll be OK," he whispered. "We'll go somewhere hot after this. I'll look after you. And the baby."

Tulip glanced at Clint. He was sitting on the edge of the bench, nervously waiting for Gawl, not listening. "We could escape now," she whispered back. "He wouldn't notice. Get away. Go to the police."

Kevin shook his head. "This is our future."

"Or our end." He smiled shakily as if that was a crazy idea. Hugged her again. "What if Gawl betrays us?" Tulip asked. "What if he abandons us at the church or kills us instead of giving us our passports and the money?"

"I thought of that already," Kevin said, lowering his voice even further. "We aren't going back to the church. On the way, we'll stop at the Elephant & Castle and demand our cut. If they don't give it to us, we'll raise hell, draw attention. They'll have no choice but to pay up. They daren't kill us in public."

"You didn't tell me this before."

Kevin smiled. "I didn't want to worry you. I've been doing a lot of thinking. I have it all worked out. From the Elephant we'll backtrack to Waterloo, catch the Eurostar to Paris, lay low, take it from there."

"And if Dave Bushinsky's men follow us?"

Kevin grinned sadistically. "They'll be busy elsewhere. We'll make a call before we board the train, tell Big Sandy where McCaskey and Clint are, sic him on the bastards, use them like they used us."

"No," Tulip said steadily. "That would mean betraying Fr Sebastian too."

"They won't harm him. We'll tell them he was an unwilling –"

"No," Tulip said, louder this time. Clint flicked his gaze at them, irritated, then looked away again.

"Keep your voice down," Kevin growled.

"Only if you agreee not to involve Fr Sebastian."

"But it's safer this way. We'll create a diversion. It will be easier to slip free." Tulip stared at him stonily. He sighed and lowered his gaze. "OK, we'll skip that part. But the rest of it's good. McCaskey said Bushinsky agreed to let us all leave the country – part of their deal – so the station probably won't be watched."

"If it is?"

He shrugged. "We'll deal with that later."

Silence settled upon them. Minutes ticked by slowly, Clint checking his watch frequently, muttering, "Where is he? Where is he?" Kevin shivering but not from the cold, half-hoping McCaskey wouldn't return, half-praying he would.

Sixteen minutes after he left them, McCaskey huffed back into view, hurrying towards them, face hidden by the scarf and hat, shoulders hunched over. He strode to the bench and tugged down his scarf. "Big Sandy's there, alone. It looks safe." He hauled Tulip to her feet and pressed a notebook into her hands. "Stick that inside yer jacket. Keep it safe. Super fucking safe, right?"

"That's the formula?" Clint sighed dreamily. "Can I see it?"

"No," McCaskey said. "That'd be a waste of time." His eyes were on Tulip. Her hands hadn't moved.

"I don't want to hand this over," she said. Looked up at McCaskey defiantly. "I know what it will do to people. I don't want to help deliver it into the world."

McCaskey blinked dumbly. Clint laughed. Kevin grabbed Tulip's elbow and squeezed hard. "Don't fuck about," he snarled. "Take it and do what you're told."

"But –"

"You don't have to take it," Clint interrupted. "We can use Kuh-Kevin for that part. But Big Sandy might take him huh-hostage and torture him for information. Big Sandy's soft on you, so I doubt he'll try anything. Of cuh-course, if you want to send in Kevin and let him take his chances..."

Tulip shot daggers at Clint with her eyes. Stuck the notebook inside her jacket. Stood and took off at a fast pace for Westminster Bridge. The men smiled at each other – *women!* – then set off after her, Gawl catching her up in a couple of long strides, Kevin and Clint just behind.

Up the steps and across Westminster Bridge, stopping at the top of the steps leading down to the Southbank. County Hall ancient and stately on their right. The London Eye impossibly tall and gleaming dead ahead. Tourists milling around, not many, but more than Kevin expected on such an overcast December day. At the end of County Hall, where the ticket office for the Eye was situated, Big Sandy, taller than anyone else, a stand-out even from their distant vantage point.

Kevin's gaze passed from Big Sandy to the tourists and street hawkers. Some of them could be the Bush's men, disguised, armed, waiting. Clint and Gawl thinking the same thing, judging, calculating. Tulip's gaze fixed on Big Sandy. He looked lonely, towering over everybody, dwarfed only by the buildings and the Eye.

Gawl snapped to attention. Nudged Kevin. "Go t' him. Bring him over. Stop ten or twelve feet from the foot of the steps. Me and Clint'll come down for the money when he gets here."

Kevin nodded nervously. It was what they'd agreed, but now that the moment was upon them he wished he'd argued for Clint to make first contact, uneasy at the thought of leaving Tulip by herself while they made the transaction. But too late to debate the issue now. He gave Tulip a final hug, kissed her chastely, whispered, "I love you," and advanced down the steps, past the tourists and vendors, towards Big Sandy.

The giant spotted him coming. He stiffened, took a step forward, stopped. He stared over Kevin's head, scanning the faces behind him until he located the two men and Tulip on the bridge. Recognised Clint from here. McCaskey's face hidden behind a scarf, hat pulled low over his eyes.

Kevin stopped a couple of feet short of Big Sandy. Sweating. Shaking. Vomit rising. He forced it down and smiled pathetically. "Hi."

Big Sandy impassive. "If anything happens to Tulip, I'll kill you."

Kevin flinched, then firmed. "I'm doing this for her. We weren't part of the original plan. McCaskey and Clint used us."

"Are they using you now?" Big Sandy asked sceptically.

"No," Kevin admitted. "I made them cut us in. I need the money to look after Tulip."

"McCaskey won't give you anything."

"I'll make him. I have everything under control." Kevin licked his lips and glanced at the bags which Big Sandy was carrying. "Is it all there?"

"Yes." Big Sandy offered one of the bags to him.

Kevin stuck his hands behind his back. "Not to me," he cried as if he was being offered a poisonous snake. Caught himself and grinned sheepishly. "McCaskey and Clint will take the bags. Clint will stay with you while McCaskey and I check the money. Then Tulip will bring the formula to you. You let her and Clint leave. Then we're through."

Except for letting Clint leave, Big Sandy thought, but said out loud, "OK." He lowered the bag. "Lead the way."

SIXTY-FOUR

Face hidden behind Fr Seb's hat and scarf, Gawl circled around the back of County Hall, slipped past Big Sandy in front of the London Eye ticket office, stopped to examine a rack of postcards. Glancing left and right as he pretended to peruse the cards, studying Big Sandy's eyes in case he looked towards a partner. If Gawl caught the scent of betrayal he'd beat a quick retreat, screw the plan, get out with his life and forget the money. But Big Sandy appeared to be alone, gaze lingering on various faces in the crowd, but casually, normal curiosity. A bit of red in his cheeks. Might have been from the cold, but Gawl thought it was more likely from walking fast once he got the call, to make sure he got here on time.

Gawl gave it a few minutes to be as certain as he could, then returned to the steps and climbed up to Westminster Bridge, paused at the top for a final once-over, hurried to fetch the others from in front of St Thomas'.

Minutes laters, back at the top of the steps, he stared numbly at Big Sandy as Kevin led the giant towards them. Big Sandy lugged the bags as if they were empty, but as he got closer Gawl could see the whiteness of his knuckles — he wouldn't be clutching empty bags that tightly. Gawl shivered as he realised they'd done it. Until this moment he hadn't truly believed in the dream. Deep inside he was sure the deal would blow up in their faces, the Bush would set a trap, Big Sandy would come packing guns instead of crisp notes. Now, as he watched the pair draw closer, clouds of serene calm filled him from the inside out. It was all going as planned. In a few minutes he'd be rich, set for a magnificent retirement, free to live out the rest of his life in unimaginable style.

Beside him, Clint less confident, twisting left and right, looking over his shoulder, expecting the Bush's men to close on them from all sides. Gawl spared Clint a pitiful glance – no place for him in Gawl's triumph – then fixed on Big Sandy and Kevin Tyne, rocking softly on the balls of his feet, eager to make the handover, abandon Clint, get back to the church, count his money, plot his betrayal of Kevin and Tulip.

Kevin came to a halt at the arranged mark. Big Sandy stopped beside him, asked Kevin should he stay here or climb the steps. Kevin told him to stay then stared at Gawl pleadingly, wanting to be relieved of his wretched responsibility. Gawl chuckled at Kevin's misery and prolonged it for a few seconds more before turning to Tulip. "Ye're clear about the plan?"

"I wait here," Tulip said. "You and Clint go down and get the money. You and Kevin come back and check it. I go down with the notebook and give it to Sandy. I come back up with Clint."

"Aye." Clint was staring at Big Sandy, mouth agape. Gawl pressed his lips close to Tulip's ear. "Think only of yerself when ye're returning. Don't worry about Clint."

"What do you mean?" Tulip frowned.

Gawl's only answer was a wink. He clapped Clint hard on the back and the young dealer almost screamed. "Are ye ready?"

A shaking Clint faced Gawl and nodded. "Yuh-yuh-yuh-yes."

"Calm down," Gawl said softly. "The hard bit's behind us. Don't lose yer nerve in front of Big Sandy."

"Buh-buh-Big Suh-Sandy," Clint croaked. "I duh-don't want to fuh-face him. Can't yuh-you go down aluh-aluh-alone?"

"If I go alone, I'll take the money alone," Gawl said coolly. "Ye want t' give up yer half? Fine. Walk now. I won't stop ye." Clint blinked at the thought of walking away from a million pounds. Grinned sheepishly. Gawl smiled encouragingly, a Judas smile. Clapped his back again, soft this time. "Let's go collect our prize."

They started down the steps, leaving Tulip alone on the bridge, watching sadly. Big Sandy spread his legs as they came, planting his feet firm, bags held by his sides. Kevin took a step away from the giant, fingers twitching, a crazy image of Big Sandy dropping the bags, drawing guns, opening fire like a Western bandito. But Big Sandy didn't even blink. Gawl and Clint kept coming. The image passed and Kevin grinned with embarrassment, tried to stop shaking.

Gawl felt like a god as he descended. Everything in his life seemed to have been preparation for this moment. The beatings he'd endured, hunger, prison, exile, hopelessness... They had a purpose now, to make this moment all the sweeter. He was experiencing something he'd never known before — happiness. He'd thrilled to the rush of alcohol, sex, murder and more. But never simple, genuine happiness. He was startled to find soft tears in his eyes and quickly blinked them away, dangerous to weaken now. Celebrate later, when he had the money and was out of the country.

Gawl hit the path. Stopped. Took a deep breath, grinning behind his scarf at Big Sandy, who stared back blankly. Another new sensation — pride. This was all his doing. It had started with Clint and Phials, but he'd taken them, directed them, worked the situation around to his own gain. Not many men went up against the likes of Dave Bushinsky and profited. So many ways to blow it, so many mistakes he could have made, so many pitfalls. But he'd avoided them all, kept a cool head, made the right calls, surprising even himself with his daring, greed and ingenuity.

Clint looked at Gawl nervously, wondering why his partner was standing there instead of moving forward to conclude the swap. Kevin nervous too, couldn't see Gawl's face, didn't know what he was thinking, fearing the worst. Big Sandy took no notice, just stood, waiting, in no rush.

Gawl sighed. He'd savoured the moment, now it was time to close the deal, take his money, ride off into the sunset. He stepped forward, taking off the hat and unwrapping the scarf, wanting to face Big Sandy unmasked, as an equal, not a hidden, cowering underling. "Gawl McCaskey. Pleased t' meet ye."

"Get stuffed," Big Sandy said and held out the bags. Clint snatched for the bag in Big Sandy's left hand, wrestled it from him, clutched it to his chest, eyes ablaze. Gawl slower to react. He smiled broadly at Big Sandy, reached up and scratched the jagged top half of his left ear, acting bored. Then, as if it was a chore, he stuck out his hands, expecting Big Sandy to lay the bag into his palms.

Big Sandy didn't react. He was staring at Gawl.

Gawl's smile shook a little but held. "I'll take that now," he chuckled.

Big Sandy didn't react. He was staring at Gawl.

Gawl's smile slipped. He glanced sharply at Clint, rubbing his bag like a cat, unaware of anything else. Looked around, stomach lurching, expecting to see armed men storming towards him or making off with Tulip and the formula. But nobody was moving in for the kill, Big Sandy alone, Tulip on the bridge by herself. Gawl frowned at Big Sandy. "Give me the fucking bag," he snapped.

Big Sandy didn't react. He was staring at Gawl.

Kevin worried. Something was wrong. He tried to slide behind Clint, using him as cover, getting ready to run. Gawl grabbed him. "Stay where ye are." Sweating and shaking, not sure what Big Sandy was playing at. He took hold of the bag and wrenched. Big Sandy let go and the bag shot into Gawl's hands. He tightened his grip on it, smiling again, then squinted at Big Sandy, waiting for him to say something.

Big Sandy didn't react. He was staring at Gawl.

"Well," Gawl said uneasily, "it's been sweet doing business with ye, even if ye seem a bit –"

Big Sandy's hands snaked forward. His fingers locked around Gawl's throat. He squeezed.

Gawl caught off-guard. He blinked dumbly as Big Sandy choked him. Kevin squealed, turned to run, crashed into Clint, slipped and fell. Clint realised something was wrong, looked up, saw Big Sandy's fingers wrapped around Gawl's throat. He gawped.

Big Sandy's fingers tightened. His face darknened. Gawl dropped the bag and snatched at Big Sandy's wrists, to jerk them apart. Big Sandy too strong, his fingers remained locked. Gawl tried to throw himself backwards, to break the grip. Big Sandy followed, collapsing on top of him, driving him to the ground, fingers loosening slightly, then tightening again, Gawl wheezing.

Around them, people gasped, ogled, nudged their partners. Nobody screamed or intervened, more curious than apprehensive. Kevin scrambled to his feet and sought out Tulip. She was watching, eyes round, a hand over her mouth. He wanted to get to her. He tried to run. Clint stopped him with one hand while holding on to his bag with the other. "What's happening?" he yelled. Kevin shook his head and tried to break free. Clint held him.

On the ground, Gawl choking, eyes bulging. He remembered the gun in his coat pocket. Willed his hand to slide down and dig it out. But his fingers wouldn't obey. They were grasping Big Sandy's wrists, tearing at them, refusing to let go.

Gawl thinking, *What the fuck?* Startled, bemused, confused. Staring at Big Sandy's creased face, lips bared in a snarl, eyes tight, naked hatred. This shouldn't be happening. It made no sense. The deal had been struck. Easiest for everyone to proceed as planned. Why was he doing this? What did he hope to gain? Not the Bush's orders, Gawl sensed that even as he choked to death. The money? Did Big Sandy plan to cross them all and make off with the two million? But then why bother coming? Why go to the trouble of choking Gawl? Why not just run with the bags earlier?

On the bridge Tulip could take no more. She turned and fled, racing across the road, cars jerking to a halt, horns blaring, Tulip slipping away, picking up speed. Kevin saw her flee. Moaned. Punched Clint, half broke free. Clint clung to him. "The money!" he roared.

"Tulip!" Kevin retorted.

"The money first," Clint cried. "We –" Stopping, heart sinking as he spotted two police officers on Westminster Bridge, a man and woman, marching towards them, alerted by the commotion. Not at the steps yet but they'd reach the top before Kevin and Clint could. Clint grabbed Kevin's neck. Pointed. "Cops!"

"I don't care," Kevin moaned. "Tulip."

"Run," Clint insisted, pulling Kevin after him. "We'll find her later."

"No. Now."

"No time," Clint screamed. He let go of Kevin, picked up the second bag, thrust it into Kevin's hands. "If they arrest us, you'll never see her again."

The warning struck Kevin like a bullet. He glanced at the pair on the ground, Gawl's legs thrashing, hands locked on Big Sandy's, Big Sandy's hands locked around Gawl's throat, Gawl's eyes all the way open, lips blue, close to death, Big Sandy snarling insanely. Then he stared at the police rushing to the steps, calling in the disturbance on their walkie talkies. Kevin groaned then nodded wretchedly. They leapt over the wrestling men and ran for their lives, Clint panting, Kevin weeping.

Gawl's strength deserted him. He found himself relaxing. Incredulous. *This isn't happening. This isn't happening. This isn't...*

"Bastard," Big Sandy grunted and it sounded like a sob. Gawl forced his eyes into focus. Another conundrum — the giant was crying.

Gawl found one final burst of strength, tugged hard at Big Sandy's hands, trying to get enough air and space to croak, "*Why?*" If he could just speak with Big Sandy, he was sure he could iron this out. Something was amiss – this wasn't what either man had planned – but he could fix it if Big Sandy just... gave him... a moment to...

The grey sky turned black. The gasps and mutters of the crowd were obscured by Big Sandy's harsh, growling breathing, the sound of a large dog as it chewed at the throat of a defeated rival. Gawl's fingers unclenched. His hands slipped away. The money forgotten. Dreams forgotten. Future forgotten. Big Sandy's betrayal forgotten. The pain forgotten.

His last moments. His final thought, which he could make no sense of, a face forming out of the blackness. A woman, calm, lips slightly lifted in a sneer, hair tied back. He recognised the face – one of the women he'd murdered – but he didn't know why he was seeing it now. Of all the faces from his past, all the people he'd known, the men he'd fought, the women he'd fucked, the women he'd killed, why did the face of *Nancy Mooney* come to him at the very end?

Before he could pick at the puzzle, life deserted him. A great stillness settled. All faded, even the woman's face. He heard nothing. Saw nothing. Knew nothing. Gawl died ignorant.

SIXTY-FIVE

Big Sandy weeping and snarling, knuckles red/white as his fingers crushed Gawl McCaskey's throat. McCaskey was dead but Big Sandy didn't stop, he wanted to rip the bastard's head off and take it as a trophy. People in the crowd were screaming and sobbing now. Half backed away, the other half pressed closer. Tourists took photos. Big Sandy saw only McCaskey's despised face, grinning hellishly in death.

Something struck his right arm hard and fast. Not much pain but the surprise made his fingers unclench. He looked up. A policeman standing over him, truncheon raised, face twisted with fury and fear. "Let go!" he bellowed. A female cop behind him, truncheon also drawn.

Awareness flooded back, where he was, what had happened, the shit he was in. The bags were gone. Smith and Kevin Tyne gone. Tulip and the formula gone. Just him, the corpse of Gawl McCaskey, the cops and the crowd. No, not a crowd — witnesses. He saw cameras flashing. Fucked.

He rose slowly. The cop's face dropped as he realised

how enormous Big Sandy was. He backed off, raising his truncheon defensively. Big Sandy ignored him. Studied Gawl McCaskey's face from a safe, sane height. Laughed through his tears. The female cop said something, trying to control the situation. The words didn't register. He turned his back on the cops, laughing, heedless. Let them take him. He didn't care. On a high. The world couldn't touch him. Arrested, locked away forever, so what? Life was glorious. The bastard on the ground was dead. Nothing else...

He caught sight of the inside of the hat McCaskey had been wearing. A name tag. Big Sandy stooped and picked up the hat, incredulous. *Sebastian Parry.* Explosions inside his head. They'd been hiding in the church! Fr Sebastian had sheltered them. No idea how that had happened, why the priest would have given them sanctuary, but Smith and the Tynes might return. They'd been safe in the church this long. No reason for them to think they couldn't hole-up there again.

Assessing his actions. He'd shamed the Bush, screwed the deal, lost the formula and the money. One chance to redeem himself — catch them at the church, recover the money, claim the formula. Not worried about what would happen to him later, whether the Bush would slip him out of the country or sacrifice him to the police, only focused on restoring his honour.

The male cop was talking. Big Sandy shut him up with a snarl. "Stay away from me." He drew a gun. Those in the crowd who'd been pressing closer shrieked and broke for cover. The cops ducked. Big Sandy ran, knocking them aside. Raced up the steps on to Westminster Bridge. Sprinted to the traffic lights. Waited for them to turn red. Stepped up to the first car that had stopped, only one person in it, a man. Walked around to the driver's door. Yanked it open. Flashed his gun. "*Out!*" The driver didn't argue, unclipped his belt and rolled out, whimpering. Big Sandy sat in. Pedestrians staring at him. The cops came flailing up the steps, shouting at him to stop, at the pedestrians to stand back. Big Sandy crashed the lights, leaving the cops, the crowds, the chaos behind, heading for the Elephant & Castle, then the Church of Sacred Martyrs. Calm now. Forcing McCaskey out of his thoughts. Professional. Focused on his job.

He parked in front of the church. Kicked in the door, disrespectful in a church for the first time in his life. Stormed up the aisle, ignoring the stares of the handful of people in the pews. Marched to the sacristy and through to the house. Failed to spot Fr Sebastian to the left of the altar, close to the pulpit. But Fr Sebastian saw Big Sandy. Knew what it meant. Sighed and offered up a prayer for his damned soul as he climbed into the pulpit, loosening his belt, crying softly but not sorrowfully, escape from this life a mercy.

Big Sandy was halfway through his sweep of the house when he heard screams in the church. He raced back, drawing his gun. Crashed in on Fr Sebastian hanging from a bar which ran along the top of the pulpit, a belt looped around his throat, legs kicking spastically, tongue extruded. One of his female parishioners ran to the priest and grabbed his legs, trying to support him, crying shrilly, "No, Father, no!" Big Sandy watched in silence for a few seconds, then walked up behind her, picked her up and set her down behind him, let the priest strangle. "What are you doing?" the woman shrieked.

"It's better this way," Big Sandy said.

The woman stared at him. "Suicide's a sin," she whispered.

"I'm guessing it won't be his worst," Big Sandy replied, figuring the priest would only have taken in the fugitives if they had something on him. Maybe Tulip was the link, Fr Sebastian one of the Tynes' clients. Or maybe he was one of Clint's junkies, which would explain why the dealer had set up shop in the church. Hell, for all Big

Sandy knew, maybe it was both.

He waited until the priest's legs went still, then turned his back on the shamed messenger of God. "Call the police," he said to the stunned woman as he passed. "Don't bother with an ambulance." Out of the church. Back in the car. A leisurely drive to the Bush's, not worried, not afraid, what must be must be.

The Bush grinning when Big Sandy entered. He got up to greet him. Caught Big Sandy's expression. Sank back into his chair. Eyes Burton had admitted Big Sandy. The Bush waited for him to leave before speaking. "What happened?"

"I killed Gawl McCaskey. Clint and the Tynes escaped with the money and the formula. They'd been staying at the Church of Sacred Martyrs. I went there. Fr Sebastian hung himself before I could question him. If the others return, the police will be there to capture them, nothing we can do."

The Bush took all that in. Dazed. Breathless. He blinked like an owl. Big Sandy stood impassively, waiting for his boss to recover. Finally, uncertainly, the Bush muttered, "Did McCaskey try to cross you?"

"No."

"Then why did you kill him?"

Big Sandy's gaze didn't flicker. "I recognised him."

"Of course you recognised him," the Bush roared. "Gawl Mc-fucking-Caskey!"

"I meant I recognised him from the past. I've been looking for him most of my life. He murdered my mother."

The Bush had been poised to bellow more abuse. At Big Sandy's statement he stopped. Stared bug-eyed. "No," he croaked. Big Sandy didn't reply. "It can't have been. That was so long ago."

"I haven't forgotten. I made him as soon as I saw his face. If the drawings had been more accurate I would have twigged before, but they were way off."

"You were mistaken," the Bush wheezed.

"I wasn't," Big Sandy said. "He went under a different name back then, Davey Connors. He hadn't lost half an ear. He was thinner. More hair. But it was him. He butchered my mother. So I killed him. I choked him to death in front of dozens of witnesses, including two police officers. I didn't care about anything else. Killing him was all that mattered. I don't apologise for it, but I regret the circumstances in which it happened."

Big Sandy lapsed into silence, waited for the Bush to respond. The Bush flabbergasted. It seemed too impossible to be real. One look at Big Sandy's granite face and he knew the story was true, but still he tried to pick holes in it. "McCaskey knew you, knew that I was sending you. If he'd murdered your mother why the hell would he agree to meet with you?"

"I was eleven years old," Big Sandy said quietly. "A scrawny kid. He wouldn't have remembered me."

"But your name…"

"My mother always called me by my full name. And she gave me my father's surname, even though she didn't bear it herself, but I doubt he was aware of that. If he remembered me at all, it would have been as Alexander Mooney, not Big Sandy Murphy."

The Bush shook his head and half-smiled sickly. "You think this was destiny?"

"Just McCaskey's bad luck," Big Sandy grunted. "I don't believe in destiny."

"This is too coincidental to be luck," the Bush disagreed. Big Sandy didn't reply. The Bush studied him. "You don't seem too agitated. You just found and killed the man you've been hunting for thirty years, yet you stand here, reporting to me calmly, like it was no big thing."

"It's the biggest thing of my life," Big Sandy said. "But it's over. Later it'll hit me hard and I'll obsess about it, cry about it, cheer about it. Right now there's my fuck-up, the lost money and the missing formula to account for."

The Bush snorted admiringly, Big Sandy far cooler than the Bush would have been in the big man's shoes. He sat back, fingers coming together, addressing the problem. After a minute of silence he shrugged. "The money's gone. The formula's history. You acted as anyone would have in your position. I don't blame you. We forget about it and get on with our lives."

"We can't," Big Sandy said. "I was seen killing McCaskey. Photographed."

The Bush frowned. "So we smuggle you out of the country, hide you somewhere safe, set you up with a new identity."

"That won't be easy. My face can be altered but not my build. People will notice me wherever I go. It'll cost a lot of money to hide me, and the danger of my being unearthed will always exist. Plus, word of what happened today will spread. Stories will be told, how you trusted me with two million pounds, how I lost it, how you rewarded me for my fuck-up. Very embarrassing for you. A lot simpler to write me off and –"

"What are you talking about?" the Bush snapped. "You think I'd betray you? You think I don't know how to be loyal?"

"I'm not questioning your loyalty," Big Sandy said, unfazed. "But business is business. You said yourself how important this deal was, how you couldn't afford to lose two million. The money it would cost to defend me... the loss of face... the aggro... I add it all up, and from where you stand I don't think I'm worth it."

"You're suggesting I have you killed?" the Bush cried incredulously.

"I'm just trying to anticipate the way you're going to think in the coming weeks, save us both time and hassle. I won't live like Tony Phials, a prisoner, with the threat of retaliation hanging over my head. You're being gracious now, but I look ahead and see your options narrowing, your thoughts turning, your people advising you to cut me loose as the liability I am."

"I wouldn't do that," the Bush said unconvincingly, but they both knew from experience that he would. He'd sacrificed loyal servants before when he'd had to. Business always came first. There were plenty of vultures waiting in the wings to swoop upon him and pick his bones clean at the first sign of weakness.

Big Sandy waited patiently for his boss to think the situation through. Finally the Bush sighed and lowered his hands. "How do you suggest I handle this?"

"Three things you can do," Big Sandy responded instantly. "One, ship me off quickly and quietly, like you were saying, pay for me to lay low, take the heat when the cops come looking for me, endure the mockery when word gets out how much I cost you. But I don't think that's a feasible course of action."

"So lay out my alternatives," the Bush smiled.

"Two, have me executed." Big Sandy spoke without emotion. "Leave my body where the cops can find it. That gets them off your back. It also puts out the message that nobody fucks with Dave Bushinsky. You'll be seen to have acted brutally and swiftly, making the best of a bad lot."

The Bush nodded, impressed that Big Sandy was able to lay it out so clearly and bluntly, as if it was somebody else's life he was talking about. "And my third option?" he asked softly.

"The Tynes and Smith are still in London. As far as I know, they fled on foot from the Eye. They can't return to their safehouse now that Fr Sebastian has killed himself. They have the money but no idea how to get away with it safely. They'll panic. If we respond swiftly, we might be able to find them, recoup your losses, maybe get the formula too." Big Sandy licked his lips, the only sign that he was nervous. "You could give me twenty-four hours. I'd spearhead the search. If I find them, I'll redeem myself, earn the right to walk away a free man. There'll be a reason for you to reward me. You won't lose face."

"And if you don't find them?" the Bush asked.

Big Sandy shrugged. "My freedom if I succeed. My execution if I fail."

The Bush raised an eyebrow. "You'd stand there and take a bullet voluntarily?"

"I'll do what's right, like I've always done," Big Sandy replied evenly.

The Bush thought it over. "How would you search for them?"

"The hounds. I wasn't taking much notice, but I think Tulip went one way, Smith and Kevin another. I'd give Tulip's scent to one of the hounds, Smith or Kevin's scent to the other."

"What if they've thought of that?"

"I'm gambling that they won't, not in the heat of the moment. While I'm heading the hunt on foot, you can put out word that they're on the loose. Offer a reward again. Cover all points of departure. Throw up a net like before."

"What if I catch them before you?" the Bush asked.

"Then it's your call. I'll accept your decision."

The Bush considered it silently. "If you're made by the cops during the hunt?"

"I won't be handling the hounds alone," Big Sandy

said. "You can have a few words with the team, tell them what to do in an emergency."

The Bush chuckled. "You frighten me, the way you're taking this in your stride."

"There's no other way to take it," Big Sandy demurred. "I'm in deep shit. I can whine and go down. Or I can keep my head and do my best to pull myself out."

The Bush decided. "Get the hounds. Fast Eddie will help. I'll send men to assist. You have until dawn. Report back here if you don't find them. Depending on the circumstances, I might grant you more time or I might not."

Big Sandy nodded obediently. Got to his feet. Struck for the door.

"Sandy," the Bush stopped him. "Did it feel good, killing McCaskey?"

Big Sandy grinned bleakly. "Yeah."

"Worth whatever you must face as a consequence?"

"Yeah."

"I'm glad for you." The Bush smiled. "Good luck."

"Thanks." Big Sandy left to fetch the hounds.

SIXTY-SIX

Clint and Kevin fled, panting, faces red, eyes ragged with terror, bags of money clutched tight, ignoring the startled stares of those they passed, looking back often for signs of pursuit. At Waterloo Bridge Clint paused, doubled over, catching his breath, moaning. Kevin stood tall, shaking, quick shallow breaths, thinking, *Tulip!* When he caught his breath he gasped, "We have to go back." Clint laughed sickly and didn't look up. "Tulip's alone. We have to find her. We –"

"Gawl's dead!" Clint shouted. A couple of pedestrians stopped and stared. He lowered his voice. "Big Sandy flipped and killed Gawl. The cops saw it — and us. We stole Dave's money — he'll want it back. The streets are going to be crawling with people looking for us – cops and Dave's thugs – and you're worried about your fucking sister?" Paused and half-smiled, impressed despite everything else that he hadn't stuttered. "Forget Tulip."

"I can't," Kevin cried.

"Then go look for her, but the money stays with me."

Kevin clutched his bag possessively. Clint sighed.

"Westminster will be crawling with cops by now, so we couldn't go back for Tulip even if we wanted."

"The church," Kevin mumbled. "She'll return to Sacred Martyrs."

"Maybe," Clint agreed. "But we can't go there until it's dark."

"Why not?"

"We were seen with Gawl. Our descriptions will be circulated by the police. People were taking photos. They could be aired on the news. If we go to the church in the middle of the day, we'll be seen by parishioners, they'll report us."

Kevin nodded wearily. "So where?"

"North," Clint decided, leading the way on to Waterloo Bridge. "We'll hide until night. Talk this over while we're waiting. Make plans."

"And Tulip?" Kevin asked, following meekly.

"We'll figure that out later," Clint said, not meaning it, caring only about getting the hell away.

Walking quickly, collars up to mask their faces, keeping to the shadows, avoiding the busier streets, saying nothing. Both men shocked and scared, but Clint the less shaken, the same strength he'd displayed in the cellar at the lab, surprisingly cool under fire. Eyes peeled, looking for a place they could hide. His thoughts kept darting to the million pounds he was carrying. They hadn't checked the bags yet. He wanted to rip them open, dig down deep, feel, smell, taste the money. But they couldn't do that in the open, so he forced himself to keep moving.

Twenty-five minutes later they came to a building under construction, encased in scaffolding, roped off, nobody at work. A quiet street, no traffic. Clint walked to one end of the building to be sure it was deserted, then backtracked and stepped over the ropes, Kevin just behind him, hurrying forward into dark cool shadows.

Once hidden safely, Clint set his bag down and hunkered over it. Kevin just dropped his bag and slumped against a wall, sobbing softly. Clint struggled with the zip, tore it open, jammed his hands inside, came up clutching *THOUSANDS!* Rolls of notes bound together with elastic bands. Clint whimpered. Focused on one of the stacks, dropping the others back into the bag. Rolled off the elastic band, fanned out the notes, checking watermarks and serial numbers, eyes glowing. He flashed the money at Kevin. "They're real." Kevin stared, dazed, then opened his bag and took out a couple of rolls. Checked them. Smiled weakly. Pulled out more. "What are you doing?" Clint asked.

"Making sure it's all there."

Good idea. Clint quickly thumbed through his fan of notes, counting them, then dumped the contents of the bag out on to the floor. Two passports fell along with the money. Clint tossed the passports to Kevin, then arranged the stacks of cash neatly. Did a quick count. Moved on to Kevin's pile. It all added up as far as he could tell. "Two million!" Clint whooped.

Kevin ogled the money, momentarily forgetting everything except the riches at his feet. It looked like monopoly money. Almost anticlimactic. It would have been more exciting if the haul had been in the form of gold or diamonds.

"Put it all back," Clint said, starting to bag his share. "If somebody walked in on us and saw this..." Kevin thought about that and began bagging even quicker than Clint. When they had the money stashed, the men stared at one another and shared a shy smile. "We did it," Clint whispered.

"Two million," Kevin giggled. Then he remembered Tulip and Gawl. His smile faded. "What the hell happened with Big Sandy?" Clint shook his head. "Was it a set-up? Did Dave Bushinsky plan it that way?"

"I don't think so," Clint frowned. "Big Sandy was alone. If it had been a trap, there would have been others. He flipped. Were you watching his eyes? He went berserk. I don't know what it was about, but it wasn't planned."

"Did he definitely kill Gawl?" Kevin asked.

Clint's features blackened. "Yes," he said, mourning his friend's loss. "Poor Gawl. He thought he had it all sussed out, every angle covered, but nobody could have bargained on Big Sandy losing his nut."

"There must have been a reason," Kevin insisted.

"Yes," Clint agreed. His eyes hardened. "But we can question it later. First we have to get out of here and figure a way to spend this money before Dave gets his hands on us. Gawl's dead, he can't help us now, we're on our own."

"So's Tulip," Kevin noted glumly.

"Where do you think she'll run if the police didn't get her?"

"The church," Kevin said without hesitation. "It's the only place she can go."

"What about friends?"

"No, she knows I couldn't..." He stopped. About to say she knew he couldn't find her if she went to her friends, since he didn't know who they were or where they lived. But what if she didn't *want* to be found? What if she chose this moment to strike out on her own? He and Clint had the money. The Bush would be looking for them, not Tulip. And Tulip hadn't been with them when the police arrived, so the cops wouldn't be looking for her either. The perfect time to ditch him.

"What's wrong?" Clint asked.

Kevin shook his head. "Nothing," he wheezed.

"You don't think she'll go to the church?"

"She must," Kevin croaked.

He didn't sound as if he believed it but Clint let that pass. "What about us?" he said. "Do we return to the church or run like hell?"

"Return," Kevin gasped. "We have to collect Tulip."

"The longer we remain in London, the greater the risk that Dave or the cops will find us."

"I don't care," Kevin said stubbornly. "I won't leave without Tulip."

Clint took that into consideration. He didn't care about Tulip or Kevin. What he wanted was to take his cut – the majority now that Gawl was out of the running, he'd only give Kevin the agreed amount, not a penny more – and keep going north, get a cab out of the city, then a train, lose himself up country, buy his way to freedom. But his passport was at the church and Dave would be mad as hell, on his heels from this day forward. If he returned he could collect his passport, get the formula from Tulip, post it to Dave, assuage his anger.

"What if Tulip doesn't show?" Clint asked. "What if the cops caught her or she kept on running?" Kevin didn't answer, unable to face that possibility. "How long do we wait?" Clint persisted. "When do we cut our losses and –"

"She'll be there," Kevin wailed. "She'll come. She has to."

Clint unconvinced, but the lure of the formula was great, still possible to make everything right, get out of this alive and rich. He didn't want a pissed-off cousin Dave on his back, chasing him, harrying him, hunting him.

"We need to act now," Kevin said, disrupting Clint's train of thought. "Tulip won't wait for night. She'll head for the church straightaway. She could be there already. If we don't show soon, she might think the worst and leave without us."

"I told you we can't go until it's dark," Clint objected. "If we're seen..."

"Fuck being seen," Kevin shouted. He lurched to his feet, furious. "The sooner we get her, the sooner we can get out. That's the priority, isn't it? The longer we stall, the more people the Bush and the cops can tip off. We have to act *now*."

Clint opened his mouth to shout Kevin down, then shut it. Kevin was right. Darkness was preferable but speed was essential. They couldn't afford to squat here for hours, giving the Bush and the cops time to gear up for a full pursuit. If Tulip was at the church they could grab her, ask Fr Sebastian to arrange a lift for them with one of his parishioners, get out quick. A risk, but one they'd have to take. "OK," he decided, standing. "We passed shops along the way. We'll buy caps and scarves, cover our faces, head for the church." He bent to collect his bag. Paused. "What about the money?"

"What about it?" Kevin frowned.

"They'll be looking for the bags. The Bush knows what they look like and the cops probably got a good look at them when we were running."

"We could stuff the notes inside our jumpers," Kevin suggested.

"Too bulky." Clint looked around the room and gulped. "The obvious thing is to leave the money here."

Kevin glanced around and gulped like Clint had. "You think it would be safe?"

"We can find some out-of-the-way hole, leave the bags there. They'll be OK for a few hours. But it means coming back for them."

"I don't like it," Kevin muttered.

"I don't either," Clint sighed, "but we can move quicker without the bags."

Kevin nodded slowly. "But we hide it together," he

said warily, "and we don't split up after this, not even to go to the toilet."

"Don't you trust me?" Clint laughed.

"As much as you trust me," Kevin said.

"Christ, that little?" They grinned at each other shakily then went exploring the building in search of a niche where they could stash the money.

SIXTY-SEVEN

With recently purchased wide-brimmed hats pulled low over their foreheads and scarves tied around their lower faces, Kevin and Clint cut south for the Church of Sacred Martyrs, leaving the money hidden behind. Even though the idea to leave the bags had been his, Clint was having second thoughts about parting with the millions and kept glancing back over his shoulder, torn between his desire to gloat over the fruits of their haul and the need to get his hands on his passport and the formula, so that he might live to enjoy those fruits.

At the river they detoured east and crossed London Bridge. Kevin smiled sourly as they slipped by the station. One way or another, he'd never be going back to work there. No more Dan Bowen. No more slapped-on smiles for Joe Public. No more slaving away at a job he hated. Some measure of comfort, no matter what happened next.

His heart beating fast as they closed on the church, thinking, *she'll be there... she won't... she will... she won't...*

They turned a corner, sighted the church and stopped. A crowd outside, and a police car. The door to the church roped off. People muttering softly, a few women sobbing, kids standing quietly and curiously with their parents. Kevin and Clint stared at the crowd. Clint lowered his scarf. "What's huh-happening?"

Kevin shook his head dumbly, thinking it must be Tulip. Had something happened to her? Had the police taken her into custody? Or was it worse than that? Crazy thoughts of Fr Sebastian snapping when Tulip returned alone, raping her, killing her. He jolted forward, ready to scream her name and barge into the church. Clint grabbed him, shoved him against a wall. "I've still got a gun," he barked. "You do anything stupid, I'll blow your fucking head off."

"Tulip," Kevin groaned.

"Change the fucking record," Clint sighed, releasing him. "We'll check what's going on, but we'll do it quietly, OK?" Kevin nodded hard. Pushed away from the wall. Clint pushed him back. "We're not doing it until you calm down."

Kevin leant his head back, got his breathing under control, forced the crazy thoughts from his head, nodded again, softly this time. "I'm OK now."

Clint studied Kevin's eyes then signalled him forward,

keeping close behind, hand on the butt of his gun. Kevin stumbled ahead, eyes flicking from the people to the squad car to the church spires. Blanking out thoughts of Tulip captive, Tulip breaking under interrogation and telling the cops everything, Tulip dead. Stopped when he reached the crowd. Looked to Clint for instructions.

Clint pulled his scarf clear of his face but kept his hat on. He leant in close to an elderly man and mumbled, "What's going on?"

The man looked around, eyebrows furrowed, lips tight with disapproval. "Fr Sebastian's dead."

Clint gawped. Kevin froze — he only heard the word *dead*.

"How?" Clint gasped.

"Hanged himself. The police are there now. They're not letting anyone in. A terrible thing. To kill yourself's bad enough, but to do it in a house of God..." The man shook his head and crossed himself.

"Dead," Kevin croaked, eyes welling with tears. He began pushing his way through the crowd, wanting to be with Tulip, to worship her lifeless body, weep at her feet, confess all, let the police do what they wished with him.

"What are you doing?" Clint snapped, grabbing Kevin's arm, tugging him back, the man and a few others staring at them, Clint smiling apologetically, yanking Kevin out of earshot.

"Tulip," Kevin cried softly. "I want to be with Tulip."

Clint stared at him uncomprehendingly, then clicked to what was going through Kevin's mind. He chuckled harshly. "Tulip isn't there. Fr Sebastian hung himself. Not Tulip — the priest."

Kevin blinked as Clint's words sunk in. "Fr Sebastian?"

"Weren't you listening? Fr Sebastian checked out. I don't know why, but Tulip had nothing to do with it."

"How do you know?" Kevin asked. "How do you know she wasn't there when he did it? That she isn't there now?"

Clint frowned. Of course he couldn't know for sure. Trying to think of a way to calm Kevin's fears. Gaze wandering as his brain ticked over. He spotted a thin, ginger-haired man, Derek James, one of his church junkies. "Keep close," Clint said, angling through the crowd.

Derek James saw Clint while they were working their way towards him. He broke ranks immediately and rammed his way through to Clint, ignoring the angry grumbles of those around him. "Where the fuck have you been?" he hissed.

"Keep your vuh-voice down," Clint said.

"Fuck keeping my voice down," James growled, but lowered it anyway. "I've been going cold turkey. Where have you been? Why didn't you tell me you were going to stop dealing?"

"I've had problems with my suppliers," Clint improvised. "I huh-had to lie low for a while. There wasn't time to –"

"What happened to Fr Sebastian?" Kevin cut in, not interested in Clint's deals. "Did anybody else die?"

James eyed Kevin. "Who's this fucker?"

"A friend," Clint smiled, flashing Kevin a look, *Shut the fuck up!* He stepped closer to James. "*Do* you know what huh-happened?" Thinking quickly. "I wuh-was coming to see Fr Sebastian to clear the way to start duh-dealing here again."

"Some hope of that," James chuckled. "Fucker's dead."

"He hung himself?"

"From the pulpit, with his belt. I heard it all from a neighbour, she was there when the shit went down."

"Any idea why he duh-duh-duh-did it?"

"Word is he got on the wrong side of Dave Bushinsky."

Clint went wooden. "Wh-wh-why do they suh-say that?"

"Big Sandy Murphy stormed into the church just before Fr Seb hung himself. The Father did it while Big Sandy was tearing apart the house at the back."

"Did the puh-police cuh-cuh-capture Big Sandy?" Clint asked.

"He was long gone by the time they got here," James snorted.

"What about..." Kevin cleared his throat. "Was there anyone with Fr Sebastian when he killed himself? A girl?"

"A fucking angel maybe," James laughed. "No girl though. Why?" Clint pulled Kevin away before he could say anything else. "Hey," James snapped. "What about my shit? When are you –"

"Come on Friday," Clint lied. "I'll be buh-back. Business as usual."

"But what about..."

Clint and Kevin passed out of earshot. Clint force-marched them to the end of the street, around the corner, out of sight of the crowd. "Happy?" he snapped. "Tulip had nothing to do with this. It was Big Sandy."

"But how did he know to come here?" Kevin moaned. "He must have got it out of her. He caught her. He –"

"Don't be stupid," Clint snarled. "Tulip did a runner."

"Then how..."

"Gawl. He must have forced it from him before he killed him. Or maybe Gawl had it written down somewhere."

"You really think so?" Kevin asked pathetically.

"I'm certain."

"So where's Tulip?"

Clint shrugged. "I don't know. But she isn't here. Come on, we have to get away before –"

"She might come back," Kevin insisted. "Or she might have been here already."

"Maybe," Clint agreed. "But if she came, saw the crowd and fled, we can't find her. And we can't stick around on the off chance that she turns up."

"But –" Kevin began.

"You can't help her if you're locked up," Clint interrupted. "We can think about Tulip later, but right now the cops are here. They'll turn the house upside down and..." He drew to a sickened halt. *And* find the body of Tony Phials. *And* find Clint and Gawl's passports. Gawl's no longer mattered but his did. Implicated in a brace of murders and a priest's suicide. A major story. Media saturation. His name and photo everywhere. A wanted criminal.

Figuring swiftly, *I'm screwed. Money won't buy me out of this mess.* Options — hit the house while the cops were there, shoot it out with them and steal his passport? Too wild. Besides, people in the crowd could identify him. He'd need a fake passport, a new identity. The only hope he had of getting one... cousin Dave.

Kevin was watching Clint intently. He saw despair/

hope, despair/hope, despair/hope flash across the dealer's face. Wondered what was going through Clint's thoughts. Said nothing, waiting for Clint to speak his mind. Which he finally did, softly but quickly. "Where would Tulip guh-guh-guh-go?"

"She has friends but I don't know where they live."

Clint shook his head. "She wuh-won't want to involve her friends in this. If I'm wrong, we're scruh-screwed. But let's say I'm ruh-right. Where else?"

"Why do you care?" Kevin asked stiffly.

"My puh-passport's in the house. Once the puh-puh-police find it, they'll know who I am."

Kevin started to smile. "*My* passport's safe with the money."

"If I go down, you do too," Clint growled.

Kevin ignored that. "What does Tulip have to do with your passport?"

"I need the fuh-formula. With it, I can cut a deal with Dave. I was going to post it to him, to make guh-good on our original deal and keep him off our buh-backs. That's no good now the cops know who I am, but I can truh-trade it for a new passport, make him huh-help me get out of the country."

"I'm not getting involved with Bushinsky again, not after what happened to McCaskey," Kevin said. "You want to cut a deal with him, you do it alone."

"Fine," Clint snapped. "But first we have to fuh-find Tulip. You want her too, even more than I do, so don't give me any shit. Where is she?"

Kevin's thoughts turned inwards. "I'm not sure," he muttered. "But the Borough is home. It's the area she knows best. She might go there, wander familiar streets, hide out in cafés or shops, at least until she decides what to do." He admitted the terrifying truth out loud. "Unless she's cleared out or gone to earth with a friend."

Clint checked his watch. It was coming up to three o'clock. With the cloud cover it would be dark in another hour. Harder to find her in the dark, but safer for them on the streets. "Let's go get something to eat," he sighed. "Hot food, a drink, rest. You can think of all the places she might have run to. Draw up a list. We'll start looking as soon as the sun goes down."

"If we don't find her?" Kevin asked.

Clint shrugged. "I'll give it until midnight, then I'm out of here with my share of the money. You can do whatever the fuck you like."

Kevin nodded, welcoming Clint's assistance, whatever his selfish motives. The two men skulked away, found a fish and chip shop, sat and loaded up on greasy food, eating mechanically, saying little, Kevin racking his brains for all the possible hide-outs where Tulip might have fled. Neither man paused to mark the loss of Fr Sebastian. Neither gave a damn about the fate of the paedophile priest.

SIXTY-EIGHT

In a van, close to Westminster, waiting for things to quiet down. One of the Bush's men in the area, mingling with tourists, reporting back to Big Sandy. The hounds in the back of the van, four men watching over them, Eyes Burton among them. Fast Eddie beside Big Sandy in the front. He'd insisted on coming, eager to get even with Clint. Big Sandy silent, thinking about Gawl McCaskey, marvelling at the twist of fate which had thrown them together after all this time, remembering the feel of the bastard's throat in his hands, relishing it. Trying not to think too much about his mother, afraid he'd well with tears and break down. He wanted to go to Sapphire, tell her everything, toast the memory of his mother and the death of Gawl McCaskey, get roaring drunk. But not while there was work to be done.

"What happens if we don't find them?" Fast Eddie asked, breaking the silence, shame-faced at having voiced the question but too curious to keep quiet.

"They get away with Phials' formula and two million of Dave's money," Big Sandy said. "It'll be my fault.

What do you think happens?"

Fast Eddie coughed nervously. "You and Dave go way back. Given what happened with your mother, surely he —"

"Business is business," Big Sandy interrupted. "Dave's always played fair by me, but playing fair means taking the bad along with the good. When a man fucks up on this sort of a scale, he must be punished. Unless he can redeem himself."

"You could run," Fast Eddie said, looking away as he spoke. "Turn yourself in to the police. Testify against Dave. They'd protect you."

Big Sandy didn't dignify that suggestion with an answer. Fast Eddie noted his scornful expression and relaxed. The Bush had phoned him while Big Sandy was on his way to the lab and explained the situation, telling Fast Eddie to sound out Big Sandy and, if in any doubt, to feed that back. If Big Sandy had for one moment considered Fast Eddie's proposal, Fast Eddie would have had to tell the Bush, and that would have been the end of the giant.

A return to silence. The day darkened into a short evening, then night. Street lights flickered on around them. Fast Eddie squinted at the lights, then at the street outside. People could see them sitting inside the van. "Want me to take out a couple of the lights?" he asked.

Big Sandy shook his head. "We'll get into the back with the others." It was a tight squeeze and the air was rotten with the foul stench of the hounds but nobody said anything, the four men bunching up to make room, Fast Eddie and Big Sandy slipping in beside them, Big Sandy having to bend sharply forward to fit.

An hour passed slowly. The men fidgeted and scratched themselves, eyeing the hounds nervously. Even the experienced Eyes Burton and Fast Eddie shifted and itched, checking their watches every few minutes, twitchy. Only Big Sandy was calm, eyes closed, thoughts focused, occasional flashes of his mother's face – imagining her smiling at the news of McCaskey's death – which he let slide, not lingering on the past until he'd dealt with the dilemma of the present.

Finally his mobile rang. He held it out blindly to Fast Eddie, who took the phone and answered, "Yeah?" Smiled with relief and hung up. "We're clear. The body's been removed, witnesses have given their statements, the crowd's dispersed. It's still a crime scene, a few officers left to guard it, but otherwise business as usual."

"That was quick," Eyes grunted.

"Murder's a turn-off for tourists," Fast Eddie grinned.

"Do we go now?" one of the men asked. Fast Eddie glanced at Big Sandy. His eyes were still closed.

"Wait another half hour," Big Sandy said. "Tell our man to hold his position and phone back if it's still quiet. If it is, we'll go then."

Half an hour later they spilled out of the van and hurried with the hounds to Westminster Bridge, to the steps where Tulip had been when Big Sandy attacked Gawl McCaskey. They stopped at the top of the steps. Fast Eddie took a dress of Tulip's from a plastic bag and stuffed it in the hound's face. The hound made alarmed snuffling noises, then got the scent and stiffened. Fast Eddie removed the dress and stepped back. The hound sniffed the pavement. People passing by stared but said nothing. The hound caught Tulip's scent, whined and jerked forward, dragging the men grasping his leash after it. "Here we go," Fast Eddie grinned jaggedly at Big Sandy.

"Keep in touch," Big Sandy replied, then hauled his hound away, to circle around County Hall. He handled the leash himself, Eyes Burton and the other man hurrying after him. At the far side of the Eye, where they wouldn't attract the attention of the police officers, he dug out a shirt of Smith's and fed the dealer's scent to the hound. He had one of Kevin Tyne's shirts too, which he'd use if the search led to a dead end, but Smith was his first priority, the one most likely to be carrying the money. The hound fixed on Smith's scent, sniffed the path with crazed zeal as Big Sandy jerked it left and right. It stiffened when it caught the smell, pissed lightly, then took off, bounding past Jubilee Gardens, Big Sandy and his men keeping pace, ignoring the bemused glances of anyone who got in their way, brushing them aside, fully focused on the hunt.

Across Waterloo Bridge, then north through lamp-lit streets, the heart of the city quiet now that the business day had drawn to an end, most of the work-force departed for home. Fast Eddie phoned. Tulip's trail had led to a bus stop then disappeared — the girl had either remembered the threat of the hounds or been too tired to run any further. Fast Eddie asked if he should link up with them. Big Sandy told him to return to the van and await further orders.

North at a rapid pace, the hound excited, memories of past hunts, mouth watering as it flashed on recollections of bloody feasts. Big Sandy was exhausted – it had been the longest day of his life – but he never faltered, breathing evenly while Eyes and the other man panted, forcing himself on.

The hound eventually came to a halt outside a large building clad in scaffolding. It sniffed the ground around the entrance, head darting towards and away from the building, growling softly. "Think they're inside?" Eyes asked, right hand going to the gun inside his jacket.

"Leave that where it is," Big Sandy said, studying the building. "Nobody draws until I say so."

The hound started forward, Big Sandy following, then stopped, spun and set off again, crossing the road, taking them in a different direction. Eyes gazed back at the building suspiciously – he would have liked to go inside and explore – but Big Sandy never paused, trusting his future to the hound, placing his life in the hands of a beast which lived only to kill.

When Big Sandy caught sight of the spires of the Church of Sacred Martyrs, he hauled the hound to an abrupt halt and experienced a faint fluttering of nerves. A squad car was parked outside. The crowd from earlier had broken up but a few extra-inquisitive souls still kept vigil.

"What's wrong?" Eyes asked.

Big Sandy didn't answer, playing the scene out theoretically. Smith and Kevin had come here after fleeing north, unaware that Big Sandy had found out about Fr Sebastian. The police most probably present when they arrived. So either they ran into the arms of the cops and had been taken into custody or they'd turned tail and fled.

The hound was straining at its leash, the scent of Clint Smith heavy in its nostrils, wanting to tear ahead and rip into the man it was hunting. But Big Sandy knew Smith wasn't here, that the hound was fixing on old scents. Glancing around, he dragged the hound back to where they'd turned on to the street, thrust Smith's shirt in its face again, then grabbed the back of the dog's neck and forced its nose over the pavement in a wide circle, gambling that Smith and Kevin had retreated this way rather than risk walking by the church.

The hound resisted at first, then let itself be led, nose working busily. It started back the way it had come, retracing the scent it had followed here, but Big Sandy dragged it back, walking the hound around in an increasing circle in search of a new trail. On the fourth circuit the hound latched on to a fresh scent and lunged across the road. Big Sandy permitted himself a rare self-satisfied smile then hurried after the hound, Eyes Burton and the other man trailing him, offering no words of advice or critique, letting Big Sandy make the calls. It didn't matter much to them whether or not they found Smith and Tyne. Their lives weren't on the line. This was just work.

SIXTY-NINE

Scouring the grey streets, searching desperately, Kevin leading the way, Clint following half-heartedly. They started with Long Lane, walked the length of it, peering left and right at the few shops – two chippers, two laundrettes, an off-licence, a pub called the Valentine – and side-streets in case Tulip was cowering in the shadows. Heads low, they hurried past Kevin's apartment block. Kevin was sure Tulip wouldn't have returned – she'd know how dangerous it was – but Clint wasn't convinced. If she panicked and sought out familiar turf, there was nowhere more familiar than home. He wanted to go up and check, but that would have been suicide, the Bush certainly had men posted there.

At the top of Long Lane, no sign of Tulip. They paused. "Where now?" Clint asked. "Tower Bridge Road?"

"I guess," Kevin said miserably. "Or Borough High Street."

"We'll do Tower Bridge Road and its side-streets first," Kevin said. "Might as well since we're up here. Unless there's some place specific on Borough High

Street you think she might be." Praying Kevin would say yes. But Kevin only shook his head pathetically.

Down Tower Bridge Road to the flyover where the New Kent Road became the Old Kent Road — no Tulip. Back up Tower Bridge Road, this time detouring, exploring the side-streets, restaurants and pubs — no Tulip. After forty minutes Clint stopped. "How wide a search area are we going to set ourselves? What's *local* for you and Tulip? Would she have gone as far as the Elephant & Castle or Waterloo?"

"No," Kevin said. "If she wants to go where I can find her, it'll be closer."

"So where do we look?" Clint pressed. "What's within reasonable range? Let's set a boundary, so at least we know how much ground we have to cover."

Kevin thought. "No further south than Great Dover Street. Not east of Tower Bridge Road or west of Borough High Street. And not north of the river."

"OK," Clint said. "How about we work it east to west, and south to north, so we end up at the Thames?"

Kevin shrugged. "Seems as good a way as any."

"But when we see water," Clint added, "that's it, I'm out of here."

Kevin nodded reluctantly. "If we haven't found her by the time we get to the river, we probably won't. I'll come with you."

Clint blinked, surprised. "I thought you'd rather die than leave without her." Kevin didn't answer, just turned away and started walking. Clint watched him through narrow eyes — he'd liked the idea of Kevin staying to hunt for Tulip, Clint getting away with all the money — then followed, checking his watch, figuring the odds on them running into Tulip were slim. As he searched he played with escape plans, ways to get a passport, get out of the country, evade the cops, make his peace with Dave. None of his plans panning out. He was a lone rat surrounded by wild hounds. As far as he could see, without Tulip and the formula he was destined to be devoured.

SEVENTY

From their southernmost point they doggedly worked their way west, back east, then west again, gradually gravitating north. Exploring the maze of narrow streets and alleys contained by the triangle of Great Dover Street, Long Lane and Tower Bridge Road on the off-chance that Tulip was resting by a fence or on a bench. Potier Street, Prioress Street, Manciple Street, Alice Street... Soon they stopped taking notice of the names, feeling their way, trusting their instincts.

Once they'd finished with the triangle – no Tulip – they checked Borough High Street, crawled along one side of the road from Borough Tube station to London Bridge, then down the other side, glancing in windows of restaurants, ducking into pubs, before taking on the warren of back streets between Long Lane and Saint Thomas Street.

Kevin torn between hope and terror. He wanted to believe Tulip was lying low here, waiting for him, but he couldn't. He kept telling himself she'd be in Guy's hospital or around London Bridge station or in Hay's

Galleria. But the more he thought about it, the less likely it seemed. More probably she was tucked up in a friend's flat, sobbing her way through her horror story, her friend listening in a mounting mixture of sympathy and disbelief. Part of him hoped she was — at least she'd be safe — but another part hated her if that was the path she'd chosen. That dark part which came to the fore when he was watching her copulate would rather she die than live without him. That part fantasized about escaping with the money then returning to track her down, make her pay for betraying him. That part almost wished they didn't find her, just so it could grow stronger within him and claim him whole.

Kevin said nothing of this to Clint. He barely even acknowledged it himself. Just kept going, alert, padding through the dark streets, heart leaping whenever he saw anyone who remotely resembled Tulip, leading Kevin, working his way back towards Borough High Street. He checked his watch. Twelve minutes to nine. Wondering how long it would take them to complete their search and if he could bring himself to slip away with Clint if they reached the river without sight of Tulip, if he could find the courage/cowardice to leave his sister behind.

SEVENTY-ONE

The hound tracked Clint Smith, Big Sandy tracked the hound, Eyes Burton and the other man tracked Big Sandy. The hound's pace hadn't dropped, tracing the scent with unwavering confidence.

The hunt led them to the Borough, up Long Lane, then down Tower Bridge Road. Big Sandy puzzled. Why would Smith come here? Was there something in Kevin's apartment that they needed? Big Sandy didn't think so. Besides, the hound hadn't hesitated in front of the building, just charged on. Had the dog led them astray, chasing an old scent of Smith's? Nothing Big Sandy could do if that was the case, except report to the Bush at the end of the night and accept what he had coming.

At the bottom of the road the hound drew to a temporary halt, sniffing the area beneath the flyover uncertainly, before returning to Tower Bridge Road. It began leading them back up the road, stopped, sniffed some more, then took off to the left down a side-street. Lots of twists and turns, backtracking, returning to Tower Bridge Road, more side-streets. Then the hound led them west to Borough High Street. They emerged slightly north of the Tube station and the hound followed the scent up the street to the top, crossed the road and started down the other side. Big Sandy checked his watch. Five to nine. By this time tomorrow he might be dead. Pushed that thought away as swiftly as it popped into his head. He had to focus, take each hour as it came, forget about the future and the price of failure. Tonight was all that mattered, all he had to play with. Let tomorrow take care of...

The thought died unfinished. Eyes had come to a halt and was staring down the street incredulously. "I don't fucking believe it," he muttered, raising a shaking finger to point. Big Sandy focused and saw Clint Smith and Kevin Tyne on the other side of the road, walking away from them. Big Sandy grinned viciously at the beauty of it. With their backs turned, the hunters could sneak up on the pair and take them before they knew what was happening.

Then the man with Big Sandy and Eyes, whose name Big Sandy hadn't even asked for, opened his stupid fucking mouth and roared, "*Stop!*"

Big Sandy groaned with disgust as Smith and Kevin spun and spotted them. He made a quick note to teach the dumb son of a bitch a very painful lesson later, then took off after their prey as fast as his massive legs would carry him, releasing the hound, which raced along beside him. Eyes and the fuckwit were slower to react and were only getting into gear as Big Sandy and the hound tore across the road and hit the pavement on the far side.

Smith and Kevin gawped at Big Sandy and the hound, then fled for their lives. Big Sandy didn't waste breath shouting. As he closed the gap, Smith broke off to the left and darted down a side-street. Kevin looked back, hesitated, then carried on down the High Street, arms and legs pumping madly. He saw a taxi and roared for it to stop, desperately waving his right hand above his head.

Big Sandy didn't wait to see if Tyne succeeded in hailing the cab or not. Smith was his target. He paused and bellowed at Eyes and the arsehole, "Go after Tyne!" Turned left and set off down the side-street after the hound.

Ahead of Big Sandy and the dog, Smith was running wildly, panting erratically, feet slipping, head jerking left and right in search of an escape route. Big Sandy zeroed in on Smith, machine mode, thinking only of how to subdue him and get him back to the lab quietly and safely.

Not looking where he was going, Clint smashed into a lamp post and crashed to the ground. Sitting up, he shook his head, fixed on the hound – several feet in front of Big Sandy now – stumbled to his feet, drew a gun and fired. His first two shots flew wide of the mark and the hound closed on him. As it prepared to jump, Clint fired again and this time struck true, taking the hound in its left flank. The dog spun away from Clint, hit the ground and slid, howling with pain. Clint took a step after the hound, intent on finishing it off, then remembered Big Sandy, looked up, saw the giant storming towards him, readjusted his aim and fired.

Big Sandy's first instinct was to dive for cover. He ignored it and kept running, the bullet whistling past, focused on getting to Smith and disarming him. Clint's face wrinkled with fear, then went calmly blank. He spread his legs, took careful aim at Big Sandy's stomach – an easier target than his head – and squeezed the trigger slowly, surely.

Just as Clint squeezed, the hound threw itself at him, having recovered. It connected with his arm, knocking it aside, sending the bullet zinging down into the pavement. Clint cursed and raised the gun for another shot, but the hound was on him before he could fire, fangs locking on Clint's other arm, trying to gnaw its way through the bone.

Clint screamed, dug the nozzel of his gun into the

hard flesh of the hound's stomach and fired off two shots in quick succession before clicking on blank. The hound yelped and stiffened, then slumped, stomach torn to shreds, blood pumping, moaning pitifully in its death throes.

Big Sandy was on Smith before he could even think about reloading. Grabbed him by his ears and pulled his head down, then slammed his knee up into Smith's jaw, but carefully, not wanting to snap the dealer's neck and blow his only chance of getting out of this alive. Clint grunted dumbly as the strength left his arms and legs, and would have collapsed if Big Sandy hadn't been holding him by his ears. Big Sandy prepared to knee Smith again, then saw his fluttering eyelids, realised it wasn't necessary and laid him flat on the ground.

While Smith twitched and whimpered and slid into unconsciousness, Big Sandy examined the hound, saw it was beyond help, took out his own gun and fired a shot through its head, putting it out of its misery. As the echo of the gunfire died away, he fixed on the sound of racing footsteps. He whirled and aimed. Saw Eyes Burton and the fuckwit. Lowered the gun. Eyes came to a stop, panting heavily.

"Tyne?" Big Sandy asked.

Eyes shook his head. "Made the taxi. I got half the

licence plate."

Big Sandy grimaced, then pointed at the idiot who'd blown their cover. "I'm going to fuck you up bad when this is over, and you'd better hope that's all I do." The man's face whitened but he said nothing. Big Sandy stooped, picked up the corpse of the hound and tossed it to Eyes, who staggered backwards under the weight. Big Sandy holstered his gun, drew his mobile phone, rang for a car then picked up the slumped Clint Smith and draped him over a shoulder like the slab of rancid meat that he was.

SEVENTY-TWO

Clint came to in the car, half sat up, groaning. As his eyes were clearing, a hand clamped over his mouth. Clint struggled, tugged feebly at the hand, then slipped back into blackness, the hand releasing him, knowing no more until he was slapped awake...

...in the lab. Clint knew where he was even before his brain kicked in fully. In the cells where the hounds were kept. One of the four hounds present in a nearby cell, chained and gagged. The other cells vacant. Clint lying on a table which had been brought in for the occasion. Naked, his feet and hands bound, spreadeagled. Around the table, Big Sandy, a small guy Clint didn't recognise, and cousin Dave.

"Welcome back," Dave smiled maliciously. Clint moaned and shut his eyes, wishing for a return to darkness. Fingers gripped his crotch and squeezed. He gasped and his eyes shot open again. Big Sandy let go. He wasn't smiling. "No more sleeping," Dave said softly. "Now's when you sing like a bird."

Clint licked his lips and tried croaking for water but

he couldn't get the words out. Dave saw what he was trying to ask for and told Big Sandy to give him a drink. Big Sandy filled a glass and poured it into Clint's mouth. Clint stretched his lips wide and gulped, savouring the water, knowing this was his final toast.

"Can you talk now?" Dave asked.

Clint nodded weakly. "Yuh-yuh-yuh-yes."

"Then talk." Dave glared at Clint. Clint stared back stubbornly, saying nothing. Dave sighed and nodded at the man Clint didn't know. "This is Michael. He's from Eastern Europe. He tortures people for a living." Michael grinned. A short man, thin, streaky grey/black hair. Dead eyes.

"I duh-duh-duh-don't know wh-wh-what you wuh-want me to suh-suh-suh-say."

"I want my money and the formula. Where are they?"

Clint looked around. No sign of Kevin. "Wh-wh-where's Kuh-Kevin?"

"Worry about yourself," Dave snapped, then leant low over Clint, so their faces were only centimetres apart. "Let's talk plain, cousin. You do not walk out of here alive. There is no hope for you. There never was. Did you know you were part of the deal I struck with McCaskey? He promised you to me. Big Sandy was to take you as well as the formula. McCaskey betrayed you."

"No," Clint sighed.

"Yes," Dave chuckled. "Because he understood what you didn't, that there can be no reward for a man who betrays his family. You think I was going to give you a million pounds for fucking me over? I'd choke first. You know why Big Sandy killed McCaskey? Because McCaskey murdered his mother."

Clint gawped at Big Sandy's stony face. "What?"

"McCaskey killed his mother years ago. Big Sandy's been searching for him all his life. A real pisser, huh?" Dave's smile faded. "Killing McCaskey wasn't on the agenda. By doing it, Big Sandy risked everything, even his life. That didn't matter. When it's personal, nothing matters except getting even." The smile returned. "*This* is personal. So I say again, you do not walk out of here alive. Tonight you die. But you can die cleanly and painlessly. If you tell me where the money is and what happened to the formula, I'll shoot you through the skull and that's all you'll suffer. Otherwise I let Michael at you and you'll squirm for hours in the kind of agony no human can dream about until they've been subjected to it. Your call."

Clint stared up at Dave, mind whirring, searching for the words to wriggle out of this. Finding none, he resigned himself to death and opened his mouth to tell

Dave about the building, the money, Tulip and Kevin. Then closed it, figuring, *Kevin and Tulip are still out there. The more time I buy them, the greater their chance of escape.* Not worried about his partners in crime – he didn't feel like he owed them anything – but he didn't want to sell them out cheaply, like a dog. This was his final hour. Soon he'd be removed from this world, quickly forgotten. He could go like a worm or he could die with dignity. His final choice.

Surprising himself, Clint chose to go down fighting, hoping if word ever leaked back to Shula that she would remember him for this, not the rest of it.

"Go fuck yourself, cousin," he said clearly, without any trace of a stutter.

Dave gawped, truly astonished. Michael smiled sadistically. Big Sandy sniffed with disinterest.

Dave's expression hardened. "So be it." He turned to Michael. "Time is crucial. I want his tongue loosened fast."

"Can I play with him after?" Michael murmured.

Dave glanced at Clint. He was lying there calmly, afraid but in control, gazing back without rancour. "No," Dave said wearily. "Just do your job. Quickly."

Michael scowled then picked a black bag up off the floor, opened it, dug out a serrated knife and something that looked like a cheese grater. He set to work.

It took thirty-seven minutes to break Clint Smith. Thirty-seven minutes of excruciating torment, Michael working swiftly, putting years of brutish experience to terrifying use, removing strips of skin from Clint's most sensitive areas, probing inside him with knives and other implements, ridding him of his manhood, slicing his left eye open and draining off the fluid. Dave turned away after five minutes and concentrated on his breathing, trying to tune out Clint's screams and the sounds of Michael's instruments as they destroyed skin, bone, muscle, tissue. Big Sandy observed silently, noting Clint's pain but unaffected by it. He'd seen men tortured before. This was nothing new.

After thirty-seven minutes, Clint crumbled. He had been savaged and ruined. His mind and tongue were no longer his own. He knew nothing of loyalty or dignity. There was only the reality of all-consuming pain and the hope via death of physical escape.

He spat out the words, unaware that he was speaking. Told them where the bags were, that Tulip had the formula, that Kevin thought she might be waiting for him in the Borough. Dave listened with his back turned, then checked with Big Sandy. "You believe him?" Big Sandy nodded. "Send a couple of guys to get the money if it's still there. You take the last hound and find the girl."

"What if Kevin returned to the building and took the bags?" Big Sandy asked. "Don't you want me to go after him?"

"The formula means more to me than the money."

"But if we get neither..."

Dave started to snap at Big Sandy, then recalled the giant's position and what he stood to lose if he returned empty-handed. "Tyne won't forget about the hounds twice. If he returned for the money, he won't leave on foot. The girl's our best shot." Big Sandy thought about that, nodded, turned to leave. "Sandy," Dave stopped him. "Send Eddie down before you go. I told him he could be here at the end."

Big Sandy left. Clint only barely aware of what had been said. The world roaring red with agony. Michael reached into his bag for another knife, eager to wring more screams out of his plaything. Dave stopped him with a curt, "No." Jerked his head. "You can leave now." Michael pouted but packed his bag and slipped away.

Dave studied the bloody mess that was his young cousin. A shame it had to end like this. If Clint had shown this sort of courage and willpower earlier, Dave could have trusted him, found a decent post for him, educated him, brought him into the fold. Why had he saved the best for last, when it was wasted?

Fast Eddie entered the cell grim-faced. Dave acknowledged him with a nod, then stepped up to Clint, produced a gun and aimed at the centre of Clint's face. "Are you ready cousin?" he whispered. Clint's one remaining eye swam into focus. He managed a jagged, inhuman half-smile. Mumbled something incomprehensible through a mouthful of blood, that sounded to Dave like *Oola*. "What was that?" Dave asked gently and Clint started to repeat himself. Dave fired and Clint's head exploded. Fragments of teeth, bone and flesh rebounded off the table and struck Dave and Fast Eddie. They stepped back, cursing, wiping off the bloody shrapnel. On the table, alone, tied down and in torment, Clint died a man.

SEVENTY-THREE

Kevin literally pissed himself when he saw Big Sandy and the hellhound lumbering towards them. It was the second time in little more than a week that he'd lost control of his bladder but he was too terrified to be ashamed. Only vaguely aware of Clint by his side, frozen to the pavement as Kevin was. Then, in unison, they spun and fled, Kevin whining and sobbing as he ran. When Clint broke left without warning, Kevin paused, almost raced after him, glanced back, saw Big Sandy closing and instinctively realised that he was going to follow Clint. Thinking only of himself, he tore off down Borough High Street. With crazy delight he saw a cab and screamed at the driver to stop, waving frantically. He didn't hear Big Sandy shout at Eyes to follow him, or look back to check if he was being pursued, just fixed on the cab and chased it like a panther. The driver pulled over to the kerb and rolled down his window. "Where you going, mate?" he asked as Kevin slammed into the side of the car, panting for breath, eyes manic.

"Anywhere!" Kevin screeched, wrestling with the

handle. He looked over his shoulder, saw two men chasing him, squealed and tugged harder at the handle.

"Easy," the driver snapped. "Let go or I'll –"

Kevin released the handle, dug into his pocket, tore out his wallet and threw it at the driver. "You can keep it all," he wailed. "Just let me in and get me the fuck out of here *now!*"

The driver hesitated, looked around, saw two men converging on his car. He didn't want to get involved in this, but the wallet felt heavy. A quick judgement call – *Can I get out of here before those tough-looking bastards catch up?* – then he flicked the locks open. The door almost came off in Kevin's hand as he yanked. He threw himself into the back, slammed the door shut, and the driver took off, squealing tyres, pressing down hard on the accelerator, grinning happily, feeling like Steve McQueen in *Bullitt*.

Kevin sat up, trembling, stared out the window, saw the men stopping in the middle of the road, stranded. He laughed, not caring about the warm damp in his crotch or the shit Clint was in or where Tulip might be. He was alive. He'd made it. He was free.

The driver kept a cautious eye on the laughing, shaking man in the back, ready to stop and throw him out if he got violent. With his left hand he thumbed the wallet open and slid out notes, four twenties, two tens, a five. Not a fortune but a nice little earner. He took the money then tossed the wallet back at his customer, credit cards too hot for his liking. "Where to, mate?"

Kevin shook his head. "Just drive... for now. I need time... to think."

"A hundred quid buys you half an hour," the driver grunted, mercenary instincts coming to the fore. "But we can stop at a cash point if you want me for longer."

Kevin trying to think straight, heart pounding, tears drying on his cheeks, crotch like ice as the piss cooled. Assuming Big Sandy would capture Clint and find out where the money was. But it would take time. Big Sandy would have to haul him off the streets, take him some place quiet where there were no witnesses. If Kevin acted swiftly he could return to the building, get the bags, ride off with the money, two million, his alone, his and... Tulip's.

Torn for a moment, wondering whether he should go after the bags or focus on finding his sister. Then he leered as he realised he could have it all. With so much cash he could afford to hunt for Tulip later, pay professionals to find her. Without the money he was as damned as Clint, Gawl, Phials and Fr Sebastian. The bags had to be his first priority. Leaning forward, Kevin gave the driver instructions then sat back, checked his watch, closed his eyes, relaxed in the gloom.

Kevin had meant to get out of the cab at the bottom of the street, wait for the driver to depart, then make his way to the building. But by the time they arrived he'd altered his plan. He needed a car but he had no loose cash and he didn't like the idea of wandering the streets in search of an ATM — time was ticking. Besides, this driver had proved calm under pressure and open to bribes. When the car pulled over, Kevin was ready. He'd read the driver's name – Dave English – and without moving he said softly, "Want to make a thousand pounds, Dave?"

Dave English stiffened warily. "How?"

"Wait for me here, then drive me out of London."

"How far?"

"Twenty or thirty miles."

Dave hesitated. "Those guys who were after you..."

"No questions," Kevin smiled. "A thousand pounds, yes or no?"

The cabbie licked his lips nervously. "In advance?"

"At the end of the night."

"Two thousand," Dave said weakly, breathless at his own audacity. "A thousand up front, the rest at the end."

Kevin nodded slowly, then opened the front of his jacket so the driver could see his gun. "So we know where we stand," he said and it sounded like somebody else talking, finding new strength and determination in his greed.

"What's to stop you shooting me instead of paying me?" Dave asked quietly.

"Easier to pay you. Less complications."

Dave Engish judged the risk against the pay-off and made up his mind. "Where do you want to go?"

"For a start, up the road. Drop me in front of that building with the scaffolding. Circle the block until I come out. I'll give you your first thousand then."

The driver did as Kevin asked, circling the block like a shark once he'd dropped off his customer, tension mounting, mad at himself for buying into this mess but ecstatic at the prospect of making a couple of quick grand.

Inside the building Kevin hurried to the room where he'd stashed the bags with Clint. Nerves jangling, afraid that the money would be gone, Big Sandy waiting for him. But the money was where they'd left it and Big Sandy was nowhere to be seen. Kevin opened both bags, smiled at the rolls of notes, counted out three thousand pounds – two for the driver, a grand for emergencies — then dumped the contents of one bag into the other, so he'd only have a single bag to carry. He hefted it, turned for the door...

...and stopped. Laid the bag down. Squatted in the darkness, thinking. He'd planned to get out of London, lay low, skip the country, look for Tulip later. But now that he paused to consider Tulip, he was loath to leave without her. If he had to he would, but he'd rather take her with him. It might be difficult — impossible — to come back. Dave Bushinsky would be looking for him, maybe the police too if they tied him in with Fr Sebastian. He'd have to go on the run. It might be months before he could launch a search for his sister, and even then he'd probably need to manage it from abroad. What would happen to Tulip in the meantime?

Trying to think it all through. Clint would tell Big Sandy where the money was, tell him about Tulip as well and why they were in the Borough. Big Sandy would race here after the cash. When he didn't find it, he'd start looking for Kevin — no, for *Tulip*. Kevin had seen the hound and how it tracked Clint. Big Sandy would assume — rightly — that Kevin wasn't dumb enough to leave here on foot again. He'd take it as given that Kevin would get the hell out of London as fast as he could. Tulip had the formula, so he'd target her. With the hound, he'd find her. Take the formula and either kill her or use her as bait to ensnare her brother.

Cut her loose, a sly part of him urged. *Forget her. You have the money. You'll find other young women, new ways to excite yourself. Get out while you can.*

But Kevin couldn't do that. Not without at least trying to find her. Checking his watch — nine thirty-six — calculating shrewdly, imagining worst case scenarios. Big Sandy would have started on Clint by now. Kevin wasn't sure how long Clint could hold out — if he'd even try — but he gave him no more than half an hour. By ten, Big Sandy would be on his way. Here by ten-fifteen. Ten minutes to ensure the money was gone. Then after Tulip with the hound. But would he start at Westminster Bridge or the Borough?

Unaware that there had been more than one hound, and not taking the Bush's other men into consideration, Kevin assumed Big Sandy would come looking for the money in person before homing in on Tulip. On that basis he figured Big Sandy would head for Westminster, where Tulip's scent was freshest. If Tulip had returned to the Borough, it would take Big Sandy time to track her east. Checking his watch again. He couldn't imagine the giant making the Borough before eleven thirty. Most likely he wouldn't get there (*if* he got there) before midnight.

Kevin thought he had time.

Standing in the darkness. Stomach and hands clenched. Trembling indecisively. *Will I/won't I? Will I/won't I?* Recalling their appointments, the sickening elation, the overwhelming high. Playing the images against those of Big Sandy capturing and crushing him.

Out of the darkness, down the stairs, through the building, on to the street. No sign of the taxi. Kevin waited, still undecided. The taxi appeared, pulled up to the kerb, Dave English solemn-faced. Kevin sat in, laid the bag on the floor, closed the door gently. Dave looked back at him. Kevin slid a thousand pounds to the cabbie then made up his mind and said, "Change of plan. Take me to the Borough."

SEVENTY-FOUR

Big Sandy, Fast Eddie, Eyes Burton and a balding, grey-haired, smartly-dressed guy Big Sandy knew only as Jimmy B, discussing their plans, standing outside a van inside of which the last living hound was strapped down.

"We should go to Westminster," Fast Eddie said.

"You said that trail led nowhere," Big Sandy grunted.

"It led to a bus stop. We can follow the various bus routes from there, get off at every stop, let the hound sniff around for her."

"That could take forever," Big Sandy muttered. "Kevin thought she'd return to the Borough. I want to try there first."

"Trouble with taking the hound to her regular stomping ground is her scent will be all over the place," Fast Eddie said.

"No," Big Sandy disagreed. "She's been in hiding for more than a week. We've had rain and wind. There won't be any old scents."

Fast Eddie shrugged. "I think Westminster makes more sense but it's your call."

Big Sandy considered it a moment longer, then decided. "The Borough. We'll start with the High Street, then take the side-streets and alleys. If we draw a blank, we'll try Westminster."

They piled into the van, Big Sandy, Fast Eddie and Jimmy B in the back with the hound, Eyes driving. Jimmy B eyed the hound nervously – the first time he'd seen one – and wondered what it was like let loose. Fast Eddie was thinking about Clint and how he'd died, glad he hadn't been there for the torture, just as glad he'd been there at the end. Big Sandy's thoughts were of Tulip and what would happen to her. Uneasy. None of this was the girl's fault. He wanted to protect her but couldn't see how, in no position to ask the Bush for favours. The best he could hope was that the Bush would be merciful when he got his hands on the formula, take pity on Tulip and let her go. Admitting to himself, *Unlikely.*

Eyes parked just off Borough High Street, slid out and opened the rear doors. The men in the back got out and stretched, then Big Sandy freed the hound and fed it Tulip's scent. The hound was uncooperative – shook its head, refusing the scent – until Big Sandy tugged sharply on its leash a few times and forced it to focus. When the hound finally fixed on the cardigan and whined obediently, they set off up the High Street, fast, the hound sniffing the pavement dejectedly — no scent.

At the top of the street, where it led on to London Bridge, they crossed and started back on the other side. As they were passing steps leading down to the riverbank the hound stiffened and growled with excitement. Big Sandy caught Fast Eddie's eye and the pair exchanged tight grins. Big Sandy checked his watch — ten thirty-seven — then the hound was leading him forward, padding down the steps to the path and forging ahead.

Big Sandy and the others raced to keep up with the hound. It was going as fast as it could, a sign that the scent was fresh. "She's near," Fast Eddie gasped.

"Or was," Big Sandy replied, not letting hope flare in his heart, just following the hound, letting events unravel as they would.

The hound ran straight for a while before turning right into an open-fronted shopping mall called Hays Galleria, dark and deserted this late at night. The hound was straining manically on its leash. Big Sandy jerked it to a standstill and glanced at the others as they puffed for breath. "I think she's here," he said softly.

"I'll call for backup," Fast Eddie said, flipping open his mobile.

"We're not gonna wait," Big Sandy said.

"Agreed. But we have guys in the area. They can be here in a few minutes to help tidy up or deal with witnesses."

Big Sandy grunted, let Fast Eddie make his call. As soon as he put the phone away he drew his gun and so did Eyes and Jimmy B. Big Sandy frowned, worried that Jimmy B might fuck up like the earlier idiot. "We take her alive. She's sixteen and unarmed. We do not under any circumstances harm her."

"What if she leaves us no choice?" Eyes asked. "She might have tooled up. What if she pulls a weapon and –"

"We do not harm her," Big Sandy interrupted curtly. "She won't have a gun and she won't open fire. But if she does, duck for cover and leave the rest to me."

"The formula comes first," Fast Eddie said calmly. "I know you like the girl – I do too – but if we can't produce the formula for Dave..."

"We'll get the formula," Big Sandy said. "But we don't have to hurt Tulip. And we won't. Understand?" He looked at each man directly, challenging them. All three nodded glumly. Satisfied, he fed the hound some slack, signalled the others to fan out behind him, then proceeded slowly into the shadows of the Galleria.

SEVENTY-FIVE

Kevin fine-tuned his plan during the ride south. Not enough time to complete a thorough sweep. Hit the likeliest spots, check for Tulip, get the hell out. Narrowing down the possibilities, deciding on Borough High Street again, London Bridge station, Hays Galleria, then get Dave to drive him to Tower Bridge Road for one last look. It would be after ten by the time he got started. He'd give himself half an hour here, max, before swinging by Tower Bridge Road. However the search went, determined to be on the road by eleven, at least a good half hour before Big Sandy showed up if his calculations were correct.

As the cab approached the Borough, Kevin leant forward. "Dave?" The driver glanced back. "I'm getting out on Borough High Street. I'll be gone no more than half an hour, maybe less. I want you to drive up the street every five minutes and pick me up when you see me."

"No problem," Dave said.

Kevin reached inside his jacket and half pulled out the second thousand pounds so that Dave could see. "I won't cry if you abandon me," Kevin said. "Plenty of cabs on the High Street. It's simpler for me to have you on standby, but if you aren't there when I need you, I'll just –"

"I'll be there," Dave snapped. "Every five minutes on the dot."

Kevin sat back, grinning smugly, liking this new side of himself. It was good to be in control.

He got out at Borough Tube station, waited for the cab to pull clear, then started up the street, lugging the bag with the millions – it felt heavier than it had earlier – looking in every pub and restaurant window, praying for Tulip's face to leap out at him. He walked up the left side of the street, down the right, no Tulip. He returned to the side-street Clint had disappeared down, staring into shadows, wondering where Clint was now and what had happened to him. Brutally clamped down on the morbid thoughts – whatever Clint got, he more than deserved after what he'd put Kevin and Tulip through – then hurried to London Bridge station, his all-too familiar work hole. He prowled the Vaults first, the shops on the lower ground floor, worked his way up to the concourse, checking all the crevices, waiting rooms, toilets (ignoring the startled cries of women who were alarmed by his presence) and shops, the station busy even this late, a variety of trains pulling in and out. No Tulip. At one point he thought he spotted her outside WHSmith, staring in at a window display. He started towards her, heart leaping joyously — then she turned and it was just a girl of similar build.

It was ten twenty-nine when Kevin trudged disconsolately to Hays Galleria. He no longer held out any hope of finding his sister and thought about simply making his way back to Borough High Street, but he still had a few minutes of his self-allotted deadline to play with and he was so close to the Galleria that he decided he might as well check, just so he could walk away with a clear conscience, having done all he possibly could to locate her.

He passed a couple of late-night pedestrians as he was entering the Galleria but otherwise the area seemed deserted. He did a quick circuit, rounding the giant, mechanical fish/boat that was its centrepiece – it looked menacing in the half-light – and started back the way he'd come, no Tulip, dejected but not surprised.

"Kevin?" The voice came from the fish/boat. Kevin gawped. "Kevin?" the voice came again and he almost fled hysterically. Then a shadow detached itself from the massive bulk of the sculpture and stood before him, wiping a hand across its tear-stained face, smiling weakly.

"Tulip?" Kevin croaked, fearing her to be an illusion.

"I prayed for you to come," Tulip said hollowly, then threw herself at him and wrapped her arms around him, hugging, moaning, weeping. And he knew she was real.

"Tulip!" he cried, clutching her ecstatically. "Oh God, I thought I'd lost you."

"I ran," Tulip sobbed. "Got on a bus. I was going to... run forever... but I had nowhere to go... and I was lonely... and... I thought you'd look for me. I *knew* you would. So I came back. I went to the church first but Fr Sebastian... he..."

"I know," Kevin murmured, kissing her ice-cold cheeks, stroking her damp hair.

"I came here next," Tulip continued. "I've been waiting all night, cold, hungry, terrified. I... I... I..." She could say no more. Tears choked her and she just clung to Kevin, trembling and crying, Kevin crying too, the pair supporting one another, weak with relief. Finally Tulip pushed herself away from her brother and smiled at him through her tears. Then she frowned. "Where's Clint?"

Kevin held up the bag in reply. "I got the money. All of it."

Tulip stared at the bag, eyes round. "What did you do to Clint?" she whispered.

Kevin half-laughed. "Nothing. Big Sandy caught him. There was nothing I could do. He abandoned me, only interested in saving his own neck. I got away. He ended up... I don't know... dead, probably."

Tulip took that in, her face creasing sorrowfully, finding pity in her heart for Clint despite what he'd done to them. "What happened at the bridge?" she asked. "Why did Sandy attack Gawl?"

"I don't know," Kevin sighed. "And I don't care. I have you and I have the money. Nothing else matters. Let's go." He stuck out a hand. Tulip didn't take it.

"Where?" she said quietly.

"I have a cab waiting. We've two million pounds and our passports. We can go wherever we want. Abroad. Somewhere sunny. Or the Alps if you'd prefer."

"They'll come after us," she said.

"We'll post the formula to Bushinsky before we leave," Kevin chuckled. "He won't give a toss about us or the money once he gets that."

Tulip gulped and gazed at her brother, troubled. "Kevin... I..."

"Wait a minute," he interrupted. "I thought I heard something." He looked over her head, scrutinising the shadowy depths of the Galleria. For a couple of seconds, nothing. Then a massive figure emerged out of the gloom, others behind him, something scrabbling on all fours in front, and Kevin groaned sickly, "*No!*"

Tulip turned and squinted. "Who –"

She got no further. Kevin grabbed her arm and ran like the devil. Tulip had no choice but to run too. Behind them someone bellowed, "After them!"

Kevin couldn't believe it. He should have had until eleven thirty, yet it wasn't even a quarter to and here they were, Big Sandy at the fore. What had gone wrong? How had he miscalculated so disastrously?

Spilling out of the Galleria, hearing Big Sandy and the others pounding after them, turning right into Tooley Street, racing for Borough High Street, telling himself Dave would be there if he made it, passing at the exact moment he hit the street, the fates would be kind if he could stay ahead of them just long enough to...

Tulip slipped and fell. She cried out and slid into the middle of the road. If a car had been passing she could have been killed, but there was no traffic. Kevin dived after her, grabbed her elbow and hauled her to her feet. "Come on," he screamed. "We have to..."

Tulip yelped with pain and slumped, clutching her left ankle. "I can't."

Kevin glared at her desperately, hatefully. Glanced up. Saw Big Sandy surge out of the Galleria, a savage-looking dog ahead of him, three or four men hot on his heels. He studied Tulip as she nursed her ankle. Gazed at the bag in his right hand. He knew what he must do, the sacrifice he must make. For almost a full second he rejected that knowledge and stood firm beside the sister who meant so much to him, who was so vulnerable now...

...then spun with a moan and struck for freedom, taking the money, leaving Tulip behind.

Fleeing cravenly, thinking only of himself, all noble thoughts washed away by a wave of self-serving fear. Sights set on Borough High Street. Praying for Big Sandy to stop with Tulip, focus on the formula, not bother about Kevin. Escaping like he escaped before, but this time he wouldn't make the mistake of coming back. Get out, lay low, put his money to good use, say a few prayers for Tulip and weep for her. But he wouldn't die for her. The lie of the last few years exposed. The threat of suicide if she left him ridiculed in an instant. The selfish truth revealed abruptly and nakedly to the world, to Tulip, to himself.

Kevin ran, sobbing, clinging to the bag, unaware of Big Sandy stopping next to Tulip, unaware of Fast Eddie drawing his gun and looking to Big Sandy for a signal, unaware of Big Sandy nodding with the slightest and tightest of grins.

Something exploded in Kevin's lower back. He gasped and went sprawling. Blood arced from the small of his back as he hit the ground face first, not losing his grip on the bag. He broke his nose and shattered his front teeth as he smashed into the pavement. Tried bringing his arms in, to push himself up, get on his feet, run. But his arms wouldn't work. He tried moving his legs but they only twitched. Sobbing pitifully he began to crawl, thinking, *If I can just get to the High Street... Dave English... freedom... millions...*

Fast Eddie stepped up behind Kevin as he painfully inched towards the promise of escape. Checked with Big Sandy again. Big Sandy nodded again. Fast Eddie put the nozzle of his gun to the back of Kevin's head. Kevin never felt it. He was focused on the path ahead. He heard a click. His thoughts snapped back into place and he realised what the sound meant. Flashed on an image of Tulip. Then a bullet, bone and his brains came screaming out through the front of his already bloodied face and Kevin died a coward, in selfish disgrace.

SEVENTY-SIX

Big Sandy stood in front of Tulip with the hound – he had to choke hard on the leash to keep it away from her – blocking her view of Kevin as Fast Eddie finished him off. He needn't have bothered. Tulip had shut her eyes and covered her ears with her hands. Her lips were moving fast but silently, praying. When Fast Eddie had finished with Kevin, dumping the body at the side of Tooley Street, having first checked his pockets for the formula and prised the bag from Kevin's lifeless fingers, Big Sandy gently pulled Tulip's hands from her ears and waited for her to look at him. When she did, he smiled sadly. "It's over."

Tulip's lips trembled and for a moment she held Big Sandy's gaze. Then she glanced through his legs, saw Fast Eddie walking towards them, spotted her brother's corpse. She shut her eyes again and moaned, rocking back and forth. Her left hand automatically slid to her ankle and rubbed the flesh around it. "You shouldn't have done that," she wept. "You could have just taken the money."

"It's better this way," Big Sandy replied. "He died quickly. If I'd taken him back..." He shook his head sombrely. Fast Eddie stepped up beside him. Eyes Burton and Jimmy B were further back, guns drawn, keeping watch, warding off the few pedestrians who were on the street. Fast Eddie passed the bag to Big Sandy, who held it in the same huge hand with which he gripped the hound's reins. Didn't even glance at the bag. "Is it all there?"

"I only had a quick look but I think so." Fast Eddie stared at Tulip. "No sign of the formula."

"Tulip?" Big Sandy said softly.

"He didn't have it," she sighed. "They gave it to me. I was supposed to hand it to you." Her tears had ceased. Placing her hands on the road, she pushed herself to her feet, wincing. Big Sandy reached out his free hand to help but she ignored it and hopped towards the pavement where Kevin lay splayed. Eyes trained his gun on her but Big Sandy grunted at him and he lowered it again. All four men moved with Tulip, trailing after her as she made her slow way to her dead brother, the hound whining with excitement at the bloody smell of the corpse.

Tulip hovered over Kevin when she reached him, gazing in silence at the back of his head. Big Sandy was glad that Kevin was lying face down. She lowered herself to the pavement and sat next to her brother, running her fingers through his hair, smoothing it over the hole in his skull. Then she opened the front of her coat and rubbed a hand over her stomach.

"Give us the formula, Tulip," Big Sandy said quietly. "You don't have to die like the rest of them. We can stop if we have the money and the formula. You can walk away. You have my word." Knowing he couldn't guarantee that – the Bush might kill her to be safe – but not making the promise lightly. He'd fight for her life if he had to.

"I'm pregnant," Tulip said. Big Sandy blinked, taken aback. "That's why Kevin struck a deal with Gawl and Clint, so he'd have money to look after us. He loved me really, despite his sickness."

"Is that why he deserted you?" Fast Eddie snorted.

"He was weak," Tulip responded evenly. "He wasn't responsible for his actions. Not all of them anyway."

"We need to get out of here," Eyes said nervously. "We're exposed. Let's get her back to the lab. She can do all the talking she wants there."

"He's right," Fast Eddie said to Big Sandy. "The others will be here soon. I'll stay and help them deal with the body. Will you walk her back to the van or do you want me to phone for a car?"

Big Sandy didn't answer. He was staring at Tulip as she rubbed her stomach. "Why tell us you're pregnant?"

Tulip smiled shakily. "I'm going to be a mother. I have responsibilities now. I have to make the world as safe for my child as possible."

"Sandy, we have to –" Fast Eddie began but Big Sandy cut him short with an angry gesture.

"Tell me you didn't do it," Big Sandy croaked, fearing the worst.

"Drugs are evil," Tulip whispered. "Kevin got me hooked. I'm still an addict. I've sworn to get clean for my baby's sake, but I know it wont be easy. I know what it's like to be trapped, to feel the *need*. Clint and Tony said this new drug would be given to people who didn't want it, that it would kill them if they didn't keep taking it. I chose to experiment, but their victims wouldn't have had a choice. Innocent people bound to a relentless, vile addiction for life. I couldn't allow that, not when I was presented with a way to prevent it."

"What's she saying?" Eyes snapped, not liking the sound of this.

"I destroyed it," Tulip said. "The formula was written down in a notebook. I ripped out the pages, tore them up into pieces and scattered them over the Thames as I walked here from London Bridge." She reached into a pocket, produced a thin notebook and opened it to show its eviscerated interior.

"She's got to be shitting us," Eyes groaned but Big Sandy and Fast Eddie knew Tulip and they could tell by her expression that she was telling the truth.

"That was very foolish," Big Sandy said dolefully.

"I couldn't allow such a wretched drug into the world," Tulip countered. "It was God's plan. He put me in possession of the formula so I could dispose of it."

"God doesn't work that way," Big Sandy said.

"I believe he does."

"She's lying," Eyes snarled. "She made a copy or this is just a notebook she bought in a shop and ripped up after she hid the real one."

"No," Big Sandy said. "I believe her."

"I do too," Fast Eddie sighed, "but we have to be sure. We have to take her in. Dave will want to question her. He'll probably sic Michael on her."

Big Sandy's left eyelid twitched. "No."

"It's not our call," Fast Eddie hissed. "We can talk to Dave, try to persuade him that she's on the level, but this is his business, not ours." Big Sandy hesitated and Fast Eddie pushed ahead swiftly. "We don't make the decisions. We'll take her back, plead her case, hope

Dave believes her. If he doesn't..." Fast Eddie shook his head.

"Enough of this shit," Jimmy B growled, stepping forward to pick up Tulip.

"Stop." Big Sandy didn't raise his voice but the menace in it stopped Jimmy B cold. He stared at Big Sandy. Fast Eddie sensed danger. His hand sneaked towards his gun. Then Big Sandy sighed. "I'll bring her." He thrust the reins of the hound – straining anxiously, wild on the smell of blood – to Jimmy B. "Take this."

Jimmy B nodded and took charge of the hound. Fast Eddie relaxed. Tulip drew away from Big Sandy as he reached for her. "Can I say a prayer first?"

"You can pray later," Big Sandy grunted, taking hold of her wrists.

"But it's not for me, it's for Kevin." She looked at Big Sandy pleadingly. "I want to say a prayer for the repose of his soul. Please. This is important to me."

Big Sandy wavered. "You're wasting your prayers on him," he warned her.

"Maybe," she conceded with a weary smile. "But God is merciful. He listens to those who plead on behalf of their loved ones."

"She's playing for time," Eyes said.

"Shut up," Fast Eddie told him and turned to Big

Sandy. "Let her pray. It can't do any harm. I'll call for that car."

"OK," Big Sandy said, releasing Tulip. He stepped back. Tulip faced Kevin, made the sign of the cross, put her hands together, closed her eyes. Eyes and Jimmy B stared at her incredulously, then at Big Sandy, but said nothing. Fast Eddie moved away and phoned for a car, telling the guy to also contact the Bush and let him know that they were coming.

Big Sandy watched Tulip praying, her face serene despite the trauma of the last week and the terror and loss of the last few hours. He imagined what would happen when they presented her to the Bush. Dave would be furious. Big Sandy knew he'd believe her story – too crazy to make up – but he didn't think the Bush would let himself be seen to believe. There would have to be proof positive. And retribution. Tulip would be tortured and killed. Dave wouldn't – couldn't – allow her to live, not after she'd cheated him out of the formula and all the millions it would have generated. Her motives were irrelevant. He'd have to punish her.

Big Sandy fixed on Tulip's lips as they moved silently. He took in the tears, the bedraggled hair, the pain in her face, the (imagined) bulge of her stomach. Sixteen years old and damned. None of it her fault. A good girl dragged through the muck by her vicious, petty, perverse brother — but not degraded. Too pure of spirit to be truly soiled. And a mother-to-be, new life in her womb, an innocent child.

Big Sandy thought of Amelie. The boy who snapped her bra. Pictured her in this position, knocked up by the spotty teenager, pregnant, a victim of a wicked man, in the grip of even worse men, damned. And he knew — he couldn't let Tulip die.

The realisation hit him suddenly, awfully. The consequences would be dire, he was signing his own death warrant, betraying all he believed in. But a few things in life were more important than duty. Killing Gawl McCaskey had taken priority over his allegiance to Dave. Saving Tulip Tyne now seemed just as essential. He could no more stand back and let her be killed than he could have stood by quietly and let Gawl McCaskey walk away from the London Eye.

The moment called for immediate action. Without dwelling on the madness of his choice, Big Sandy drew his gun, took aim at Eyes Burton and fired twice into his chest. As Eyes went down in a silent, puzzled heap, Big Sandy drew a bead on Fast Eddie. But Fast Eddie had reacted to the first shot and darted towards the Hays Galleria, head down, running at top speed. Big Sandy fired a couple of shots after him but both flew wide. He could probably have taken his time and fixed firmly on Fast Eddie but he chose not to. Fast Eddie was a friend and Big Sandy didn't really want to kill him.

He turned on Jimmy B, gawping at him, still holding the hound's reins, too astonished to defend himself. Big Sandy put a bullet through the man's forehead before he wised up and Jimmy B went down hard, letting go of the reins as he fell. Big Sandy prepared to shoot the hound too, but it was past him before he could take aim, launching itself at the corpse of Kevin Tyne, knocking Tulip out of the way – she'd stopped praying and was staring at Big Sandy, bewildered – then trying to gnaw at Kevin's head. It couldn't, because of its muzzle, so it settled for gulping his blood.

"No!" Tulip shrieked, trying to pull the hound away. Big Sandy didn't waste time arguing with her. He transferred the bag to his right hand, wrapped his huge left arm around her waist, picked her up and backed off, eyes on the Galleria, ready to drop the bag and start firing if Fast Eddie poked his head out. "Kevin!" Tulip wailed. "Don't let that beast –"

"Quiet," Big Sandy snapped. "If we act quickly we might get out alive. Otherwise we're both dead."

Tulip stopped struggling, paused to analyse what was

happening, realised what Big Sandy had done and gazed at him, awestruck. "*Why?*" she whispered. He didn't answer, there was no time. Thoughts churning as he backed away from the carnage. They could make for Borough High Street and hail a cab. But Fast Eddie had called in support, the men were almost here, they might be coming from that direction, Fast Eddie would be on the phone to them now, telling them of Big Sandy's betrayal. Alternatives? London Bridge station directly behind them. Dash in, grab a Tube or train, try to stay ahead of the Bush's men.

Backing into the station, grasping Tulip, the money and his gun. Train or Tube? He opted for the former, space to run if Fast Eddie caught up with them — didn't want to get trapped underground. "Can you walk?" he asked Tulip, angling for the entrance to the platforms.

"I can maybe hobble."

"Let's try. We'll attract less attention that way." Lowering her, he let her lean on him for support. Tulip tested her ankle, smiled bravely at him and the pair scurried up the escalator and down the corridor to the rail platforms as fast as they could, Big Sandy glancing over his shoulder with every few steps, holding the gun close by his side so as not to alarm others in the station.

Lots of platforms and trains. The numbers meant

nothing to Big Sandy. He passed two platform entrances before stopping and squinting at an electronic departures board. Checked the time and next available train. There was one due to depart from platform five in two minutes, lots of stops. They could ride it for as long as they wished, get off anywhere, connect with another train or grab a cab.

They lurched for platform five, Big Sandy holding Tulip up and giving her a big swing forward to quicken their pace.

The train was pulling into the platform when they arrived and for the first time since he was a child Big Sandy offered up a silent prayer of thanks to God, even though he didn't truly believe that God had intervened to help them. Tulip sensed the prayer or saw it in his eyes and smiled knowingly but held her tongue. They stumbled along the platform to the rearmost carriage, where Big Sandy bundled Tulip aboard then climbed in after her, slamming the door shut, sliding the window down, standing guard, ready to fire if they were followed.

Tulip relaxed against the opposite door, taking the weight off her injured ankle, studying Big Sandy in wonder and grateful amazement. She started to ask why he was doing this, then stopped. It was a question she didn't need to voice. He was doing it because he cared, because he was human, because he'd been touched by God, even if he'd never admit it. "Where are we going?" she asked instead.

"I don't know," Big Sandy said, not looking around. "We'll jump off after a few stops, get out of London, hide."

"And then?"

"I haven't thought that far ahead."

"My passport's in the bag with Kevin's. If we need to get out of the country I could use mine, you could alter his and use that."

"Maybe." Not concerned about such details. Wary of thinking too far ahead when their present crisis was far from behind them. If this train got moving and they weren't seen and they got out of London ... *then* he'd start considering the long-term difficulties.

The tannoy crackled into life and the voice of a bored driver came over it. "Ah, sorry about this short delay, ladies and gentlemen. We have some signal problems on the track ahead. Nothing serious, we expect to be moving again within three or four minutes. Thank you for your patience and once again, sorry about the delay and any inconvenience it might cause."

Big Sandy drew back from the window and looked at Tulip. She saw defeat in his eyes and an unvoiced sneer,

So much for God.

"It's only a short delay," Tulip said nervously. "We might still make it. Or should we grab another train?"

Big Sandy thought about that and shook his head. "We're safer here. They won't know which platform we've come to, maybe not even that we came up here instead of down to the Tube. We'd be vulnerable outside. Better to..."

Stopped by familiar howling on the platform — the hound. Big Sandy lurched to the window and peered out. Fast Eddie at the platform entrance, three more of the Bush's men behind him, the hound just ahead, snout red with blood. Fast Eddie must have thought fast, dragged the hound off Kevin once the backup had arrived, gave it Tulip's scent, followed her here. He wouldn't have been able to if Big Sandy had shot the hound. Letting the creature live — dumb move, not like him.

Big Sandy leant out the window and fired, but he was too far away to make the shots count. Fast Eddie and the others ducked back. The other people on the platform dove for cover. Big Sandy glanced at Tulip, who stared at him resolutely, unafraid. "They've found us?" she asked.

"Yeah."

"If the train starts now..."

"It won't. Even if it does, they know where it's going. They'll have men waiting for us at the next stop. They'll get on and hunt us down."

"You could give me back to them. They might forgive you."

He smothered a disrespectful snort. "No."

"Then it's over," she said, resigned. "Will we surrender or make them fight?"

"Which would you rather?"

Tulip hesitated then made up her mind. "Surrender. You might kill one of them in a fight and I don't want that. There's no need for it now."

Big Sandy nodded. "They might still torture you. If you want, I could..." He left it hanging.

Tulip smiled sadly but firmly. "Life's too sacred to discard cheaply. I'll take my chances. God will look after me."

"Like he's looked after you so far?" Big Sandy grunted. He glanced out the window again. One of the men with Fast Eddie was creeping forward. Big Sandy fired and the man scrambled back into cover. "Lousy trains. To get this far and be undone by –"

Stopped by another announcement, this time coming from the station speakers. "The next train on platform six is an express train. The train on platform six will not be stopping in this station. Please stand back from the edge. Thank you."

Big Sandy paused. Platforms five and six were joined. Crazy thoughts of jumping aboard the oncoming train with Tulip, but express trains screamed through at top speed. He reached for the handle of the door, preparing himself to go and surrender...

...then stopped as another thought hit. This one crazy in its own way too, but sobering at the same time. There *was* a way out of this. Maybe God *was* looking down and offering Big Sandy a bittersweet choice, testing his resolve, maybe even offering him the chance of...

Big Sandy thought quickly. Both damned if he did nothing, him definitely damned if he went with his plan, Tulip probably damned — but only *probably*. She might get away.

He decided. Opened the bag, yanked out several rolls of notes and thrust them at Tulip. "Stick those inside your jumper."

"What are you —" she began to ask.

"Do it," he barked, pulling out more rolls, forcing them on her. Tulip stared at Big Sandy, confused, but did as ordered, stuffing the money down the neck of her jumper, hundreds of thousands in total, maybe half a million, he couldn't be sure. She looked like the Michelin Man by the time he was finished. He almost laughed. Her passport was in the bag. He tossed it to her. He also emptied his wallet of cash, so she'd have some smaller bills.

"Where's the notebook?" Big Sandy grunted. Tulip handed it to him. "Do you have a pen?" She shook her head. Big Sandy cursed then stomped down the carriage. Three people, cringing in their seats, staring at Big Sandy as if he was the devil. "I need a pen," Big Sandy shouted, flashing his gun. Hands were thrust into pockets and pens appeared like magic. Big Sandy grabbed one, returned, checked the action on the platform to make sure no one was sneaking up on them, then tore a page out of the notebook and scribbled a hasty message. *All that you've earned for me over the years is Amelie's now. Give it to her when she's old enough, help her make the most of it. This girl needs your help too. Invest the money that she gives you. Keep it safe for her. Let her draw from it whenever she asks. Do this for me and we'll be even forever, all debts paid. Sandy.* On the back of the note he wrote Julius Scott's name, address and phone number.

"If they don't come after you, get off somewhere random and find a hotel," he told Tulip, handing her the note, then riffling through the rolls of cash left in the bag, thumbing the elastic bands off them, leaving the bag half-open. "Once you've checked in, stay in your room for a few days, don't go out, treat yourself to room service. Then call Julius. Arrange a meeting, take the money to him, show him the note, discuss your future with him. He'll invest the money safely and make sums available to you whenever you ask. You can trust him."

"What's happening?" Tulip asked, more scared now than she had been when her situation seemed utterly hopeless.

"Ask Julius to help you get out of the country," Big Sandy continued. "He can set you up somewhere, arrange for regular payments to be sent to you, plenty for you and the kid to live on. You'll be safer abroad, but don't spend too much, you won't want to draw attention to yourself. If the payments ever stop, forget about the money and find another way to pay the bills. Never come back looking for it."

"Sandy, what –"

Big Sandy leant forward and kissed her chastely. "Will you pray for me?" he asked as he pulled away. Tulip nodded. She'd started to cry again. "Good girl," Big Sandy smiled, opened the door before she could say anything and jumped out. He fired his final couple of shots at Fast Eddie and his cohorts – they'd been creeping forward cautiously – then moved away from the train, across to where platform five became platform six.

He kept to the edge of the platform and ran, willing the express train to be on time, challenging God to prove himself as interventionist and benevolent as Tulip believed he was.

Fast Eddie leapt to his feet and shouted at the men behind him. "He's making a break for it. He has the bag. Stop him!" They needed no further encouragement. Racing ahead of Fast Eddie, they opened fire, ignoring the screams of the people on the platform, focused on the giant further ahead, each of them keen to be the one to claim such a valuable scalp.

Big Sandy heard the retorts of the guns and the zings as the bullets struck the floor and platform pillars. He willed the bullets wide of their mark. If they killed him, they'd be able to check the bag and his plan would be ruined. Where was that fucking train! He was getting near to the end of the platform. If it didn't arrive soon...

And here at last, as if sent by God, it came. An express train thundering towards platform six like a steel angel on wheels. Big Sandy sighed with relief when he saw it coming, began to slow, then remembered this had to look genuine. Picking up speed again, he raced for the end of the platform, confident that the train would get there before him.

He thought about Sapphire as he ran. Winced at his

thoughtlessness. He should have given Tulip her number, asked the girl to ring her and tell her that Big Sandy had said goodbye. Sapphire would hear about this anyway, but she was worthy of a personal farewell. A regretful oversight. His last. No putting it right now.

Just before the train hit the platform, a bullet struck Big Sandy's left thigh. He'd planned to fake a trip and throw himself beneath the wheels, but now there was no need. The force of the bullet knocked him sideways and he fell into the path of the onrushing train. He hung mid-air for what couldn't have been more than a fraction of a second but which felt longer, flashing back on the life he'd led, the sins he'd committed, his actions of the last few minutes, how and if they'd affect his standing with God.

Then the train smashed into him. Everything stopped. The world disappeared. His intention made real. A bad man sacrificed so a good girl might live. Big Sandy died messily but quickly and painlessly, wondering in his last moment, *Any chance of redemption?*

world without end, amen

i

Fast Eddie walked slowly down the platform to where Big Sandy had been struck by the train. The driver had applied the brakes and the train was coming to a screeching halt along the tracks beyond the station. People on the platform were standing, shocked, slowly graduating towards the scene of the accident, heedless of the four men with guns and the wild, howling hound.

Fast Eddie stopped at the approximate spot where Big Sandy had been hit. Banknotes were drifting through the air like confetti. Fast Eddie watched the wind playing with them, rising and twirling them high above the platform. A small, romantic part of him thought that the particles might represent Big Sandy's soul, freed and hovering above the place of his death. The greater, realistic part of him thought, *Fuck!*

One of the men with Fast Eddie caught a few of the notes and scrutinised them gloomily. "Two million pounds," he muttered. "The Bush'll go apeshit."

"Maybe we could pick up all the notes," one of the other men deadpanned but nobody laughed.

"Who shot him?" Fast Eddie asked. No response. He glanced around wryly. "Nobody wants to take the credit?"

"We were all shooting," one of the men said uneasily. "You too, Eddie. Any one of us could have hit him."

"It wasn't our fault," the second man said. "He was too close to the edge of the platform. If he'd fallen the other way, everything would have been fine."

"You don't think the Bush will blame us, do you?" the third asked nervously.

"No," Fast Eddie sighed. "This was beyond our control. We did what we could. Fate was against us."

"There's still the girl," one of the men noted.

Fast Eddie's gaze slid to the train on platform five. It was just starting to pull out, the driver unaware of what had happened on the adjacent platform, official word not yet circulated. From here he could see Tulip Tyne's face as she stood by the door of her carriage, staring at them. It would be a simple task to make a phone call, have men waiting at the next station to get on and take her quietly. Deliver her to Dave for questioning, interrogation and execution. He didn't like it but it was his job. The formula was still unaccounted for. Dave wouldn't look favourably upon him if he returned and said he'd taken Tulip at her word when she said she'd destroyed the notebook.

Fast Eddie was reaching glumly for his phone when he stopped and frowned. Who was there to tell Dave about Tulip ripping up the formula? Of the men who'd heard her confess, only he remained. The truth could be whatever he decided to make it.

"Forget the girl," Fast Eddie said, turning for the exit, raising the collar of his coat, only now thinking about CCTV and witnesses. The Bush had contacts at the station. The security tapes would go missing or be erased, but the witnesses might cause some problems for Fast Eddie and the others on the platform. A long holiday beckoned, perhaps further than Margate this time. Fast Eddie wouldn't complain. He was tired of London.

"What about the formula?" the man who'd mentioned Tulip asked.

Fast Eddie steeled himself for the lie. "She gave it to us. It was in the bag with the money. It's lost."

The man shook his head bitterly then followed Fast Eddie from the platform, the others close behind, dragging the hound, which was howling miserably after the departing train and the rapidly evaporating scent of its prey.

ii

Tulip found a seat in a row halfway down the carriage – the other three passengers eyed her warily but kept their distance and said nothing – and sat next to the window, staring out at the darkness of the city, studying her reflection in the glass, thinking about Big Sandy, crying and smiling at the same time as she considered the magnitude of his sacrifice. She was sure it wouldn't go unrewarded, that whatever Big Sandy's previous sins, God would show compassion for a man who had given his life for a girl he owed no actual allegiance to.

She was hot and would have liked to take her coat off, but didn't dare, afraid the bulges of the rolls of money would show. In two minds what to do with the cash. On the one hand it was blood money – many men had died for it – and her first impulse was to get rid of it, give it to charity, wash her hands clean of the whole dirty affair. But Big Sandy had given the money to her at the very end. He'd wanted her to have it, not just for herself but for her baby. To give it away would be a betrayal of his final act of kindness. She'd think about it in more depth later, but she was pretty sure she'd settle on a compromise, keep enough to provide for herself and her child — at least for the next few difficult years — and donate the rest to a good cause.

She slid a hand beneath her coat, up under her jumper and the rolls of money, and rubbed her stomach, thinking about the foetus, giggling softly as she realised she now had a name for her unborn baby. Alexander if it was a boy, Alexandra if it was a girl, but as far as everyday use went, regardless of its gender, *Sandy*. A reminder — not that she'd need any — and a tribute.

Frightened as she looked ahead, sixteen years old, a single mother, alone in the world. It wouldn't be easy, no matter how much of the money she kept. But she'd pull through, of that she was certain. She had endured more than most girls her age and hadn't been crushed or consumed. The world could surely throw no worse at her than it had these past couple of years.

Despite her confidence in herself, residues of fear remained. So, as the train chugged towards the suburbs of London, Tulip did what she always did when she was afraid, anxious or unsure — she prayed. At first, closing her eyes and crossing herself, she prayed only for good luck and safe passage. Then, as the train picked up speed and she left the nightmares further behind, her thoughts turned to Big Sandy and she asked God to show mercy and accept the dead giant's tarnished soul. After that she prayed for Kevin, her poor, sick brother. He'd hurt her more than he probably ever knew but the sickness wasn't his fault and she prayed to God to understand that and forgive. And then, relaxing back into her seat, feeling sleepy from the heat and exhaustion, she extended her prayers to include the others who had died in the name of the awful drug and cursed money, pitiful Fr Sebastian, the greedy dreamer Clint Smith, prisoner of genius Tony Phials, even the brutish and truly wretched Gawl McCaskey. Figuring, as she rode her train to freedom, hovering on the verge of sleep and humbly intervening with God on their behalf, *If* I *don't pray for their lost, damned souls, who will?*

THE END

written between 25th april 2001 and 10th august 2013

Printed in Great Britain
by Amazon.co.uk, Ltd.,
Marston Gate.